BEST
KEPT
SECRETS

BEST
KEPT
SECRETS

A Novel

TRACEY S. PHILLIPS

Fam. Noir

**CROOKED
LANE**

NEW YORK

Published in the United States by Crooked Lane Books, an imprint of The Quick Brown Fox & Company LLC.

Crooked Lane Books and its logo are trademarks of The Quick Brown Fox & Company LLC.

Library of Congress Catalog-in-Publication data available upon request.

ISBN (hardcover): 978-1-64385-227-0
ISBN (ebook): 978-1-64385-228-7

Cover design by Melanie Sun
Book design by Jennifer Canzone

Printed in the United States.

www.crookedlanebooks.com

Crooked Lane Books
34 West 27th St., 10th Floor
New York, NY 10001

First Edition: October 2019

10 9 8 7 6 5 4 3 2 1

For Mom
And for Michael, who stood beside me during
my many fractured moments

Your perspective on life comes from the cage you were held captive in.
—Shannon L. Alder

CHAPTER 1

MORGAN

Detective Morgan Jewell outpaced her partner by several car lengths.

"Hold up, Mo. I didn't get enough sleep, thanks to you. You could at least wait for me!" A seasoned detective, Donnie James had been Morgan's partner for ten years. Now he was fifty and would rather ease into retirement than take any risks.

Morgan snapped over her shoulder, "I can't wait. This is the one, Donnie. I know it." Pulling the front of her jacket closed against the cooler than normal temperatures, she took in every detail of the rural street. On one side of the road, oaks towered over Victorian-style houses. Across from them, fields of tall, end-of-season corn browned in the sun. Fresh country air filled her lungs with the bright smell of autumn.

"Is that what you think?" Donnie strolled along at a slower pace.

He and Morgan had been partners for almost ten years but his time as a detective was drawing to a close. He had been offered the position of their lieutenant, who was retiring at the end of the year. Donnie hadn't accepted yet but was seriously considering it. Morgan had called him before five this morning. She had had to dial his number three times before he answered, groggy and resistant to taking a case outside of their jurisdiction. Furthermore, it was Saturday. He would rather have stayed at home with his wife and two teenaged daughters. Behind him, farm tractors kicked up dust clouds that dissipated in the breeze.

Half a dozen police cars in the road indicated that most of the law enforcement in this little farming burg had come out for the show. In the driveway, EMTs were trying to console a hysterical woman sitting on the bumper of an ambulance with the back doors open. Morgan heard her cries and winced.

The night before in Hendricks County, dispatch had reported a 911 call. Upon returning from an out-of-state work trip, Rebecca Harrington, the weeping woman, discovered her partner's broken, blood-covered body in their bedroom. Because of this crime's similarities to an ongoing Indianapolis investigation, Detective Morgan Jewell of the Indianapolis Metro Police Department, Homicide Division, had been granted special access to this crime scene in Danville.

Fueled by coffee and self-confidence, she bounded past a group of officers gathered around the steps of the light-blue, Victorian house. This little town had never seen a murder so gruesome, and Morgan didn't like the attention it was getting. She snarled at them, "What is this, some kind of party? Have some respect for the dead, will you?" A pair of them took the hint and peeled away.

Inside the house, the officer on duty greeted her. "Morning, Detective Jewell." Behind him, several Hendricks County cops milled around the living room. Too many crime-scene investigators were dusting, tagging, and labeling every surface.

Donnie ambled in a few minutes later, his voice booming, "Who's in charge?"

The officer nearest the door updated them. "Nothing in the lower level was disturbed according to Ms. Harrington," he said. "We've sealed off the crime scene. Forensics is on its way."

Morgan wandered past the officer, who had seated himself in a chair near the front door. Behind him, an oriental rug covered the living-room floor beneath an IKEA-style smooth-as-swede couch and matching chair. The ottoman was topped with a flat blue tray holding a candle and a stack of coasters. A vase of flowers sat in the corner. Little china cups and saucers filled the gaps in an ornate bookshelf. On a side table, a photograph of two women posing cheek-to-cheek and smiling widely took prominence. Morgan looked closer without touching. They looked so happy. She remembered feeling that way once.

"What's upstairs?" she asked.

"Upstairs . . . Lieutenant Werner is upstairs. That's where . . ." Color left the young officer's face.

Donnie had come in and was standing in the doorway texting someone on his phone. Morgan asked, "Your daughter?"

Donnie nodded and followed Morgan up a narrow staircase. At the top of the stairs, the lieutenant greeted them. "We've been here since midnight. What took you so long?"

"Got caught in that construction traffic on I-465." Donnie was bending the truth. In fact he had dragged his feet and taken his time, his way of showing Morgan that he didn't want to be there.

"They're always working on something, aren't they? Even on Saturday." The lieutenant looked past Morgan at Donnie.

"Especially on Saturday," Donnie concurred.

Morgan felt like a ghost as the lieutenant chatted casually with his same-sex peer.

"I've heard a lot about you, Detective James, but no one mentioned your stature. Did you ever play ball?"

"Too clumsy. Call me Donnie."

"Lieutenant Werner." He reached past Morgan to shake Donnie's hand—indeed as if she wasn't there. "Call me Tim."

"I'm the detective in charge." Morgan intercepted the handshake. "And I'd like to see the body."

Limp and cool, the lieutenant's hand slid from hers as he looked her up and down. She was wearing a black fitted suit with a red blouse. Her long brown hair was pulled into a tight ponytail. Thick black lashes framed dark-brown eyes emphasized by her porcelain complexion.

"Hope you haven't had breakfast yet, Detective," he said to her.

"Burger and fries on the way here, lots of ketchup." She privately hoped to see the lieutenant pale at the thought. When he didn't, she continued. "What have we got?"

Werner led the way down a tight hallway wallpapered with pink flowers. The trim, painted periwinkle-blue, bordered hardwood floors that groaned under Donnie's weight. Werner stopped before entering and held up a hand.

"Her name's Hallie Marks. She's the owner of Hit the Mark Design. I heard she was one of the best interior decorators in the state."

"Yes." Impatient, Morgan wanted to go into the room. "It was her partner who found her like this, isn't that right?"

"Rebecca Harrington," Werner said, "is the owner of the house. She said she's been out of town for a few weeks."

"How long ago was Hallie Marks killed?"

"Probably in the past day or so."

Donnie lifted the back of his hand to his nose. In the airless hallway, he looked a little pale.

The lieutenant gave a final disclaimer. "This is ugly. Just warning you."

Morgan pushed past him. "I'm ready for it."

Light colors and country lace decorated the small master bedroom. It looked like no one had slept in the antique four-poster bed the night before. Eyelet curtains framed the bay window where dark, dried spots of blood splattered the light-blue cushion on the window seat. Outside, the sun shone on ripe cornfields across the street.

Beside the window, the body of Hallie Marks sat strapped to a Queen Anne chair. Her bloody face hung down forward between her shoulders. A drying red stream ran from her destroyed face down her chest and between her breasts. Hallie's broken, bloody hands were tied to the arms of the chair. Her bare feet rested in a sticky pool of blood.

Morgan's hand grazed a soft spiral notebook in the pocket of her pants. Donnie stood beside her looking down at the body. As he shook his head, she knew he was thinking about retirement. In the car he had let her know how upset he was to be riding along with her. It wasn't even their jurisdiction, he'd said. But Morgan wanted Donnie's opinion. She had enormous respect for him and his ability to solve crimes. And crazy as it sounded, Morgan hoped this case could be the connection to her past.

"What do you think?" She asked him.

"Me?" On his wide forehead, his eyebrows were raised up to his trim hairline. "This is all you, Morgan. I'm following your lead."

Morgan stepped as close as she could to the woman in the chair. "She wasn't just beaten. She was tortured." *I think I've caught up to you, you fucker,* Morgan thought. *I've finally caught up to you.*

"The killer is an animal," Werner said.

Riveted to her spot, Morgan answered, "Not an animal, Lieutenant. A sick-minded, fucked-up human being. Animals don't behave this way." She squatted down for a closer look. She had seen these kinds of injuries before. The memory made the hair on the back of her neck stand at attention.

At least the victim was wearing underwear, a lacy red pair of panties and fancy bra. Her clothes, a pair of jeans and a plain white shirt, were laid on the bed as if she had been getting ready to go out. Or perhaps she'd just taken them off?

Gazing at the female victim's smashed, bloody face, Morgan shivered. Blood covered most of the injuries, but it was clear that anger had driven the killer to destroy this woman's face. Years ago, Morgan's best friend, Fay Ramsey, had been murdered similarly. Every day since her death, Morgan had scanned the news for possible reports of the killer's capture. And she still looked for the killer herself, needing closure. But for now she pushed the horrid memory aside to focus on the task at hand.

The victim was wearing a braided silver ring with a malachite stone on the pinky finger of her left hand. But her crushed metacarpals had caused the long, slender fingers to lie askew. Swollen, black-and-blue flesh indicated that those injuries had been inflicted hours before her death. *That,* Morgan thought, *seemed to be the killer's mark.*

On her face, numerous impact sites were about two inches in diameter. One blow had crushed Hallie's nose. Another took several teeth. Fay's killer had done the same things to her.

Under her breath, Morgan muttered, "So much hate and passion."

"Passion isn't the word I'd use." In the doorway, the lieutenant watched her work.

"Me neither." Donnie went out into the hallway.

Morgan took a pair of gloves from her pocket and slid them onto her hands. She lifted Hallie's cold, stiff fingers to examine her fingernails. They were long but not painted. All were trim, filed, and clean, except for the index and middle finger, which had something dark underneath them.

Had Hallie clawed at her attacker? Is that his blood? A chill went down Morgan's spine.

"Have forensics swab her nails and send me the results."

"Sure thing, Detective."

"Do you study serial crime, Lieutenant Werner?" she asked, standing.

Werner picked at his own fingernails. "Nope. Not my thing."

"The killer has done this before. There is precision in each knot, each loop of rope, and in every blow." Morgan removed her gloves.

"Can we get the body out of here?" Donnie called from the hallway.

"We were waiting for you detectives. Hey, Richardson!" Werner hollered out to the officer stationed at the bottom of the stairs. "Go tell Lemay that we're ready for the coroner."

Donnie started for the stairs and Morgan followed. "I want to talk to Rebecca," she said.

"Wait." Lieutenant Werner touched the back of Morgan's arm. "We found a possible murder weapon."

Morgan turned on her toes. She wondered what hard object had been used. Something sturdy and heavy would do it. The butt or barrel of a gun. A mallet. A hammer.

"There's a meat tenderizer in the dish rack by the kitchen sink. It's been washed. We're spraying the sink for traces of the woman's blood."

CHAPTER 2

MORGAN

Morgan stood beside Donnie's messy desk holding a new cell phone. "I'm calling her again." With a nice-sized screen and a black jelly casing, the latest android was large for her small hands. She raised a finger to dial.

Donnie's brows knitted together. "How many times have you tried? Since yesterday? Since Danville?"

"Seven," Morgan admitted reluctantly.

"Seven times?" Donnie looked at his watch. "And it's only ten. You know she has every right to refuse to talk to us until she's proven mentally sound."

"She was in shock." Morgan conceded.

"Right. So give her some space. The paramedics said it could take her a few days." Sometimes Donnie had to be Morgan's voice of reason.

But this case was different. Call it intuition, maybe. *It's been so many years . . . and now . . . I'm so close,* she thought. "We don't have a few days. That killer is still out there."

Donnie lowered his chin, talking to Morgan like she was one of his teenage daughters. Like this was the twelfth time he'd given the facts-of-life talk and she was pregnant.

"Rebecca Harrington may have never met the killer. Did you think of that? She might not have known him." It was, at least, the twelfth time he'd talked her down from this ledge.

Donnie's use of the masculine pronoun caused Morgan to stop and think. "*Him?*"

"The murderer," Donnie said.

"I know who you meant." The revelation hit her hard. "I've been assuming all along that Fay's killer was a man too." *Fay Ramsey.* She tried to put the past behind her, but it always had a way of sneaking back. And rather than fading away over the years, Fay's brutal murder continued to plague her. It had become more than a mild obsession.

"Not Fay. Hallie Marks. Don't do this, Morgan. Don't go down that road again. I'm too old to be caught up in your ancient vendetta."

She turned toward the window and ignored Donnie. Fay Ramsey had been killed—her life interrupted—and the event had changed Morgan's path. Originally signed up for literary fine arts, she switched to criminal psychology and law to try to make sense of what had happened to her friend. Since Fay's death, Morgan had been searching for a man named Larry Milhouse. Fay had gone to meet him and never returned.

Hallie, like Fay, seemed ready for some kind of encounter. It seemed she was dressed and preened for intimacy, unless Hallie wore fancy undergarments on a daily basis. Rebecca Harrington, her partner didn't arrive home until the following day. Morgan asked Donnie, "Was she dressed as if she was expecting a sexual encounter?"

"I see what you're getting at, but I can't imagine a woman killing like that." Donnie leaned back in his chair, making it creak. "No. This killer is a man."

She respected Donnie and listened to his advice, but lately she had to argue her point to get through to him. She wondered if he was losing his detective's edge. He didn't seem that interested in chasing down killers anymore. Morgan had requested access to Hallie's crime scene because she'd been waiting for something like this. She thought Donnie resented her for dragging him into it.

"Regardless, we need to move on this now, Donnie. Rebecca might have key info on this investigation. You know, we need to act quickly." Morgan paced back and forth in the small area between their desks.

"When is the funeral?" he asked, spreading the file folder from Hallie Marks's crime scene across his desk.

"Forensics won't release the body for another week or two. I can't wait that long." Morgan put her phone back in her jacket pocket and placed her hand on Donnie's desk. On her left little finger was the thin silver band her brother gave her when she graduated from Indiana University with a degree in criminology.

She shook her head, causing her dark-brown ponytail to swing over her shoulder. "Look. None of the information in the forensics report surprises me. She died from blunt force trauma to the face and head. The blows were deliberate and deadly. And I believe that the killer's signature is in how he treats the hands. He smashes the victim's hands hours before killing her. Why do you suppose that is?"

"Hands can represent a lot of things."

"Tenderness? Hand-holding?"

"Without them we are less able. Impaired." Donnie fiddled with the pen on his desk. "But the imprints on the body didn't match the checkered pattern on the meat tenderizer. They dismissed that mallet as a possible murder weapon."

"I know what the murder weapon was," Morgan said.

"A hammer." Donnie completed her thought.

"Just like Amy Dufresne."

Then he nodded. "It does remind me of Amy Dufresne."

"It does, doesn't it?" Morgan wanted the confirmation. "It seems too farfetched, but the similarities can't be coincidental, can they?"

"And Sara Evans, too," he said.

Morgan exhaled. At last she had connected with Donnie on this. After ten years as a beat cop in downtown Indy, Donald James had received a promotion to detective in 2001. Several years later, he was assigned a murder case that made slasher films seem like a night at the symphony. Amy Dufresne was bludgeoned to death, but not by a hammer. Or at least forensics couldn't prove what the murder weapon was. The Indianapolis woman was also left with mangled hands. She was so brutally beaten that her swollen features made her unrecognizable.

Worse than that, she had remained alive for four days before succumbing to dehydration.

Determined to help with the unsolved Amy Dufresne investigation, Morgan had transferred from Bloomington to Indianapolis Metro Homicide. She saw a loose connection between her friend Fay and Amy, but the killer didn't leave a trace or a hammer in Amy's apartment. The case went cold. Five years later, another victim was found with similar injuries.

Sara Evans had sustained similar, life-ending blows to her face. A singer in a band, she worked late nights at downtown bars. Both her hands had been crushed during the attack. Because of the impact sites on her skin, and the size and depth of the blows, the murder weapon was determined to be a Stanley wooden-handled, twenty-four-ounce hammer. It too, was never found.

Back then, Donnie had told Morgan that he believed Amy's and Sara's attackers were the same person. However, the DA had a strong case against the thug who was arrested for Sara's murder and was sentenced for it. Morgan suspected he wasn't the killer, but the man had a long rap sheet of rapes and violent behavior that played against him.

"That case was closed, Morgan," he reminded her. "Both cases are closed."

With Sara's killer behind bars and no connection to Amy, no investigator in the state wanted to link the two cases. Morgan and Donnie were alone in their belief that the man found guilty was not the killer.

Morgan faced Donnie and leaned back on the edge of her desk. "I know that hammers are used to kill people all the time. But in both those cases, not just *any* hammer was used. It was a Stanley twenty-four-ounce hammer."

Donnie toyed with a pen, rolling it between his fingers. "Every household has a hammer."

"Right." Morgan looked down at her black, high-heeled shoes. "It's an essential tool in every home. And yet—"

"Yet there were no hammers on the site at Hallie Marks's house," Donnie said.

On Morgan's order, forensics searched every drawer, cabinet, and container in the house. "It was almost as if the missing hammer is a deliberate omission."

Donnie looked up from his cushioned, black-leather desk chair. "A clue," he agreed. He set the pen down and spun it like a top. "It's bugging you, isn't it?"

"God yes."

"I know. Me too." Donnie touched his cell phone with the index finger of his right hand.

"We scoured that house, Donnie. There wasn't a scrap. I'll bet the fingerprinting lab doesn't have shit either."

"We'll find that out tomorrow."

Morgan turned to the window. "Everything we know about this murderer is in the killing. That's his process. For one thing, the victim is always a woman."

"It was a seduction." Donnie leaned back in his chair and crossed his arms.

"A setup, that's for sure," she agreed.

"And . . ."

"It's always the hands and face," they said in unison.

Morgan shook her head. "Specifically the hands. But why? Crushing someone's hands isn't meant to kill them."

Donnie explained. "I don't know."

They'd had this conversation several times before. He didn't want the cases to be linked because of the work involved. When Donnie took his promotion at the end of the year, he didn't want to leave any loose ends. He was trying to make a clean transition between the two jobs. But Morgan couldn't stand the idea of losing him. He was her mentor. He'd taught her most of what she knew.

Donnie sat up, holding his cell phone, poised and ready. "Okay. My turn," he said, and dialed.

"You're calling Rebecca?"

Smiling, he said, "Yes, sweetie pie."

"Thank you." Morgan put her hands together as if in prayer. They waited for the call to connect as Morgan whispered "thank you" again. For a moment, she basked in the pleasure of knowing that Donnie agreed with her. It had been months.

Donnie shook his head. Voice mail picked up, and he started to leave a message. "Rebecca, I'm Detective James. We met briefly the other day. Detective Jewell and I need to discuss Ms. Marks with you. I can be reached at—"

"Detective?"

On hearing Rebecca's voice, Morgan perked up.

"Yes. Good afternoon." Donnie put the call on speakerphone.

"Oh, not really." She sniffed.

"I'm so sorry if I caught you at a bad time." To Morgan, he mouthed, "She's crying."

"Ha." Rebecca gave a shrill half-laugh. Then they heard her blow her nose. "Please tell me you've found the killer."

"Not yet. We're working on it," Donnie explained.

"I haven't been home in weeks. And now . . . I *can't* go back there."

"My partner and I have been trying to reach you. We need information about your fiancé to continue our investigation. Is there a time we can get together and talk, Rebecca? The sooner the better." Donnie rolled a pen between his fingers.

"I . . . can't. I . . . This is too hard."

Donnie spoke to her in a soothing, deep, mellow tone. "You loved her. I understand. I'd like to help. This is an important case, Rebecca. May we come by this evening to talk in person?"

A few seconds passed. Impatient, Morgan crossed her arms over her chest.

Donnie rolled the pen, letting it hover over a notepad. "Rebecca?"

"This has ruined my life, Detective. Ruined everything," she cried.

"We need to meet with you tonight," Donnie stressed while nodding to Morgan.

"You'll find the person who did this?"

"We will certainly try."

Between sobs, Rebecca finally agreed. "Okay."

"Thank you, Rebecca. Thank you," he said.

Rebecca gave him the address.

CHAPTER 3

MORGAN

Homes on the near-north side of Indy were sturdy, handsome, and covered in ivy. Rebecca's sister lived in a brick colonial with an ancient oak tree in the front yard and red fall mums blooming around the front stoop. On the way there, Morgan's car engine made loud, knocking noises.

The 1998 Toyota Corolla had clocked over five hundred thousand miles from road trips to her parents' in Bloomington, Indiana. As Morgan pulled into the long driveway, the car ground to a halt, then sputtered and moaned.

"Why did I let you drive?" Stuffed into the passenger seat with his arms clutched to his chest, Donnie swept his head from side to side.

"You let me drive because your wife needed the SUV."

"I don't know much about cars." He unbuckled his seatbelt. "But it may be time for a new one."

Morgan parked the vehicle. "Don't say that. I'll take it into the shop again." As she turned off the engine, a small explosion jolted the car. Steam erupted from around the edges of the hood.

Morgan leaped out. "No, no, no. No, Thomas. No."

Donnie had always driven because Morgan's car was often in the shop. And he'd never heard her address Thomas by name. Donnie squeezed through the car door. "Did I hear that right? Did you actually give your car a name?"

"Yes." Morgan stood in front of the vehicle with her hands on her head. Too upset to be embarrassed about it, she explained, "His name is Thomas Toyota." Soothing the car's wounds with two hands, she air-patted Thomas like a dog, knowing it was too hot to touch. "Oh, Thomas," she cried.

Donnie chuckled. "Sometimes, Mo, you are such a kid."

"Don't die, Thomas." Morgan fanned the steam away from Thomas's hood.

Donnie shook his head and started up the walkway toward the house. "Just like you're still in high school," Donnie jested. "Come on. We'll call a tow truck after the interview."

Concerned for her old friend, Morgan looked back at Thomas and then followed Donnie past bright red mums up to the house. "I got this car in high school."

"That was a long time ago." From his heart, Donnie said, "You need a new car, Mo."

A paunchy, middle-aged man with graying hair at his temples answered the door. "Evening, Detectives," he said in a hushed voice. He trundled outside, and furtively looking back inside the house, closed the door.

Donnie thrust his hand toward the man. "Detective James."

He gave Donnie's hand a limp, gratuitous shake. "Davis Hearst, no relationship to the famous Hearsts." He said it as an automatic disclaimer and a part of his given name. "Look, Alex would kill me if she saw me talking to you."

"Alex?" Morgan asked.

"My wife. Rebecca's sister. She runs the show. With me, with her sister, she's trying to keep this whole murder business quiet."

Morgan introduced herself, then asked, "Is Alex protecting Rebecca?"

"Reba didn't kill Hallie, if that's what you're here to find out. Reba doesn't have a cruel bone in her body. She's a basket case. We're always taking care of her."

"Why's that?" Donnie crossed his arms, towering over the man.

"Reba's in denial about that relationship. She and Hallie were always on-again, off-again. It was normal for Hallie to be out with friends when

Reba returned from work trips. Sometimes Reba stayed here for weeks in a row."

"But she owns the house in Danville," Morgan said.

"She'd practically given it to Hallie. Alex and I don't approve. She gave everything to that woman." Davis slicked back the few hairs he had on top of his head.

"Did Alex approve of their relationship?" Morgan asked.

Davis turned toward her. "Of course she did. She's her sister."

"Tell us about it," Morgan encouraged him.

Nervous, Davis looked back at the house. "I don't tell secrets, Detectives, but I want this to end for the kids' sake and for my family's sake."

Donnie cocked his head to the side while fixing Davis with a pointed look. "Sure, sure, we get it," he said.

"What I've heard is that Hallie held this relationship over Reba—Rebecca—like it was her ticket to ride. She threatened Reba with it, used it against her. Told her repeatedly that she'd leave her for this other . . . person."

Morgan looked up at Donnie and elbowed him. "Was Hallie seeing another woman?" she asked Davis.

"Of course she was. She didn't take the relationship that seriously," Davis said.

Morgan stood taller. "Mr. Hearst, right now, we have a very short list of suspects. Do you know who Hallie was dating? Can you give us a name?"

"Truthfully, I don't know who Hallie's latest conquest was. She flitted from bed to bed."

"Does Rebecca know?" Donnie asked.

"She might." Davis moved past them and opened the heavy oak door. In front of him, three children, two boys and a girl, stampeded down the stairs. The tallest boy yelled, "I'm first!"

"Not if I get there first!"

"No, me!"

"It's my game!"

The man ignored the children as they pushed past him through the narrow hallway toward the back of the house. "Rebecca's in the kitchen," he said.

A woman's voice rose above the shouting. "Where are you going? Allen! Lexi! Aaron! Stop running!"

Davis ushered them into the kitchen with an outstretched arm and then disappeared through another door. The kids talked all at once, each voicing a different complaint. Morgan and Donnie heard the fray before entering the low-lit kitchen.

The children stood in a semicircle around a woman with long, light-brown hair, playing referee and mother. "Aaron goes first. It's his turn. Yes, Lexi, you get a turn too. Allen, you're in charge. Be fair. Play fair."

After grumbling, the children ran off again, the little girl following the two boys.

Their mother introduced herself with an apology. "Sorry about the kids. I'm Alex, Rebecca's sister."

Morgan shook her hand. Then she noticed Rebecca Harrington sitting at a wood-block table in the center of the underlit ultramodern kitchen. She looked up when Alex introduced herself. There were dark half-moons under her bloodshot eyes. Hunched over, she dragged out her stool, looking sleep-deprived and tortured. Though it had been a warm fall day, she wore a heavy, gray knee-length sweater wrapped around her square-shaped body. She clasped it tightly and asked Alex, "Is it okay if we talk in here?"

"That's fine. Whatever you need, sweetie." Alex hugged Rebecca, then rested her hands on her shoulders. "Do you want me to stay?"

"I'll be okay, thanks."

Alex nodded and left the room.

"Have a seat, please." Rebecca waved at the table and sat down heavily. She'd lost her fight against gravity, and like a big, floppy pillow, she balanced on the stool.

Donnie stayed near the doorway, giving Morgan the lead to question Rebecca. Morgan sat herself down on a rustic wooden stool close to Rebecca. "We need to discuss Hallie. Anything you can tell us will move the investigation along."

"I don't think I can help you." Rebecca stared into a coffee cup, slicking back her short brown hair with one hand.

Sensitive to Rebecca's emotional state, Morgan asked carefully, "Hallie had a secret life, didn't she? Receipts from her wallet indicate that she'd been frequenting several bars in Indianapolis."

Rebecca nodded, biting her lip.

Morgan looked down at Rebecca's left hand. She wore a green malachite ring that matched the ring on Hallie's pinky finger. Rebecca wore hers on the ring finger, like an engagement or wedding band. "Were you two engaged?" She asked.

Rebecca's mouth screwed up tight. She nodded.

The question was hard to ask. "Are you aware of any relationships she may have had on the side?"

Rebecca sniffed, but didn't falter when she answered, "You know how relationships are, Detective. We loved each other. Some days, we were made for each other. Others, we went about our business like two strangers shopping at a Walmart. On those days, we'd pass in the aisle and barely acknowledge each other."

Never having been in a lasting relationship herself, Morgan wondered how they could have been engaged if that was the case. She placed her elbows on the counter, mirroring Rebecca.

Donnie shifted his weight. "You're a reporter, is that right?"

"I'm a midwestern news correspondent for Channel 6 News in Indy. They send me to locations in the four-state region. In a good month, I'm home for two or three weeks. Lately, I've been working more than that."

"Tell us about Hallie."

Rebecca fingered the malachite ring with her right hand. "What do you want to know? She was an interior designer. She kept all her catalogues and samples at her office in Indianapolis. That's where she made her magic happen. People from all over the state knew about her."

"What about her friends? Did she have a group she liked to hang out with?" Morgan kept her voice low. The noise of the kids playing a video game came from the other room. She watched Rebecca's facial expressions.

"No. She didn't have a group of friends." Rebecca's eyebrows lifted, but her gaze remained on the ring. "She was always busy. Hallie was planning our wedding."

"When she went to these bars, did she go to meet someone there?" Morgan asked.

"She met with her clients sometimes. Or I was with her. I don't think she went out as much as you're implying."

"When was the wedding going to be?"

Rebecca's cheeks reddened. "Next year. In June." She buried her face in her hands.

Morgan turned to make eye contact with Donnie. He nodded his okay, which meant Morgan had free rein to continue as she felt necessary. She took a breath before delving deeper. "First, where were you in the days before Hallie's murder?"

"Ohio. I have flight receipts."

"Hallie wasn't as devoted to you as you were to her, was she, Rebecca? I see that it bothered you."

"I loved her," Rebecca whimpered.

"But you hated what she did to you. It hurt, didn't it? Hallie screwed around and that angered you."

Rebecca peered over her fingertips at Morgan. "What?"

"Did you really go on a trip? I think you could have been lurking around Danville and following Hallie. I think you could have been stalking her and when you found her with someone else, you killed her."

Color washed from Rebecca's face.

Donnie cleared his throat.

"My crew walked me to my car in the airport parking lot on Friday night," Rebecca said.

Morgan leaned in. "Do you understand that, right now, *you* were the closest person to Hallie? We can't find her killer unless you cooperate with us."

"I want you to find her killer." Rebecca's hands floated in front of her face. Tears rolled down her cheeks. "How can you think that I…"

Alex poked her head into the room. "Reba, darling, you okay?"

Rebecca shook her head.

Alex rushed to Rebecca's side, put a hand on her back, and massaged her sister's shoulders. "This has been awful, just awful," she said to Morgan. "Hallie's family came into town this morning. They treated my sister so badly. They didn't accept the relationship."

The defeated woman's shoulders heaved with her sobs. As Alex comforted her, Rebecca inhaled a ragged breath.

"We'll make it as quick as we can." Morgan stood up and nodded to Donnie.

"Hallie had credit card receipts from The Blue Room dated August twenty-eighth. Did you go there together?" Donnie asked.

Redness from crying flushed Rebecca's cheeks. She peered out from behind her hands. "That's the jazz club where we first met. Do you think that's where she met the killer?"

"It's possible." Morgan persisted. "Who would she have been going to meet?"

"I really don't know. We lived a very quiet life together. When I was in town, we cooked dinner together and watched movies. I didn't know she went out without me. She loved me." Rebecca's hands went back to cover her face and a new stream of tears.

Donnie tugged at Morgan's arm but she resisted.

"She just needs closure," Alex said.

"We'll see what we can find out." Donnie moved toward the door and beckoned Morgan to follow.

"Thank you, Ms. Harrington. We'll be in touch," he said.

CHAPTER 4

MORGAN

By the time Rebecca finished telling Morgan what she knew, and by the time Lawrence towed Thomas to the shop and Donnie's friend, a patrolman, came to pick them up and dropped Morgan off at home, it was after ten o'clock.

Inside, the house was just as she had left it: boots and socks in a heap beside the garage door and her cereal bowl in the kitchen sink. Her housemates, the Raffertys, had flown south for the winter with the flock of elderly retirees. It was a sweet living arrangement for Morgan, who took care of their house and paid no rent during the months they were in Florida. She went to the kitchen, poured herself a hefty serving of Cabernet, and made microwave popcorn. She took a big swig before carrying the glass and popcorn bowl up to her bedroom. The wine would put her right to sleep. Setting her phone on the bedside table next to the glass, she unbuckled her holster and placed the SIG Sauer 9mm on her dresser along with her badge. She tossed her red scarf on the foot of her bed before sitting down next to it.

Since the Raffertys had left Morgan hadn't bothered to clean up or do laundry. The floor had become one big pile of clothes. Like most nights, she didn't feel like cleaning. As she unbuttoned her shirt, her cell phone rang. She checked the caller ID.

"Kinda late, isn't it, Rob?"

"Hello to you too." Robert Gibson never called unless he was lonely and horny.

Morgan picked up her glass of wine. "And it's a weeknight."

"Yeah, well, I was working late and heard about you and your car."

"What about my car?"

"No need to get defensive. I've got nothing bad to say about that old beat-up piece of . . . Toyota."

Resigned, Morgan said, "It died tonight. Again. Do you think I need a new one?" She sniffed the rich aroma of her red wine before lifting the glass to her lips.

"Probably. You gonna need a ride to work tomorrow?"

Morgan and Rob almost dated. For six months they had seen each other once a week for sex and a drink, but when he wanted more of her time, she couldn't give it to him. Rob had asked her to move in with him, but she had declined. She couldn't get her head out of her work.

"Yeah, I guess I will," she answered. "You don't have to go to work early, do you?"

"It's okay. I think I'll be in the area."

"You think?"

"I miss you," he said.

"I miss you too, Rob." She did miss his warm body in her bed. She missed his comforting nature and his friendship.

"You miss my tongue," he told her.

She laughed out loud in agreement. "What are you doing calling me this late? Aren't you seeing Allie from Child Services?"

"Ah, that didn't work out."

Rob worked in the Indianapolis Mounted Patrol. He and Morgan had met one year earlier at the Indy 500 while he was on horseback working the event. He was a down-to-earth cop, and the best part of his job was that he had regular hours.

"So you're hitting on me again?" She had also missed the light banter between them. What she didn't miss was the pressure to maintain the relationship.

"Are Bill and Adrienne gone for the winter?" This one question held so many others. He was asking if she was home. If he could come over. If she would see him tonight.

A dog barked through the phone line.

"They're gone," she answered.

"Yes. Hush. Hey, now. Shush," Rob said.

"But it's late," she said, wishing it wasn't.

A dog barked again.

"It's not that late," Rob said.

This time, Morgan heard a dog barking outside the house. "Is that Gretta barking?" The dog sounded nearby. "Rob? Are you here?" With her free hand, Morgan picked up her glass and padded barefoot down the stairs. She saw a shadow through the frosted panes beside the front door.

"Will you stop? You're giving me away," Rob said to Gretta.

"What are you doing here?" Morgan peeked through the peephole at Rob's distorted, enlarged nose.

"Can I come in?"

Morgan turned off her phone and shoved it in her back pocket. With one hand, she turned the dead bolt and opened the door. Gretta, a medium-sized shepherd mix, was first to greet her with a wagging tail.

Rob stood there, handsome and tall. His brown hair was mussed up, and a thin layer of stubble framed his soft lips. "I knew you'd be up," he said, indicating the glass in her hand.

"What are you doing here?"

"Are you inviting us in?"

Morgan squatted on the floor and gave Gretta some loving scratches between her ears. She responded with a smooch and a sloppy lick. "I'll invite *you* in," she said to the dog. "But why'd you have to bring *him*?"

Gretta barged forward, heading for the kitchen and making it impossible for Morgan to turn them away.

Rob removed his coat and hung it on a stool as Morgan poured him a glass of wine. While they caught up, Gretta lay watching them from the floor. An hour later, as the conversation slowed and the wine was drunk, Rob put a hand on Morgan's back.

"What do you think?" he asked.

Morgan looked into Rob's dark-brown eyes. "I'm no good at this. That's what I think."

His hand traveled to her shoulder, and he turned her toward him. Earlier tonight, she'd thought she wanted a man. Now that he was here, she feared the commitment.

He spoke in a whispered breath. "I missed you, Mo."

Morgan couldn't resist those lips. Her hand moved to his cheek, and she kissed him. His lips were soft, sensual.

It had been too long.

CHAPTER 5

MORGAN

From a window stage in The Blue Room, a soulful four-member band played the language of lovers. On the cramped little stage, a stout, voluptuous woman dressed in a low-cut, floor-length gown crooned the words to a tune by Billy Holiday as her electric-red lips grazed the microphone. The guitar player, wearing a tattered green army jacket over a tight black tank top, made love to his guitar with his eyes closed. Hunched behind them, a giant wearing a black suit plucked his acoustic bass. The keyboard player with frond-like dread locks pressed his back against the wall to give more of the tiny stage to the others.

Their music filled gaps in the crowded bar, taking up space where there wasn't room for anything more. Near the stage, a group of six paid the doorman and filtered into the club, mingling with the existing standing-room-only crowd. Another group waited to be let in to the narrow, runway-shaped nightclub. The bar ran the length of the long wall. Morgan sat in the center of it, where she could see everything.

Donnie, like the keyboard player, leaned against the wall. Across the room from Morgan, he held a sweaty energy drink in one hand. Morgan had turned on her stool to see the room and noticed how Donnie wriggled to the music and tapped his foot as the caffeine hit his bloodstream. He wasn't used to going out this late. Family life and years had settled him down and tamed him.

Hallie had had a receipt for The Blue Room in her wallet. Rebecca said it was where she and Hallie first met. Once they moved to Danville, they stopped coming to the club. Perhaps Hallie needed more entertainment than she could find in the small town of Danville. Rebecca hadn't known that when she was out of town Hallie went out alone.

Because relationships were not Morgan's forte, she could only imagine the nuances that were necessary to keep love alive. A handful of short-lived relationships—discards—littered Morgan's past. She swept the memories away to focus on Hallie Marks.

Applause erupted in the bar.

"Thank you. All my people, thank you." The singer scanned the crowded room. "Ladies and gentlemen, we're gonna take a short break. Please stick around, cuz there's lots more where that came from." She replaced the microphone on its stand and whispered something to her guitar player.

Morgan turned on her stool and made eye contact with Donnie as the singer parted the sardined people and headed straight for him. She leaned close to his ear and touched Donnie's arm in a familiar and seductive manner. Morgan wished she could read her lips.

Though the band had stopped, the noise level was high. For a weeknight, The Blue Room was packed. She wondered if the band had drawn the crowd.

"How's that Coke?" one of the bartenders asked Morgan, raising his voice over the din.

Morgan swirled what was left. "I'll take another, please."

He took the glass and filled it with a scoop of ice. "What's a nice girl like you doing in a dump like this?"

"Dump? Looks like you do good business. Is it always this crowded?"

"Almost always." He set the refilled glass on a fresh napkin. "Name's Mike. Let me know if you need anything else."

"Thanks." Morgan discreetly flashed her badge then leaned forward so she didn't have to shout. "Can I ask you some questions?"

Mike nodded. "Figures." He held his hands in the air like he was under arrest. "I swear, if she—"

Morgan shook her head and handed him a picture of Hallie Marks. "I was wondering if you've seen this woman in here."

He took the photo and raised a hand at a customer at the end of the bar. "Hold on a minute," he shouted then glanced back at the photo and dropped it on the bar. "She comes in here all the time, usually on week-nights. She in trouble?"

"You could say that."

He went back to work, filling drinks and handing out beers.

"Hey, Mike! Get me a gimlet, will you?" The singer's voice carried from the far-right end of the bar. Donnie stood next to her waving a twenty-dollar bill.

Mike reached into the cooler, then passed three beers to a man behind Morgan. He traded for a credit card then slipped over to the centrally located register. He handed the receipt and card back to the man, then asked Morgan, "Hallie, right? On Wednesday nights she sits where you're sitting now." Mike looked down at the photo, then moved away to take someone else's order.

Morgan looked around the bar. If Hallie was a regular, perhaps her killer was too. *Would the killer return here after murdering Hallie?*

The bartender passed another bottle to a customer who traded it for a handful of ones. When he returned, Morgan asked, "Did she usually come here alone? Or was she with friends?"

He flipped two glasses onto the counter and scooped ice into them. "She was always with her fiancé."

"You mean Rebecca Harrington?"

Mike shook his head, "Who? She's been dating a tall skinny guy for months. He proposed to her right here."

"Really." Morgan pushed the photo toward him. "Are you sure?"

"Positive. He gave her a ring and everything. Nice-sized diamond."

Morgan wondered why she hadn't been wearing it at the time of her death. Quickly, she jotted a note to have forensics do one last search for an engagement ring. "Got any idea what his name is?"

He shook his head. "Something happen to her?"

"Murdered," she said.

"Damn." He stopped pouring to raise his eyebrows and look up at Morgan. "Damn. I mean, no shit. She was just here, right there." He tapped the bar and shook his head. Returning to his duties, Mike poured from a bottle in one hand and sprayed mixer with the other.

The singer called from the far end of the bar. "Hey Mike, where's my gimlet?"

"Coming, Rosie."

Mike took the drinks and set them down in front of Donnie. While they conversed, Morgan studied the room. She singled out a woman with long, blond, straightened hair and watched her lean on a man. Her arm wrapped around his as she laughed. Morgan imagined she was the cheerleader type, with her athlete boyfriend—*correction, fiancé.* She wore a ring. *How easy it would be to lead someone on, wearing their ring. Had Hallie planned on dumping Rebecca? Had Rebecca known?*

When Mike returned, she asked, "Is he here tonight?"

"Naw. He'd be right up at the bar if he was."

Morgan dug into her wallet and peeled out her debit card. She tried to hand it to him, but he pushed it away.

"Don't worry about it, the Coke's on me."

"Thanks for your help, Mike."

He smiled, "The pleasure's all mine."

CHAPTER 6

MORGAN

"How could Hallie have been planning your wedding when she's engaged to another man?"

"Rebecca hasn't done anything wrong." Alex Hearst took a stance behind her sister, who had crumbled. Rebecca's head lay on her forearms on the kitchen counter and her shoulders heaved up and down with her sobs.

Morgan's feet remained planted on Alex's kitchen floor. Right now she needed every shred of information Rebecca could give her.

Alex's mouth fell open. "Why are you harassing her?"

"Because she lied to us. I think Rebecca knew there wasn't going to be a wedding."

When Rebecca lifted her head, Morgan looked her in the eye. "I think you knew she was with someone else."

Alex took a step to the side, her long flowing pants grazing the floor. Physically she was tall and graceful, the polar opposite to her sister.

Donnie had taken the stool across from Rebecca. With one finger, he slowly typed notes into his tablet. Morgan needed him there for support. He reduced the tension by saying, "Mrs. Hearst, we don't have any evidence for an arrest. We're here to ask questions, that's all."

"Rebecca, I need answers." Morgan said. "Did you know that Hallie had recently become engaged? To someone else?"

Rebecca may have nodded. It was hard to tell.

Davis had gone with the kids to another room, but one must have escaped. Their little girl stood with her cheek pressed against the kitchen door. Alex glanced her way. "It's okay, Lexie." The girl ran to her mom and threw her arms around one of Alex's legs.

Morgan took a shot. She voiced her suspicion with the next question, hoping it would provoke Rebecca to tell what she knew. Morgan said gently, "Help me, please, Rebecca. I wonder if you didn't go to bars with Hallie because you two had broken up months ago."

"I let Hallie stay at my house in Danville. I thought that maybe she'd eventually want me back," Rebecca said.

Alex had lifted her daughter up on her hip. "Rebecca is living with us. She's been staying here for two months. Hallie invited Reba home after Ohio. Right, Reba?"

"Hallie wanted to talk. She even said she missed me. When she told me to come home, I thought we'd be getting back together." Rebecca turned the wadded-up Kleenex in her hand.

"Is something wrong with Aunt Reba?" The girl asked. Alex put a shushing finger to her mouth.

"Hallie walked all over you, didn't she?" Morgan persisted. Rebecca's head finally came up. Her eyes, more swollen than ever, had leaked a puddle of tears on the granite countertop. "She was still wearing my ring!"

The statement touched Morgan's heart. Nearby, a box of tissues sat on the counter. She handed the box to Rebecca, who nodded a thank-you and used a clean one to dab at the continuous stream pouring from her eyes. By now, Morgan suspected that Rebecca's tearful behavior was an act of avoidance. The woman couldn't face the real fact: Hallie hadn't loved her. But this gave her a motive to kill Hallie, tears or not.

Rebecca had been in transit between news stories on the night Hallie was killed. Her cameraman verified her statement. She'd done a story about the green movement in Springfield, Ohio. Organic farms and sustainable farms there were influencing eastern Indiana farmers. The story had aired about the same time Hallie was killed. Rebecca was no longer a suspect, but she was withholding crucial information.

Morgan said gently, "You know Hallie was seeing someone else, but you failed to tell us."

Protectively, Alex draped her free hand over Rebecca's shoulders. "Do you have to do this now, Detective? Look at her."

"Mrs. Hearst, I will ask you to leave the room the next time you interrupt," Morgan said, less harshly than she intended.

"No. Please let her stay." Slumped on the stool, Rebecca sniffed.

"Then answer the question." Morgan was pissed off enough to raise her voice. "Who was the man in Hallie's life?"

Rebecca held the crumpled tissue to her cheek and moaned. "She saw lots of other people. There was Charlotte. There was an Ed or Edward, and someone named Ceecee. She never talked about them. Why would she?" She reached for a new tissue.

"I think his name was Edmund, not Edward." Alex offered. "Or something like that."

"Are you sure?" Morgan asked. She nodded toward Donnie, who typed it into his notes.

After blowing her nose, Rebecca cried: "She was having affairs. She was cheating on me. And I wanted to marry her. I loved her." More tears.

"She wasn't planning your wedding, was she."

"In the state of Indiana?" Alex threw her head back. "We tried to protect my sister from the haters."

When Donnie and Morgan stared at her, she continued. "Hallie wanted a white wedding. She wanted to get married, and that would never happen with Reba. Not in this state, anyway."

Rebecca looked up at her sister for the first time since Morgan had arrived. The pain on her face indicated that she had never known Alex felt this way. "What do you mean?"

"Honey. I love you, but Hallie wasn't right for you. She turned your cute little house in Danville into a love shack." Alex's brutal statement got a reaction from her sister.

"Why did you encourage me to stay with her?"

Alex's mouth opened but nothing came out. She shook her head.

Alex Hearst, Rebecca's sister and caretaker to a degree, worked a full-time job as a medical assistant. Davis ran his own business as a

marketing consultant. Both had been removed from Morgan's list of suspects because of solid alibis. Both had willingly turned over their phones
and computers for inspection. Nothing of interest had been found.

Morgan balanced her need to know with a modicum of sensitivity.
She was too close to solving her own past to let this go, so she leaned in
and placed her hands on Rebecca's arms. Face-to-face with Rebecca, she
said in a lowered voice, "This is your chance to get even." She whispered
to emphasize her point. "I'm invested in catching this fucker too. I've
been chasing him for my entire career. Tell me what you know."

In Rebecca's red, swollen eyes, Morgan saw a spark of something.
She believed she had gotten through to the woman.

Rebecca tilted her head, nodding slowly at first, then more vigor-
ously. She sniffed and straightened her back. Alex removed her hand
from Rebecca's shoulder.

Morgan sat on the remaining stool and dug her hand into the pocket
of her black blazer. Her fingers grazed the soft edges of worn paper. Her
hand rested for a second on the familiar spiral notebook, and when
Rebecca began talking, she was ready.

"She said he lives in Lafayette. He's an accountant. I don't know why
she would want that, because she was so creative. She made everything
beautiful. I loved that about her."

Donnie encouraged her to stay focused on the man.

"Yes," Morgan agreed. "What did he look like?"

"I never saw him. But Alex isn't right. His name isn't Edmund, it's
Ekhard. Ekhard Klein."

CHAPTER 7

MORGAN

"Stop calling me!" The line went dead.

Morgan stared at the name on her cell phone, trying to connect psychically with Victoria Ramsey, Fay's mother.

I'm sorry, she wanted to say. For almost fifteen years, every time she had called this number, she got the same response. The definition of insanity is repeating the same task over and over and hoping for a different outcome. That's what this was, and Morgan knew it.

She set the cell phone on the couch beside her and stared into her lap at pictures of two girls with happy smiling faces: Fay Ramsey, a close friend in those days, and the younger version of herself. It was the summer before their first year of college. They were so stoned that day at the amusement park. That summer—the summer of weed, they'd called it—they were always stoned.

Pictures from that little Kodak 110 camera were terribly blurry. Still, with long brown hair blowing in her face, Fay looked frightened. In line, waiting to go on the Son of Beast roller coaster at Kings Island Amusement Park, Fay told her that she had never been on a ride like that. When Morgan had coerced her with ridiculous death threats—*I'm gonna kill you if you don't go with me*—Fay had reluctantly agreed.

"If I live through it," Fay had said with a smile, "then you can kill me." The photos were taken two days before Fay's abduction and subsequent murder.

Guilt and shame surrounding Fay's death surfaced again. After all this time, the same feelings rose to heat Morgan's face. *My best friend died because of me.*

That summer they had spent every day together, window-shopping, listening to music, driving around, and walking along the park trails. They spent hours designing their dorm room and planning their schedules. Together, they had saved enough to buy a small papasan chair and had purchased a purple tapestry to hang in a room they never moved into.

Morgan still owned that tapestry. It remained folded, just like when she bought it, with the price tag still pinned to the corner. And just as she had held onto those material reminders of that day, so she had also clung to feelings of guilt.

She pushed the books aside and thought, *I should have taken better care of Fay. I never should have let her go. Fay Ramsey died under my watch.* They were the same thoughts that had driven her to become a detective. They were the same words circling and circling around since Fay's life had ended. But something was hidden there. Something dark and sticky remained behind the cloak. If only she could remember. If only she could speak with Mrs. Ramsey.

Morgan was one of the last people to see Fay alive. Though Victoria Ramsey blamed her for Fay's death, the police had found nothing to incriminate anyone. They questioned Morgan and her parents for hours, even searched Thomas the Toyota and Morgan's bedroom. Fay died from blunt force trauma to her face and hands. Then the killer left her body to rot beside the creek.

Morgan chilled at the memory. Something about Hallie's murder pulled at her, compelling her to search for the answers to the irrational thoughts driving her. Though there was nothing concrete to go on, she couldn't separate these cases from Fay's murder. If she found Hallie's killer, she could solve the mystery of Fay's death, too.

She rubbed the backs of her arms and realized she hadn't eaten yet.

On her way to the kitchen, her cell phone rang. She doubled back to retrieve it from the coffee table.

"Miss Detective Jewell?"

The call came from Lawrence at Conner's Auto Shop with the word on her precious Thomas. "Lawrence. What's the verdict? Will Thomas live?"

"Not without major reconstruction. I located the parts. They were hard to find, Miss Detective. My estimate, for replacing the transmission and starter, for a new thermal coupling and exhaust manifold, will be sixty-two hundred."

"Dollars?" Morgan was in shock.

"Yes, ma'am. Dollars."

Morgan placed a palm on her forehead. "I can buy a new Thomas for that."

"Not a new one. Used, though."

Unable to justify the expense, Morgan had poured just under two thousand into the car this year alone for new brakes, new tires, and an air filter. "I'm sorry." She put her head in her hand. "How much will it be to tow him to the dump?"

"Nothing, ma'am. If you'll let me keep the Toyota for parts, I won't charge you anything," Lawrence added.

It was a no-brainer. "Deal. Thank you, Lawrence." A fitting end for beloved Thomas. Now he was an organ donor.

"Yes, Miss Detective. Thank you."

The news hit hard. Morgan hung up and lowered her head. The death of her car was the end of an era. Images of that time floated in and out. It was like flipping through pages of an old, familiar book. Bits of conversation came and went, memories of Fay's laughter and their worries. And the way she looked in Morgan's flowery sundress.

CHAPTER 8

MORGAN: 16 Years Ago

"Fill me up." Fay Ramsey held her empty plastic Solo cup at arm's length. Pink drops of fruit punch dotted it inside and out. The ice had long since melted and gone.

"Atta girl." Morgan Jewell closed one eye for better focus. She leaned, unsteadily, toward Fay. The nearly empty rum bottle in her hand swayed over Fay's plastic cup. "We're outta punch," she said.

"Oh no." At the last second, Fay pulled her cup back, causing Morgan to pour the last of the rum on Fay's sandaled foot.

"What d'you do that for? Now it's gone," Morgan whined. Music thumped, resounding in her chest. She closed her eyes and floated away on the beat of the song. When she opened them again, Fay was setting her cup on the coffee table next to a half-dozen just like it. She rolled off the couch onto her hands and knees, scattering empty beer cans across the floor as she crawled to a corner of the room, where she put her head in a potted palm.

Across the room, Elaine, who belonged to the house, was straddling a boy with her back to them. Morgan couldn't see the boy's face. The two bodies became one blurry, Medusa-like creature.

"I jus' puked in a plant," Fay said, returning to the couch.

"You feel better then," Morgan consoled her friend.

Laughter erupted from the kitchen. Morgan's gaze was drawn to a few kids who were still standing, drinking beers and munching on corn chips.

Cigarette smoke lingered in the room, lazy curls drifted here and there. Beer bottles and cups half full of pink liquid littered the square wooden coffee table and matching side tables. She wondered what time it was.

"I should go home," Fay said.

"That's a good idea. Your mom's going to be furry . . . furry . . ." Morgan looked at the ceiling as if it would reveal the word. "Furious!"

Fay giggled. Wearing Morgan's flower-printed sundress, she looked super cute tonight. Morgan wanted to kiss her. Instead, she laughed with her. Even sober, Fay was rarely happy. It cheered Morgan to see her friend this way. Somewhere in the back, clouded reaches of her mind, she saw Fay coming out of her overprotected shell.

"C'mon. I'll get you home safe." Morgan rolled to all fours and, making her way to her feet, stumbled a little. "Bye, Elaine. Call tomorrow if you need help cleaning."

Elaine's mouth was firmly attached to the boy. She didn't answer.

Fay took Morgan's arm, helping them both balance. "I don't think you should drive, Mo."

Staggering to the front door, Morgan realized Fay was right. Arm in arm, the young girls helped each other out the door and down the quiet neighborhood street toward Morgan's car.

"Did you have fun?" Morgan asked.

"Absolutely. Bes' night ever."

Fay's response elicited an ear-to-ear grin. "College will be so awesome." Morgan looked forward to getting out on her own. More than anything, she wanted Fay to feel good about it too.

"Maybe."

"It. Is. Believe it, Fay."

"And terrifying."

Morgan let go of Fay's arm. "Why terrifying?"

Fay looked at the grass. "I dunno. It just is." Their destination in sight, Fay stumbled toward the car.

"Because?" Morgan shouted at Fay's back.

"Because it's such a big place. Because there are so many people. Because the classes will be hard. I don't know, Morgan. Just because."

Fay ran the rest of the way to the car and bent over, collapsed, onto the hood.

When Morgan caught up, she looked at her brand-new red Toyota. Mom and Dad had made a big deal of her high school graduation present. She needed a car, but it had cost a lot of money. Tonight she knew better than to drive it. Her parents would be devastated if anything happened to it. If she had only smoked weed, she thought, she could drive safely. *I've had three . . . or was it four? . . . rum drinks at the party.* She couldn't remember.

Dropping her purse on the ground, Morgan collapsed to her bare knees in the grass. She kicked off her sandals and smoothed out her sleeveless top.

Fay smiled at her. "What're you doing?"

"I wouldn't be much of a guard dog if I drove you home right now."

"Guard dog?"

"Yeah." Morgan sat back on the soft, plushy green lawn. "I'm your desi . . . desi . . . I appointed *me* as your personal guard dog. *I* will take care of you when we get to IU. *I* will help you get to classes and help you with homework."

"Why?" Fay leaned back against the red car and crossed her arms over her chest with a scowl on her otherwise delicate features.

"Cause it's scary. Your words, not mine."

Fay shook her head. "Some guard dog. You look more like a miniature poodle than a German shepherd."

Morgan crossed her legs Indian style and leaned back on her straightened arms. Her short, light-green skirt flounced over her legs and her dark-brown hair lay loose, brushed out and long. "That doesn't matter. I'm still furry . . . furry . . . fe*ro*cious."

Fay burst out laughing and collapsed in the grass next to Morgan.

"I said it on purpose that time," Morgan explained. "And I mean it. Don't worry, Fay. I will be there for you. I promise."

"My mom will be there every day too. Count on it." Fay plucked a long blade of grass.

Morgan shook her head. "I hope not. Your mom is the fun police."

Fay sank a little lower. Vic treated Fay like a six-year-old. She set strict curfews and maintained a list of places where Fay wasn't allowed to go and people she wasn't allowed to see. Morgan had once graced that list. Over time, Vic had reluctantly warmed up to her.

Cicadas buzzed and purred in the night. Their loud song filled the silence as Morgan planned what to say next. "We'll show your mom how strong and independent you are," she told Fay. "We'll show her you can do it on your own." What she didn't say out loud was, *I'm rescuing you from your monster-mother.*

Fay lay back in the cushiony grass. "You'll help me?"

"Yes! I will be there for you." Taking Fay's hand, Morgan said, "You can do this without her." Her heart filled with tenderness. She wanted to see Fay step into the real, adult world with confidence and command. In helping her friend, Morgan could also begin that phase of life fearlessly. She had fears too, though nothing like Fay's. "You know, I'm a little nervous too."

"You don't seem like it."

Morgan lay back next to Fay. "'Cause I know it will be awesome." These were words she needed to hear herself.

For several hours they lay in the grass talking about the future. About decorating their dorm room. About boys and parties. Morgan pointed out Orion's Belt and the Big Dipper. Time seemed to stand still.

The cicada song diminished, and crickets stopped chirping when the horizon lightened behind the maple trees. Morgan rolled to her feet. "Hope your mom isn't mad. I think I kept you out all night."

"My mom is always mad," Fay admitted with a good dose of cheer.

"Time for your guard dog to take you home." A little dizzy but more sober, Morgan stood up and stretched.

"Are you sure you're okay?"

"I'm fine. Look what time it is." Morgan picked up her purse and reached inside for the keys. "Anyway, this car will get me and you home safely. I promise. This is a great car."

Getting to her feet, Fay asked, "Have you given it a name yet?"

"A name?" Morgan asked, unlocking and opening the door.

Fay climbed in the passenger side and closed the door. "I think Thomas. Thomas Toyota."

As Morgan started it up, she said, "I like it. Thomas is a strong name. It makes him sound reliable."

"Dependable."

"Unwavering."

"Like you," Fay said.

CHAPTER 9

MORGAN

Morgan traced her finger along the chrome edge of a used Honda Accord's window . "It doesn't have very many miles on it," she said. That meant the previous owner hadn't loved it as much as she had loved Thomas Toyota.

"The owner was local, and she only drove to and from work. You're lucky. A car like this doesn't come into the dealership every day. Did you enjoy driving it?" The salesman wore a green blazer over a light-blue golf shirt.

Unlike her old car, this one had sexy curves and a shiny interior. Morgan opened the door and stuck her head inside again. It was too clean.

Nearby, Rob said, "It has smooth transitions. Good handling."

With his gray hair cut short and combed to perfection, the salesman's thin smile and relaxed demeanor were well rehearsed. He started his spiel. "The Accord is one of the most highly . . ."

Rob cut him off. "We know the specs."

"Will this be a family car?" the salesman asked, pressing for more information. "I noticed that you have a dog in your truck."

Morgan laughed. "No." She stood up and closed the door. "Thank you. I'll be in touch."

"If there's anything I can do for you, please." With a flourish, the salesman drew a card from his pocket. "Name's Jeff. Call me."

Morgan walked back to the truck. Rob shook the man's hand, then jogged to catch up with her. "Didn't like it?"

"Nah. It's not what I'm looking for."

In the passenger seat, Gretta greeted them with a hearty tail wag.

Rob hopped in on the driver's side. "What are you looking for?"

"I don't know. But I'll know it when I see it." Morgan didn't like shopping for a car. It was time-consuming, and eventually it would be expensive.

He started up the truck. The sun had sunk below the horizon and the sky turned purple. Evenings were coming earlier and the days were shorter. Turning on the headlights, Rob drove out of the lot. He took a long, heavy breath, "Was there *anything* on the lot you liked?"

Morgan looked at the sea of new and used cars. "No. Not really." Aware how frustrated Rob was, she tried to lighten his mood. "I'll go online and look. There must be cars for sale on the Internet. Besides, I have to work on the computer tonight."

"That case?" he asked.

"I want to check databases. If I can locate someone, I'll call tomorrow to set up an interview." Earlier that day, Morgan had searched every database in the state of Indiana and still came up with a big zero for the elusive Ekhard Klein. One man she found, Ekhard Marcus Klein, had been born thirty-eight years before in Indianapolis on Halloween. But after a short stint as an eighteen-year-old at Butler University, he vanished. Those early records listed his mother, Anna Clare, and father, Theodore Joseph Klein, who were divorced before Ekhard was in high school. He had a younger sister, Caryn, but no other siblings.

Morgan checked public records from the surrounding counties, including Hendricks County where the small town of Danville is located—where Hallie was killed. No one with that name appeared. It seemed Hallie Marks would have married a ghost.

Sandwiched between Morgan and Rob, Gretta stared out the windshield. Morgan stroked her soft fur. "Thanks for taking me car shopping. And sorry I haven't made a decision yet. It's not easy."

"No problem. I'm trying to help. And I'm happy to answer your questions," Rob answered.

"Can I buy you dinner?" Morgan wanted to repay him for taking the time. It didn't occur to her that Rob might just enjoy being with her.

"Sure. As long as I'm not keeping you from work," he said.

She looked up at his inviting smile and decided that work could wait.

* * *

"How've you been?" Rob shouted over the cacophony.

"Busy." Loud pop music playing over continuous arcade-game racket drowned out Morgan's voice. They were waiting their turn to shoot pool at the new hot spot, a dream destination for families with school-age children and gaming nerds alike. The restaurant and combined video arcade for adults had a fully stocked bar and an eight-page dinner menu. Kurt Cobain sang melodramatic lyrics of Nirvana's "Lithium" in the background. But the loud arcade sounds weren't enough to drown out Morgan's thoughts.

"I killed you / I'm not gonna crack . . ."

Rob sat across the round bar table, attentive. "I heard about that case you're working on. That's fucked up. Have you got any suspects?"

"Not yet." Morgan pulled a frosty, glow-in-the-dark green drink toward her, leaving a wet trail on the table. She sipped the sour-apple slushy wondering, *Where could Ekhard have disappeared to?*

While her mind remained on work, Rob shifted in his seat, seeming uncomfortable. "I heard you rented a Mazda," he said.

She welcomed his question, a refreshing change of subject. "I just wanted to try it." Morgan was pretty sure nothing could replace Thomas. "But I don't know what to get," she admitted. In the sprawling city of Indianapolis, being carless was not an option.

"Do you need help?" Rob had a way of asking that showed he cared yet wasn't pushy or smothering.

"I think I can figure it out." She shrugged, not sure if she should accept the offer or not. Rob had already put in enough time on the car-buying project.

He watched the pool table while sipping his foamy draft. The two men playing took shots at the eight ball.

"How's life in the mounted division?" she asked.

"Good. With Halloween coming, the creeps keep life interesting."

After several shots and misses, one man sunk the black ball in a corner pocket.

Rob hopped off his stool and slid a stack of quarters onto the table. He placed the balls and arranged them inside the triangle. Although Morgan had never become proficient at the game, its familiarity grounded her and reminded her of home. For many years, her parents had had a pool table in their basement.

Rob handed her a pool cue. "Are you breaking?"

She took it from him and positioned herself at the end of the table. Sliding the stick back and forth over her thumb, she aimed at the triangle of balls in the center of the table. With a crack she hit, causing the balls to explode apart. The yellow one-ball disappeared into a side pocket.

"Nice," Rob commented.

Morgan surveyed the lay of the balls. Grouped in a clump, solids landed in the middle of the table. None of them were in position for a shot. Stripes, on the other hand, were spread over the table, leaving many possibilities. She planned her next two shots and aimed at the red-striped eleven-ball. When she sank it, the cue ball rebounded, leaving open the yellow-striped nine-ball.

As it fell neatly into the side pocket, a young man nearby said, "She'll run the table."

"You're right," Rob said. He stood next to Morgan, smelling of soap and shaving cream.

Morgan took aim at the orange twelve-ball at the far end of the table. It wasn't the best shot she had, but she didn't care to win this game tonight. "What are we doing, Rob?"

Soft guitar notes of Pearl Jam floated above the din. Eddie Vedder crooned indecipherable words.

"We're dating," Rob answered.

The cue ball bounced off the orange one and into the far corner pocket.

"Are you giving that to me?" Rob asked, referring to her missed shot.

"No. We're dating?" She handed him the cue.

Rob gave her a soothing smile and let his hand linger on hers.

"I don't know how to do this," she said.

"Seems like you've played the game before," he said.

Was he talking about pool or romance? Morgan wasn't sure.

Rob took the cue and bent over, spreading his legs wide, positioning himself for the shot. Morgan's gaze traveled to Rob's rear end. Behind her, a video game sounded with explosions and gunfire as Rob's ball thundered into the pocket.

"What game are we talking about?" Morgan wanted to run away.

The next ball bounced off the rim and knocked the black eight ball into the side pocket. "Oh look. You win." Rob handed the cue back to Morgan.

"You did that on purpose," she said.

"People have accused me of being a nice guy, but never of letting someone else win." He finished his beer.

She could see spending time with this man. It frightened her how easy, homey images came to mind—walking the dog, cooking dinner together.

"Why don't we go someplace quieter? Where we can talk," he whispered in her ear.

Morgan nodded. "I like that idea." She laid the stick on the table for the next players. "Where do you want to go?"

"My place? Gretta loved the treats you sent and wants to tell you how much she misses you."

Morgan's heart beat faster, but not because she wanted him.

CHAPTER 10

MORGAN: 16 Years Ago

"Oh my God!" Fay cried out.

Morgan sprinted ahead of her friend through a neighbor's yard. She had parked Thomas a block away from Fay's house. "Come on. I'm breaking you out of jail."

"I can't believe you talked me into this."

When Morgan reached Thomas, she bent over, breathless. Fay followed her closely and hid with her behind the car. "Hurry! Open it!"

Morgan had to fumble with her keys before unlocking the passenger-side door. "She can't see you from here."

"I don't care! Just get me out of here!" Head lowered, Fay crawled into the car.

Out of breath, Morgan ran around to Thomas's driver's side and slid in as fast as she could. Curled in a ball, Fay looked up at her from the floor of the car. "What are you waiting for? Drive!"

Morgan started the car and looked in her rearview mirror. "No one's following us. Don't worry."

"Are you sure?"

"I'm sure." Driving away slowly, she looked back once more. "Oh wait. Here she comes."

"What?" The look of sheer panic on Fay's face was priceless.

Morgan burst out laughing. "You should see your face."

Fay pulled herself up to look out the rear window. "Where is she?"

"I'm just kidding. She's not following us. You're safe." At a stop sign Morgan stopped the car, using the time to gain her breath and wipe the tears from her eyes. Fay spun around and planted herself in the seat. "Don't scare me like that." It took a moment for her to recover, but when she did, her frown grew to a wide smile. She giggled. "I can't believe we just did that."

"Why not? I can't believe she grounded you." Morgan drove away.

"We stayed out all night. My curfew is at eleven."

"Curfew? Are you serious? In less than a week you're moving to campus with me and you still have a curfew at home?"

"Mom doesn't like me to be out late."

"She doesn't like you to have fun." Morgan turned onto the main road. "You're eighteen, Fay, an adult by most standards. Live a little. And speaking of, there's a joint in my purse, in the makeup bag."

"Oh, I don't know . . ."

"Yes, you do. Can you get it out? There's a lighter in there too."

Fay found the desired objects, then cranked up the radio, Nirvana's "Smells Like Teen Spirit."

Fay wriggled down low in her seat. Before lighting the joint, she asked, "Where are we going?"

Morgan reached for the joint. "I want to shop for a papasan chair for the dorm room." She put the joint between her lips and inhaled. On the exhale, she squeaked, "And posters for the wall."

Fay hummed along with Kurt Cobain. By the time they reached the store, she had become thoughtful and quiet.

"What's up? Still worried about your mom?" Morgan asked.

"No . . . there's something I . . ." She stopped talking as they crossed the street together and entered the building through the glass doors.

"What?" Morgan asked. She worried that Fay's mom put too much pressure on her. Morgan wanted to help her dig out of that grave.

Fay didn't answer. They stood shoulder to shoulder admiring a colorful, visual spectacle: wine glasses and blue china plates on bright-green place mats, cheerfully accented by silk orchid flowers tossed around the table.

"I love the colors," Morgan said.

"When would you set a table that way?" Fay asked.

"I don't know. For a romantic dinner?" Morgan giggled.

Fay didn't answer.

Morgan wistfully leaned her head on Fay's shoulder. "I know, some-day, right? Someday we'll have romantic dinners with our lovers. We'll have boyfriends or girlfriends. They'll become fiancés . . ."

"Mo, I . . ." Fay gently pushed Morgan away and strode past house-hold decorations and candles to the back of the store.

"What?" Morgan chased after her. She thought she knew everything about Fay. The back of her neck tingled with anticipation. *Does she have a secret?*

"I think I met someone," Fay admitted.

Morgan seized her friend's wrist and tugged. "Who? When did this happen? Who?"

"At orientation." Fay caught Morgan's eye, then glanced away.

A wave of shock hit Morgan. "When were you going to tell me?"

Fay shrugged while turning toward a four-foot stack of colorful papasan pillows.

Morgan pressed for details. "What's he look like? What's his name?"

"I like this color." Pointing to a light-green pillow, Fay avoided the question.

At this point, Morgan didn't care about the chair anymore. "You're making me crazy. Tell me." Her loud voice caught the ear of a store employee, who frowned at her.

"Listen, it was nothing," Fay comforted her friend. "It *is* nothing."

Morgan wanted more and carefully weighed their friendship in her mind. Fay got really pissy when pushed beyond her comfort zone. Her mother had ruined her that way. Morgan had to give her friend much-needed space. Besides, Fay was so incredibly shy that she had trouble meeting people.

"It's nothing," Morgan echoed. She figured it was probably all in Fay's imagination because if it had been important Fay would have told her right away.

"If anything comes of it, you'll be the first to know," Fay said, tugging on the green pillow.

Morgan decided not to interrogate her any further. Then she asked, quietly jealous, "Promise to tell me when you're ready?"

"I promise," Fay assured her.

Wicker papasan frames were stacked together like giant baskets in a pile as tall as they were. "Are we splitting the cost?" Fay asked.

Jealousy burned Morgan's neck and chest. In a last effort, Morgan asked, "I'll be the first to know, right?"

"I'll tell you everything as soon as there's something to tell," Fay reassured her.

Fay said it was nothing. It's nothing. It's nothing . . .

CHAPTER 11

MORGAN

Two bloodhounds, led by Indiana K9 patrol detectives, sniffed the frosty, leaf-covered ground. Parked behind a pile of dirt and upturned tree roots, a bulldozer sat like a silent, sleeping monster.

Morgan yawned, tired and regretful that she wasn't exactly at the top of her game this morning. Rob had stayed again last night. Still sleeping, he had been in her bed when she got the call before sunup. She'd quietly dressed and given Gretta a bowl of water before Donnie picked her up.

Rob was a good bet for a steady, normal, and predictable life. He had all the best qualities: he was honest and hardworking, dependable and supportive. He was every girl's dream guy. But it scared her that she was falling for him. Stability and security weren't exciting. When they dated last year, Morgan had requested a "break" while Rob worked the night shift. He'd made it clear that she was right for him and told her he'd give her all the time she needed. What she really needed was time to decide if the relationship was right for her. His idea of a future together might not fit into her career dreams. Morgan didn't see herself always working as an Indianapolis detective. But for now she liked waking up next to Rob. And she had left him a note on the kitchen table inviting him to stop by any time.

Half awake, she stumbled over rough terrain. Rocks and broken branches lay covering the uneven ground at the site, slated for development of a new strip mall. The planned urban growth should be standing here by next year, and now it was delayed. A body exhumed late yesterday lay in a scoop of earth in front of one dozer. The discovery halted all progress.

The forensic squad was in process of digging remains and rotten clothing out from the upturned earth. They placed garments and bones on a clean black tarp, attempting to reconstruct the bulldozed body as it had been before the digger scooped it up. A dirt-soaked blanket pulled from the pile lay in a heap near two faded, pinkish jelly shoes.

A weathered man wearing a camouflage hunting jacket blew smoke from his cigarette toward Donnie. "How much longer?" He scratched his shaved head with yellowed fingers that held a burning butt.

Donnie waved the cloud of smoke away from his face. "I can't tell you exactly. These things take time."

The construction project manager eyed Morgan up and down. His glare stopped at her breasts. "Well, look. My crew has another job next week. I can't afford to hold off progress. The investors are breathin' down my back to get this thing movin' again."

Morgan stooped to make eye contact with the man. "What you've uncovered here are likely the remains of a murder victim. Those remains are part of a crime scene, you understand. We can't let you disturb anymore of the area until we've finished scouring it."

The man looked back down at Morgan's chest covered by a black leather jacket. He squinted and flicked his cigarette butt into the dirt and stepped on it. To his right, four acres had been scraped by bulldozers. Behind him, a stack of tree trunks and brush the size of a small building was ready to be chipped and hauled away. About two acres of the woods to his left remained untouched. The two teams of cadaver dogs moved between the trees.

"So, Jerry, is it? We have to remove the body and check the area for evidence," she explained.

Donnie added, "It might take weeks. We just don't know."

Pointing nicotine-stained fingers at Donnie's face, Jerry said, "We got to prep this for development by the end of October. You better get done in a hurry. My men need to get paid." He walked away mumbling something derogatory under his breath.

"Lowlife," Morgan said to no one in particular. "I can't believe Holbrooke sent us out here this morning. Didn't she have someone else? Stanley Williams, for instance?" She blew a cloud puff in the cold morning air.

Donnie eyed Morgan with suspicion. "I know why I didn't sleep last night. What's up with you?"

"Oh, nothing." Morgan looked at the ground and kicked a dirt clod as they walked toward the bulldozer.

"You know you can't lie to me. Who is it?"

Morgan held back a smile as Donnie fired a half-dozen names of likely candidates. The last guess was Rob Gibson.

"Rob Gibson? Why would you think he has anything to do with my late nights?"

"Just a lucky guess."

"By the way, I wanted to let you know that nothing but dirt was found under Hallie's fingernails. But forensics did discover a couple of short hairs that didn't belong to her. They were in her sheets."

"That's good," Donnie said.

"The hairs were dyed brown with some cheap over-the-counter hair product." Morgan stepped around a small boulder.

There were dark half-circles under Donnie's eyes. "What color was it originally?"

"Blond."

"So we're looking for someone who dyes their blond hair brown? That's easy. Half the women in the country dye their hair."

"Remember, she's engaged to a man, Grumpy."

"Damn energy drinks. I think I fell asleep around three."

"You shouldn't drink that shit at night, Donnie."

"Now you tell me. Etta drinks it all the time," he said.

Morgan put her hands in her pockets and strolled over toward the forensics team. "Etta shouldn't drink it either. Tell your daughter it's full of toxic chemicals."

The pair walked, careful of where they stepped, to the mound of earth where a tall, lanky man crouched over the ruined body.

"What have we got, Lyle?" Donnie asked.

Nearby, a filthy North Side High School sweatshirt lay on the tarp. Lyle Erikson, the forensic specialist, patted off his gloved hands. "Well, it's a young girl, fifteen to twenty. Two ribs and left clavicle are broken from blunt-force trauma. The face of the skull was destroyed."

"Could the bones have been broken by the bulldozer moving them?" Morgan asked.

Lyle shook his head. "These fractures happened before death. Including the ones to the face."

"Cause of death?" Morgan knelt and looked closely at the skull. Dragged into the bushes beside Jackson Creek, Fay had been struck in the face with a heavy object. The creek bed was searched for a weapon, but no evidence was found.

"Look at this." Lyle pointed to the skull. "There was significant traumatic impact above the teeth. You can see how the blow cracked the surrounding bone. Over time, decay and nature dissolved the tissue and these bones fell apart," he said. "This wouldn't have killed her, but likely the blow to her nose did. Her face was destroyed."

Indeed, Morgan gaped at the shattered bone between the eyes and above the teeth. *Like Hallie and Fay?* She looked for the corpse's hands.

"A gunshot might do that." Donnie said.

"There's no exit wound." Lyle knelt down beside Morgan and pointed at the skull. "Also, there're no buckshot or bullets inside the skull." Three upper and three lower teeth were missing or broken, creating a circular hole.

"It was a brutal act then." Donnie shifted his weight and yawned.

"This was no accident. The body was buried two feet underground," Lyle speculated.

Morgan had an incredible, crazy thought. It had to do with Fay again, so she knew it was part of that old obsession. Her gut churned at the possible connections to this case and to Hallie. She had to know . . . "Were her hands intact or broken?"

"The bones aren't shattered if that's what you're asking. However, since the site was plowed up by a bulldozer, it will be impossible to tell if her fingers were broken at the joint before she died. Why do you ask?"

"Hallie Marks had been struck in the face too," she said to Donnie.

Donnie gave her a look that Morgan took to mean he didn't want her drawing too many conclusions just yet.

She turned to Lyle. "How old are the remains?"

Lyle answered, "Fifteen or twenty years."

"Are you sure?" She asked.

"I'm sure." Lyle told them, "She was attacked from the front. The impact wounds are all on her face. Either she was surprised and attacked head-on, or . . ."

Donnie finished the sentence, "someone held her while another person bludgeoned her to death."

"Are two killers working together?" Morgan voiced the question in her mind.

Lyle removed his soiled latex gloves and stepped down from the mound of earth. He was still a good three inches taller than Donnie and towered over Morgan. "Inform the developers that this is a homicide. The investigation will halt their progress. We have to scour this area for a weapon."

"What was she hit with?" Donnie asked.

"Something heavy. Something like . . ." Keeping his gaze on the skeleton, Lyle bared his teeth and sucked air between them.

A rock was the first image that popped into Morgan's mind, and it frightened her. She took a step backward and said, "Like a hammer."

"That would work." Lyle nodded

Morgan looked out at the woods. The dogs led by the canine patrol were sniffing along the edge of the uncut woods about forty yards away.

CHAPTER 12

CARYN

Adding one to the number of times she had driven to the Oak Creek Condominiums parking lot, Caryn Klein committed the number 2,034 to memory. It had been after dark 1,382 times. Also, she'd parked in this particular parking spot 867 times. She liked to keep track. It made her feel more in control.

"Caryn! Caryn! You okay?" Brad Olafson, a neighbor knocked on her car window.

She shut off the engine, popped the trunk, and then climbed out with her purse in tow.

"You okay, Caryn? Geez. I knocked on the window, like, a hundred times."

It wasn't one hundred. It was forty-two, Caryn thought.

"You okay?" Brad, the condo association manager and self-proclaimed on-site handy man, lived in the next building. They had met at the pool the first summer she lived here, four years and five months ago—1,582 days.

"I'm fine." she answered, as nicely as she could manage, and stepped around to the trunk of the car. While lifting the hatch, her sleeve pulled back, exposing a trickle of blood dripping down the back of her hand.

Color drained from Brad's face. "What's that on your arm? Did you hurt yourself?"

"It's nothing, Brad." Caryn had scraped it on the sharp edge of an open drawer at work. A little blood didn't bother her, she'd wiped it off with a tissue and thought it was fine. Apparently, the cut was deeper than she thought. She wanted to get inside to examine it in private. Removing a green army-issue shoulder bag from the trunk, she closed the hatch and turned toward her building.

"Are you sure? I could bandage that up for you." He followed at her heels, panting like a good little dog. "I hate for you to be all alone. You seem out of it. Want me to stay for a while? To make sure you don't . . . you know . . . pass out or something. Maybe you lost a lot of blood."

She reached the outer door to her building and unlocked it, eager to get away from the idiot. With a calm, placating voice at the tip of her tongue, she said, "Thanks for checking on me, Brad," but concluded with a heavy dose of patronizing, "You can go off and find someone else to bother now." He never got the hint no matter how cruel she was. If they had dated, she would have dumped him hard. But Caryn had said no the first, fifth, and twentieth time he had asked her out. He was still trying.

"Hey, I've got brewskis in my fridge. I'll bring them to your place. We can—"

"No, Brad. Mack is coming by."

"Is he your boyfriend? Is Mack your boyfriend?"

Without answering, Caryn ducked into the foyer and let the outer door swing closed on Brad. Climbing the stairs to the third floor, she counted: five on the first flight, twelve after that, and then ten and ten. Thirty-seven total. She knew the exact number of steps up to her floor because, every time, she counted. Every time, the total was the same. There was security in that.

Her landline was ringing as she opened her door. Thinking it was the single-minded and persistent Brad, she answered, "Brad, I said—"

"There you are. Hey." It wasn't Brad. "I tried your cell. You didn't answer."

"I shut it off." With the cordless pressed to the side of her face, Caryn walked into the dark living room and flipped on a light. "Hi,

Mack." Gilroy Mackintosh and Caryn had been seeing each other for over twenty months. Twenty months, two weeks, and five days. Or 622 days.

"Brad bothering you again?" The voice on the other end of the line soothed her nerves like cool running water over a burn.

"You guessed it." She placed the green satchel on the floor and sat down on the new couch, barely sinking into the soft cushions. "What time is it?"

"Six thirty. You just get in?"

"Just."

"How was your day? Did you enjoy tormenting and torturing the employees of Garrison Electric? I suppose you sufficiently whipped them into submission?"

Caryn loved her job. She was an associate CPA for the Indiana Office of Accounting. She got to spend her day with numbers, not people. Numbers never lied. And they never left you. "Yes. They cower in fear, the little lackeys." A thin smile graced her lips.

"I'll let you whip me if you want," he invited cheerfully.

Caryn hoped he meant it. "Are you coming over?"

"Am I?" Mack was easy.

"Can you get away from her?" she asked.

"I'll make it happen."

With the phone in one hand, she peeled a multicolored infinity scarf off over her head. The scarf matched everything she owned. It had little flecks of blue, green, red, and yellow. And orange, the color of the itchy wool sweater she was wearing. Mack had bought them both for her. "Can you bring dinner? I didn't have time . . ."

"To go to the grocery," he finished her sentence. "Of course I can. Do you want carryout from Chang's?"

Her stomach growled. "I don't care. Sure."

Seriously, Mack queried, "What would you eat if I didn't keep bringing you food?"

"Nothing. Pop Tarts. I would probably starve." She smiled to herself. "See you soon."

Mack hung up. He wasn't one for goodbyes on the phone. Leaning back on her comfortable, colorless couch, Caryn brushed the fibers in one direction, erasing any marks. It was new, like most of her furniture, and had a soft-as-suede finish. As a result of Mack's pitiless nudging she'd finally sprung for upgrades to her living arrangements.

Before Mack, she had slept on a futon on the floor. Her dresser was one she'd found on the street during her college years. Her neighbor gave her three wooden barstools for the kitchen when she moved away to New York. And she had owned a ratty, flower-print chair that she bought at Goodwill while shopping for clothes one day.

It wasn't that she didn't have the money. Her job at Indiana Office of Accounting paid well. And being single, she accrued very few expenses. Comfort wasn't in her vocabulary before Mack. Truthfully, Caryn didn't care how her apartment looked. Mack did though. And he was on his way over.

She pulled back her sleeve. The two-inch gash was just below her elbow on the top side of her arm. It was deep. On the way to the bathroom, she took off her orange sweater. Blood had soaked the inside of the sleeve, so she threw the sweater on the floor, planning to soak it in Woolite later. Without waiting for the water to warm up, she plunged her arm under the faucet, splashing fresh, red blood on the countertop.

CHAPTER 13

CARYN: 6 Months Ago

Cold blew right through her jacket. Caryn had forgotten to wear the infinity scarf Mack had given her. The glass outer door of the accounting office where she'd worked for five years was heavy against the wind. Debris flew in with her.

"Good morning, Caryn," the receptionist greeted her.

Caryn allowed her lips to curl upward. "Morning," she said as she slithered to her cubicle. She had no time to set her briefcase down before her boss, Harry Randall Monroe, sped to her desk.

"Morning, Caryn. Through with those reports?" He rubbed a hand across his shiny bald head. Each of the women at IOA had stories about their boss. Behind his back they called him Harry the Hairless Dick. He never hit on them, but he had a way of implying something sexual.

"Yes, Mr. Monroe, they're done." Caryn said, and she turned on her computer.

"Good. The IRS is hammering on me for those. The hearing is next Monday." He stood a little too close for Caryn's comfort.

With her shoulder, she nudged him out of the way. "Give me a chance to get the files up. I just walked in," she said, wanting him to leave her alone.

"Sure thing." Harry leaned his hip against her desk. His large hands gripped the edge.

Caryn tried to ignore him hovering over her like a big hot-air balloon. She shifted a few folders from her briefcase to a drawer while waiting for the computer to boot up.

"Nice weather we're having. I love these cool fall days. I'm driving down to Brown County this weekend. It sure is beautiful down there. Don't you love being outdoors this time of year?" he said.

Don't, she thought. *Please don't talk about hiking.* Harry would talk a stream about his nature walks and fix-it projects. If she let him go on, he'd invite her again.

He didn't wait for her response. "Can't wait for hunting season to open. Do you hunt, Caryn? For some reason you strike me as a hunter."

Caryn interrupted him. "I'll have these reports for you in just a minute, Mr. Monroe." Subtlety was a new skill for her, sought on Mack's advice and not yet well developed. Caryn was never sure how far to let things go before telling someone off. Mack had explained the nuances of it and why she shouldn't be rude to people, like her boss.

Please don't talk about hiking . . .

"Anyway, I found a great hiking trail in the National Park. The trails lead up to this old lodge, the Abe Martin Lodge . . ."

"Listen." She turned to face him. "I'll bring the report to you as soon as it's up. Just give me some space. Please," she added.

He moved away from her desk. "Just remember, those IRS guys don't care about lipstick and high heels. They wanted the report yesterday."

Caryn watched him saunter back to his office like a fat woodchuck going back to its hole in the ground. She refused to play his flirty game or spend time alone with him. She had to be a hard-ass.

The Garrison Electric file blinked open on her computer, and she did one last check-over. Scrolling through the report, she neared the end where Garrison Electric's accounting firm signed off. Double-checking her work to cover all her bases, and to delay talking to Harry, Caryn went to the company website. There, a photo of a familiar face slowed her down and turned her blood cold.

Listed among the chief financial officers seven years ago was a CPA named Nathaniel Johnson. The name, *his* name, was absolutely wrong.

She dragged a box containing Garrison Electric accounting paperwork from six years ago out from under her desk. Several payroll sheets were signed by this person, Nathaniel Johnson. *He is not Nathaniel Johnson.* This man was someone from her past. She knew him. A chill crept up her spine and out to her fingertips.

Back on her computer, she scrolled through the next two years of data. He was not listed among their employees in the following year or any subsequent years. She found, looking back, that Garrison Electric had hired him in 2010, and he had only worked there for four years.

Caryn zoomed in on the photo. There was no mistake. She knew that face better than anyone else's. This was Ekhard Marcus Klein, her brother.

With the printed file in her arms, Caryn walked to Harry's office. Her stomach churned. In front of his desk, she placed the stack in his hands, unable to hear a word he said. Out the window, treetops waved under a light-blue sky and sunshine. A square of sunlight spotted the floor, brightening the gray carpet in the shape of a grave dug especially for Caryn.

"Caryn? What do you think? Will the IRS go for it?" Harry asked.

She hadn't heard the question; her ears were ringing. "I don't feel good," she said.

Harry came to her side. "You look kind of pale, Caryn. Why don't you sit down for a minute?"

"Eks." Caryn's stomach lurched. "I need to go home, Eks."

"What's that?" Harry put his hands on her shoulders and led Caryn to a black leather sofa where she dropped to her knees and started to heave. Her stomach rejected its contents, splattering remains of Pop Tarts and coffee across the floor and the side of the couch.

Harry backed away from his employee, calling urgently, "Riannda, come quickly! Oh no. Oh no. Please, Riannda. Get in here, now!"

CHAPTER 14

MORGAN

Piles of dirty laundry, bright-colored clothes, whites, and towels covered the floor at the bottom of the stairs. In the mudroom past the kitchen, the washing machine churned with the first load. Morgan sat cross-legged on the couch with a pillow in her lap. On the couch beside her, a manila file folder contained all the missing persons' reports in Marion County from the years 1995 through 2005. Printouts were spread out on the coffee table and floor in front of her.

Adrienne and Bill Rafferty were in Florida until the first of May. And even though Morgan could hang out in her pj's all day without evoking Adrienne's parental, pitiful gaze, she missed her. Adrienne would have cooked up casseroles and roasts and other mouth-watering delights. Morgan's stomach growled.

With a couch pillow clutched to her breast, she searched the documents for a missing high school girl from Indianapolis. If twenty-five years had passed, that case was cold. Moving chronologically from past toward present years, she'd begun with the folder dated 1999. It had been Lyle's hunch that the girl was killed fifteen years ago, around 2004. But after reviewing cases from that year, she realized his intuition had been off.

Intuition, she thought, do I trust it? *My intuition has been off before. Only once . . .*

Morgan bent forward over the pillow in her lap. From the coffee table in front of her, she picked up the 1999 files. Sixteen girls went missing during that year. Nine girls ran away, two were taken by family members. Murder and kidnapping accounted for a small fraction, but those cases were solved or closed. She placed the folder back on the table and tossed the pillow aside.

It had been a week since they recovered the body near Fishers. She'd eagerly waited for the forensic department to find a DNA match. She hated waiting. It reminded her of those terrible days after Fay went missing.

She raised her arms overhead and stretched. When she uncurled her legs and stood up, her stomach rumbled. Cereal seemed an easy option for dinner. If she had made time to go to the grocery, she wouldn't be eating cereal for dinner. She hadn't been to the grocery store in weeks.

Donnie phoned as Morgan was pushing soggy Life cereal squares around the bowl.

"Lieutenant Holbrooke just called, Mo. They found a hammer up near Fishers."

His news lit another beacon inside her. "You're kidding!"

"They're sending it over to forensics to have it examined. I can meet you at the station."

"Ah . . ." She didn't want to drive the Mazda. "Can you pick me up?"

"Not like it's the first time."

Morgan ran up the stairs to dress. A pair of jeans from a pile on the floor didn't look too dirty to wear. She slid into them and threw a soft cable-knit sweater over her head. She teased her fingers through her hair and pulled it into a ponytail. It could be another late night. She hoped it would be a late night. Because Hallie Marks had been killed with a hammer too, she hoped this was the clue she'd been waiting for.

Statistics were staggering: according to an FBI crime table, hammers and other blunt force instruments—even fists—had killed nearly five hundred people in the last year. It wasn't uncommon. Morgan knew it. What was uncommon was the way the hands of her victims had been broken before they were murdered. Perhaps with this tool, she could isolate fingerprints, or even a serial number. The excitement made her heart beat a little faster.

*   *   *

"If she hadn't died of those external wounds, she would have suffocated after being buried under two feet of dirt." Olivia Hawthorn, leader of the forensics team had her dark-brown hair pulled into a knot. With her white lab coat over a black skirt, she looked like an actress playing the part of lab technician. As she spoke, she pointed to the aged, rusty tool lying on sheet plastic on a white worktable.

"It's an old Stanley number 52 twenty-four-ounce hammer. Traces of the victim's blood were embedded in the rusty head," Olivia said. "They still make this model with the wooden handle." Daily, she surprised detectives with her extensive knowledge of just about everything.

Morgan held her breath, taking in every detail: orange rust on blackened steel, wood streaked with gray, and black where the metal head was attached. She longed to touch it and feel its weight. The paper wrapper around a warm sub sandwich crinkled in her hand. On the way, she had Donnie stop at a sandwich shop.

The natural wood triggered something in the back of Morgan's mind. *Could it get any simpler? It could.* Anxious for details, she urged Olivia to continue. "And . . .?"

"And what? This hammer was the original model for those that came after it: rip claws and framing hammers, serrated, titanium, and masonry hammers." Olivia picked up the tool and turned it in her latex-gloved hands.

"There are so many kinds." Donnie chuckled, pretending to know as much as Olivia did about tools.

Morgan gave him a sidelong glance. "So it's old," she said with her mouth full. No pretending. She didn't know shit about hammers.

"Before 1970 this hammer was in every household."

"There's no way to trace it. That's what you're saying," Donnie said.

"Right." Olivia set the hammer on the table and moved across the room to her computer. "We also found long blond hairs in the girl's hands. It isn't the victim's."

"Great!" Donnie said.

"Two girls got into a fight. One of them beat the other's face in with the hammer." High school girls overflowed with emotions, good and bad, Morgan remembered.

"I don't think so." Donnie shifted his weight from one foot to the other, then back again. "In the nineties, nothing surrounded that field but farmland and a few distant homes. They'd just begun building that Target store off 126th street. It was a K-Mart back then, remember? So, what was she doing with a hammer in the middle of the woods?"

"Hanging up signs for the prom?" Olivia suggested.

"No. Someone intended to kill our victim," Morgan said. "She deliberately brought a hammer to the fistfight." She turned toward her partner. "Donnie, I have a feeling about this. Both Hallie and this girl had their faces crushed in. Their murders went way beyond accidental killing. The amount of anger it would take to strike someone's face—to crush it like that—is vengeful and deliberate. She brought that girl into the field to kill her, I'm sure of it."

"Why do you think it's a woman? That blond hair could belong to anyone. Boys grow their hair long too." He pointed to the corner of his mouth, indicating that Morgan had mayonnaise on her face.

With a wadded napkin from her pants pocket, Morgan wiped her mouth. "You ran the hair through the database?"

"It's almost impossible to get DNA from a strand of hair. Luckily there's enough follicle on the end to run a good test."

With her mouth full, Morgan said to her partner, "Do you think they're linked, Donnie? What if this blond hair matches the blond hairs found in Hallie's bed? I have a good feeling about this."

"I'm not sure."

"We're building a case that Hallie's lover killed her. He smashed Hallie's face with some kind of mallet. A hammer seems the most likely. And how many cases have we seen where the victim's hands were broken and the face was beaten in?" Morgan argued. "We've seen at least four since I started working with you."

"You're trying to link them all?" The pitch of Donnie's voice rose.

"Detectives!" Olivia interrupted. "Mind if I finish?"

Both Morgan and Donnie turned back to the specialist.

"So, our victim here was on the North Side cheerleading squad. Like I said, she died of these external wounds. If she didn't, she suffocated after being buried under two feet of dirt."

Morgan stopped short of stuffing another bite into her mouth. "Wait. How do you know she was on the cheerleading squad?"

"The sweatshirt," Olivia explained.

Donnie's eyebrows went up.

Olivia explained, "I went to high school at North Side. For years they decorated the gym hallway with the old cheerleader outfits. Her sweater design was from the late nineties. I even verified it with pictures from the web."

"Late nineties," Morgan repeated. "What year?"

"That sweatshirt was part of the uniform they wore from 1996 through 2000. After that, they switched to the white one."

"Thank you so much, Olivia. You've been extremely helpful." Donnie turned toward the door.

"We can do a dental check for records."

"We don't have time for that." Morgan leaped after him.

"Good night, Detectives." Olivia closed her door.

These days, Donnie hated to work late. Though Morgan hoped they would. This case had been cold for too long. And Morgan wanted to open it back up.

"I brought the missing persons' files from the nineties with me. I've looked through the first five years of records, and this case isn't with those. Help me sort through the rest. It's in there, Donnie, it has to be."

"Computer records are easier. I wish someone had taken the time to file these." Donnie spread the paperwork from 1995 through 1999 out on his desk.

Morgan held a folder in her hands. "In 1995 there were no cheerleaders, missing or otherwise," she said.

"In June of ninety-six a high school girl was abducted from a gas station in Plymouth, Indiana. She was a cheerleader for a different high school. Her body was found in 2001."

"Here it is. March 1997, Suzanne Aiken from North Side High School disappeared and was never found. She was a cheerleader." Morgan looked up at her partner.

Donnie sat in his desk chair with his hand out. "Give it to me."

Morgan held it as Donnie read aloud, "Her parents were Benjamin and Leeanne Aiken. She had two little sisters, and Mom stayed at home."

"Aiken owns a furniture store in Castleton."

"She had lots of friends. Police interviewed ten of them," Donnie continued.

Morgan leaned closer. "There was a long session questioning her best friend, Becky Lewis. Afterward, the detectives determined—she was abducted at the mall, near the movie theater. How on earth did they figure that?"

Donnie waved his hand in front of his face. "Morgan, you smell like onions."

"Sorry." She covered her mouth.

"Let's see. Search teams scoured the area, but no one saw a car. No one saw anything. Looks like Becky said she waited for her at the movie theater, but Suzanne never showed."

Morgan kept a hand at her mouth, directing onion breath away from Donnie. "They had nothing else to go on. Her boyfriend, Ekhard Klein, had an alibi too." She politely stood back and pointed to the page. "What's that say?"

"He was with his dad in the hospital. Dad was treated for an overdose of painkillers."

"That sucks," Morgan said. "Ekhard Klein was Hallie's supposed fiancé. Coincidence?"

Donnie leaned back in his chair. Morgan stepped around the desk and picked up her half-eaten sandwich.

"I think we start with Suzanne's family." He picked up a phone book. "Her parents are still alive and living in Indianapolis."

Morgan spoke while chewing her food. "Call them."

"Ask nicely," Donnie teased.

"Please?"

CHAPTER 15

CARYN

Breezy air cooled Caryn's cheeks. She stood in front of a coffee shop near the IOA where the warm smell of pumpkin pie permeated the air. She had her purse and a briefcase in her hands and vaguely remembered Harry and Riannda ushering her to the door. "Go on home. Come back when you feel better," they had said.

The effects of the ipecac syrup, kept in the back compartment of her desk for just such an occasion, had worn off. In the bathroom, she'd vomited two more times. The feeling was wretched, but worth it to get off work at a moment's notice.

Pie. Caryn took a deep breath of the fragrance. She opened the door of the coffee shop to the sound of bells. The bakery shelf held a variety of enormous muffins chock-full of blueberries and chocolate chips. Scones sprinkled with cinnamon and dotted with raspberries. There were little cakes decorated with pretty frosting lines, and marzipan flowers sat on top of yellow squares.

"May I help you?" A college-age blonde with her hair in two braids faced Caryn from the other side of the case.

"Pie. Do you have pumpkin pie?" Caryn asked.

"Oh. No. But we are featuring our pumpkin spice latte right now. Iced or hot."

Caryn nodded. "A large, please. Hot."

The blonde handed her the warm cup topped with a heap of whipped cream. Not pie, but it would have to do.

In the corner of the low-lit coffee shop, Caryn got comfortable. She took off her jacket, pulling the left sleeve over the bandage on her arm. With her right hand she scooped her laptop out of her briefcase and set it on the small table. After it booted up, she typed his name into the search bar.

Never in a million years had she expected to see him again. Yet here was Ekhard Marcus Klein within a tap-tap of her fingers. Eks, whom she had written off and given up for dead. Eks, who had changed his name to Nathaniel Johnson.

And so he wasn't dead. *Just dead to me.* She hadn't seen him since the day of her graduation from high school. Ekhard was her only sibling and only living relative.

Seventeen years, four months, and twelve days was how long. She knew the number of days. He had dropped her off at graduation at 9:04 in the morning on June fourth in 2001 and said, "See you in hell." And she hadn't seen him since.

He didn't call. He didn't stop by, not for holidays or birthdays. She remembered being very angry with him. It had taken eighteen years, four months, and seventeen days to say that without wanting to kill him.

Kill him.

There was an idea.

Ekhard/Nathaniel currently lived in Lafayette, north of Indianapolis. He worked for a small accounting firm with a ridiculous name, Baker and Baker. Everyone knows there's no *baking* at a CPA office. Caryn thought it should be called Checks and Balances, or Numbers-Are-Us. Nevertheless, he was hired in 2014, replacing William Baker as the one in charge of small business bookkeeping. Before that, he had worked in eastern Indiana for another accountant, Gary Pritchard. That job came after getting the sack at Garrison Electric.

Research was a cinch for Caryn. Easy as pie, she thought—her mother's saying. She breathed in the warm scent of her pumpkin spiced latte. Though pie wasn't easy at all. Like her mother, Caryn couldn't bake if her life depended on it.

She remembered that her mom always bought cold, grocery-store pie-in-a-box. *That* was easy. Mom talked about recipes that her mother and grandmother had made when she was a child. Apple and berry pie. Even sugar pie. Caryn wondered what that was. She imagined that it was full of creamy white pudding and topped with mountains of white, fluffy whipped cream. Heaven to a seven-year-old.

I never got to try it, she thought, and bitterness boiled up again, the flavor of vomit.

Ekhard hadn't left a trail. Except for Garrison Electric, it was almost like he didn't exist before working at the accounting firm. Caryn muttered to herself, "And where are you now, dear brother?"

Two women at the round table next to Caryn's looked over at her. The one wearing white horn-rimmed glasses with little jewels on them sneered at her. Or smiled. Caryn couldn't tell which, so she grinned back, picked up her paper coffee cup, and toasted the woman as the ladies went back to their conversation.

Caryn sniffed at her latte, then took a cautious sip, scalding the tip of her tongue. She licked cinnamon whipped cream off her lips and reset her focus.

Nathaniel Johnson had an address: 6818 Hyacinth Court in Lafayette. It would take an hour and a half to drive up there, but it might be worth it. To see him again.

Maybe, just maybe, he'd want to see her. They could go out for dinner. Or drink lattes together. Or just drink. Perhaps she should bring him a gift. A new tie. Or a bottle of wine. She wondered if he drank wine. Maybe he was a bourbon drinker like Dad. Caryn decided to stop at the liquor store on the way.

In the recent picture of Ekhard on the website of the Baker and Baker Accounting firm, he looked older, though not any heavier; his skin was mottled, and he hadn't shaven. "You look like shit," she said out loud.

The lady in the horn-rimmed glasses looked over at Caryn again, as if defending Ekhard.

"What?" Caryn asked her.

Without answering, the woman turned back to her friend.

He was thirty-nine. The same age as Mack, and he looked bad for his age. His thinning hair was slicked back and too long. He had died it dark brown and the color did nothing for his skin tone. The picture of him from the waist up showed that he was thin—too thin for a man his age. The one redeeming feature was that he looked genuinely happy. And *how* could that be? Caryn wanted to see for herself.

6818 Hyacinth Court. She committed the address to memory and shut off her laptop.

The lady at the next table stared over her horn-rimmed glasses and watched Caryn tuck the computer into her bag while carrying on a discussion with her friend: "So Madeline talked to the principal. I tell you, she is a real piece of work. Mrs. Von Broche told my daughter she imagined things. Can you believe it?"

I hate being stared at. Caryn's furrowed her brow. "What?" she asked. Hackles up, she didn't expect an answer. She slung her purse and computer bag over her shoulder, and with her free hand picked up her coffee.

The Horned Lady placed a hand on Caryn's arm just as she was about to walk past. "Excuse me, I know you. You were a friend of Amy Dufresne, weren't you?"

Caryn stopped. She *had* known Amy Dufresne. She'd been a dear friend, until . . . "Amy is dead."

"I know. She and I were college roommates at IU in Indy." The woman touched her glasses, adjusting them.

"How do I know you?" Caryn asked.

"We met at The Blue Room. Remember?"

Perhaps it was the memory of Amy, or the shock of being connected to Amy this long after her murder. The cup of hot coffee slipped right out of Caryn's hand and landed in the woman's lap.

Like a cat having kittens, the woman howled and jumped to her feet.

"I'm so sorry." Caryn tried to brush the coffee off her, but it had already soaked into her shirt and jeans.

"What were you thinking?" she shrieked. She took off her glasses and set them on the table, as they were splattered too. Her friend ran for some napkins.

"I'm so sorry." Caryn fussed over her.

The Horned Lady hunched her shoulders, peeling the blouse away from her chest. A dollop of foamy whipped cream ran down her thigh. The friend returned a moment later with a thick stack of brown-paper napkins. She pressed them into the woman's stained blouse, saying, "It was only an accident. I'm sure it was just an accident. We'll get this all cleaned up."

Caryn apologized and made her way for the door, moving quickly to get away from that coffee-pie smell.

Outside, she tucked the white horn-rimmed glasses into her pocket.

CHAPTER 16

CARYN

Caryn unlatched the clip from the belt loop on her jeans and flipped between the five keys to find the right one. On the ring were keys for each important part of her life. Ekhard wasn't among them. But he was only a short drive away.

They had been close growing up. After Mom left them, Dad spent most of his time sucking down booze. As a parent, he became so useless that by the time Caryn was in high school, Ekhard had to take on the role of parent, chauffer, and guardian. He was the only one who gave a damn.

Inside her Hyundai, Caryn slouched in the driver's seat and pushed her bags to the passenger side. After closing the car door, she took a breath, her mind spinning in all directions.

She thought about her drunk, useless father and her mother. At least Anna Clare had gotten away. Like Ekhard, her mother had escaped and disappeared too. But that was another story, one Caryn didn't wish to revisit, ever. When she did, it made her angry.

Gripping the steering wheel with one hand, Caryn started the car with the other. A woman's voice bellowed over the radio, drums beat a danceable rhythm to the words. And she stiffened, reminding herself that consequences, whatever they might be, were still within her control. She had decided to reconnect with Ekhard, with her childhood.

Traffic was forgiving for a change. The Genesis bumped along, rolling like a billiard ball toward its destination. I-465 was clear through the exit to I-65 North, and the drive to Lafayette didn't take as long as she had anticipated. Gliding into town on the curved exit ramp, she made a quick stop at Walmart for a bag of lollipops. It was just the thing to help settle her stomach. It had always worked when she was a kid. As a last-minute decision, she grabbed a bottle of Kentucky's finest for Ekhard. A peace offering.

Taking a scenic route through Lafayette, she circled into Ekhard's neighborhood like a hawk. How long had he lived here? She turned left on Hyacinth where neat, single-story houses lined clean streets and mature trees extended like battered umbrellas over each yard. She parked in front of 6825, a white house with faded green trim and too many potted plants near the front door. Ekhard's house, two doors diagonal from that one, had no potted plants on the stoop.

As it was dark inside the house, she couldn't tell if he was home or not. She decided to stay in the car, staring at his front yard and the browned, mid-fall grass, cut short, and his bushes, squared off. Light-brown circles dotted the trunk of the maple in his front yard where limbs had been trimmed off. Caryn chuckled. So Eks did yard work. He had grown up. She shut off the car and busied herself with visions of Ekhard as a good homemaker and happy husband.

Puffy clouds drifted in front of the sun, alternately creating the need for sunglasses and the need to remove them. His street had very little traffic. One carful of teenagers passed with the radio blaring so loud that her car shook. She wondered what classes those kids were skipping. No one came or went from Ekhard's house. It was 10:37 in the morning.

Her cell phone rang, and she jumped out of her skin. "Hello?"

"Caryn? It's Riannda. I was just checking on you. Feeling any better?"

One advantage Caryn had was the ability to feign illness when she needed to get away. Ipecac syrup was a perfect antidote. She shifted the phone to her left hand and reached for the Walmart bag. "Thanks, Riannda. I'm much better."

"Did you go home?"

"I . . . yes."

"You get yourself some chamomile tea for your stomach. That will settle it down right away. And calm your nerves."

"I will. I'm working from home on my computer." She had done it in high school. Lied and pretended to be sick. Now she did it sometimes at work.

"Doesn't sound like rest to me. That chamomile is what you need. Do you have any? I could bring some tea by when I get off work."

"I'll be fine." Caryn had a body type conducive to a sickly persona. She was thin. Fit, but thin. Not too muscular. When she pretended she was ill, people fell for it readily. She would cough or go in the bathroom and stick a finger down her throat. It was also easy to lose a little extra weight if she needed to.

"I'll get better, Riannda. See you tomorrow."

It was dark before Ekhard came home. As soon as he pulled into the driveway, Caryn took a swig of the bourbon. The cap had fallen between her feet on the floor of the car. The open bottle, sitting on her lap for some time, had provided less than interesting reading material during the long afternoon. It just gave her a break from her memories, rotten carcasses that floated to the surface of the swamp of decay that was her consciousness.

What was he like now? Did he have children? "Ha! No way." Caryn laughed out loud at the thought. Ekhard would not have any children. Not considering their own upbringing. And who were his friends? Did he hang out with a bunch of gun-toting thugs wearing leather jackets with chains hanging from their belt loops? Or were his friends neatly pressed, churchy folk? She imagined them with clean-smelling hair, a cappella singers able to harmonize in any key.

Another fine image of Ekhard Klein thrown in the trash. *If he goes to church at all, I'll be a baboon's ass.*

His garage door opened. In the low light, Caryn couldn't see the make of his car. For some reason, that mattered to her. *Is it a better car than mine? Is it newer?*

There were no other cars in the garage. No children's Big Wheels or bicycles. Ekhard lived alone. He got out of the car. An older man now, he looked thin and tired. He opened the trunk of his car and lifted out a duffle bag and a plastic grocery bag. Shifting them into one hand, he grabbed a gallon of milk with the other and shut the trunk with his elbow. He looked vulnerable. Hunched over, he made his way to the house, and the garage door shut.

Now what? So she had seen him. Caryn had been sitting there all afternoon, flipping through scenarios in her head. Should I knock on his door and say hi? She held up the bottle and tipped it back again. "To you, Eks." She didn't want to give him an open bottle. And now she was tipsy.

The light came on in his living room, blue light from a TV. It flickered from bright to dim, blinking, then turning completely dark. She screwed the cap on the top of the bottle and tucked it back in the bag.

I could call him, she thought. Caryn recalled the number she had written down earlier today. She dialed slowly and watched the shadow of a man move across the living-room blinds. The shadow reminded her of her father.

"Hello?"

Blood drained from Caryn's face.

"Hello? Who's there?"

She could hear him breathing. It was odd that he sounded exactly the same. Exactly like she remembered. But her mouth hung open, refusing to form any words. She was an empty kettle, hot and dried out, without any steam.

CHAPTER 17

CARYN: 28 Years Ago

The sticky-slick pleather car seat was sweat-glued to the back of Caryn's thighs. She was slumped down in the spacious back seat of her mom's Pontiac station wagon with the window down. The wind blew her shoulder-length hair in all directions as she stared out at the passing fields. Michael Jackson sang in high-pitched falsetto over the radio, *"Keep up with the pup, don't stop. Don't stop till you get the pup . . ."* That's what she thought he was saying, anyway. Over the crackly radio it was hard to tell.

Caryn's mother Anna drove, white-knuckling the steering wheel. From the back seat, Caryn watched the muscles in her jaw bulge to the beat of the song between puffs of her cigarette.

Eks sat in the front seat with an ice pack wrapped in a pink kitchen towel pressed to his cheek, his head tilted to the side. She wanted to pull his short blond hair. She wanted to hit him in the head. If he hadn't made Dad so mad, they might not be leaving.

Early in the morning, Caryn had heard her parents yelling. When she went downstairs to investigate, Dad slammed his fist on the kitchen counter. He was saying things like "You bitch!" And, "A man's got a right . . ."

Mom cried out, "I've been reading magazine articles about it. I have rights. You can't say that to me."

Caryn wanted to hear the fight, so she had made herself invisible behind the dining-room wall.

"My house, my rules. I don't want to see any more of those fucking magazines, do you hear? That shit is messing with your head."

Eks snuck into the dining room behind his sister. "Whatcha doin'?" He walked all the way around the table to stand next to her near the doorway. He was hiding too.

"Listening." Caryn looked up at him. Her brother's body had stretched out that year. He was lanky and about a foot taller than she was.

"What's going on?" he asked.

"They're fighting again." She peered out into the kitchen just as Mom threw a coffee cup at Dad and it exploded on the wall tile over the counter. Caryn and Ekhard backed away.

"Duh. At least you aren't a total imbecile." Eks put a hand on Caryn's arm. "Come on, let's get out of here."

Tearing herself away from him, she crossed her arms tight over her chest. "No," she whispered. "I want to hear what they're saying."

Dad growled at Mom, "Where are you going to go? You have no one."

"Come on, Ceecee." Ekhard tugged at Caryn's arm. His eyes widened further with every word their dad said.

"Stop it, I can't hear." She leaned toward the kitchen in order to hear without being seen.

Mom blew her nose into a tissue. "I have friends. I have my cousins. I'm taking the kids, and we're leaving you."

"Goddammit, Anna. You can't . . ."

Next thing Caryn knew, Eks had an arm around her middle and was scooping her up by her waist, pinning her arms to her sides. With his free hand over her mouth so she couldn't scream, he carried his little sister out of the dining room. She kicked him in the shins and screamed into his sweaty palm. He didn't set her down till they got to the living room.

As soon as he let his hand go, she shrieked, "Mo-om! Da-ad!"

Eks shoved her to the floor. "You little traitor. I'm going to kill you." He bent over his sister with his fingers out like claws.

Caryn pulled her knees up to her chest to protect herself and, out of the corner of her eye, saw Anna Clare, her mother, running into the living room.

"What's going on in here? Ekhard, what are you doing?" She waved the tissues wadded in her hand, a white flag of surrender.

From the floor, Caryn watched her dad, his face red as a tomato, swoop in and pull Ekhard back by his shoulders. Then he wound up and slugged him. Right in the jaw.

Mom shrieked, "No!"

Eks fell back into the china hutch, rattling the dishes. Something fell over and broke. His hand went to the side of his jaw, which was already turning purple. Screwing his mouth and eyes closed tight, he ran out of the room.

"Goddammit, Theo!" Anna raised a hand to slap him.

Theo caught her hand in the air. "Don't you dare!"

Their eyes locked on one another.

Anna wrenched her wrist away and said, "I'm leaving you. Now." In one big swoop, she took Caryn by the hand and stormed out of the room.

It felt like her arm was being ripped out of its socket. Anna Clare had such a tight grip on Caryn's small hand that the bones ground together.

An hour and a half later, in the back seat of the car, Caryn absent-mindedly rubbed her sore, bruised knuckles.

"Keep up with the pup. Don't stop. Don't stop till you get the pup."

Anna had doted on Eks before pulling out of the driveway. She made sure he had the ice pack and cooed, "Poor baby." Bitterly recalling those moments, Caryn slouched forward to press her knees into the back of Ekhard's seat. She moved her knees in time to the music's beat, rocking his seat and jolting him.

"Stop it, Caryn." Eks turned around, showing his blackened, swollen cheek.

"Make me," she taunted.

"Caryn Clare, you stop that right now." Anna's long arm snaked over the seat. Though Caryn ducked, Anna smacked her in the face, hard.

"Ow! What did I do?" Caryn lifted bruised hands to her throbbing nose. The last time she had teased her brother Anna had smacked her hands until they turned bright red. They were still sore.

"Leave your brother alone. Can't you see he's been hurt?" Anna took another drag on her cigarette.

"Where are we going? Are you leaving Dad?" Ekhard asked.

She flicked her cigarette butt out the window. "That's none of your business. Your dad and I just had a little argument, that's all."

Caryn put in her two cents' worth. "You were fighting."

"We were fighting," Anna agreed.

"Are you leaving him?" Eks sounded hopeful. And scared.

Anna didn't answer. She slowed the car and turned onto a dirt road, put the car in park, and leaned her head on the steering wheel. Caryn sat up and scooted to the middle of the back-seat bench, draping her elbows over the front seat for a better look. The three of them stared silently out the front window.

"Where are we?" Ekhard asked.

No one answered.

In front of the car was a faded-gray old-fashioned, two-story house with dirty white pillars on either side of the front door. The no-longer-white trimmed windows and doors hung broken against the pale, weathered siding. A shutter lay on top of dead bushes near the steps.

The front porch stretched around the house, as did the railing, missing posts here and there. Caryn thought she could make out a rocking chair at one end. Above the roof of the porch, the shred of a flowery curtain billowed out one open window. Inside, it was dark. Like no one was home. Like it had been abandoned.

For a while, Anna shook. Her hunched shoulders bobbed up and down to the music, no longer Michael Jackson. Neither of the children spoke a word. Then, as if nothing had happened, Anna sat up and sniffed. She wiped her nose on her sleeve and turned that big station wagon around.

Eks threw his towel and ice pack on the floor in front of him. "Where are we going now?"

"Home. We're going back home."

CHAPTER 18

MORGAN

"Is Angie upset? It's Friday night."

"No, she's not mad. I dropped Etta off at practice. As long as I do whatever the girls need when they need it, we're good. And by the way, tomorrow is Etta's forensics meet. She and her team are debating the pros and cons of a democratic government. I plan on being there."

"So you're not spending Saturday with me? I swear, Donnie, where are your priorities?"

Donnie grumbled something under his breath.

"Just kidding. Geez, ever heard of sarcasm?"

"Not when it comes to my family." He drove his SUV up a long, winding, tree-lined driveway. The Aikens' home sat tucked in a gated community in the near north side of Indy.

"You're a good dad. The girls are lucky to have you." Morgan adjusted her jacket.

"Sometimes I'm not so sure."

"Trust me, I know," Morgan assured him.

The Aikens' home, a majestic white two-story with columns on either side of the front door, emerged from behind trees. Two huge black Labradors in the front yard saw the vehicle and ran toward it. Together they surrounded the car, barking ferociously and baring their teeth.

Morgan's eyes widened at the sight of the huge animals. "How did Mr. Aiken react to the news? Maybe they don't want to talk to us."

"No, no," Donnie quelled her worries. "He was relieved. He said they needed the closure."

"How are we supposed to get to the house?" The larger of the two dogs was up with its front feet on the door and growling through the closed passenger-side window. "I'm not getting out. Call them. Tell them to call off their guard dogs."

While Donnie dialed, the front door of the house opened. A man in green-plaid slacks and a navy blazer stepped outside. A thin woman wearing a peach-colored sweater dress rushed past him and toward the car. She called to the dogs, "Bernie, Conan, come here! Get over here!"

The dogs trotted to their mistress, tails wagging. She took both dogs by the collar and led them back to the house.

"Look, they're friendly," Donnie encouraged Morgan. "Come on."

Mr. Aiken approached the car. Donnie stepped out of the vehicle and greeted him.

"Good evening. Detective James is it?" Mr. Aiken shook hands with Donnie.

"That's right. Thanks for seeing us, Mr. Aiken."

Morgan also shook the man's hand. His strong handshake was vigorous.

"Call me Bennie," he said. "Not Bernie. That's the dog's name. My wife always gets us confused." A deep, soft laugh accompanied this statement.

"Nice to meet you." Morgan pulled away and surreptitiously rubbed her hand.

"Come on inside." Bennie led the way into the house.

The grand entryway had marble tile floors and high ceilings. To the right was a decorator's showcase dining room complete with table settings and a floral centerpiece.

"Expecting company?" Morgan asked.

"No, Leeanne likes to keep it that way. I don't ask questions."

Bennie led them to the left into a high-style living room. The plush-carpeted room was painted light-green so that the white trim popped. A pair of matching dark-green sofas faced each other in front of a gas-burning fireplace surrounded by black marble. A brick patio confined by thick brush and tall trees could be seen through a set of windowed French doors. Outdoor furniture was covered in fallen leaves.

Mrs. Aiken swept into the room. "Thanks so much for coming over, officers. Sorry about the dogs."

"It's detectives," Morgan said. "Detective Morgan Jewell."

Leeanne's bleached-blond hair was frizzy, the result of years of processing chemicals. She appeared physically fit for her age and wore bright-pink lipstick. "Please have a seat. Can I get you anything? Coffee or . . ." She checked her watch. "It is happy hour somewhere, isn't it?"

Bennie went directly to a wet bar. "And it's Friday. How about a drink?" He dug ice from a bucket and dumped it into a wide glass.

"None for me, thank you." Donnie shook hands with Leeanne; then, careful not to disturb the numerous decorative pillows, sat down on one of the twin sofas.

Morgan also declined a drink as Leeanne poured herself a glass of wine. Leeanne and Morgan sat on the sofa across from Donnie, and Bennie settled into a straight-backed, flower-printed wing chair. There was a collective release of breath.

"You found her. You found our baby Suzy," Leeanne said.

"I hope you find closure in knowing that. But Mr. and Mrs. Aiken," Donnie said gently, "the discovery of her body has reopened the investigation."

"Of course, of course." Bennie set his drink down on the cluttered table next to his chair.

"Not on the table, Bennie," Leeanne scolded.

He moved the glass to a pink coaster next to a gold lamp, probably a valuable heirloom, that included a pair of porcelain figurines—a man and a woman wearing garb from centuries ago dancing around a tree trunk. The lamp and gilded shade shook as Bennie nudged the table. He said, "Ten years after her disappearance we held a wake. We wanted the search to finally be over."

Morgan reached into the inner pocket of her jacket and pulled out her tattered notebook and fine-tip pen.

"It's not like we gave up on her," Leeanne explained. "But we have two other beautiful girls. They both felt forgotten by us. It took years of counseling to help them recover. I think they still resent Suzy for leaving us."

"Let's not get into that, Leeanne." Bennie picked up his drink.

"We know she was murdered," Morgan said, coming directly to the point.

"She didn't run away, you see. I knew she wouldn't leave us." Leeanne waved her arms, almost spilling her wine before guzzling half of it.

Donnie pushed aside the sofa pillows and said, "We need to ask you a few questions about that time."

Bennie rattled the ice in his glass. "Go ahead. The search was mismanaged from the start."

Leeanne added, "For one thing, they took little Becky Lewis in for questioning. They held her at the station for a whole day, poor thing."

"Becky Lewis was Suzanne's best friend," Donnie stated, holding a pillow in his lap.

"That's right." Bennie took a big swallow of his drink. "Becky and Trina Kierra. The three were cheerleaders and inseparable. And I'll have you know, neither of those girls would hurt a fly."

"Becky never recovered from it. Her mother and I had a falling out because of it, but I kept tabs on her through friends for many years." Leeanne held her wine glass in a shaky hand.

Morgan wrote, "Trina Kierra," in her notebook, as the name wasn't listed on the report. "Do you have a picture of them? Becky and Trina?" she asked. She hoped one of them had blond hair.

"Yes, of course." Seeming relieved to have something to do, Leeanne set her glass on a nearby table and skipped out of the room.

Uncomfortable, Donnie leaned forward over the pillow in his lap. On either side of him, more pillows toppled toward him, encroaching on his space. He shifted one of them to under his arm.

"I tell you, they weren't the ones the police should have been targeting. I would have questioned those Klein kids if it had been up to me."

Bennie finished his drink and stood up. "You sure I can't get you something?"

Both detectives shook their heads.

"Who were they? The Kleins." Morgan spun around on the sofa to look at Bennie behind her at the bar.

"Ekhard Klein and his little sister, Caryn. Like Karen, only pronounced weird. Caryn was a creepy kid."

"I read the files. Ekhard was Suzanne's boyfriend, wasn't he?" Morgan asked. She wrote, "Creepy Caryn," in her book.

"Suzanne did that to get back at us." Leeanne had reentered with a thick photo album. "You know how teenagers love to act out their frustrations. Dating Ekhard was Suzanne's rebellion against us." Sitting down on the sofa next to Morgan, she opened the book on her lap.

"Tell us about him," Morgan said.

"Ekhard wasn't a bad kid," Bennie answered. "He was kind of a dope, though. His dad didn't help them out either. Theo was an alcoholic, and in fact he died the following year." Bennie asked his wife, "Did Ekhard go to college, sweetie?"

"He went to college for a year." Leeanne picked up her glass, finished what was left, then handed the empty glass to her husband.

"After Theo died, the kids sold the house. I don't know what became of them after that," Bennie continued.

"They sold everything, the house and their dad's warehousing business, and moved across town to an apartment," Leeanne explained.

Bennie stood behind his wife, looking at the album. "That's right. I dealt with Theo as a business associate for a few years."

"Ten. It was ten years, Bennie, and we knew their mother, too, before she left them. Her name was Anna."

"Their mother left them?" Morgan asked.

Donnie mouthed to Morgan, "Write that down."

"It was so sad," Leeanne said. "After that, Theo went to the doghouse."

"The liquor store, you mean," her husband corrected.

"What kind of business did you do together?" Morgan asked Bennie.

"Theo owned a small warehouse just outside of town. At times, I had large shipments of furniture coming from the West Coast. He stored our overflow."

Morgan lit up. "You own that furniture store near the mall."

Bennie burst into song, *"We treat you like family,"* and handed a refilled glass to his wife.

"Now's not the time, Ben." Leeanne sipped again.

"So back to Ekhard and his sister," Donnie said. He pushed aside the pillows, now piled up on his right side.

"Ekhard had an alibi. His sister vouched for him," Bennie said.

"But Suzy spent lots of time with him. He picked her up in his car and she came home at all hours." Leeanne pointed to a photo of three young girls in cheerleading outfits. "Here are Becky and Trina with our Suzy."

Donnie half-stood to look, then leaned back on a pillow. He stood up again and shifted three pillows that had fallen back into his seat.

The girls looked like every American high school cheerleader. Becky had black hair, and Trina's was brown and long, down to her elbows.

"Do you think Ekhard had something to do with her disappearance?" Morgan asked.

"Yes," Bennie said.

"No," Leeanne said. "Ekhard didn't have a wicked bone in his body. I think it was his sister. If anyone should be investigated, it's her. Caryn Klein was a scary kid."

CHAPTER 19

MORGAN

Sheets lay across Morgan's bare body, cooling the heat that lingered between her legs. Rob took care to make her happy. The warm afterglow of satisfying sex filled her with a sense of contentment that she was sure she didn't deserve. She didn't mean to lead Rob on. And having promised him nothing yet, she wondered what she'd have to give up if she settled down with him. Lately she'd been thinking about applying to the U.S. Marshals. If she did get the job—and she knew it might take a few years—she couldn't imagine how married life would fit in with it. But she wasn't ready to give up the dream.

Ever since Fay's murder, Morgan had had only one goal in her life. That was to find the killer. Much like Suzanne and Hallie, Fay had been bludgeoned to death. Police never found the killer. The only clue had been a name written in Fay's journal—Larry Milhouse. Yet Larry Milhouse, like Ekhard Klein, didn't exist. No one by that name was registered at IU in Bloomington. He didn't live in the city of Bloomington or anywhere in the state of Indiana.

Morgan had been in such denial that Fay was seeing someone that she thought Fay had made up the name. She even told police she thought so. And until recently, Morgan's memories from the time of Fay's death came from photos and diary entries. So much of it had been blocked out. Not forgotten. Just erased.

Her psychiatrist, Dr. Taylor, had said that it was Perpetration-Induced Traumatic stress syndrome. The PITS. Which was the truth. She predicted that the memories would surface again someday. And now . . . seeing Hallie's face had triggered the awakening.

Deep in sleep on her bed, Rob snorted and turned onto his belly. Far from ready to join him, Morgan's mind buzzed with questions. She slid out from under the sheet and felt her way to a pair of jeans on the floor. The rough seams rubbed her inner thighs as she pulled them on. On the foot of the bed, Gretta lifted her head, then rolled over on her back. It took Morgan several minutes' groping in the dark to locate her tank top that had been tossed on the desk chair. She put it on before realizing it was inside out, then left it that way and padded down to the kitchen.

The coffee pot burbled on the counter next to Morgan's laptop. Blue light from her computer lit up her hands and the green coffee cup she'd filled. Morgan dragged a stool to the end of the counter and climbed up on it.

At the time of Suzanne's death, Rebecca Harrington had been attending a private college in Louisville, Kentucky. Due to the precision of the strike patterns on both Hallie and Suzanne, and of Rebecca's alibi, Morgan removed Rebecca from the list of suspects to focus on the one person she couldn't find: Ekhard Marcus Klein.

On the screen, his name had bounced back to "No Records Found" in every search she had tried. He didn't show up in rental records or as a property owner, and there were no arrests or court records. Yet his death wasn't recorded either. At his last known haunt, Butler University his course load had been heavy in mathematics for one semester, then he had vanished.

Morgan sipped her coffee and made a note to look in public records stacks in the courthouse.

Ekhard's sister, Caryn Klein, might know something about him. Morgan made a note to connect with her first thing in the morning. *Does she know where her brother is?* Morgan typed the number into her cell phone and wrote down her work address. In another search, Morgan found that Trina Kierra had married Randall Tanner in 2010. They had one child, a seven-year-old boy, and lived in Crown Point, Indiana. Her husband worked in Chicago. Perhaps Trina would have some more insights. Morgan wrote her address on a pad of paper and the next one too.

Becky Lewis, who lived in a crappy neighborhood in downtown Indy, had been the one most questioned by police after Suzanne's disappearance. Now, Becky owned a house in a neighborhood that Morgan wouldn't visit unless necessary. And it was.

Morgan yawned. The coffee had sustained her for an hour, but now she was tired. She closed her laptop, plunging the room into darkness. Feeling her way back to bed, she found Gretta spread out along the foot and Rob curled up on his side. She loved the way he smelled. Without waking them, she slipped out of her jeans and under the warm covers. For a long while, she lay awake thinking about how she also loved the way Rob looked at her when he wanted to touch her. And how he approached her with such tenderness.

But now she was sleepy. She didn't have time to plan her future. She couldn't fathom what that would look like. In the dark, the only thing she could see was the dead girl Suzanne. She was only a few years younger than Fay had been.

CHAPTER 20

MORGAN: 16 Years Ago

Fay slung her backpack over her shoulder and stood up to go. "See you tomorrow then."

"What?" Sitting cross-legged on the floor with a small stack of books in her lap, Morgan looked up from the box she'd been packing. "You're leaving?"

"Yeah." Fay checked her watch.

"I didn't know you had to work tonight." Morgan moved the stack to one side.

Fay checked inside her pack, moved things around, and pulled out her headphones. As she looped them around her neck, Morgan noticed she was blushing.

"Yeah. They called this morning. I'm covering for Dimitri. He's on vacation or something."

No. Morgan thought. *That's not right. Fay's lying.* "Dimitri, huh? Well, that sucks."

"Yeah." Fay's voice was entirely too singsong. "Well, gotta go." Her cheeks had become the color of cranberry juice.

Like a kangaroo, Morgan sprung to her feet. "Fay. Wait."

Fay moved quickly to Morgan's bedroom door. Before Morgan could catch up with her, she was down the stairs and putting on her yellow high-tops.

Morgan touched her friend's arm, trying to make eye contact with her. "Fay. Where are you really going?"

"Work. Like I said." Fay's gaze remained lowered and focused on her yellow high-tops. Morgan had a matching pair, only hers were blue.

"I thought your mom didn't let you work the night shift at The Hamburger Stand." Morgan didn't understand why Fay was lying.

"Today she did." Fay still avoided Morgan's gaze and opened the front door.

A new tactic was necessary. Morgan let a sly grin cross her lips. "The other day you said you met someone."

Now Fay looked her in the eye. "I did not! Leave it alone, will you?"

Morgan released Fay's arm and raised both hands in surrender. "Okay. Don't get mad. Geez."

Fay looked at her watch again. "Look, I have to go or I'll be late."

"Do you need a ride?" Morgan offered, hoping to get the truth out of her on the way.

Fay thought this over for a moment. Then, irresolutely, she said, "No. I'm taking the bus." She slipped past Morgan and out the front door. "See you tomorrow."

"Okay, bye." Morgan waved.

How weird was that? It was obvious that Fay was lying about something. Work? Or maybe . . . could Fay have actually met someone? Morgan's lips sagged at the corners. *Who? Where had they met? Who?*

CHAPTER 21

MORGAN

As she zipped between semitrucks on I-65 northbound, Morgan's fingertips grazed the smooth, black-leather steering wheel of the Mazda RX-8. On her way to interview Trina Kierra-Tanner somewhere between cities and surrounded by cornfields, she decided that she loved the car. She loved it right up till lights of a state patrol car flashed behind her, pulling her over. This wouldn't have happened if Donnie had been driving. Yet Morgan couldn't blame him for spending the day with his daughters.

Though embarrassing, it had been easy to get out of the ticket by flashing her badge. The officer had caught her going 103 in a 70-mph zone. He recognized her too, because he used to work in Indy with Rob Gibson. *Rob will hear about this and I'll never live it down*, Morgan thought.

A half-hour later, in the town of Crown Point, Indiana, she parked the red rental car in front of an old brick Tudor-style home where Trina Kierra-Tanner lived with her husband and son. The heavy front door opened before she could knock, and out of the house ran a blond boy followed by a black puppy. The kid whipped past Morgan, but the floppy-eared dog stopped with tail wagging and tongue lolling. Morgan bent to pet the dog as he sniffed her shoes.

A lithe teenage girl bounded out after them and almost ran Morgan over. She apologized before asking how she could help.

"Is Mrs. Tanner at home?" Morgan asked.

"She's in the breakfast room. Follow me." She shouted out to the kid, "Stay in the front yard, Charlie."

Inside the darkened house, the girl led her to the back room, a sunny, cozy kitchen. "Mrs. Tanner?" She called out. "Someone is here for you." The girl waved her thin arms in the direction of a room full of potted plants.

Trina emerged from behind a small palm tree with a watering can in one hand and a pile of dead leaves in the other. "Hello, Detective Jewell. I didn't expect you so soon." Her hair, bleached and wispy, gave her an angelic glow. She set the watering can down on the counter and placed the leaves in the trash can under the sink. Then turned to the sink and washed her hands and dried them on a flower-print towel that hung on the stove handle. "Thank you for driving all the way up here."

"There wasn't any traffic. Must be because it's Saturday," Morgan fibbed. An unexpected yawn opened her jaw wide. She covered her mouth with the back of a hand. "Excuse me." Sleep hadn't come easily over the last week. It was catching up with her.

With warm, clean hands, Trina welcomed Morgan as if they were old friends. "Can I get you a cup of coffee?" she asked.

At a small wooden breakfast table with sunlight pouring in on them, Morgan and Trina faced each other, sipping espresso from dainty cups decorated in ornate colorful patterns.

"There were four of us at first. Suzanne and I told Becky and Julia what to do. At the beginning of senior year, Suzanne kicked Julia out of the group. Today they'd say Julia was bullied. She was, you know." Trina looked at her lap, her hair a halo in the sunlight. The large window behind her was a perfect spot for the numerous indoor plants and potted flowers that covered every surface and hung from the ceiling.

"Was Suzanne the leader of the group?" Morgan asked.

"I guess so. We were terrible people. All of us were bullies. Becky and Suzanne loved to pick on underclassmen. They got off on watching kids die of embarrassment." Trina toyed nervously with her hair as if she still carried guilt from all those years ago. "I . . . did too. I wasn't an innocent bystander, Detective."

"None of us were, Trina," Morgan said. The strong taste of coffee lingered on her tongue. She hoped the caffeine buzz wouldn't affect her driving on the way home as she lifted the delicate cup to her lips and finished it. "What about Ekhard? What was your take on Suzanne's relationship with him?"

Trina shook her head. "Gosh, I forgot about him. The way I remember it, their relationship was an experiment."

"In what way?"

"Suzanne planned on dumping him hard. Poor guy. He was a dork. He had no idea what was coming. What would have come, you know, if . . ."

Charlie burst into the room with the puppy after him. "Mom, Mom! I got him to sit! Watch!"

Drool dripped from the panting dog's mouth. It sat down, needing a rest.

"Sit." The boy commanded. "See? Can I give him a treat?"

The swift-footed teenager sprung into the room. "There you are!"

"Can I, Mom? Please?" he begged.

"I'm sorry, Mrs. Tanner. Charlie wanted treats for Nemo."

Pointing toward the kitchen, Trina smiled. "That's fine. Do you know where they are, Jenna?"

"Yes. Come on, Charlie. Nemo, come on." Charlie and the dog followed the girl into the kitchen.

Trina picked up her cup. "Empty. Would you like a refill?"

"No, thank you. Any more caffeine and I won't sleep at all tonight," Morgan said. *I might get stopped again for speeding* was her thought.

"So, where were we?" Trina stood and cleared the empty cups from the table.

"You were telling me about Suzanne and Ekhard," Morgan reminded her. "Perhaps Ekhard saw Suzanne's ulterior motive."

"Well, if you're wondering if he could have killed her, I don't think so." Trina stepped into the kitchen and returned with a plate of muffins.

"What happened to him anyway? Where did he go after college?" Morgan eyed the sweet snacks hungrily because she hadn't yet eaten.

"Oh, Ekhard and I weren't friends. I have no idea."

Morgan had been burning to ask this next question. "Who do you think killed Suzanne and buried her body in the woods?"

Trina shook her head. Her blue eyes remained fixed on Morgan as she said, "Honestly, it could have been any number of kids. Girls and boys hated her. Suzanne wasn't nice, and she didn't care how many enemies she made."

CHAPTER 22

CARYN

"Oh, Riannda, tell Harry I can't make it today," Caryn said in her practiced, puny voice. "I feel so . . . I just can't get out of bed."

"Are you taking any echinacea? It helps your immune system fight off bugs. Is it your stomach again? You probably have a flu virus."

"I don't know what's wrong. I'll call the doctor's office as soon as they open."

"Could I bring you this ginger tea with honey?"

"No thanks, Riannda."

"Did you try that all-day cold medicine? It works wonders for me. I can even get things done. Last March I had the worst cold . . ."

"Thanks. You're a real sweetie. But I don't want pills. I drank grapefruit juice this morning and got nauseous again. I'll have to wait it out."

"You're not pregnant, are you? Could it be morning sickness?"

"Oh, God, no!" Caryn bellowed her answer a little too loudly.

"Okay. Well, I hope you get better soon."

Caryn hung up. Easy enough. She'd woken early to look for information about Ekhard, aka Nathaniel Johnson, online. So far, she'd discovered that he was an accountant and a single nerd who kept to himself. But Caryn had ways of learning about people's private lives. And now she had a sick day.

Two hours and sixteen minutes later, she parked her car on Hyacinth Street in Lafayette, three houses from Eks's place.

The thought troubled her that her brother lived in a house. He owns the home, she thought. *And I live in a condo. I don't care. It was never a competition.*

Who was she kidding? It was always a competition.

She closed and locked the car, ducking behind it, and checked the street for signs of life. Past his house in the next yard, a tall elderly man stood with his back to her. His blue windbreaker flapped in the breeze. In one hand, he held a hose that was showering water on orange and red mums. In a month, winter weather would take those flowers, so Caryn wondered why he bothered.

The man stepped out of the shade into bright sunlight. Behind his back, she zigzagged into Eks's yard as the man turned. In four long gazelle-like strides, Caryn made it between the houses and out of his line of sight.

She stopped to put her hands on her thighs, breathing hard. *I'm not nervous,* she told herself while her heart drummed a jazzy beat. She looked at the dark windows of the house next door. Dry grass crunched under her feet as she crept to the backyard. The sounds of children play- ing nearby forced her to a stop behind a bush before proceeding. Behind Ekhard's yard and across the chain-link fence, two toddlers wearing bright-colored clothing sat in a sandbox, playing. One wore a ruffled hat to protect her face from the sun.

Where is the parent?

There. Ten or twelve feet from the sandbox, their mother sat in a folding lawn chair with a white cup in one hand and a magazine in the other. She faced Ekhard's backyard, watching the children giggle and coo.

One scraggly crab apple tree grew in the center of Ekhard's exposed backyard. The fruit from it covered the ground where several birds pecked at the fallen berries. Other than that, one small shed tucked into the farthest corner didn't block the woman's view. With no plantings or rail around the deck, Caryn remained behind a deciduous bush that had already lost half its leaves.

A phone rang. The plump woman in the lawn chair set her magazine on her lap and flipped open a cell phone. "Hi, Mom. Nothing. Letting Emily and Eric play outside in the sandbox. I don't know how long this nice weather will hold."

Caryn watched the breeze whip several leaves off the bush. They tumbled across the yard, beckoning the toddlers into a game of tag. With her back pressed against the dingy white aluminum siding, she hoped her black long-sleeve shirt and camouflage pants would hold up to their reputation.

"What? You're kidding. I despise that woman. Hold on a minute." The mother looked right at Caryn and then, with an effort, lifted herself out of the lawn chair. "I'll go turn on the TV."

Caryn breathed in relief as the neighbor waddled into her house. The kids, who appeared to be near the ages of two and four, remained playing outside while their mother watched them from a window. Caryn couldn't risk an entry through Eks's patio door.

She ducked back to the front of the house, keeping an eye out for the man watering flowers. As luck would have it, he was gone. Across the street, homes were quiet. It was 11:27. Quickly, she hopped up to Ekhard's faded-green front door.

The solid door had no windows or sidelights. She pulled two straightened paperclips out of her pocket and got to work. As she was a little out of practice, it took her over a minute to jimmy the deadbolt because the knob was loose and wobbly. Once unlocked, the door opened and closed behind her without a sound. Her heart pounded loudly as if trying to send a message to the dead while Caryn stood in Ekhard's darkened foyer.

A boxy glass and gold-plated light fixture hung from overhead. On her left were dark-walnut closet doors, and next to them the door to the garage. She peeked inside to confirm that Ekhard was indeed gone for the day. Cool air and the smell of gasoline leaked into the house before she shut the door.

On her right, the once-white carpet had a brownish-gray path from the kitchen to a chair in the living room. His decrepit leather recliner faced a big-screen TV and reminded her of the one their dad had had. Given the age and wear of this chair, it might have been the very same one in which Theo had drunk himself to death.

Except for the hum of the refrigerator in the kitchen, the house was quiet. Caryn took a step forward. Worn floorboards creaked under her feet. Ahead of her, she recognized a long, dark table in the dinette with four straight-backed chairs around it. Every morning before school she had eaten breakfast at that table.

Scratches on the corner took her back to a memory of the ten-year-old Ekhard when he had been making a model airplane and decided to saw the pieces apart with his Boy Scout camping knife. He was grounded for two weeks for cutting into the table. He also took a beating from their mother. His bare bottom had turned bright red and blue while Anna Clare paddled him.

Caryn ran her fingers over a dent in the surface, a perfect circle, about the size of a quarter. The edges of the dent had softened with age; now it was smooth where it had once been splintery. Near it was a mound of model glue about one centimeter in diameter. The dents and bumps connected her to a distant history hidden behind a heavy theater curtain.

Daylight poured in through the sliding door. Out past the deck, Caryn watched the neighbor woman rejoin her children in their yard. The smallest one had begun to cry. The drama unfolded like a silent movie. The mom picked up her child and patted the girl on the back while talking to her. The child calmed and wiped her eyes with a tiny fist.

Caryn couldn't imagine what was being said. She didn't remember Anna Clare ever holding her that way. The memory of her mother turned black-and-blue. She would rather forget.

In the kitchen, the old Formica counter was peeled and cracked as if harsh cleaners had regularly been used to scrub it. It struck her how clean it was. Spotless. There wasn't a crumb of toast or a drip of coffee on it. The stovetop, too, sparkled and shined in the sunlight.

She wondered if Ekhard still cooked. After Anna Clare left, circumstances had forced him to do most of the cooking and cleaning. Not that Theo cared. He didn't. But they had to eat. Instead of starving, Ekhard made the choice to take care of those things while Dad sucked down more bourbon.

What does Ekhard eat now? Caryn peeked into the fridge. Eggs, milk, and an unopened package of Colby cheese. A twelve-pack of beer opened on its side. Bread and a pot of leftovers that smelled like meat or spaghetti sauce. She closed the door.

Around the corner, a closed door led to the basement. She'd save that for last. She hated basements. A yellow phone hung on the wall with a spiral cord that, stretched to its limit, hit the floor. Next to it hung a whiteboard with "Gold's Gym membership dues" written on it in blue dry-erase marker.

Pictures covered the wall in the darkened hallway past the dinette. Here, Caryn flipped on a light. Framed in plain wood was an old family photo. In a posed studio picture with fake trees in the background, Theo wasn't smiling. Mom, with her long, straight hippy hair, looked more worried than happy. And, grinning and ignorant, Ekhard and Caryn sat on an orange pillow.

A rattling sound startled her. One picture hit the floor with a crash. Her chest felt tight as she bent to pick it up. At least the glass hadn't broken. It was of Anna Clare, bronzed tan and smiling with her arms around Ekhard, who was about six. Next to them in a pink ruffled bathing suit, sun-bleached-blond Caryn pouted. She was maybe three years old.

Disgusted, Caryn moved to the bedrooms. A stale-stagnant smell hung in the air. No more pictures. Not even decorative paintings hung on the walls. Only one large full-length mirror stood against the wall beside her mother's dresser. A king-size mattress lay on the floor, made to perfection just like Mom had taught them, the sheets and blue blanket pulled into perfect nurse's corners.

Eks's bathroom was white and pristine. The sink was clean, without a single hair or smudge. Two white towels folded neatly over the towel bar appeared unused.

When did my brother become such a neatnik?

Back in his bedroom, Caryn rummaged through the top drawer of her mother's dresser. Oddly, it still contained things that she had coveted as a child: a small perfume bottle, a cheap gold locket with a picture of her grandmother in it, a black rosary that had belonged to a friend. She picked it up and remembered that person giving it to Anna Clare. She remembered her mother's black, swollen eye.

A silver tube of lipstick lay next to the rosary. Though the sticker had fallen off, Caryn knew the color: Frosted Pink Rose. She twisted the tube open. About half remained. It wasn't too dried out. The tube made its way into the cargo pocket of Caryn's camouflage pants.

Caryn had seen enough. She rubbed her aching hands together. Psychosomatic, the pain always started when she thought of her mother. It went along with deep feelings of anger.

It was time to meet with Ekhard face to face. Time to face the past.

CHAPTER 23

CARYN: 27 Years Ago

It was a dog. The best one Caryn had ever drawn. It had brown-and-white fur, though the white crayon didn't show up on the white paper very well. She drew small black dots for eyes, just like the dog that lived in the blue house down the street. The fuzzy white dog that barked all the time.

"That looks good," Ekhard complimented her drawing. "Yours is better than mine," he admitted. He was right. Across the kitchen table, he had drawn a dog too. But his looked like a horse with stick legs.

Ekhard crumpled his paper and threw it across the room. "I'm better at cars." He reached for the box of crayons, but his hand hovered over them indecisively. "Should I make a yellow or a red Corvette?"

Caryn didn't know what a Corvette was, but she liked red better. "Red," she told him. She had a dark-green crayon called Pine Tree in her hand and worked on the grass under her dog.

Mom strode into the room wearing a plaid miniskirt and removing a jean jacket. Underneath, she wore a sheer chiffon blouse with ruffled short sleeves. "What would you like for lunch today?"

"Peanut butter and jelly," Ekhard said. He had begun drawing a yellow car.

"Coloring?" Anna Clare slung the jacket over her left arm. The wadded-up piece of paper that Ekhard had thrown scooted across the

floor as she kicked it. It landed under the table and stopped dead. "Who told you that you could color on the kitchen table?"

Caryn's eyes remained on her paper. "We're not coloring the table, Mom. We have paper."

"Don't get smart with me, Caryn. Is that your paper on the floor?" Their mother pointed at the crumpled-up paper under the table.

"No." Caryn admired the grass around each of her dog's feet. She put the green crayon away, then chose one called Pumpkin Orange and added a flower.

Mom waited. "If I have to pick the paper up, you will both get grounded. Understand?"

"It's not mine. Ekhard did it," Caryn said, focused on her drawing.

"Someone get that trash off the floor." Mom's voice rose.

Ekhard ignored the mounting tension and continued working on black wheels for his Corvette. Caryn felt it coming and crouched over her paper. Mom was having a bad day. An angry day. On days like this, Mom could hurt you. She would do it without regret and without saying she was sorry. Once, Caryn got in trouble for asking too many questions. Mom had taken her hands and hit them with the round part of a spoon till they were red and bruised. Caryn stopped asking questions.

"Pick it up," Mom commanded. Her face had turned red.

"Eks?" Caryn pleaded.

Silent, her brother remained engrossed in his project.

Mom hovered over the table. She had hung her jacket over the back of one chair and placed her hands on the table. "That's a nice dog, Caryn. Very nice."

For a fleeting moment, Caryn appreciated the praise. But the grateful feeling didn't take hold before her stomach went cold. Her mother paused, calm before the storm.

Ekhard looked up and met Caryn's eye at the moment Anna struck. Their papers were torn from under their hands, and Mom raged, flinging torn little pieces like confetti across the table. On days like this Caryn knew to stay small and hidden. She would remain quiet. Watching. Invisible.

When she was through shredding Caryn's drawing, their mother spilled the box of crayons and scattered them violently across the room. "I said, pick up the paper! Pick up the goddamn paper!"

Ekhard cowered.

Caryn shouted, "Do it, Eks!" Mom's tantrums could last for a whole day, and no one could make her stop. Caryn slid off her chair and under the table, out of reach.

Ekhard yelled, "Stop it!" and pushed his chair back with a grating sound. "Why do you have to be like this?"

Caryn looked up at him. His gaze seemed to burn a hole in his mother's head. *What was he doing?* They both knew she'd just get worse if you stood up to her. And it did. At the sound of skin on skin, Caryn shrank into a ball.

Once, twice, three times.

His chair fell over backward as Ekhard jumped to his feet. He shrieked, "I hate you! I hate you!" Then he bolted for the door. Caryn saw him trying to get past their mom, trying to go to his room, but she caught his arm and yanked him back.

"Where do you think you're going?" Their mother gripped his thin arm with one hand as he struggled to get away.

Anna squeezed his smaller hand and made a white-knuckle fist. Ekhard screamed.

Over the sounds of his cries, Caryn carefully picked up every last crayon and tiny shred of paper, including the broken Pumpkin Orange crayon. While doing so, she decided never to be like her mother. Mom was crazy. If you didn't do things her way, she got so angry. Just like today. She threw things and hit you.

Black-and-blue bruises peppered Caryn's arms and bottom. Ekhard's too. Once, she even broke his fingers. Caryn remembered waiting in the emergency room that night. When the doctor asked how it happened, Mom had lied and said Eks fell. She told us to keep it a secret. Caryn was surprised that Ekhard did. If anything, she would grow up to be tough like him. She would *never* be like her mother.

CHAPTER 24

MORGAN

Tiny snowflakes floated through the air, an early show of winter in October. Morgan zipped her red winter jacket up to the neck and peered through a smeared, dirty glass window, shading her eyes from the glare. The two-story, inner-city house was three miles from Monument Circle in central downtown.

"No one is home," she said.

Donnie, out on the concrete sidewalk, craned his neck to see the upper windows. "Someone's upstairs."

Weathered sheets of plywood boarded over two windows on this house-turned-apartment. This area was inhabited mostly by druggies and poor folks, and most houses were aged beyond restoration. Residents didn't have the opportunity or the know-how to rise above their conditions, nor the money for decent repairs.

Somewhere inside, a door shut. Morgan knocked again and pressed her forehead to the dirty glass, trying to see inside the house. A shadow emerged. A hunched-over person wearing jeans and a dark-green hoodie approached the door.

"Someone's coming." She tapped the glass.

A woman opened the deadbolt first, then two sliding locks.

"Yeah?" A cloud of cigarette smoke accompanied her. A burning butt hung from bitterly thin lips.

"Good afternoon, ma'am." Morgan's breath clouded the cold air. "I'm looking for one of your residents, Becky Lewis. Is she in?"

"I'm Becky, and it's not Lewis anymore. It's Parks. What do you want?"

With Becky's police record she had been easy to find. Nowhere did it mention her marriage. Around thirty-seven years old, Becky Parks had aged dramatically. She looked closer to fifty. Her gray-streaked black hair was pulled into a knot at the back of her head. It looked and smelled like she'd slept on it for days.

Both detectives flashed their badges. "Hi, Becky. I'm Detective Jewell, and this is my partner, Detective James. We just wanted to ask you some questions about someone you went to high school with."

"If it's Craig Flynn again, I don't know anything. I told them a hundred times . . ."

"No, ma'am. It isn't about him. We wanted to talk to you about Suzanne Aiken," Morgan said.

In an instant, Becky's body language changed from up on her toes and leaning in their faces to fallen, stricken from her perch.

Morgan offered a handshake.

"Oh." Becky weakly shook Morgan's hand with two fingers.

"Do you remember Suzanne?" Morgan asked.

Becky nodded.

"Would you mind talking to us about her?" Donnie asked. He remained on the sidewalk.

"That's all right. Sure. Let me get my smokes. It's cold out today, but we can sit on the porch if you don't mind. My son is sleeping upstairs."

"We'll wait here," Donnie said in his deep, soothing voice.

The weathered front porch was broken like the building. There was a rotten, ripped-up couch that smelled of mildew even in the cold wintry air. Morgan put her hands in her pockets and leaned on the porch rail, which needed more than a good coat of paint. Trash, a broken beer bottle, and fast-food wrappers littered the small front yard. A plastic grocery bag caught on a twiggy bush waved in the breeze.

Donnie approached the porch step but then remained on the concrete. Morgan feared his weight might further compromise the structure.

Becky returned a few minutes later wearing an unzipped, dirty, black coat and carrying a pack of Camel cigarettes and a lighter in one hand. A newly lit cig burned in her other hand as she closed the door.

She faced the detectives, inhaled from her cigarette, then blew a cloud of smoke into the air. "High school. Humph." Becky half laughed. "Sure was a long time ago. Senior year really sucked for me."

"How so?" Morgan leaned back. The rickety railing loosened under her weight.

"Oh, those cops made a big deal of me and Suzy going to that movie. Which we never did."

"You never went to the movie?" Donnie placed his hand on the rail, supporting it where Morgan leaned.

"Yeah. We wanted to see *Disturbing Behavior*, which none of our friends would go to. Me and Suzy had a thing for scary movies." Becky grimaced, then inhaled deeply from her cigarette.

"But you never went?" Morgan persisted.

"Naw. Life was rough after that day. I barely graduated—so depressed about losing my friend. Other kids blamed me too." She puffed on her cigarette. "Couldn't get my shit together after that. Didn't go to college. Couldn't keep a job. See this?" She waved a hand at the building. "This is all I have. I got pregnant and married a fucking drug-dealing deadbeat. He's dead now, by the way. Overdosed. And me and my son get rent. And we survive."

"The investigating detective spent a long time questioning you."

"Fuck. I never been so scared in my life."

Morgan rubbed the notebook in her pocket. "You told him that you *ditched* Suzanne. Those were your words."

"Look. I did what I did. You can't arrest me for it now, right?"

"Arrest you for what?" Donnie asked.

"I was with Mark and some other boys from school. We broke into someone's house that night. We stole their stereo and a bottle of vodka. We got so drunk I hardly remembered it the next day. And when the police came to question me . . . Shit. I froze. I didn't want to get caught."

"Where do you think Suzanne went?" Morgan asked.

Becky nodded and looked out into the distance. Her head followed a car driving past the house. "If she didn't see me there, she would have gone to see Eks. Ekhard Klein was her boyfriend of the moment. But he said she never came over. His sister vouched for him. As if she was trustworthy."

"Why didn't you trust Caryn?" Donnie asked.

"Who?" Becky tapped another cigarette out of the pack.

"Caryn Klein, Ekhard's sister," Morgan explained.

"Is that her name? Shit, everyone called her Ceecee."

Donnie nodded. Morgan didn't pull out her notebook. She didn't want to scare Becky into thinking she was under investigation and clam up. "So you didn't trust Ceecee? Why not?"

"Ceecee was dangerous. She was the kind of bitch who kept to herself. Unless you crossed her. Then, ha ha! Then you'd be expecting bad shit to happen." Becky's open-mouthed laugh revealed yellow teeth.

"Like what?" Donnie asked.

"If she was mad at you, she'd come at you in the lunchroom with a handful of food and shove it down your shirt. Hell, once she cut off a girl's ponytail in a crowded hallway between classes. We couldn't prove it. No one would say they saw her. But I was sure she did it."

"Why was Suzanne dating Ekhard?" Morgan knew the answer from Trina's point of view but wanted Becky's.

"I don't know. I didn't get it. He was a world-class loser. And trust me, I know losers." Becky lit a new cigarette. "So they found her body. After all this time. She was murdered, wasn't she?"

"That's right," Donnie answered flatly.

Becky shrank back toward the door. "You don't think I did it, do you? I didn't kill her. I told them that back then. If you can find Mark Whitby, he can vouch for me."

Morgan stood up, causing the rail to moan. "No, Becky. We aren't investigating you."

The front door opened, and a tall, scruffy young man stepped out with eyebrows arched in concern. "Mom? Everything okay?"

Becky's shoulders dropped two inches at the appearance of her son. "Yeah, it's fine. Go on back inside."

"You sure?" He scratched his shaggy, unshaven face.

"I'm sure," she reassured him and took another long drag.

After he closed the door, Becky said, "Reggie's a good kid. Looks after me."

"Mrs. Parks, is there anything else you'd like to say about the day of Suzanne's death?" Donnie shuffled his feet. Toying with his car keys, he looked ready to close the meeting.

Becky took a quick drag and blew smoke at the floor. "I just wondered if Ekhard found out that Suzy was going to dump him. He was the quiet type. Too quiet, you know what I mean? I never liked him."

CHAPTER 25

MORGAN

With the stealth of a serial rapist, the assailant descended on Morgan. Stan's reputation preceded him by the dozens. Known for wet, unfulfilling relationships that didn't last the night, the man couldn't see the error of his ways. Yet, women lined up around the block to sleep with him. And now, Stan snaked his arm around Morgan's neck in a choke hold.

His hot breath on the back of Morgan's neck made her cringe. The nasty faded smell of cologne permeated his sweaty shirt. "I finally caught you, Minx-y Morgan. When are you going to go out with me?" Stan hissed into her ear.

Stan had asked out every single woman at Indy Metro PD. Though Morgan had repeatedly said no, he kept trying. Through gritted teeth, Morgan replied, "Never, sleaze."

"I know you want me," he oozed. Stan, who was a foot taller, stooped over her.

"Like hell, I do." His strangle technique was poor. It gave Morgan the perfect opportunity. In preparation to take him down, she tucked in her chin. She placed a firm grip on his choke-hold arm, then slid one foot backward and pushed his leg out from under him, simultaneously dropping to her knees. Morgan used gravity and her short stature to her advantage. As she went down to the mat, she forced him into a head-first flip over her shoulders.

Stan somersaulted and hit the floor hard and flat on his back. His long thin body splayed out on the mat while Morgan held his arm taut. As practiced, she pulled his arm straight out above his head and flattened his palm against the mat. She kneeled on the soft part of his inner arm, causing him to arch his back and cry out.

"Stop asking me out, you asshole." Morgan whispered the command, giving it intensity.

Stan smiled at her. "Gotta keep trying. You know that, don't you?"

She put her weight on his arm. "I could dislocate your shoulder."

Through squinting eyes and pursed lips, Stan cried out, "Uncle! Uncle! Shit, Morgan, let go."

She released him and stood up to a smattering of applause around the gym. Other female officers hooted and cheered. Training had ended. She walked to a folding chair where she'd parked her gym bag and bottled water.

"Nice job, there. You've been practicing." A familiar man's voice startled her.

Water splashed from the bottle down her chin. Morgan turned, surprised to see her brother Jeremy and his wife Dierdre standing at the edge of the mat. "Hey. What are *you* doing in town?"

"Just here for a visit. Donnie told me you'd be here." He approached with open arms, offering a hug.

Morgan backed away with the excuse, "I'm all sweaty."

"Do you think I care?" Jeremy swept in and wrapped his arms around Morgan. At his side, Dierdre smiled.

Morgan stepped away to look at him. A healthy new growth of stubble covered his chin. Brown eyes sparkled with his smile.

Dierdre said, "We came up for the Coldplay concert Saturday night. And we were hoping to spend some time with you beforehand."

Morgan embraced her sister-in-law. "It's great to see you. Can I take you out to dinner?"

"Let us treat. We have some news to share," Dierdre said.

"News?" Morgan asked.

Jeremy said, "I know you haven't talked to Mom and Dad, they told me you never call."

"I haven't. What is it?"

Dierdre took Jeremy's hand and said, "We'll tell you at dinner."

"Where are you staying? Adrienne and Bill are gone for the winter, you can stay in their bed." Morgan offered.

Jeremy tilted his head and gazed toward his brunette wife. She nodded agreement to the unspoken question. "That would be great," he said. "We were going to drive back right after the concert."

"The concert won't be over till late. Now you don't have to." Morgan beamed. She had missed her brother. Jeremy had been there for her during the roughest part of her life. He had lifted her up after Fay died. Now that Morgan lived two hours from Bloomington, they didn't see each other as often. She regretted not making time for it.

*　*　*

Jeremy and Dierdre followed Morgan back to the Raffertys' where she showed them to their room. After she showered and changed, they drove to Broad Ripple, the hipster center of Indy's north side. Once he had parked along the canal, the three walked, scoping out menus to the newest eateries and brew pubs. They decided on a Greek restaurant and were seated near a window overlooking the patio beside the canal. Chilly breezes blew clusters of brown and yellow leaves between the patio chairs.

Sitting opposite her brother and Dierdre, Morgan looked at the wine list, but she couldn't wait to ask the burning question. "Well? What's this news?"

The way Dierdre looked at Jeremy, Morgan knew instantly. Her eyebrows lifted with joy. "Am I going to be an aunt?"

Jeremy blushed.

"Yes!" Dierdre said. "We're due in April," she beamed.

"I am so excited for you!" Morgan said. It was true.

"It means you'll have to come visit more often," he said.

Morgan wanted to, but she was instantly torn between that and her work. "I'd love to . . ."

Jeremy leaned in, "But?" He seemed to have sensed her hesitation.

Morgan shook her head. "You won't believe me." *Will he be proud of me? After all this time?*

When Morgan had graduated from IU with her degree in criminology, she and Jeremy talked about her desire to find Fay's killer. Because he'd been there when it happened, he knew what Morgan had gone through. When Jeremy found out Morgan's reason for pursuing this career, he told her to get help. He asked her to see a shrink. Six months of weekly visits hadn't helped at all. Morgan didn't think it was necessary to continue, so she quit. Jeremy found out and they had gotten in an argument about it. Ultimately, Morgan won. She never did go back to her doctor. She didn't see the need to.

Their waiter came and poured water, giving Morgan time to think about how she wanted to share her news with Jeremy. She ordered a glass of Cabernet and listened to the waiter explain the chef's specials.

When he'd taken their orders, Jeremy picked up right where they'd left it. "I'll believe anything. Remember, we have no secrets."

Morgan looked at Dierdre. Her chin-length brown hair was streaked with purple. *How much of this has Jeremy told her?* "I'm working a new case."

"You're always working a new case. That can't possibly keep you from Bloomington." The way he joked, Morgan knew he didn't suspect what she was about to tell him.

She took a deep breath and gave him her news in a whisper. "I may have found him." She twisted her napkin out of the ring and smoothed it out in her lap.

"Who?" Dierdre asked.

Jeremy's grin faded. "This isn't what I think it is."

If Jeremy wouldn't give her encouragement, she'd have to lift herself up. Morgan nodded to spur herself on. "It is." She looked into his dark-brown eyes and said, "I may have found Fay's killer."

Jeremy let out a breath.

"That's great," Dierdre said supportively.

"No it isn't." Jeremy argued. "I thought we were done with this," he said to Morgan.

Dierdre's eyebrows raised in confusion. Clearly, she didn't know anything about this, which was fine with Morgan. Because of the distance between them, Morgan hadn't taken the time to get closer to her sister-in-law. Now she wished she had. Perhaps she would be on Morgan's side. If Jeremy wouldn't be, Morgan needed someone. "I know you think it's crazy . . ."

"It is!"

"The strike patterns are the same."

"What's the point of revenge, Mo? Nothing can come from that." Jeremy gulped down some water. Dierdre did too, cowering a little behind her glass.

"It's an unsolved crime," Morgan stated.

"Leave it alone. It's just going to make you crazy."

Morgan raised her voice. "I have to know who killed her, don't you understand?"

"I think you need help." His statement echoed off the ceiling. It looked like other patrons had stopped to listen. Morgan's ears began to ring.

The angry look that Jeremy gave Morgan was cooled by the arrival of their wine. He thanked the waiter pleasantly then rested his fingers on the stem of his glass. Morgan copied him. She needed Jeremy to understand.

"I hope Coldplay plays *Magic* tomorrow night. I love that song." Dierdre sipped a coke and tried to change the subject.

Looking down at the table, Jeremy shook his head. "We need to talk."

Morgan didn't want to. "I thought you understood."

"I guess I don't," Jeremy said. He was looking Morgan in the eye.

Morgan couldn't explain how driven she was by this. She had lost days when Fay disappeared. The hole in her memory burned her. It fueled her motivation and had become an addiction desperately seeking the next fix. Somehow, she felt connected to Fay's disappearance, but she didn't know how. *If only . . .*

Dierdre took Jeremy's hand. She looked up at him through thick dark lashes, giving him a signal.

Softening, he relaxed his shoulders and sat back in the chair.

"You don't know how it was for me," Morgan said. "How it is."

CHAPTER 26

MORGAN: 16 Years Ago

"What's going on, Mo?" Hunched over with his elbows on his knees, Jeremy sat on the edge of Morgan's unmade bed. Piles of dirty clothes littered the floor, making it impossible for anyone to walk into her bedroom. The stench in the room came from an old pizza box under the desk, numerous fast-food bags in various corners, unwashed sheets, and foul body odor.

A hoodie pulled over her head hid greasy plaits that hung lifelessly on her cheeks but could not disguise the smell. She hadn't bothered to shower in over a week. Even then, her mother had badgered her relentlessly to wash.

"Please," Jeremy whispered. "Talk to me."

Morgan slouched, practically horizontal, in a hard, wooden desk chair with her feet up on an overturned laundry basket. She shrugged.

"What's going on here?" Jeremy asked. One arm swept a wide arc indicating the entire room, the entirety of Morgan's life.

Beneath her hood, she sniffed back her answer.

Sadness filled his eyes. "This isn't good."

She didn't answer. Empty plastic pop bottles and beer cans littered the desk to her right. Close to the edge, on top of a small spiral notebook with the picture of a kitten on the cover, headphones from a Walkman squeaked out a rhythm.

"Mom and Dad are worried."

"So. What do they know?" The words croaked from her dry throat. Out of the corner of her eye, Morgan saw a shadow cross her bedroom door. "Go away, Mom."

Her mother chirped, "I'm going." She shut the door.

A bitter thought came to Morgan. "Did Mom call you? Is that why you came?"

Jeremy sat up tall. "No. Don't even think that. I came here on my own."

Morgan threw him a sideways glance.

"I ran into your friends last weekend."

"Who?"

"Elaine and Trevor. Remember them? You used to hang out with them all the time. Elaine says you haven't been taking any calls. She hasn't seen you since . . ." He stopped.

He almost said since I found Fay's body, Morgan thought. She hunched down, letting the hood slide forward over her eyes. Since that day, she hadn't left her bedroom except for once: the day she joined the search party, the most devastating day of her life.

Jeremy kicked a towel and a pair of jeans out of the way, clearing a spot on the floor in front of him. "I came over to help. And damn it, Morgan, I'm not leaving till we figure this out."

Without moving a muscle, her gaze met his.

"I know what happened. Everyone knows what happened."

How can he know? I don't even know. Bile rose to her throat as her stomach clenched.

He waited for her to reply.

She glared at him from under the hoodie.

"Fay is gone, and that's the cold hard truth."

Under her hood, Morgan's eyes filled with pools that overflowed and dripped down her cheeks without a sound. Her throat closed, making it impossible, even if she'd wanted to, to say a word. Had she cried since Fay left? She couldn't remember.

After several minutes of her silent sobbing, he continued. "There is something. But . . ." He reached for the laundry basket under her feet and tugged at it. "But . . . you don't want to hear it."

She kept her feet on the basket. *Reverse psychology,* Morgan thought. *He says I don't want to hear it, so of course I do.*

He tugged. She resisted.

She asked, "What?" with a breath.

"There's something you can do. Something you can do to help find her murderer." He tugged harder, removing the basket from under her feet, which forced her to put her feet on the floor and sit up straighter.

Though unresponsive, Morgan listened.

"Whether you like it or not, the ghost of Fay Ramsey isn't going to appear and change your life. And the truth is, I don't expect you to want to change this situation." He flipped the basket and started filling it with dirty clothes. "I mean you've got a pretty sweet deal here. Mom and Dad love you. They'll let you stay here forever like this. You don't have to go to school or get a job. No one expects anything of you."

This is bullshit. Morgan sat up and sniffed back the tears. "Why don't you leave me alone?" she said, reaching for the headphones.

"No." Jeremy stood, towering over his sister. He stopped her from putting on the headphones and went on, "I'm *not* leaving you alone. I figured a way out for you."

Morgan shrank, looking up at him. "What?" She pushed back her hood a little, revealing her tear-streaked face and matted, dirty hair.

"It won't be easy. Count on that. There isn't a simple solution. My way will be harder than hell."

Her gaze locked on his. Jeremy was serious.

"Whatever." Morgan pulled the Walkman into her lap. To shut him up and shut him out, she was about to put on the headphones when Jeremy reached for the kitten notebook.

"Hey!" Morgan wasn't quick enough to stop him. "Give that back!"

He pulled it away from her, then sat back down on the bed. His glare dared her to come take it away. But Morgan didn't have the energy to stand up and fight. He opened the small spiral notebook to examine the contents.

On the first page, Morgan had written:

Who Killed Fay
Who Killed Fay
Who Killed Fay

Past that, page after page of handwritten notes filled more than half the book. There was a hand-drawn calendar, a timeline that marked the whereabouts of Morgan's friend for the whole summer of '95. There were lists of phone calls she had made, and even several photos.

Morgan sat up and held out her hand, fingers flicking. "Give it back."

Jeremy threw it to her. "There *is* something you can do."

She folded the notebook closed and placed it inside a cluttered drawer. "What?"

"Mom told me you've called the homicide division at the police station downtown. She told me you call every day."

"She's such a liar." Morgan winced, but it was true. Sometimes she called homicide two or three times a day. She needed to know if they had found the killer. She wanted someone, anyone, to be arrested for Fay's murder.

"Here's what we're going to do. And I say *we* because I'm going to help you."

Jeremy laid out a plan to clean Morgan up and get her functioning. Then he'd help her sign up for classes at Indiana University, where she had already been accepted. The university had a criminal justice department and classes in criminology and psychology. The first goal was a degree and, in the future, a job as a police detective. "We're doing this together," he said.

The idea had merit. Since Fay's death, Morgan had spent weeks ciphering the facts around Fay's last days. And though she hadn't solved the puzzle yet, Morgan had loved every minute of the process. It was the one activity that made her feel alive. "You'll help me?"

"Yes."

"What if it doesn't work?" She had many unspecified doubts. Though it sounded difficult and impossible, his idea awakened something inside her.

Jeremy stood, picking up the filled laundry basket. "Do you want it to work?"

Morgan trusted her brother. They had always been close. She could tell him things that she didn't want to tell her parents, and since he was three years older, he almost always had fitting words of wisdom to share.

If he would help, she'd make the effort. And though it felt like a hard road to tread, someday she could track down her friend's murderer.

She followed Jeremy to the laundry room.

"Do you want it to work?" he repeated.

"Yes. Yes, I do." A weight lifted from her shoulders. For the first time in four months, Morgan looked forward to something.

CHAPTER 27

CARYN: 6 Months Ago

Weeks crawled by before Caryn had a plan. She needed to see Ekhard to prove that their childhood had been real. Otherwise, why did he parent her and coach her into independence? He never went back to college. Instead, he had stayed with her, working two jobs till she graduated from high school.

On the day of her graduation, Eks had dropped her off. In her cap and gown, standing in the parking lot of the event center, she had no idea what he meant by goodbye. Caryn had always thought they would take on the world together. But what he had said was: "You thought this was your day? You're wrong. Today is my day, and I'm going to celebrate. Until next time. I hope we meet in hell." He had laughed a crazy, Jack Nicholson laugh. "Good luck with your life, Ceecee."

She remembered it like it was yesterday.

Theo was dead by then. He died the fall of her sophomore year, when she was sixteen. By then, Eks had barely taken one semester of college but had to drop out. That year, he listed the house and sold it. They moved into a small apartment near Fall Creek on the west side of Indy. The money from selling the house paid the rent. Eks cooked and cleaned and worked his butt off, making sure Caryn applied to colleges. She was brilliant at math, and with Ekhard's coaching she received a scholarship to IU.

He had guided her every step of the way.

On the way to Lafayette, Caryn stopped for a large cup of coffee, then took the loop to I-65 northbound. Traffic was stop-and-go, with eighteen-wheelers intercepting her path. Once in the city, she parked in front of Baker and Baker's, the small accounting firm in a strip mall on the west side. Five employees worked at the firm: David Baker and his wife Cheryl, Ann Grayson, Matthew Milkey, and Nathaniel Johnson, also known as Ekhard Klein.

If she went inside, he'd recognize her. That was the point, wasn't it? After so much time, how would he react to seeing her?

Unsure, she watched, and waited. No traffic came into the parking lot. Next to the accounting firm was a darkened sandwich shop. At 9:07 AM it was too early for them to be open. On the other side, one lone employee sat still as a statue inside a mattress store with the lights on.

Caryn's coffee had gone cold, but she finished it anyway. Clouds cleared from the sky, and as the sun beat down on her dark-blue car, it warmed the inside. As she unfastened her seatbelt and struggled to remove her jacket.

A car pulled in beside her and parked. The driver, a man in his late fifties or sixties, got out and walked into the accounting firm. The door closed behind him.

It was now 9:43. She waited five more minutes, which seemed like an hour, until she couldn't stand it anymore. Caryn had nothing to lose. She had to see him. She had to say hello to her long-lost brother.

* * *

"May I help you?" The middle-aged redhead looked up and adjusted her pale-gray blazer.

"I'd like to see Ek . . . Nathaniel Johnson."

The redhead checked her calendar and shook her head. "He's busy this morning."

Caryn spun a quick lie. "My name's Martin. Patricia. Patricia Martin. I called for an appointment, but they couldn't fit me in. I have the day off today. I don't have time tomorrow."

The receptionist flipped through pages of her calendar. "Mrs. Baker is available today."

"Mr. Johnson has spoken with me on the phone. I can take my business elsewhere." Caryn pretended to leave and turned to go.

"Wait. It looks like he'll have a few minutes between meetings this morning. Let me call him." The receptionist picked up her phone.

"You do that." Caryn crossed her arms in front of her chest.

"Mr. Johnson, can you fit a new client in? Ms. Martin says she spoke with you?" The redhead pursed her lips. "Thank you, I'll let her know. Please have a seat," she said to Caryn after hanging up. "Mr. Johnson will be with you in a few minutes."

With her arms still crossed, Caryn turned away from the desk. The waiting room in this strip-mall accounting firm was tiny. The furniture looked like it had been stolen from a 1986 garage sale. Two chrome-legged chairs, upholstered in a greasy-gray weave, were arranged on either side of a heavy wooden table. On the light-oak-paneled wall was a lavender print in a silver frame. In the picture, white and pink feathers and pastel-colored halos surrounded a Native American Indian chief.

Caryn sat down in the chair without a bent leg, and when the phone rang, she eavesdropped.

"Baker and Baker, how may I help you?" The receptionist wrote something on her pad. "Please hold for a moment." *Click.* "Cheryl, it's Gary Protheimer calling again . . . Okay . . . Sure." *Click.*

Caryn dug through her purse and found the pair of horn-rimmed glasses she'd swiped from the lady at the coffee shop. Neatly arranged on the table was a stack of family magazines, one inviting readers to learn about raising triplets. Next to the stack sat a purple vase stuffed with mismatched, fake flowers that appeared to have been dragged through the parking lot.

It was a lame disguise, but she donned the glasses and pretended to read the article on triplets. The glasses made everything blurry. She looked over them at the picture of a mother wearing a pink T-shirt holding perfectly coiffed infants, one with a pink headband, one in a blue ruffled dress, and one wearing a frilly yellow top.

Down the hallway and out of Caryn's sight, a door opened, and the voices of two men rumbled. "I'll get those receipts to you later in the week. I'm sure the quarterly payment stub is in a file at home. I'll have Shannon send that tomorrow. Thanks, Nate."

Caryn strained to see around the corner as the men walked toward the waiting room.

"Sounds good, Charles. Hey, are you going to be at Quincey's tonight?"

That voice. Caryn recognized her brother's voice and sweat broke out under her shirt and around her neck.

"Not tonight. I have to stay home with the kids. I promised Mary. She's got some jewelry party to go to. Probably spending last week's income. You know how it is."

Ekhard/Nathaniel laughed as they rounded the corner from the hallway. Caryn saw his cheese-eating, smiling face and looked back down at the magazine.

"I know. Women, right? Can't live with them . . ."

How would Ekhard know anything about marriage or parenthood? *Faker. What a phony.* Caryn grew the courage to look up again and stared right through his dandy little act. That wasn't the real Ekhard Marcus Klein.

Her heartrate nearly doubled in speed at the sight of him. The Ekhard she knew didn't appear to have gained any weight. He was about five feet ten and weighed maybe 150 pounds. When he was younger, he had looked wiry. Now he appeared starved, malnourished, and sickly. His dyed dark-brown hair thinned around his temples.

The client patted Eks on the arm. "How about Saturday? Happy hour? The IU game will be on. It's a late one this week."

"I'll be there."

"Great. See you then."

Ekhard shook the man's hand and glanced over at Caryn as she looked away. *Did he recognize me?* she wondered. *How will he react to seeing me? Had Ekhard become like their mother? Unpredictable and violent? Or was he an angry drunk like their father?* Neither option filled Caryn with hope. It was that random chance that terrified her most.

When the client had gone, Ekhard stepped toward the receptionist. Caryn's fingertips quivered with the anticipation of his inviting her back to his office. Then what? She hadn't planned that far ahead.

"Mr. Johnson, Ms. Martin is here to meet with you." The receptionist whispered something to Ekhard.

Caryn kept her chin tucked in and lifted the magazine up to hide her face. She felt Ekhard eyeing her.

"Give me a few minutes to file Charles's paperwork. I'll be right back."

As soon as he disappeared down the hallway, Caryn had seen enough. She wasn't ready to face him. She had no idea how he would feel about her coming here. The uncertainty of his reaction terrified her. She knew what he was capable of. Dropping the magazine back on the table, she ducked like a bunny out the door.

She drove fast. Matching her vehicular speed, her internal wheels spun like a combustion engine on methamphetamine. To think she had idolized Ekhard as a teenager!

All this time, eighteen years, four months, and twenty-seven days, her past had stayed with her, a bundle of dead, useless limbs. In the worst-case scenario, the past manifested as a cancer eating her from the inside out. It was likely, considering how things had been going. Her life sucked. Steady job; nothing exciting there. Steady boyfriend; married to another woman for Chrissake. Lord knows there's nothing thrilling about *that*.

Since Ekhard left her she had wanted to prove him wrong. And now . . . now Caryn had a choice. She could use this new information about Ekhard, her brother, to turn her life around. She could use the knowledge to move her life forward. Back then, he'd said she was just like her mother. *But Mom abandoned us. I won't abandon you, brother, because I am not my mother. I will not abandon you, Eks. Like Mom did. And like you did to me.*

Caryn laughed out loud. She could put a positive spin on all of the negative shit from her childhood. She could make a fresh start. The plan was clear, and it included her brother. They grew up together. They shared the same history.

They also shared secrets.

CHAPTER 28

MORGAN

In a coffeehouse near the Indiana Office of Accountants Morgan's breath caught in her throat at the sight of Caryn Klein's blond hair. She occupied a small, round table filled with her computer and personal effects. Morgan leaned over her, a tiger hunting prey, and said, "You're a hard woman to connect with, Ms. Klein."

The presence of police officers in the coffee shop evoked uncomfortable stares and nervous shifting from a few patrons. Not from Caryn, though, who answered, "I work on location all over the state of Indiana." She didn't look up from her computer.

"We're aware of that." Morgan's fingers grazed the tattered notebook in her jacket pocket. "This is my partner, Detective James."

Behind her, Donnie flashed his badge.

Caryn's hands remained poised over the keyboard, her eyes on her computer screen.

"We want to ask you a few questions," Morgan stated. She noted that Caryn wore an orange sweater and black slacks. Her shoulder length blond hair was not dyed like the shorter hairs found in Hallie's bed. *Did Ekhard have blond hair too?*

"You have questions about my brother?" Caryn's focus remained on her laptop.

Morgan gently pushed the laptop closed. "We'll only take a few minutes of your time."

Caryn grimaced. "Of course." She seemed reluctant but tucked the laptop into the case and set it on the floor by her feet.

Morgan pulled out the chair where Caryn's purse rested. "Do you mind if I sit?"

"Not at all." Caryn moved stiffly when she put her purse in her lap and wrapped her arms around it. A shield.

To be friendly, Morgan scooted the chair closer to Caryn's and leaned forward on her elbows like she was getting the gossip from an old friend. "Does Ekhard live in Indianapolis?"

"We had a stressful childhood. My mother left us when I was ten. My dad died before I graduated high school. And Ekhard left me the day of my graduation."

"That's awful," Morgan said, noting the sad expression on Caryn's face. But when Caryn reached for a tissue it seemed overplayed.

Donnie hovered behind Morgan with his hands folded in front of him and said, "You must have been fifteen when your dad died."

Caryn's expression was blank when she said, "Fifteen and a half."

"My daughter Annabel is fourteen." Donnie said. "I can't imagine her without parents. And my older daughter isn't equipped to survive on her own. How did you do it?"

"We did what we had to do," Caryn said.

Morgan expressed condolences and then said, "You and your brother must have been very close."

"On the contrary," Caryn said. "I haven't seen him in years."

With the notebook in her hand, Morgan's pen spun like a whirling dervish. "You had a falling out?"

"We did." Caryn sat back and crossed her arms. "What, exactly, are you looking for?"

"Suzanne Aiken," Morgan said. "You may remember her from high school." When Caryn shook her head Morgan added, "She was a cheerleader, and she dated your brother."

"Maybe that jogs your memory," Donnie added.

Morgan thought she could get more out of this witness if Donnie wasn't towering over them. She turned around. "Hey, Donnie, can you get me a pumpkin spiced latte with extra whipped cream?"

"Uh . . ."

"I'll pay you back."

"Okay."

Morgan watched Donnie walk to the register, then turned back to Caryn. Leaning forward as if she had a secret, she told her, "The parents are seeking closure. You understand, Caryn. Is it okay if I call you Caryn? Or do you prefer Ceecee?"

"No one calls me Ceecee."

Morgan weighed the response. Irritation? Something was bothering Caryn, and now she was holding back. "Okay. Caryn then." Morgan wrote that Caryn might have lied about the nickname. "That's an unusual name."

"What's this got to do with me?" Caryn asked, chafed.

"Can you remember a few details about Suzanne? Since your brother dated her, I thought you could tell me about their relationship. I know it's been a long time since then." Morgan held her pen at the ready.

"Twenty years . . ." Caryn stopped short of saying something else.

Morgan's brow furrowed. *Is that how long since she's seen him?* She wrote, "20 years" in her notebook, then made a note to find out.

"Or something like that," Caryn said.

"Something like that." Morgan drew in a breath. Later she'd look up the dates to see if they matched.

Donnie returned to the table. "Did you want regular or soy milk?"

Morgan averted her gaze from Caryn and looked up at Donnie. "Regular. When have I ever put soy milk in my coffee?"

"Angie's been doing the soy thing. I forgot," he replied.

"Medium, okay?"

"I know better than to get you a large."

Morgan chuckled as Donnie returned to the counter. "This won't take long, I promise," she said to Caryn. "Let me ask you a few more questions."

"Sure." Caryn shook her head no in contradiction to her answer.

"Look. Do you remember any details about Suzanne? Particularly about their relationship? Was Suzanne cruel to your brother? Did they hike in the woods? What more can you tell me about them?"

"I don't remember."

As Morgan observed Caryn, she recognized evasive behavior. Her back was rigid and neck muscles tight. Morgan didn't want to scare her away. She planned on having solid evidence before arresting anyone because this was the most important case of her life. She played her cards strategically. "Do you keep track of local news, Caryn?"

"I'm more of a big-picture person."

Morgan noted the shifting back-and-forth of Caryn's green eyes, the telltale sign of a lie. "Then you didn't see that we found her body up near Fishers?"

Caryn raised her eyebrows and shook her head.

She thought it unlikely, but perhaps by explaining the horrific details of Suzanne's discovery, the decaying, rotting corpse, she wanted to shock Caryn into telling the truth. "She may have been buried alive. Someone crushed her face in with a hammer then buried her in the woods. I can't imagine what a teenage girl could have done to deserve that."

"People disappear all the time."

"Like your brother."

Caryn raised her eyebrows in agreement.

"Your brother, Ekhard, dated Suzanne for what, almost the whole school year?"

"No, I'd remember that. Ekhard didn't date anyone."

"You don't say?" Morgan wrote that down too. It was a flat-out lie, if she could believe the other witnesses.

Morgan looked at the small silver ring that Jeremy had given her and noticed that Caryn, too, wore a sparkling diamond ring on her pinky. It looked like an engagement ring. Hallie's ring—the one that the Blue Room bartender had seen—had never been found. "That's a beautiful ring."

Caryn spread her fingers and looked at her left hand. She took a quick breath and said, "Thank you."

"It looks very special."

"It was a gift."

"Oh?" Morgan was sure there was a story. If someone had given her a ring like that, she'd be sure to tell everyone. "From who?"

"My boyfriend gave it to me a few months ago. Can we get to the point? I need to get back to work." Caryn looked at her watch.

"We know what the murder weapon was," Morgan reiterated. "We know what killed Suzanne."

The response was a glare.

"Where is your brother, Caryn?"

In her seat, Caryn shifted, not uncomfortable but clearly agitated. "I told you I haven't seen him. We're estranged."

With each question about Ekhard, Caryn sat a little taller, so Morgan wondered if she was nervous or hiding something. She hoped this next question would push her over the edge. She switched gears. "You don't know a woman named Hallie Marks, do you?"

"Did she go to North Side too?"

"No." It irked Morgan that Caryn remained so calm. "Hallie used to hang out at The Blue Room."

"That bar's been around since 1986."

"You've been there?" Morgan asked hopefully.

"I do like jazz. I go there once in a while."

"Does your brother go there?"

"How would I know?" Caryn had become impatient. "Where is this leading, Detective?"

Morgan dug a photo of Hallie out of her jacket pocket then slid it on the table in front of Caryn. "Do you know this woman?" She watched Caryn's reaction closely, but Caryn gave her nothing.

"No." Caryn downed the last sip of her coffee. "I have to get back to work. My lunch hour is over, and I haven't gotten a thing done."

Detective Jewel stood up. "One more thing, Caryn. When was the last time you saw your brother, Ekhard?"

"Eighteen years, five months, and twenty-three days ago." Caryn packed up her computer.

"That long?" To Morgan it sounded like she had counted the days since losing him. If that was the case, she had obsessed about it, too. And *that* was something Morgan knew a bit about. Obsession could take over a person's life. "Thanks for meeting with us, Caryn," she said.

When Donnie returned with two steaming cups, Caryn dismissed herself. Morgan felt confident that Caryn had more information than she was letting on. She waited for her to leave, keeping an eye on her empty paper coffee cup.

Once she'd left, causing a flurry of jingling doorbells, Morgan dug the cup out of the trash can to submit for DNA tests.

CHAPTER 29

MORGAN

"No disassociated DNA was found under Hallie's fingernails," Donnie said.

Disappointed, Morgan said, "I know. I saw that report. The murderer wiped Hallie's fingertips with a concentrated oxidizer."

The lingering smell of pizza wafted from the cardboard box on the dining-room table. Morgan pushed away her plate of crusts. The detectives had gone to Donnie's house to kill two birds. Angie and their daughters wanted to spend the evening with Donnie, and he and Morgan needed to organize their notes and come up with a plan.

"This is no average criminal, that's for sure." Donnie yawned.

"Just to be clear, the follow-up investigation for Hallie Marks is associated with Suzanne's death as well. We're treating the two crimes as a single investigation."

"Right," Donnie said shortly, then changed the topic. "So tell me . . ." He raised his eyebrows.

"What?"

"You know. What's going on between you and Rob Gibson?"

Morgan leaned back in the dining-room chair, unable to put off answering him. Donnie had pressed the issue relentlessly. She covered her face with her hands and, with a dramatic exhalation, mumbled, "We're dating."

"What was that?" Donnie leaned forward. "It sounded like you said you're dating him."

"Mmm-hmm." Brushing her hair back, Morgan pulled the rubber band from her hair and retied her ponytail.

"Good. Good. That's good. Rob is a great guy." Donnie nodded with enthusiasm.

"Then can we get back to work?" Morgan smiled. Donnie cared, but their discussions about her private life remained skin deep. She'd said enough. She picked up her dog-eared notebook with the faded picture of a kitten on the cover. "Something's nagging at me."

"What's that?" Donnie leaned forward, more interested in the left-over pizza.

"Where is Ekhard Klein?" Morgan asked.

Donnie stood and, hovering over the table, examined the remnants of the pizza. "Disappeared. I looked for records too. He's vanished. Not an easy feat in this day and age." He picked two circles of pepperoni from the last piece.

"But, why?" The enigma that was Ekhard had become a hole in the investigation.

"Perhaps he killed Suzanne then went into hiding. If I was eighteen and killed someone, that's what I would do." Donnie stood up straight. "Did Trina Kierra know what happened to him?"

"She said they were never friends. She also said everyone hated Suzanne." Talking about it triggered a memory. "Also, Trina told me that Suzanne's plan was to humiliate Ekhard. I wonder if Ekhard found out about that. What if he knew, then took her to the woods?"

"That's an interesting scenario. I like it. Write that in your little book." Donnie pointed a finger at Morgan's pen. "We could put out an APB with high school photos of him. See if anyone has seen him in Indy. If he's not here, we may have to reach out to the US Marshals and turn this into a fugitive investigation."

"I'm not ready to turn the investigation over to another division." The mention of U.S. Marshals reminded Morgan that she wanted to apply there. Hunting fugitives was a dream job for her. Perhaps when this was all over? Morgan dug the familiar notebook out of her pocket and stared at it. She wasn't done yet; she had an idea to bounce off Donnie. But because she suspected what his reaction might be, she wanted to segue into it gently.

He sat back in the chair and stacked file papers that had been spread around his plate.

"So . . . I found a couple cases that might link us back to Hallie Marks. If Suzanne and Hallie Marks were killed by the same man, then he may have killed others too."

Donnie stared at her, tired of the conversation, or just plain tired. Morgan couldn't tell anymore.

"In 2013, Jenny Delacourt was beaten in the face. The strike pattern was similar . . ."

Peppered with sarcasm, Donnie threw another name into the mix. "Don't forget Sarah Evans,"

"Yes, you're right." Morgan picked up the ballpoint pen and opened her tattered book. While flipping through it, she explained, "But Jenny Delacourt survived. If we could talk to her, show her pictures . . ."

Donnie glared at her and at the notebook. "Are you okay, Mo?"

"I'm fine, why?"

He concentrated his gaze on the book. "I'm worried that you're too emotionally invested in this case."

Morgan looked up from her notes. "What?"

"You know what I mean," he said.

Fay.

"Stop it," Donnie said. "I see what you're doing."

Morgan didn't stop. "Jenny's husband was a drug dealer. Blaine Delacourt took the rap for it. His involvement with local gangs turned him into a likely suspect. Yet he pleaded innocent . . ."

"You're trying to link these cases to your friend Fay."

"Listen, Jenny survived! She's still alive!"

"Mo."

"I can interview Jenny . . ." She needed to convince him of this.

"Morgan!"

"What!?" She barked. She locked her undivided attention onto Donnie.

Donnie placed his hands on the table and leaned toward her, mollifying. "I'm not sure this is connected. If you take this route, I can't support it." He glanced toward the kitchen door before adding, "Angie and I have been talking."

Morgan had an idea where this was going.

"I'm taking Holbrooke's position when she retires at the end of the year."

"I figured." She looked down at her lap. She ached at the prospect of losing her partner. *Who could fill his place?*

He continued. "You're grasping at nothing. Random slayings." In a low, convincing voice he said, "You need to take one possibility into account."

She didn't want to hear it, but the question fell out of her mouth regardless. "What possibility?"

"There's a possibility that Fay's killer will never be caught."

Morgan slammed her notebook closed. "No, Donnie. I've got a weird feeling about this one. There's something missing that I can't put my finger on. Look, I understand you think Bloomington is too far from the trail, but I've been mapping out these crimes on a timeline. Let's say the killer went to school at North Side, then he went south and left a body trail."

"Then there could be others," Donnie argued. "But not Sarah Evans. Brian Carter is serving a life term for her murder. And I still have faith in the system. Carter was tried and convicted. Take these people off your list."

Her face heated with anger. "If our serial-killer theory holds, he's the wrong guy. Come on. The system fails sometimes. We have to look at this through a different lens."

His tone was sharp, aggravated. "Right. Then the FBI or US Marshals needs to get involved."

"Never mind then." Morgan closed the kitten notebook and slammed it down on the table again.

Donnie shook his head. "Our lives could be so much easier if we turn it over . . ."

"Don't say it again, Donnie." Morgan lowered her voice to a near whisper. "No fucking way. This is my deal. I'm going to find this f-----." Red-faced, she looked over her shoulder. Angie stood in the doorway, her long straight light-brown hair a shade lighter than it had been two weeks ago.

"How late are you two working?"

"I don't know, honey. Till we get it figured out." Donnie stretched his arms over his head.

How can Donnie, of all people, think I won't find Fay's murderer? Morgan thought she'd never get through to him. Now she wanted to be done with the conversation and stood up to clear their plates. "Thanks for letting us do this here, Angie."

"It's no problem. The girls are always looking for an excuse to eat pizza." Angie collected the pizza box and two glasses, then followed Morgan into the kitchen. "Are you making any progress?"

"I think so. We've created a timeline, so to speak."

"*You've* created a timeline." Donnie followed them to the kitchen.

He was a smart cop, and Morgan respected him because he had mentored her. In the past he had always guided her in the right direction. But now, the dynamics between them were changing. Morgan rinsed the plates in the stainless-steel sink. Steam rose from the hot water; so, too, did Morgan's temper.

"Morgan," Donnie's tone softened. "Can we please work on one case at a time? Let's solve these two before assuming that the rest are linked to it."

After stacking the plates in the dishwasher, Morgan spun to face him. "But it's right in front of us. He . . . she . . . the killer is here. I can feel it."

After Fay died, Morgan had had a series of emotional setbacks. When she was diagnosed with PITS—a post-traumatic stress disorder associated with Fay's murder and with Morgan being so close to her when she died—the psychiatrist had told Morgan that she had a hole in her memory. She explained it away as the shock of losing her friend. *"The memories will return some day,"* the doctor had said. She had dismissed Morgan's visions and dreams as forms of an imagined psychic bond between them. Because of this, Morgan lacked trust in her own gut feelings.

When the possibility entered her mind that Ekhard could have changed his name, she didn't tell Donnie. Fay's boyfriend Larry had disappeared, and investigators said he changed his name and left the country. Or left Indiana. She thought Ekhard could have killed Fay too. But she wouldn't mention that to Donnie either. It was a crazy idea and she knew it.

They faced off. Morgan saw Donnie's point of view but wouldn't relinquish her own.

"Okay, guys," Angie said. "It's late. Get some rest and in the morning look at it with fresh eyes."

"What's wrong, Dad?" Annabel, Donnie and Angie's fourteen-year-old daughter stood at the bottom of the stairs. "Don't fight with Mo." She hopped to Morgan's side.

Morgan smiled up at Annabel, who she'd known since the girl was four years old. She had sprouted in the last few months; she was taller than her older sister Etta, and now, taller than Morgan too. Thin, with graceful arms, she had on a pair of red pajama pants and a matching Elmo T-shirt.

"Dad says you're always right," Annabel revealed.

Morgan looked from Annabel to Donnie, her eyebrows rising to her hairline.

"He says it all the time. He trusts your instincts, and so do I." Annabel gave her a quick, generous hug.

"Thanks, Annabel. I'm glad someone trusts me," Morgan said with a spoonful of smug.

"Annabel, whatcha need, sweetie?" Angie asked.

The girl shrugged. "I heard them arguing."

"We're not arguing. We're just expressing our opinions," Donnie said to his daughter.

"Strongly," Morgan added. She thought they were arguing too. Her mouth stretched wide with a yawn that she couldn't hide. Three late nights with Rob this week had made her irritable.

"You're investigating that cheerleader from North Side High School, aren't you? She was, like, my age." Annabel's brow creased with worry.

"Don't you have a test tomorrow? I was just coming to say good night," Angie said.

"Daddy, you'll find the person who did that, won't you?" Annabel pressed.

Donnie soothed Annabel's worries. "It was a long time ago."

Still, his daughter fretted, "It's really scary how she died. Kids at school said someone hit her with a sledgehammer."

This time, Donnie looked at his partner.

"It was on the news," Morgan said.

His comforting voice lifted the tension in the room. "That's not true. It wasn't a *sledge*hammer. Those reporters don't know anything. They just like to talk and talk." He embraced his daughter, and she hugged him back, wrapping her arms around his wide middle.

"You'll protect us, won't you, Daddy?"

"You got that right, sweetheart." Donnie gave her another bear hug. "Baby Bell, Morgan is solving that case. She's figuring it out."

Heat rose to Morgan's face now for a different reason—embarrassment. Donnie's unspoken apology went straight to her heart.

"All right, off to bed." After saying good night, Angie whisked Annabel away and followed her up the stairs.

"Annabel is growing up." Morgan watched them go.

"Scares me." His gaze lingered on his wife and daughter.

With a gentle concession, Morgan said, "No. Don't be scared. You and Angie are doing a great job. Both your daughters are strong young women. You should be proud."

Uncertainty clouded his expression.

"It's true."

"Annabel trusts your judgment." Light returned to Donnie's eyes.

Morgan's mouth curled upward; she couldn't help it. She shook the crumbs off the pizza box over the sink and set it near the recycling bin. Still, she needed closure. "So where are we with this thing?"

Donnie let out a long breath. "As long as we talk to each other and communicate . . ."

Her head hung in exhaustion. The search was taking a toll. She had a plan, and she would stick to it no matter what Donnie said. For now she conceded, "Let's run a few more searches for Ekhard, then put out an APB."

"You're running the show."

"We're almost there. I can feel it. We're this close." She pinched her thumb and index finger together.

Donnie's doubt gave way to a goofy expression. He pursed his lips and made a funny noise. "This close." He held up his hand, mirroring Morgan's gesture.

CHAPTER 30

MORGAN: 16 Years Ago

On the floor Morgan's yellow phone drew her attention as she packed the last boxes. She was waiting for Fay to call. Tomorrow was move-in day, and Morgan was giddy with anticipation. With shorter days, it was already growing dark. She hadn't seen Fay today, but Morgan suspected she had chores to do. Some nights Fay didn't call till after eleven, when her mom had gone to bed.

"Do you need any boxes?" Morgan's dad stood balancing three more in his arms, then set them outside her room.

"No, I don't think so." She placed a folded towel in the bottom of an empty box beside her knees.

"Dinner's almost ready. How's it going?" Dressed in jeans and an old IU sweatshirt, he stuck a foot inside the door.

"It's going," she answered. Piles of towels and bathroom supplies, books and bedding, surrounded her. Morgan surveyed the area. The scent of fabric softener wafted toward her from brand-new, light-blue sheets that had just been washed and folded.

His gaze swept the room. "We need to load the car tonight. Check-in at the dorms is between nine and three. I thought you'd want to get there early."

"I do." Morgan stood up and massaged her legs. "We have to drive to Fay's house first so we can caravan. Fay and I have this planned out."

He grinned, seeming full of pride. "I know you do. Are any boxes ready for me?"

Morgan looked over her right shoulder. "Should we load the papasan chair first?"

"Sure. I'll take that to the car." The floor was so covered with college supplies, there wasn't room for her dad to enter. He took one more step between books and bottles, then reached out. "Can you hand me the pillow?"

Morgan stepped between the sheets and another half-filled box to reach the papasan. She loved the lime-green color that Fay had chosen and imagined Fay curled up in it with a book. She folded the heavy pillow in half and heaved it toward her dad.

"Got it! I'll be back for the rest in a minute," he said, and disappeared down the hallway.

Morgan checked her watch. Six o'clock. Fay would be home by now. Her shift ended at five. To Morgan's left, a super-sized suitcase filled to the brim stood open. She tucked the remaining shampoo bottle and two bars of soap into the side. She didn't think there was room for anything else so flipped the lid closed.

"Is that ready to go?" Her dad was back.

She struggled with the zipper. "I think so."

"I'll take it next," he said. Sidestepping through the room, he forced Morgan to dive out of his way and onto her bed. After making sure the suitcase was tightly closed, he hefted the bag onto its end. "What have you got in here? An entire library?"

Morgan couldn't suppress her smile. "Something like that," she giggled.

He groaned, exaggerating the weight of the bag. Morgan laughed. As he carried it out of the room, her phone rang.

She leaped off her bed. Expecting Fay's call, she answered cheerfully, "How was work?"

"Morgan?" It was Fay's monster-mother, Victoria Ramsey.

"Yep, it's me."

"Where is she? Is Fay at your house?"

Morgan took the phone to her bed and sat down on the edge. "Why? Isn't she home?"

"I swear, if you're hiding her . . ."

"Mrs. Ramsey, I'm not hiding Fay. Didn't she come home yet?" Morgan checked her watch again. 6:05 PM.

Victoria kept strict curfews and expected Fay to come home directly from work. Her tone grew shrill. "This is her last night at home, Morgan Jewell. If you don't send her home right now, I'll request a dormitory switch in the morning."

Morgan considered this an impossibility. Mrs. Ramsey's overreaction was nothing to sweat over. "If she were here, I'd bring her home. I'm sure she's been delayed at work or the buses are running late," Morgan stated, although unsure.

"When you hear from her, tell her to get home." Mrs. Ramsey hung up.

*   *   *

Morgan didn't hear from Fay. After her parents had loaded the car, Morgan told her parents she needed mascara and face-wash from the drugstore to complete her last-minute packing. It was the first of many lies. Instead, she got behind the wheel of Thomas Toyota and pressed her foot down on the accelerator. "We've got to find Fay, Thomas," she said to the car.

Victoria had called back again during dinner to tell Morgan that the kids at the Hamburger Stand said Fay hadn't come in. So Fay had lied too.

But Fay never lied. Something was wrong.

Dead set on finding her friend, Morgan sped past the drugstore and tilted the rear-view mirror to deflect the glare of the setting sun behind her. First, she would drive to the Hamburger Stand and interrogate the people Fay worked with. Maybe they knew something. Fay didn't have any other friends—besides Morgan and Morgan's friends, Fay had no one. *Was that really true?* A pang of self-doubt shot through Morgan at the arrogant thought.

Morgan had stood up for Fay in the lunchroom at school. Jules Tanner had turned rage-red after Morgan threw a chunk of apple at her back. But Jules had taken a handful of Fay's French fries. So uncool. Morgan had felt sorry for Fay then. But the more she got to know her, the more she liked her. *Really* liked her. And ever since, they had become allies. Partners in crime.

Traffic was light tonight. Morgan ran an almost-red light. "Come on, Thomas. We've got to find Fay." She remembered that just last weekend, Fay had named the car Thomas for being reliable and dependable. *Like Morgan,* she had said.

Tomorrow would be the start of a new life. Morgan had already planned her breakfast, a tall cup of coffee with cream and extra sugar. Then she'd caravan to Fay's house followed by her parents. Morgan smiled in anticipation. She couldn't wait to start this new life with Fay.

But first, she had to find her. In the empty parking lot of the Hamburger Stand she parked near the door and noticed that Fay's bicycle wasn't locked on the rack. Morgan opened the door, triggering a ding-dinging doorbell. The smell of greasy fries turned Morgan's empty stomach as she sped to the counter. Fay had said she was covering for Dmitri tonight. Yet there he was, with his back to Morgan, his frizzy dreads hanging to his shoulders and a yellow cap on his head.

"Hey!" Morgan said.

Dmitri spun around. "What's up?" He smiled.

"Where's Fay?" Morgan planted her feet near the register.

"I don't know. She didn't come in tonight. I covered for her and did a double shift."

"No, *she* was supposed to cover for *you.*"

Dmitri shook his head, jiggling his dreadlocks. "Shouldn't you know where she is? You're always with her."

Cold realization cascaded down Morgan's arms. It was exactly what she feared. "Fay didn't come in?"

"That's what I told her mom. Looks like she gave you both the slip!" Dmitri smiled, which made Morgan angry.

"What do you mean?" Morgan couldn't fathom Fay wanting to deceive her.

"I just mean, she . . ." Dmitri squinted at Morgan, who squinted back. "Never mind. Can I get you something?" He stepped closer to the register.

"No thanks." With that, Morgan darted toward the door.

Back in her car, Morgan's heart ached. *Fay never does anything without telling me!* The blow hit hard. Last weekend Fay said she'd met a guy. Had she really? Morgan couldn't imagine her best friend with anyone else. Raw emotion heated her neck. Embarrassment? Anger? Betrayal.

Putting the car in reverse, Morgan backed out of the parking spot. Trying to guess where Fay went, she turned left into the late afternoon sun. A million questions went through Morgan's mind. *What guy? Who was he? Where did they meet?*

Then, green-eyed jealousy surfaced. *Why didn't Fay tell me?*

After parking on the street, Morgan walked to the bicycle locking area where dozens—blue ones, red ones, and an old rusty Schwinn—leaned against the bar. None of them was Fay's yellow Trex. Morgan jogged through the building to see if Fay was sitting at one of their favorite tables. A half-hour later—after looking in every corner and at every table—she panted hard, like having just run a race for the track meet. Fay wasn't here either.

More anxious, Morgan walked down the street to a bookstore and coffee shop where she and Fay told stories and drank chai tea lattes together. These were their favorite places to hang out together. *Would Fay take someone else there?* The mere idea stabbed Morgan in the heart.

Lights were turned off in the bookstore. Of course, it was past seven on a Thursday night. As she looked around, most places were closed or closing. So where could Fay have gone? One possibility after another raced through Morgan's mind but she dismissed them all. *Where would Fay have gone without telling her mother and without telling me! Where did we go to get away from the world?*

Jackson Creek Trail. *Yes!* The creek was quiet and secluded. If Fay went anywhere, it would be near the water. She loved being beside the creek with the trees rustling overhead. This summer she'd told Morgan that she felt safe there.

She had considered telling Fay her true feelings that day. They had shared a joint and begun talking about what they loved best about each other. They had been sitting beside the creek bed on a red plaid blanket. Morgan remembered the heat from Fay's thigh against her own. The touching memory made her kick herself for not having told Fay then.

Now she regretted it.

Morgan had seen female lovers on TV but never met any other girls who were gay. And that's what this was, wasn't it? Now Fay was missing, Morgan's true feelings for her friend surfaced. She wished she'd told her sooner.

Jealousy ate at Morgan's heartstrings all the way to the trail head. With plenty of time to think about what she wanted to say, she decided that when she found her, she would tell Fay she loved her. I'll say, *I love you, Fay. Don't ever run away from me again. Then I'll take her hand. I'll hug her.*

The setting sun reflected in Thomas's rear-view mirror. Morgan tipped the mirror and imagined Fay's reaction. Would Fay hug her and be *so* happy? Fay loved her too, didn't she? Fay would understand, Morgan hoped.

Thomas slowed down behind the city bus. Atop the back of the bus a sign read "Jackson Trail Head." Fay would have had to take the bus to come this far out of town because it was too far to ride her bicycle. Morgan passed the bus, and when she arrived at the trail head parked beside two other cars. From the driver's seat, she waited for the bus to arrive. A few minutes later, it stopped beside the parking lot. The doors opened. No one got off.

After several minutes the doors closed. The bus turned around and drove back to Bloomington. *Where is she?* Morgan wondered.

Head hanging, Morgan got out of her car. She didn't know if Fay would be here or not, but she had to go looking for her. She wanted to tell her she loved her before tomorrow. Before they moved into the dorms. It was the fair and honest thing to do. The fast beating of Morgan's heart couldn't be wrong.

Morgan's red high-tops carried her to the trail head, where she looked out across the field. Fay had a canary-yellow pair just like them.

Where are you, Fay? I have to tell you. I have to tell you I love you! In the last light of the sun, the field ahead was devoid of people. A long line of old oaks and weeping willows bordered the trail to her left. On the other side of those trees the creek meandered through the woods. On the path near the trees one jogger in a bright green T-shirt moved toward her at a quick pace. Beyond him, two people were walking together . . . *was that Fay's tan jacket?*

Yes, she was sure it was Fay's long brown ponytail. Those were definitely her yellow high-tops. She'd found her! Longing to tell her the truth, she rushed toward her best friend.

CHAPTER 31

CARYN

Caryn climbed the steps to her apartment, counting each one along the way. When she reached her doorway, she heard music playing and smelled food cooking. She didn't have a sound system and sure as hell hadn't invited anyone over. She pushed the door. Inside, the thunderous guitar sounds of Korn's heavy-metal band rocked her condo.

In the kitchen, Mack fussed over a skillet. Wearing faded, ripped jeans and a tight, long-sleeved black T-shirt, Mack's shoulder muscles rippled as he bobbed to the beat.

Caryn set her purse and laptop case on the kitchen desk, wondering how he had gotten inside. She hadn't given him a key.

"Hi, Caryn. I wanted to surprise you with dinner." Mack approached for a kiss, as though they were married or living together.

Without accepting his invitation, she pushed him away with both hands. "What are you doing here?" she shouted over Jon Davis's dark vocals.

Mack darted into the living room, where a brand-new set of speakers was hooked to his laptop. He turned down the music. "Check it out. We could use some music in here to lighten the mood. So I bought these." Mack swung his arm around pointing to the speakers, then rocked his air guitar, strumming with the song. "Sound great, don't they?"

Caryn hadn't budged from her spot since she walked in. Her arms remained crossed over her rib cage, and on her face was a stoney scowl. *Did he take my extra key?*

Something on the stove boiled over. Mack leaped toward it to control the damage. "What's wrong?" he asked, turning off the stove and removing the pot from a burner.

"Wrong?" Caryn asked. "What's wrong is you broke into my apartment. What's wrong is you didn't tell me you were coming over, and what's wrong is you invaded my home with your . . . music."

Mack looked like she'd slapped him in the face. "I did this for you."

As if chewing a saw blade, she spat, "Why aren't you home with your wife?"

"Erin drove to Merrillville to see her mom for the weekend. I wanted to see you."

"How did you get in?" Stuck on this detail, she thought he had picked the lock.

"Oh, that was easy. You know that maintenance guy? The one that's always stalking you?"

"Brad?"

"Yeah. That's the one."

"Brad let you in?" Another strike against that loser.

"Yeah. So what? Jesus, Car, I thought you'd be happy to see me."

"Only if you have something for me."

"I always have something for you." Mack's hand slid to his crotch.

Caryn warmed up to him. Her arms came unbound from her chest and she slid them around him. "Next time, call me. Then I can be ready for you." She kissed his rough, stubbly chin, not minding that it scraped her lips. She liked rough sex. In fact the more it hurt, the better.

Jon Davis screamed to announce something terrifying. "Are you ready?" followed by fast drums and bass guitar.

* * *

An hour later, an open bottle of wine stood on the red-tile counter. Caryn held a glass in her hand and breathed the warm cherry tannin. "Got any bourbon?"

Mack held a steaming plate, and the aroma of roast pork filled the kitchen. "When did you start drinking bourbon?"

She shook her head. "I didn't. I was just kidding."

Mack put the covered plate in the oven and stirred a small pot simmering on the stove. "I think I saved dinner. The sauce didn't curdle." After tasting it, he danced toward the sink, washed and broke the ends off a handful of asparagus spears, then tossed them on a plate.

"How was work today?" In her pajamas Caryn sat on a counter stool, relaxed and wearing an after-sex glow. She sipped the wine.

"Okay. Not too stressful. How about you?" He arranged the spears on a white plate and sprinkled Parmesan cheese over them.

She ran her fingers through her hair and rated her day from one to ten. It was a nine. "I had a pretty good day."

He put the plate in the microwave. "Got any new clients?"

"No, but . . ."

After a several-second pause, Mack said, "But, what?"

The blood-colored wine stained the sides of the glass as she swirled it. "It's nothing."

"It must be something. I recognize that look on your face."

Caryn shot a glance at him. It continually surprised her how observant he was. It was an unnerving trait. "What look?"

"That *look*." For the moment, he stopped cooking to pick up his glass. He swirled, sniffed, swirled again, and then sipped and swallowed. "Your going-in-for-the-kill look."

The microwave beeped, signaling that the asparagus was done. Mack winked and smiled at Caryn. "Dinner's ready."

Feeling exposed, Caryn stood. "So it's something I've done before? This . . . look?" She couldn't imagine what he was talking about. She thought she held a tight rein on her emotions. His observation made her curious.

Mack handed her a plate. "There's béarnaise sauce on the stove and," with a flourish, he lifted a linen napkin off a bowl, "baked potatoes."

Caryn loaded a potato, pork, and asparagus onto her plate, then sat down at the kitchen counter set complete with a burning taper candle and red linen napkins. "Tell me more. I didn't know I . . ." *gave myself away like that,* was her thought.

"Remember that night last summer? We went to dinner at an Italian restaurant. Martinelli's." He smoothed out his clothes, then joined Caryn at the counter.

"No."

"At the restaurant there was a woman who knew you. Said she went to high school with your brother, Edward. Don't you remember?"

She almost corrected his mistake but decided against it. She shook her head.

"She kept calling you Ceecee. That woman was positive she knew you. She went on for ten minutes about it. I'm surprised you don't recall." Mack took another sip of his wine.

She did remember the incident; she just wouldn't admit it. Caryn spooned béarnaise onto her asparagus. She remembered the woman who had recognized her too. She had known Trina in high school. Trina was one of Miss Popular's groupies. But after what had happened, Caryn wanted nothing to do with Trina or any of her friends. Ever again.

"She said she knew your brother Edmund, or Edward," Mack continued. "But you don't have a brother or you would have told me. So I knew she mistook you for someone else."

"I must have one of those faces. That kind of thing happens a lot," Caryn deflected. *The look* Mack referred to was hatred, sheer and simple.

For Caryn, high school had been more about learning life skills than the three Rs. No parental figure at home made growing up a bit like *Lord of the Flies*. In fact, what happened to Miss Popular had played a bigger part in Ekhard's leaving than anything else. He'd been dating her, after all, and for the first time in her life, Caryn wondered if Ekhard had loved Suzanne.

Mack droned on. "I have no idea why it stuck in my mind. It wasn't that big a deal. She must have sparked something. Maybe she just pissed you off." Mack laughed. "Now and then when you're mad, though, you do this thing with your eyes. I call it your going-for-the-kill look."

Caryn laughed with him, trying not to sound forced or fake. *I know why it stuck in your mind. I wanted to kill that woman. I would have, too, if . . .*

"I don't remember," she lied.

"It was nothing, Car. I hope you never give me one of those looks." Mack smiled a nervous smile.

She narrowed her gaze. "I gave you that look when I came home tonight."

Tilting his head to one side, Mack teased, "Did you?"

"I thought so," she bantered. *I can pretend to joke about this. Mack has no clue.*

Mack sat back, sipping his wine. "Whatever it was, it was pretty damn sexy."

CHAPTER 32

CARYN

Mack's ringing cell phone woke Caryn the next morning. As he crept out of bed to answer the call, she heard him say, "Hi, Erin," in a low whisper. "That's okay, I was getting up for work anyway." He closed the bathroom door.

The sheets cocooned Caryn in a warm nest that she couldn't stay in forever. Her eyes drifted open. Six fifteen according to the clock. *What kind of wife calls her husband at that hour?*

Mack's voice rose and fell in the bathroom. Was he arguing with her?

Caryn peeled off the blanket, exposing her naked body to the invigorating morning air. She pushed herself up on her elbows and dropped her feet over the edge of the bed. A black silk robe hung over the chair in the corner. She poured it on, a cool liquid coat with ruby-colored roses embroidered up and down the back. Mack had bought it for her on a trip to Dubuque where he went for a conference last summer. Dubuque, Iowa, the hotbed of luxurious and exotic garments. The robe was something a mistress or kept woman would wear. Mack didn't stay overnight at Caryn's often. This was only the second time she'd worn the robe.

With the sash tied, she tiptoed across the cold kitchen floor in her bare feet and turned on the coffeemaker he had prepared last night. A bowl of fruit sat on the counter. He must have gone grocery shopping for her too. She took a banana.

Leaving the lights off in the semi-dark room, she opened her laptop case on the kitchen counter. While the computer booted up, she ate the banana. Overnight she'd had a dream that she and her brother reconnected. They were drinking Kool-Aid of all things. Caryn remembered the last time she had seen Ekhard after he betrayed and abandoned her. The smell of cherry blossoms had filled the air as she stood pressed against his apartment wall. Caryn remembered the cold, hard brick against her shoulder blades because she'd forgotten to wear a jacket that day. Ekhard had been dressed in a gray blazer over a dark-blue golf shirt as he strode toward the apartment. She had slipped to her car as soon as the door to the building closed behind him.

She didn't talk to Eks that time. They didn't reconnect. She'd never phoned. Over the years she had been watching him, keeping track of every movement, every job change, every alias. By staying in Indiana, Ekhard made it easy for her to find him. Caryn wondered if he regretted leaving her. *Did he stay in Indiana to remain close to me? Is he stalking me? How would he take it if I showed up on his doorstep?*

Mack opened the bathroom door. "Oh, you're awake," he said and padded to the kitchen while zipping up his pants. "Cup of coffee?"

"Yes, please." The green light from her computer screen lit the countertop.

Mack set two cups on the counter and poured. "One black cup of joe for my sweetie." He leaned over the counter and kissed her on the nose.

"You're chipper this morning," Caryn said without a smile.

"I woke up next to you. It's going to be a beautiful day."

"Beautiful? Funny, I thought I heard you arguing with Erin."

He stirred cream and sugar into his coffee. "About that . . . Listen, Car, I'm asking Erin for a divorce."

This is new! Caryn's heart skipped a beat, not in a good way. Every nerve ending stood at attention as his statement jolted her nervous system. Eyes wide, Caryn shook her head. "You can't be serious."

"I want to be with you, Caryn. Erin is so . . . demanding. I can't be who she wants me to be anymore."

She closed her laptop lid. "You're suffering from postcoital brain damage."

Mack's eyebrows shot up. "It's not brain damage. I'm in love with you."

Was that even possible? "No, you're not."

"Can we at least discuss it?" he pleaded.

"No." She shoved the stool aside and stomped out of the kitchen.

Love. It wasn't a word she used loosely. In fact, she never used it. As if she knew what that feeling was.

Mack picked up his coffee and strolled after her.

Caryn fumbled with a pair of pants. She then stripped off the robe and pulled a shirt over her head.

Mack placed a hand on the small of her back. Something told Caryn she had hurt his feelings. *Shouldn't I be the one consoling him?*

"Don't." She moved away. She was not ready for this. And probably never would be.

"I want to move in with you."

An ancient image of her parents made its way to the forefront of her mind: her dad so severe, and her mom, with a cigarette between her lips, with the same look as the woman in the famous *American Gothic* painting—only Dad held a drink in his hand instead of a pitchfork.

"You have a wife. Don't expect me to be that woman for you." She pushed past him into the bathroom as a frightening thought came into her mind. "Did you already break up with her? Is that why you were arguing?"

Mack lowered his head. "I might have mentioned something."

Caryn spun around. "What did you say to her?"

"Nothing. She called the home phone." Mack gripped his coffee cup in both hands. The sad look on his face reminded Caryn of homeless dogs in the humane society—animals with no place to go and no one to love them, animals about to be euthanized.

The reality of the situation, *his* situation, dawned on her. "She knew you weren't there. *She's* dumping *you*. You piece-of-shit liar! She dumped *you*, didn't she?" Their affair had lasted for over a year and a half. How had Erin *not* noticed it before?

"She told me not to come home tonight." His head hung a little lower.

Caryn had been alone since high school. Single. Solitary. That was the way she liked it. She had no intention of sharing her life with anyone. "You need to go back to her."

"Come on, Car. I love you." He leaned toward her, his big soft-brown eyes saying, "devoted for life."

"Don't do this, Mack. Don't pressure me." Caryn backed away. She didn't want anyone to be so close to her. Anyone who might want her to share her secrets.

"Why not? I'm ready to move forward with you."

"Mack, you're married. You ought to have kids by now. *That* would be moving on—the perfect wife, family life—I will never be that for you. For God's sake, go back to your wife!"

CHAPTER 33

CARYN

It was another overcast, white-skied, midwestern day. An unforgiving wet drizzle soaked the car and everything else in central Indiana. Leafless trees stood dormant, dripping, ready for the long sleep of winter. In the city of Lebanon, Caryn pulled into the Quincey's Brewery parking lot.

She drove to the far end of the lot and parked away from other cars, a long-time habit. When Ekhard was still in school, the track team had keyed his Buick Skylark. The scratches ran the entire length of the car. To get even, he stuffed socks into the exhaust pipes of three of the team members' cars during a track meet. Two suffered carbon monoxide poisoning. The third, who drove a '62 Mustang, started his car with the windows closed. There must have been a hole in the carburetor. When the kid lit a cigarette with the engine running, the car exploded. The boy sustained third- and fourth-degree burns on his face and arms. He didn't complete the school year. Ekhard had always been vindictive. No matter the cost, he would get the last laugh.

Wary of approaching him, she kept her head low, strolled into the pub and found a seat at the bar. On the TV screen overhead, the IU quarterback pitched a ball high into the air. First and ten.

"Bourbon on the rocks?" The bartender, a soft woman with ash-brown hair, flipped a glass onto the bar and scooped ice into it.

156

"Yeah, same as usual," Caryn said. When she overheard Ekhard/ Nathaniel talking to his client, they had mentioned this bar. Every day since, Caryn had been leaving work early to catch a glimpse of her brother. She was trying to build up the nerve to speak to him.

"You got it." The bartender busied herself, filling the glass while staring at the TV. "Hope IU wins- tonight. Record's been crap so far."

Caryn hated small talk. More than that, she didn't care about football. When the bartender had finished pouring, she sat back and scanned the room.

A few minutes later, the door flew open and Ekhard tramped in, stomping the wet off his feet and shaking out a long trench coat. He made his way toward the table behind Caryn where a woman sat with a big box.

What a stroke of luck. Caryn would be able to hear everything they said.

"Hilary, I'm so glad you could make it," he greeted her.

Ekhard folded his coat and placed it neatly over the back of one chair. While Hilary struggled to lower the box onto the floor, he sat down.

"Hi," she said, red-faced from the effort. "Thanks for meeting with me. I can't wait to hand this over to you. I brought the statements from my mutual funds. But I have bad news. I didn't have time to get the bond certificates you requested."

Ekhard slid onto a stool. "Okay, okay. Hold your horses. Let me order a beer for you first." He waved to the waitress.

The waitress meandered over to their table. While he ordered beers, Caryn took a big swallow of her bourbon. She dug the horn-rimmed glasses out of her purse and put them on. It was okay that she couldn't see the TV clearly anymore. She wanted anonymity.

"Tell me what you have here." Ekhard waved at the box on the floor.

"I brought everything. The statements from the last two years and from all my husband's accounts." She stopped, placing her fingers to her lips.

Caryn cocked her head and listened, watching out from under the corner of the glasses.

Ekhard touched Hilary's arm sympathetically. "It's hard to let go of our loved ones."

A near sob escaped as she said, "I don't know what I'd do without you."

"I will help you through this. I promise," he said.

Help her? Caryn doubted it.

When their beers arrived, Hilary took a long drink. Ekhard gazed down at a piece of paper that looked to Caryn like a financial statement.

"Is this all he left you?"

"Plus the bonds," she said.

"Next time bring those and sign them over to me, okay? I promise, Hilary, I'm going to make you a lot of money."

"I'll need all the help I can get. My job at the convenience store doesn't pay that much." She sipped her beer.

Caryn waved at the bartender and asked for another drink. She downed the first one, then peered over her shoulder at them through the glasses.

"I go to the gym every Friday." Ekhard said to Hilary. "I've been trying to put on a little weight." After a pause, he added, "I play racquetball and recently started lifting weights on the off days."

"Where do you go?" Hilary asked. She seemed too enamored of Ekhard. Caryn wanted to pull her aside and slap her out of it. She'd tell her what a loser her brother was. And what he had done.

"Gold's Gym," he said. "They have the best weight equipment. I can do traditional or nautilus."

"Is it working? Are you putting on weight?" Hilary's high-pitched voice grated on Caryn's nerves. She appeared frail. Weak. Ekhard would probably like that about her.

He guffawed, "I hope so."

Hilary said, "It's nice of you to help me with all this. I need someone like you to take care of the financial part of things. I'm so stupid about all that."

Ekhard answered, "I'm doing something I'm good at. I enjoy numbers."

Caryn choked on her bourbon and spit it across the bar as a sudden torrential outburst of laughter erupted from her. Ekhard? Enjoying numbers? That had always been Caryn's forte. She reined in her laughter to hear what was said next, adjusting her glasses and wiping her mouth with a napkin. Out of the corner of her eye, she saw Ekhard peering at her. A cold chill washed over her. *Had Eks recognized her? Was this it? Would he finally speak to her after all these years?* Caryn held her breath and tried to plan her escape.

Hilary had started laughing too. "To me, numbers are impossible. Hugh, my husband, handled everything. I never thought to ask. Now that he's dead . . ." Hilary sniffled. "You are rescuing me just like he did."

Another laugh erupted from deep inside Caryn. This time she trained her gaze on the television, pretending something she'd seen there had caused her outburst. She could feel his cold gaze on her, and it made her want to run again. To finish her drink and get the hell out of there.

Ekhard smoothed his features and the collar on his light-blue, button-front shirt. "I'm here to take care of things for you, Hilary." He stacked her statements and put them aside. "But let's put the paperwork away for now. It's been a long week for me. I can look over your statements tomorrow. I don't mind working on the weekend."

"That's really sweet of you." Hilary batted her nonexistent eyelashes. "By the way, you never said how much it will cost for your services."

"My services?" Ekhard looked at the statement again. "For you, I'll make it affordable."

Hilary put the pile of papers back in the box at her feet and pushed it toward him.

Ekhard was going to steal money from this widow, Caryn thought. She finally had something she could use to get even with him. Peering over her glasses, Caryn dared to turn and make eye contact with her brother.

Hilary picked up her beer. "Then the business meeting is over. I'd like to find out more about you, *Nathaniel Johnson*. Tell me about the man behind the name."

With his beer glass in his hand, Ekhard stared back at Caryn. "Ask me anything."

Caryn wanted to know too. Who was Nathaniel Johnson? Emboldened, Caryn held up her glass of bourbon, mirroring Ekhard/Nathaniel. They studied each other for a long minute.

"Tell me how you became an accountant," Hilary said.

"That's a long story."

"It appears that I have plenty of time, now that Hugh is gone." She shrugged.

Caryn flipped her hair back, and that's when she saw the blood drain from Ekhard's face.

CHAPTER 34

CARYN: 26 Years Ago

A group of girls at the bus stop pointed and giggled. Clouds of breath billowed out of their mouths as they talked. Caryn, standing apart from the group, made another foggy puff in the crisp morning air. As it flew away, she wished she could too. Like Mom did.

It was January. Her first day at a new school. She was wearing her favorite dress, the one with the big purple flowers, the dress she'd worn at her aunt's third wedding. It was a summer dress. Caryn's brown winter boots hit the bottom of the ruffle. Mom would have said the boots didn't match the dress. If Mom had been around, she would have told her not to wear any of it. But Mom was gone.

The group of girls faced each other, whispering secret things not meant for Caryn. Two of them glanced at her and laughed. Caryn knew they were talking about her as the bus rumbled to a stop. When they lined up to climb on board, one of the girls asked, "What's your name?"

"Caryn." Another cloud puffed into the chilly air.

"You want to sit with me? My name's Ellen."

Caryn sat next to Ellen, wishing she could have had the window seat. Instead, she got the aisle. The school bus was noisy. Kids were talking and laughing. It was the middle of the school year, just after Christmas break. Of course everyone in the bus knew each other. To Caryn, they were a bunch of strangers.

She hadn't wanted to go to this school, but Dad had moved them to a different house during Christmastime. Originally, Mom was supposed to have moved there with them. Caryn thought she would like it. From what everyone said, Mom wasn't coming back. She and Dad had been fighting the night she left. She had packed a small suitcase and driven off. Just like that. Because she was gone, this Christmas had been the worst ever. They didn't put up a Christmas tree because Dad couldn't find the box of ornaments. Instead, he put their presents on the dining-room table in the shopping bags they came in.

Ellen pointed to the enormous box of tissues in Caryn's lap. "Do you have a cold?"

Caryn didn't answer. Her backpack was bulging full of new boxes of crayons, markers, and notebooks, and there hadn't been room for the tissues. None of the other kids had their first-day-of-school stuff with them. Embarrassed, she leaned on the lumpy backpack and stared straight ahead.

"Are you sick?" This time Ellen had to shout over the noise.

"It's my first day."

Ellen held a lunch box with Cinderella in her blue gown on it. "You'll like our school, Karen."

She lurched with the motion of the bus. "No. My name's Caryn. Like car-in." She hated having to explain it. It was a terrible name. Her face felt hot. If Mom had been home, she would have driven Caryn to school. She'd always driven her to school before.

Ellen got up on one knee and turned toward the back of the bus. "Hey Deedee, her name's Car-In. Like… cars, you know?"

"That's a stupid name."

Caryn looked back at Deedee laughing. She was sitting in the center of the back seat. Center stage. Caryn wanted to go back there and pull her hair, but she was surrounded by all her friends. And suddenly, she felt silly in her flowery dress. The embarrassment turned to anger.

Someone else called out, "Car -wash." He started a flurry of name calling.

"How about Car-parts."

"Car-tire."

"Wait!" Deedee shouted above the others, "Car-seat."

Everyone laughed. Caryn shrank back, mortified, trying to make herself as small as possible. She wanted to be invisible. But the bulky supplies in her backpack made it impossible to shrink. Even though she dropped the giant Kleenex box on the floor and kicked it away, Caryn couldn't make herself disappear. The sound of their laughter made her mad.

When the bus stopped in front of the school, kids piled into the aisle. They laughed and poked at her as they went by. Caryn didn't get up.

Next to her, Ellen went as far as she was able to, blocked in by Caryn. "Come on. Get out."

Caryn stared at the dirty green leather of the seat in front of her. Someone had written "Jason Whitaker" on it with a heart next to it.

"Come on," Ellen repeated. "Let me out."

After the last kid had stepped down off the bus, Caryn asked, "Why'd you have to do that?"

"Do what? Let me out!"

She sat like a lump, refusing to move.

The bus driver called to them, "Come on girls. Let's go."

"She won't let me out." Ellen started to push.

The bus driver, an angular woman, stood up. "Don't make me come back there," she said.

Still Caryn wouldn't budge.

Ellen pushed harder. She was a little bigger than Caryn, taller and stronger. But when Caryn stood up, she locked her arm straight and pressed her hand onto Ellen's face. Ellen backed into the window and whimpered. Drawing blood, Caryn dug fingernails into the girl's soft cheeks.

* * *

Still wearing her bulky winter coat, Caryn sat on the wooden bench in the principal's office. She watched as the bus driver, teachers, school nurse, and Principal Thompson fawned over Ellen. The girl cried when they wiped the blood from her cheek and bandaged her. Every time she looked at Caryn, she burst into tears again. The principal called Ellen's mother. When the woman arrived, she hugged her daughter and held her for the longest time. They looked sideways at Caryn and pinched their lips closed. It made Caryn hate Ellen even more.

After Ellen and her mother had gone home and the flurry of activity died down, Principal Thompson called Caryn's house. Teachers returned to their classrooms. The secretary took her seat at her desk, and the nurse and principal went to their offices.

"Is my mom coming?" Caryn asked the secretary. She knew she wasn't. But she didn't want to say it out loud.

"We left her a message."

After an hour had passed, the secretary said, "Why don't you take your coat off, honey?"

She didn't want to. Caryn was hot but kept her backpack on, a life preserver.

At noon, the secretary brought her a tray with a school lunch on it. There were tater-tots, green beans, and slimy-looking meat. She held it out to Caryn, who didn't take it.

"Did you call her again?"

"Yes, Caryn. We've called your house a few times." She jiggled the tray in front of Caryn, as if trying to entice her.

"My dad is at work. Did you call him?"

"We tried. He told us . . . Well, he can't pick you up right away." The secretary's face turned pink.

Caryn imagined that her dad had said more words than that. He yelled and screamed about everything. "Why can't I go to class?"

"Principal Thompson has issued you a suspension. Do you know what that means?"

"I can't go to class?"

"You can't come to school for three days. Have some lunch. Are you sure you don't want to take your coat off?" When Caryn still didn't take the lunch tray, the secretary set it on the bench beside her. "You do know that what you did was bad, don't you?" She placed her hands on her hips.

Caryn had been thinking. She had known it would come to this and had already decided how she needed to react. A third-grader, she was considered very bright. And whether her parents told her or not, she knew it. She was able to figure out what was expected from her. She knew that kids hated it when their mothers left them. She knew they cried.

So Caryn began to cry. It started as a trickle. "Don't tell my dad I got suspended. He'll be so mad." Now she let it out, and decided that crying felt really good. She began to moan out loud, "Please don't tell my dad. Please."

The principal came out of his office. "What's going on out here?"

The secretary whispered something to him, but Caryn couldn't hear what over the sound of her own howling. Kids stopped in the hall to see what was going on in the office. The secretary went to her phone again. Caryn wailed even louder.

Dad and Ekhard arrived later that afternoon, after the other kids had gone home. While Theo talked to the principal, Ekhard sat beside Caryn on the hard wooden bench.

"Where's Mom?" she asked him.

Ekhard looked at his feet. "You know she couldn't come."

"Why not?" Even though she knew Mom would probably give her a sore bottom for what she had done, Mom was the only one she wanted.

"She's gone, Ceecee. What happened today?" Ekhard asked.

"I got mad." She wiped her face where tears had left a sticky film.

"Did you hurt someone?" He helped Caryn out of her backpack.

Her shoulder blade was sore where the box of crayons had been poking her all day. She made a sour face.

"Caryn, are you okay?" Ekhard asked.

She bit her lip and nodded yes. She wasn't hurt. Nor was she sorry for scratching Ellen's face, or even sad about having to stay in the principal's office all day. She wanted to go home. And she wanted her mother.

They could hear Theo talking with the principal, explaining the situation at home.

On an instinctual level, Caryn knew her mom had run away. She knew it when their dad said she wasn't coming back. Anna Clare had left them alone with their awful father. And Caryn hated her for it.

Ekhard set her backpack down on the floor. Then he did something he had never done before. He embraced his sister. He put an arm around her and drew her close to him. She dropped her blond head on his chest and stayed that way until it was time to go.

CHAPTER 35

MORGAN

With the television volume muted, Morgan watched the IU football team kicking Michigan's proverbial ass. The quarterback sailed the ball downfield and directed it into the arms of a teammate. In slow motion they danced. Halloween commercials slotted between plays were frequent and distracting.

Unable to concentrate on the game, Morgan curled up on the couch with her laptop resting on her thighs. Her fingers poised over the keys as she played and replayed the meeting with Caryn in the coffee shop. Tapping, they restlessly waited a command. Her phone rang, interrupting the process. She slid the laptop to the couch and dug into the front pocket of her hoodie. She wanted it to be Rob. She looked at caller ID and answered, "Hi, Mom."

"Hi, dear. Are you watching the game?" Morgan could hear their TV blaring in the background.

"Oh . . ." Morgan looked at her screen as the Michigan quarterback got sacked. Through the phone, she heard her dad and Jeremy cheering.

"Do you have plans with your friends today?" her mother asked.

"Donnie invited me for dinner with his family, but I'm not going. Besides, it's cold and rainy. It's a pajama day."

"Well, your aunt Lucy is coming over in about an hour. We're working on the Thanksgiving menu. You're coming for Thanksgiving, aren't you?"

"I'm planning on it," Morgan said.

"Oh good. Then you can help too." As her mother ran off the scheduled agenda for the day, Morgan's mind wandered to holiday traditions. "When my mother cooked the turkey . . ." Listening to her mom's prattle comforted her.

She felt bad about arguing with Jeremy in front of Dierdre. She hoped to reconcile when she went to visit for Thanksgiving.

Jeremy worried about her, that's why he didn't understand. But this time he didn't need to. Morgan knew what she was doing. She was trained for this. Her degree in criminology would not go to waste. Jeremy could be thankful for that. Eventually.

She heard him laugh in the background. Happy memories of growing up with such a supportive brother made Morgan smile. It also made her wonder what holiday gatherings had been like in Caryn's house when she was younger. Did her mom cook? What about after she left them? Did their alcoholic father cook? Who took care of the household chores?

"In a few minutes it will be halftime. Do you want to talk to your dad?" Morgan's mom asked.

If Morgan could find Anna Clare Klein, what would she say about her children? About the past? Thinking out loud, Morgan asked, "Mom, if you had to leave Dad, where would you go?"

"What? What kind of question is that?"

"I'm working on a case, and the mother left her children to escape an alcoholic husband. I suspect he beat her. If it was you, where would you go?"

"Well, not far. I'd want to keep an eye on my kids, even if I couldn't have physical contact with you anymore. Why didn't she take her children with her?"

"Good question."

With the phone pressed between her shoulder and ear, Morgan dragged her computer closer to search databases.

"I can't imagine any mother leaving her children."

"Unfortunately, it happens all the time, Mom," Morgan said. "Let me call you back, okay? I'm working."

"On Sunday?"

"Yeah. Tell Dad and Jeremy I said hi, okay?"

After hanging up, Morgan's fingers flew over the keyboard. She searched death records first, then titles to land. When nothing appeared, she typed in hospital and emergency room admittances. The woman didn't show up in any hospital or police records in Marion County.

The game was wrapping up before she found an emergency room record in 2015 at the Ball Memorial Hospital in Muncie, Indiana. Anna Clare Klein was still using her married name.

*   *   *

Morgan hopped into a new, rented Toyota. After she'd gotten a speeding ticket in the Mazda, she'd exchanged it for a safer, more familiar vehicle. She headed to Muncie, where Anna Clare was living and dying in a hospice-sponsored facility. Through tracing the admittance records at Ball Memorial Hospital, Morgan had been able to follow up with nurses in the pulmonary wing. Condemned by lung cancer, Anna Clare did not have much longer to live. The cancer had moved in and taken residence. The nurses let Morgan know that the last time Anna Clare Klein had come to the hospital, she had been released to hospice care.

On arriving at the hospice facility, Morgan had to show her badge to get inside, something she hated about her work. She didn't enjoy harassing sick, weakened people. Anna Clare had told them she didn't want any visitors. When Morgan explained that she was investigating a murder, they let her in.

Frail and small, Anna Clare slouched in her bed with blankets bundled around her. A bony shoulder peeped out from under the covers. Alert, bright-blue eyes targeted Morgan as she entered.

Morgan sat near the bed in a chair she had brought in from the hallway. She explained who she was, and Anna didn't seem to mind. Nor did she seem surprised that Morgan had questions about her children.

"I never wanted to leave them, you know." Anna cleared her throat again and coughed. Her raspy voice didn't have much wind behind it. "Lung cancer has spread. Surgery, removing both lower lobes, has only made me weaker. The cancer returned last year in the upper half of my lungs."

"I can come back later," Morgan said with a twinge of regret. Th truth was that if Anna didn't talk now, Morgan might never have anothe chance. And she hoped that Anna knew where her son was.

"It's fine. I don't mind. The way it looks, I might not be here if you came back another day." When Anna smiled, it began another coughing spasm. When the worst of it subsided, she continued. "Funny how things change, isn't it? Once, all my secrets seemed so important. None of it matters anymore." The loud hum of her oxygen condenser filled the quiet spaces. "Back then I'd have made a huge stink about answering your questions. I wouldn't have told you a thing." She closed her eyes.

Morgan knew something about secrets. She wouldn't share hers no matter who asked.

"I want you to know, I had to be free of Theo. The decision to leave had nothing to do with Ekhard and Ceecee," Anna said. "I wanted to kill their father. He was a mean man."

"Did he beat you?"

"Oh yes." Anna closed her eyes.

Perhaps she had dozed off for a moment. Morgan couldn't tell. She looked down at her lap. *Patience,* she thought.

Ten minutes later, Anna continued, drowsily and slowly. "He beat me all right. He beat the kids too."

Morgan's lips met in a frown.

"No harm in telling you now, I suppose." Anna nodded, continuing. "I bought a gun. A big Sig Sauer semiautomatic. A forty-five. The bullets were as big as my little finger. I suppose you'd know that. I wanted to, but I never shot him. I could hardly handle the gun for its size. When I learned about his death years later, I was happy that drinking took him. But, by then, I couldn't go back to the kids. They were so grown up by then. They weren't mine anymore."

"Ekhard and Caryn were in high school."

"I know what they went through. I was Eks's age when my ma died." Anna coughed again. This time she sat up.

Morgan handed her a water bottle and a box of tissues. The spasm stole Anna's energy. When it was over, she slept.

So, Morgan waited, watching her from the hallway. One nurse stood nearby, and Morgan asked her if Anna had had any other visitors.

The nurse responded by saying, "I haven't seen a soul come by for her. No surprise. She's got no gratitude, no remorse, and is certainly lacking in the kindness department. Pretty sad if you ask me." She took a home-baked cookie from a tray near the coffeepot and shoved half of it into her mouth.

The oxygen pump worked, breathing life into the dying woman, cycling and releasing. When Anna woke, she continued talking as if she hadn't been asleep for over an hour. "The gun was too big for me to handle. I took it to a shooting range, got some lessons on how to use it. I couldn't even pull back the shuttle, let alone shoot and hold the thing steady."

"You wanted to kill him. Things were that bad for you," Morgan said with sympathy.

"Let me finish." With much effort, Anna wrestled her arm out from under the covers. She placed her cold, boney hand on top of Morgan's. "Your hand is so warm."

Morgan leaned forward, resting her notebook on the side of the bed.

Anna continued with renewed energy. "I became afraid. Afraid that he'd find the gun. Afraid that he'd wrestle it out of my hands. I thought, Theo will shoot me and there will be no one to take care of Eks and Ceecee."

"So you left him."

"It was my only choice. Then he cut me off from all our finances. He took my name off our checking and savings accounts. He canceled the credit cards. All of them."

"You had to make a new start," Morgan said.

"I did. It was hard, but I didn't call those kids after I left. I just couldn't recover anything after leaving or after Theo died." Her solemn expression was sorrowful. "He wasn't the only mean one, though."

"How so?"

"Theo wasn't alone. I was just as wicked as he was. Probably why we married in the first place. I think back on it now and wonder if I must be going to Hell."

Morgan cocked her head and gently asked, "Did you beat them too?"

"Aw, you know, sometimes they deserved it. Kids are sometimes stupid that way." Anna looked away. "And sometimes I just couldn't help it." She pushed herself up on the pillows.

Morgan stood up, ready to help if necessary. "Caryn was only fifteen when Theo died. From all accounts, Ekhard dropped out of college to take care of her. They sold the house and moved to an apartment on the west side."

"I heard. Ekhard was a good kid. And Caryn? I never worried about that girl. She could hold her own." Anna fussed with her pillows.

"What can I do to make you more comfortable?"

"Nothin'. If I get too comfortable, I'll fall asleep again." Anna struggled with the pillows before settling into the bed.

Morgan sat back down in the hard, plastic chair.

"Ekhard came to visit me after Ceecee graduated from high school." Anna closed her eyes. Her eyelids fluttered as if she were watching an internal movie of memories. "He had changed his name by then, and he'd called me out of the blue."

"He changed his name? To what?" This news gave Morgan renewed hope of finding him. She opened her little notebook and clicked her pen.

"I think it was Linus, or Larry. I can't remember now."

Larry was the name written in Fay's journal. At the time of her death, no one with that name was registered at the university. No one by that name even lived in Bloomington. Morgan wrote the names Linus and Larry on her notepad. "Was it Larry Milhouse?" She asked.

"Maybe. I couldn't figure him out. So much time had passed, I didn't know him anymore. I remember he looked so much like his father. That's when I knew it was too late." Anna closed her eyes, lost in the memory. "He told me all kinds of stories about his sister. It warmed my heart to know they'd stuck together. That girl was quite a prankster. I think she got it from me.

"As Eks told me some of the stories, I remember he laughed. I'm not sure what tickled him. But when he laughed it reminded me of when he was a boy. It was good to hear, because it sure seemed like something big was bothering him. Something heavy." She chuckled at the memory and held back another cough.

"What kinds of things did Caryn do?" Morgan asked, thinking that her early behavior might shed light on her adult personality.

"Aw, you know, the usual kid-stuff." Anna's mouth turned downward as another thought saddened her. "Thank goodness Ekhard stood by her. I think he set her right."

"What do you mean?"

"Ceecee was a little bully, even in first grade. But I liked that about my Ceecee. She didn't take shit from anybody. After I left them, I heard she got suspended from her new school. Dug her fingernails into some poor girl's face. That girl had it coming from what I heard. She teased Ceecee too much. I was like that when I was young too. Until I met Theo." The coughing began again.

Morgan held back her question until Anna had stopped. "When was the last time you saw Ekhard or Caryn?"

"Caryn didn't come find me. That's okay. And I never saw Eks after that once." Between coughs she added, "He sometimes sends a card. At least I think it's from him." Anna Clare nodded toward the get-well card on the bedside table. Morgan lifted it from behind Anna's water bottle and opened it. The front of the card showed a bouquet of pastel flowers covered in sparkles with "Get Well Soon" written in cursive lettering. Inside, the printed sentiment read, "Wishing you a speedy recovery." No handwritten note. It was signed, "Nathaniel Johnson."

"You think this is from Ekhard?"

"I don't really know."

No envelope was with the card or on the table. Could it be in the trash? Morgan took a pair of latex gloves from a box and then dug around in the wastepaper basket. When she didn't see what she was looking for, she asked the nurse in the hallway.

"That card came over a week ago. The envelope is long gone," she said.

When Morgan returned to Anna Clare's bedside, she had fallen asleep again. Her breathing sounded thick and gravelly, adding to the musical purr of the oxygen converter.

Reluctantly deciding it was time to go, Morgan stood up and stretched. She left her business card on a table under a small vase of flowers. Then she looked around the cozy hospice room once more.

Outside, Morgan wrote down another name in her notebook.

CHAPTER 36

MORGAN: 16 Years Ago

Hope lit Morgan up and she walked much faster. Fay and the other person were almost the length of a football field away. But who was that with her? It wasn't a guy. The woman wore a clingy brown dress and jean jacket. Morgan saw Fay follow her into the trees and began to jog.

Morgan knew what lay beyond those trees—a picnic table and a rock big enough to sit on. The creek bed was nearby. She and Fay had smoked their first joint there because it was secluded. But why would Fay go to their secret place with another woman? *Could Fay be gay too? How did I not know?* Morgan wondered.

She jogged to catch up. As she closed in on them, doubt filled Morgan's mind. What if Fay loved this other woman? *What if Fay doesn't love me?* At this distressing thought, Morgan reduced her speed. She decided to approach slowly and listen to them talk before announcing her presence.

In the growing darkness, Morgan stepped lightly so as to make no noise as she snuck up on her friend. Under the trees, she smelled cigarette smoke. Fay didn't smoke. Morgan heard Fay's nervous laughter and crept a little closer to hear their conversation. Something about *Larry.*

The glowing coal of the woman's cigarette lit up her features. The blonde wore dark eye makeup. When she exhaled, she moved the cigarette away from her face and the darkness disguised her again.

"How long have you known him?" Fay sounded scared.

"Since we were kids. We grew up together," she said.

Crouching behind a tree, Morgan listened and watched.

Fay said, "And you've kept in touch all these years, that's great."

"We haven't kept in touch," the woman said. She tossed her cigarette into the creek.

In the darkness, Morgan squinted to see.

Fay said, "Look, I guess I should be going. I should get home to my mom. She'll be expecting me, and Larry's really late."

"Larry's always late."

CHAPTER 37

MORGAN

A mixture of ice and hard rain crackled against the third-story window near Donnie's desk.

"You're an hour late." Donnie greeted Morgan.

"I've been grieving." She wasn't kidding. Donnie, she hoped, would think she missed her car. The truth was that she'd been obsessing about Fay again.

"Because of a speeding ticket?"

Lucky. Hands flew to her hips. "How did you hear about that?" If she had slept at all she'd woken in a bad mood. Suzanne, Hallie, Larry, and Fay—they were all connected, Morgan was sure. The strike patterns on Hallie's and Suzanne's faces were the same. Fay's might be too. Morgan had laid awake wondering whether to get an exhumation order for Fay's body.

"Rob told me," he revealed. "It's nothing to be embarrassed about. That Mazda is a sweet car. I would have been going one hundred miles an hour too." Donnie smiled and nodded his approval.

She inhaled sharply. "I wasn't going one hundred."

Donnie filed the crime photos in a manila folder on his desk. "So you're not buying a sports car?"

"No. Absolutely not," Morgan grumbled. "I'm leasing a Toyota now."

"That's safe. Kinda like your old car."

Morgan dropped into her desk chair. Their desks faced each other, and now she noticed how clean his was compared to hers. The sight unnerved her. "You're really taking Holbrooke's job?"

Donnie nodded. "It's a big decision, but it's time to settle down a little."

With straight fingers, she smoothed her brow. This wasn't something she wanted to deal with right now. She had to remain focused.

Donnie kept talking, "And you too. Buying a car is just a start. It's time you began thinking about your future. Dating Rob, that's a no-brainer. I think he's perfect for you."

Morgan glowered at Donnie. "How do you know Rob anyway? Since when are you two such good friends?"

Donnie sat back and folded his hands behind his head. "I bumped into him outside the station. That's all. He asked about you. Don't get so sensitive with me. I've known you for a long time, Morgan. Will you let me care a little?"

Morgan stifled a yawn. "Sorry, I appreciate your perspective, Donnie. I'm just grumpy. I haven't slept well since this thing with Hallie Marks started."

Morgan stared at the raindrops on the window reflecting the overhead light behind her. Each single drop stood alone until it rolled down the windowpane and joined the rest in a puddle on the sill. It reminded her of the blood pools of each of the victims. Eventually, they would form a single body of evidence.

Suzanne held the secret in her hand: hairs that belonged to her killer. Processing thoughts that arrived between fits of slumber, Morgan had tied together similarities of the two murders: Hallie Marks and Suzanne Aiken. Their faces had been crushed beyond recognition. Ekhard Klein was a clear suspect in both cases—if they could find him. Fay remained in the distance, waving from the trees beside Jackson Creek.

Bloomington was too damn far from these Indianapolis crimes to pin Fay's murder on this person. Or was it? Two facts forced Morgan to question her judgment: the time between the killings and the distance. And yet, if the same person murdered them, he—or she—had been killing for twenty-two years. What did the killer do during those gap years? Not needlepoint.

Over the years Morgan and Donnie had spent hours looking at similar crimes. At any given time, there were more than fifty serial murderers living in the United States alone. They mingled with the working crowd, pretending to be normal. In Morgan's mind, they were one step from screwing up and getting caught.

What kind of person would kill young women so brutally? The thought sickened Morgan. How does a person like that think? How do they interact with friends, lovers, and victims? Morgan thought she knew. Her left hand dipped into a crowded pants pocket. Wedged inside, the pawed, pocket-sized spiral notebook with softened edges filled the space, allowing no room for her hand. She pulled it out by the corner and caressed the booklet with her thumbs.

On his wooden desktop, Donnie's cell phone vibrated once. "Oh, Etta. She isn't supposed to text during school."

Morgan smiled at the little distraction. "Did something happen?"

"No. She's got Driver's Ed tonight. She was reminding me I'm supposed to drop her off."

Morgan stepped toward his desk and lifted a framed photo of Donnie's daughters, Etta and Annabel, while Donnie texted a reply to Etta. When he looked up, he seemed to sense her brooding. "What's wrong?"

Morgan set the picture down and began paging through her notebook. She opened it at the names she'd written down while talking to Anna Clare. "Anna Clare admitted that Ekhard has changed his name. She didn't say why. I have some calls to make." She explained about the name on the card.

Donnie tilted his head to the side. "Sure everything's okay?"

"I'm sure." Researching Nathaniel Johnson, the name from the get-well card, Morgan found twelve men with that name in the state of Indiana. Five within the right age range lived in Indianapolis. After calling them all and dismissing them as possible suspects, she extended her search. It was late afternoon before she began working on a CPA in Lafayette, Indiana. Nothing came up when she cross-referenced his name with Anna Clare's. But before giving up, she ran a search with his name and each of the victims, Hallie Marks and Suzanne Aiken. Unable to find any links, she called his workplace. The receptionist at Baker and Baker told her he was no longer working there.

"How can I get hold of him?" Morgan asked.

"Are you a client of his?"

"I'm with Indianapolis Metro Homicide. Can you give me his personal number?"

"Certainly." After the receptionist gave Morgan Nathaniel's number, she explained that he'd left the firm to branch out on his own.

*   *   *

The next morning, when she asked Donnie to try the number again, Nathaniel answered. Eyebrows raised in excitement, Donnie waved her over to his desk. After the initial greetings, Donnie put the call on speakerphone. "Nathaniel, I'm investigating Suzanne Aiken's case. Have you heard about it?"

Right away, Nathaniel began coughing. "Yes," he said when he had caught his breath. "You'd have to be living in a cave to miss it."

"You would. Horrible what happened to her, wasn't it? She was tortured, then killed with a number of hammer blows to the face."

"Horrible." Nathaniel agreed. He coughed again, then apologized for his asthma.

Sympathetic, Donnie said, "Aw, that sucks. My father has asthma. Sometimes just the cold air will trigger it."

Morgan loved the way her partner could comfort a person before laying siege with questions.

"Let me get to the point of my call. My partner interviewed some people associated with the Aiken girl when she was alive. Your name came up." Donnie relaxed back in his chair.

"It did?"

"It did." Donnie paused between these little bits of information, giving Nathaniel plenty of time to say something. And plenty of opportunity to ingest the details.

"Did you know Suzanne socially?" Donnie asked, circling like a hawk.

Nathaniel answered decisively, "No. I'm sure I didn't."

"Did you grow up in the state of Indiana, Nate? Can I call you Nate?"

"Yes I did. If you don't mind my asking, how did my name come up?

"Ah. Members of the Klein family mentioned you."

Nathaniel seemed to choke on the word. "Who?"

"How do you know Anna Clare Klein?"

"Anna Clare?"

Morgan noted the agitation in Nathaniel's voice.

He coughed again before answering, "She's an old friend."

"How long have you known her?"

"Many years. I used to do her taxes for her."

Morgan shook her head. Anna Clare lived in Muncie, a good two-hour drive from Lafayette. She doubted either of them would have made that long a drive to do taxes. Quickly, she jotted a question on a sheet of paper and dropped it on the desk beside Donnie: "Does he know the kids?"

Donnie glanced at Morgan's note and asked, "Do you know her children?"

This time Nathaniel's coughing spasm lasted several seconds before subsiding. Donnie repeated the question.

"I can't help you, Detective."

Morgan wondered if he couldn't, or wouldn't.

* * *

Morgan told Donnie her plan to drive to Lafayette to talk to Nathaniel while he took Etta to Drivers Ed. On her way out of town, she stopped in to see Rebecca Harrington at the Channel 6 News building downtown. Rebecca had left her a message saying she had found something that might help the investigation.

A pleasant young security officer at the information desk directed Morgan to the third floor. Open cubicles formed a maze of desks that Morgan navigated with the help of three different people. When she finally reached Rebecca's desk, it was vacant. Morgan hadn't called ahead, but she knew that Rebecca frequently traveled for work.

"She had to go to a live shoot on the north side," a woman at a nearby desk informed her.

Morgan turned on her heel. "I should have called."

The woman's round cheeks sagged. Her blue blouse had a greasy stain down the side. "Rebecca's been a little forgetful lately. Hallie's death hit her hard, you know."

Morgan did know. She glanced at the top of Rebecca's messy desk. Stacks of paper spilled out of a file box. A half-dozen yellow sticky notepapers drew attention to the bottom of her computer screen.

"Can I help you with something?"

Morgan flashed her badge. "I'm investigating Hallie's murder."

"Oh." The woman raised her chubby hands in the air.

"I'll just be a few minutes," Morgan said, then sat down at Rebecca's desk.

The sticky notes bore a variety of announcements and reminders. *Call Doug re: Carmel Cupcakes. Oil change—OVERDUE! Gerald needs final report on Sampson story. Call Detective Jewell re: receipts.*

What had Rebecca found? Morgan unclipped her phone and dialed Rebecca's number.

"Detective Jewell. I was hoping you'd call." Wind was obviously blowing across Rebecca's phone, making it hard to hear her.

Morgan nodded. "I got your voicemail and stopped by your office. I'm there now."

Wind scraped across Rebecca's receiver. ". . . inside my desk."

"Can you please say that again?"

". . . second drawer." This time, the connection went bad.

Morgan waited to see if the static cleared, but the line went dead. She hung up and tried calling again. The call didn't go through. She pushed away from the desk. Looking around the office to see if anyone was watching, Morgan began quietly opening drawers. The second drawer on the left was filled with junk food—Doritos, Keebler cookies. A dozen or so airplane-sized bottles of whiskey and vodka were buried at the back.

On the right, the second drawer was full of strips of paper. Credit card receipts from restaurants and hotels in a jumbled disarray filled the drawer. It looked like Rebecca had just thrown them in. Was this her filing method? Morgan took out a handful and looked through them. On top were several from a Clarion Hotel in Bloomington. Some under that were from a restaurant in Illinois. These must be her work receipts.

Morgan's phone rang again. Rebecca.

"Sorry about the bad connection. So listen, I wanted to tell you I found something. I had completely forgotten about this. About six months ago, I was emptying the trash in our bathroom and noticed some bar receipts. I always save those for tax purposes, so I took them out and put them in my desk drawer. The other day I was looking through them and found credit card receipts that don't belong to me. There's a blank envelope at the front of that second drawer."

Morgan pushed papers aside, digging for it.

"I don't know how Hallie got them, they aren't hers either." Static returned to the line. "Those are for you." Rebecca said something else, but it was drowned by a loud crackle.

"Thanks Rebecca," she said. "I'll be in touch."

CHAPTER 38

CARYN

The sunless Indiana sky shed grainy gray light, making the world appear barren and uninteresting. The incongruity with her colorful thoughts rubbed Caryn raw.

Before picking the lock, she had checked the time. This time, she picked the deadbolt in twenty-two seconds, the doorknob in sixteen. With her sleeve pulled over her fingertips, she turned the knob. Prepared for the proverbial swarm of bats to come rushing past her, Caryn pushed in the door to Ekhard's house.

In the basement, cut wood odors lured her to Ekhard's hobby room. The door stood open with just enough space for her arm to reach through. She felt along the wall for a light switch. When she found the familiar, smooth switch plate, she flicked. Loud buzzing came with illumination.

She stepped into the room. The smell of fresh sawdust mingled with other odors. Paint or stain, perhaps? Something metallic. In the center, a large table filled the room with a table saw and a lathe affixed to it. Pieces of cut wood filled a trash can in the corner, and an unfinished project, a stool or small table, lay on its side on top of the table. The workmanship was fine. The legs were ornate in the way of antique furniture. Decorative. Beautiful.

Ekhard has a hobby. A giggle caught in Caryn's throat.

Books and catalogs of the trade filled shelves along the back wall. Coveys of cans containing stain, paint, and oil stood like sentinels. Small finished projects like cutting boards and platters were nested and stacked, a bowl full of finials, polished driftwood. The counter underneath was clean; as in the kitchen, there was no dust. Stacked sanding blocks and rags folded in a neat pile on the left spoke volumes of careful cleanliness.

A white pegboard covered the wall to her right, and hanging from it were tools of the trade: handsaws and screwdrivers, carving knives and paintbrushes. Categorized and organized into groups of similar objects, each item on the board was carefully outlined with black marker.

Nothing was out of place. Not a scrap or wood chip on the floor. Caryn ran her fingers along the edge of the table, smooth as a baby's bottom, or so she figured.

One end of the pegboard contained hammers. With the organization and care so obviously taken to clean, it seemed conspicuous that among the many mallets and percussive devices placed and definitively organized one was missing. One astonishing thick black outline of a hammer remained empty of its filler. A bowl with no soup. A coffin missing a body.

The sight triggered a memory. The memory triggered something like feelings. Where the hammer was missing, Caryn felt loss and abandonment.

She had to see him.

This time, she would wait for him.

*   *   *

Her fingers drummed on the old wooden breakfast table—the one from the house she had grown up in. Caryn counted, passing the time. Drum, drum. Four hundred thirty-two. Four hundred thirty-three . . . It kept her from counting the number of ways this would play out. There were too many. Ekhard had always been unpredictable.

Hours ago, the sun had set and lights had come on in the house across from Eks's backyard. It was a happy scene. When the man came home, he joined his wife at the sink and kissed her. The couple puttered around the kitchen, taking care of their two small children and making dinner. Did people actually live like that?

Children were not in Caryn's future.

The low rumble of the garage door opening sent a warning siren through her spinal column and out to the far reaches of her nerve endings. Caryn sat straighter, stiffening with anticipation.

The engine shut off. A car door opened. Closed. Did she hear him walking toward the door? A rattle of keys. The garage door closed.

Ekhard shuffled into his entryway and closed the door. He took off his coat, hung it in the closet, and turned on the light. Caryn couldn't have been breathing. Then Eks turned and saw her there, and their eyes met. Silence ensued. He had warned her.

His hair was longer, and he had grown a beard that didn't match the color on his head. Caryn thought she was the only one who would know that. She was the first to speak. "Hello, Eks."

Her brother stood in the hallway, planted there. He seemed to grow roots in the eternity that passed before he spoke. "What are you doing here?"

Caryn had imagined this scenario, hadn't she?

"You know why I'm here, Eks. They dug up Suzanne's body. The police have located and questioned me. I'm afraid they might have me under surveillance." Caryn held her fingers poised over the table like she was ready to type on a keyboard. "It's over."

Ekhard's eyes lit up. "That's because you fucked up."

"*I* fucked up?" Caryn raised her eyebrows.

Ekhard ran a hand through his hair. "You shouldn't be here!"

"I needed to see you. It's been . . . so long, brother."

"Oh, you haven't been counting the days?"

"Six thousand seven hundred twenty-seven," she admitted.

"There's my Ceecee. And how about since the last time two weeks ago?"

"Fourteen days and fifteen and a half hours. Let's make a new plan. We were always good at planning things together."

"You'd like to think that, wouldn't you?" He sucked air through bared teeth, then coughed.

She put her hands in her lap.

Ekhard took a step toward his sister. "Here's the plan. You get out of my house. Take this opportunity to run like hell away from me."

"Why would I do that?" she asked in the most innocent voice she could summon.

His wide eyes narrowed, and his brow furrowed. "Because otherwise I'll kill you."

"You wouldn't do that to me," Caryn teased.

"I would." He lunged at her, his hands ready to grab hair or choke and strangle.

Her legs uncoiled like springs. Caryn stood up so fast that her chair tipped over and fell to the floor. She sprung to her right toward the sliding door, strategically putting the table between them.

He stopped at the table, gripping it, his knuckles white and his face red with rage. "Get away from me, Ceecee."

Caryn placed her hands on the table, mirroring her brother. "I needed to see you. To warn you. The police questioned me about you and Suzanne. It's only a matter of time before they find you."

He spit out, "That's your problem."

"Can't we make amends?"

"Amends? Ha!" His mouth opened wide with the insanity that lit up his eyes. "There can be no amends."

"You can't run from me your whole life." She tilted her head in the same scolding way their mother had.

"I won't have to." Ekhard coughed, and his chest rose and fell as he took huge gulps of air.

"What does that mean?"

Ekhard took a step to his right and, keeping his gaze riveted on his sister, kicked the chair out of his way.

Caryn also stepped to her right and pushed a chair in to create a clear path of escape. "Ekhard, tell me what's next."

"I'm telling you to get out." He leaned to the left, anticipating her next move.

"And what about you?" She thought she cared what happened to him.

"There aren't enough words in the entire English language to fix what you've done to me." Ekhard took another step.

"You're blaming me? After what *you* did?"

"You are toxic, Ceecee. You are poison." Ekhard's lips flared, showing his teeth between thin lips. "Just like our mother."

"Don't *ever* say that! I am not like Mom." The idea inflamed Caryn. She took another step to the right. "Do you know how many times I've wondered how we could patch things up. How we could live life differently. And you throw that at me? I'm like *Mom*?"

Ekhard spoke in a low, seething tone. "Don't you dare come near me ever again."

Caryn let go of the chair on the opposite side of the table from where this began. She wanted out now. The front door, which she had unlocked earlier, was five, maybe six long strides to her right.

Perhaps Eks noticed her taking stock. "Get out of here! Get the hell out of my house!" His voice steadily grew louder. "I don't want to see you! I don't want to hear from you!"

Caryn suppressed a smile. Ekhard caught the glint in her eye and jumped to his right, shoving chairs out of his way. He bounded toward her like a hungry carnivore.

Caryn reached the front door in five strides and grabbed the knob. The worn mechanism jammed as she tried to open it. Ekhard got to her before she could pull the door open and slammed her face and the front of her body flat against it.

"Let go of the doorknob." His forearm dug into the back of her neck, pinning her right cheek and jaw to the door.

She choked out, "Get off me."

"Don't play stupid with me. You don't get to see me. Ever. Do not come back here."

"Fuck you," she grunted, biting the inside of her lip.

Ekhard pressed his weight against her. Tucking his left forearm around her neck, he put his sister in a stranglehold. With his right hand, he pried Caryn's hand off the doorknob. While keeping her immobilized, he jiggled the knob, then yanked her over to the opening.

"You better prepare for the hell storm," she croaked.

Ekhard released her with a violent shove over the threshold, shouting, "Stay away or I'll kill you!"

Caryn stumbled onto the stoop, then fell. As she hit the pavement, her jeans ripped at the knee and she felt the sharp sting of concrete scraping the skin of her palms. Before she had time to recover, Ekhard slammed the door with a loud bang. Bleeding and bitterly angry, she stormed back to her car.

CHAPTER 39

CARYN: 20 Years Ago

Ekhard sat at the crowded bar with his head hanging like an empty banana peel. Their dad's death two weeks before seemed to have taken a toll on him. Theo died in the hospital of liver failure, lung failure, and kidney failure. A triple whammy. His death didn't take long in the grand scheme of things, but he left a wake of disaster that needed tending: a failing business and several near-empty accounts, a stiff mortgage, and large hospital bills. Someone had to sell the house and the business to pay those bills. Caryn was only fifteen, so Ekhard became that someone. He stopped going to college to take care of his dad's remains and the remains of his life.

The bartender and sole owner of Billy's Bar invited Eks and Caryn to hold Theo's wake at his establishment. Theo had spent a good deal of his money and time there. Billy hosted the wake free of charge. Inside, fixtures with bumpy orange glass and black metal hung from chains but didn't throw enough light. Candles in dirty glass globes threw flickering circles onto the tables. The vinyl benches were brown, maybe. Or red.

Many of Theo's coworkers and friends had stopped by to express their condolences. Billy and the other bartenders held court, telling stories of "Good ol' Theo." Still, no one was too broken up by Theo's passing. While Ekhard sat at a stool nursing a Coke, Caryn watched them all from the comfort of a booth. People she didn't know talked about their dad. What a *nice* guy. Only she and Ekhard knew how he really was.

189

"You doin' okay there, Ekhard?" Billy refilled his Coke with the spray nozzle.

Ekhard nodded.

"How 'bout you, Caryn? How's that sandwich?" Billy called out across the room.

"Great," she called back. With her head resting on one hand, she held up a fry.

Ekhard slid off the vinyl-covered stool, ambled over to Caryn's table, then poured himself into the booth. "You okay?" he asked.

"Better than you. Did you try the fries here? They're actually pretty great. How come Dad never brought us here?" Caryn had just picked at her sandwich. Bread and lettuce lay on the table, rejected from her plate. She dipped French fries in a dark-brown smear of ketchup.

Ekhard focused on a ragged fingernail.

"How much longer do we have to stay?" she asked.

Ekhard checked Theo's heavy watch now dangling from his thin wrist. He twisted the face around so he could read it, squinting in the low light. "Maybe another half hour."

"Billy's paying for this, right?" she asked.

"That's what he said." Ekhard worked the fingernail between his teeth, biting, picking, and spitting.

"I have homework to do. I have a project, a report due on Monday for biology," Caryn said.

"Well, you've got the rest of the weekend. Once we're done here, you have the rest of your life."

That seemed an unimaginably long time. "What are we going to do, Eks? I mean I still need to do Driver's Ed this winter. I can't get there by myself."

"I know, Ceecee." Ekhard crossed his arms on the table and leaned toward her, making eye contact for the first time in days. "I won't leave you. Listen, we'll get through this."

Caryn pushed the uneaten bread around on the table. She picked up the lettuce leaf and flapped it back and forth.

"You shouldn't worry. I've always been there for you, haven't I?" Ever since Mom had left, Ekhard had taken care of his sister at his own expense.

His grades fell through the floor, but he always had dinner on the table. He did things like laundry for their dad when Theo could no longer do it himself. Ekhard drove him to the doctor and made sure he took his medications. And Ekhard always showed up to take care of Caryn.

"You're the best," she said.

Ekhard chewed his nails, seeming distracted.

"What's wrong?" Caryn could read him like an open book.

"Nothing," he lied, looking at his nails.

Caryn pushed her plate to the far side of the table. "Bull. What's wrong?"

Not making eye contact, Ekhard shook his head and muttered, "It's just that . . . I thought . . ."

"What? Spit it," she demanded.

"I thought Anna Clare would come." For a long time they had referred to their mother by her given name. It had been more than seven years.

"Today?" Caryn's mouth scrunched into a grimace. She shook her head. "I haven't thought of her in over a year."

He plunged what was left of his fingernail back between his teeth.

"Maybe she's dead," Caryn said.

"You're right. She doesn't care about us," Ekhard said, the corners of his mouth turned down. "Maybe she never cared. She was probably a crazy, cold-hearted bitch."

"Why would you say that?" His flip statement made Caryn worry about herself. She had learned about genetic traits in school and the idea that her mother was crazy felt uncomfortably right.

Ekhard didn't answer.

"Most of the time I don't care," she admitted. "I don't give a flying fuck about any of my friends. I don't care that Dad died either. Good riddance, you know?"

"That's not true. You cared about him. You care about me. If you didn't, you would have run away a long time ago," Ekhard reassured her. "You always wanted to when you were little."

In full entertainment mode, Billy was laughing out loud and making a show of his bartending skills. A different crowd entered, not Theo's friends, and the hostess seated them for dinner.

Ekhard examined his nails. "We should go."

Caryn slid out of the booth and stood, stretching her legs. Ekhard trudged to the bar and shook hands with Billy, thanking him. Caryn waved from the door.

Outside, her eyes adjusted to the light. The setting sun brightened the crisp fall day. After the wake, they stopped at home to change out of their dress clothes and get warm jackets. Ekhard had planned something fun for the evening.

While he drove south on the interstate, away from Indianapolis, Caryn wrote her report in a spiral notebook in her lap. It was dark when Ekhard slowed down and turned onto a dirt road in the middle of nowhere.

"Where are we?" Caryn asked.

The car bumped up the unlit road. "Somewhere between Brownstown and Salem."

"Massachusetts?"

Ekhard laughed. "No, silly. Indiana."

"We were on the road for a long time," Caryn said.

"Not that long," he responded. "Forty minutes."

Caryn put her notebook in her backpack. In the headlights ahead of them, a battered house missing half its roof appeared. "I hope you know how to get home."

"You know I do." He reached behind Caryn's seat and lifted a heavy brown paper bag to his lap. "I brought something for us."

"What is that?"

He took a large bottle out of the bag. "Bourbon. From home. Consider it a gift from Dad." Ekhard's mouth twisted into the first smile in weeks. He removed the cap and raised the bottle to his lips. After taking a hearty swig, he smacked his lips, then handed the bottle to his sister.

She tipped it back, spilled some down her front, and coughed. "Ugh. Who would want to drink this?"

Ekhard took the bottle and a second swallow. "It's better after a couple drinks. It gets smoother."

She grimaced in disbelief. "If you say so."

"Come on, Ceecee." Ekhard turned off the headlights and hopped out of the car. He zipped up his jacket, the bottle under one arm.

For miles, the sky and surrounding land were pitch-black without a single light or hint of civilization to be seen. Ekhard flipped on a flashlight and led the way up the road. The only noises were the sound of their shoes crunching on the dirt road and the very distant hiss of cars on the highway.

"What is this place?" Caryn could see her breath in the cool air.

"This is the house that Anna Clare grew up in," he explained.

"How do you know?" Caryn took the bourbon bottle from Ekhard and swigged.

"I've been here before." Ekhard hurried up the path.

"When?"

"Mom brought me a few times." He shined the flashlight ahead on the front porch of the house. Broken in spots, the railing and porch ceiling had begun to collapse, but the windows were intact. "You were here, too, when you were really little."

"Nobody lives here now?" Caryn ran to keep up with her brother.

"Nope." When Ekhard halted, Caryn's trainers lost traction on the gravel. She slid to a stop beside him.

The light circle shone on a closed front door.

"Is it locked?" She asked.

"I have an idea." He handed the flashlight to Caryn, then ran back to the car to retrieve something. An owl hooted while Caryn waited. Light from the flashlight died into the blackness surrounding her. Ekhard returned with a hammer in his hand.

"What are you doing with that?"

He took another hit from the bottle, then leaped up onto the porch. "You'll see. Hold the flashlight."

On the porch, he stepped over the loose floorboards and looked around. With a hand held above his eyes, he tried to see inside the dark house through the grimy glass. In his hand, the shiny new steel hammer glistened.

"Check it out," he said and raised his hand high.

"You gonna do home repairs?" Caryn giggled. The warm feel of bourbon made her feel happy. Loose.

"Dad asked me to buy it a year ago. Said his old one went missing." He laughed, shaking the porch. "I bought this before he went to the hospital and forgot all about it." Eks took another swig. "Long story short, it's been in my car ever since. I have no idea what Dad wanted with it." Ekhard raised the hammer in the air and let it fly with an amazing clatter and shatter into the window. A million little shards of glass fell to the porch floor, freeing a ghost of a curtain to flutter in the breeze. "Now we can go inside."

Ekhard cleared the broken glass from the base of the window then leaped into the darkened house. Caryn thought better of climbing through the window and tried the door handle. Unlocked. The front door groaned as she pushed it open. "You could have just . . ." but Ekhard was nowhere to be seen. To her right, the living room had some broken furniture. At first glance, she thought there was an animal curled up on a ripped sofa, but it was only the cotton stuffing exploding from the couch cushions. She flicked a switch; lights didn't work.

From another room, Caryn heard the crash of something breaking. It sounded like Ekhard was in the kitchen. She entered with an arm over her eyes to protect them from flying debris. Torn wallpaper peeled from the wall, and there was the smell of mildew and old wood. And smoke.

He reached into the cabinets and scooped the dishes onto the counter, letting them break. Then he picked one up and, threw it like a Frisbee at the wall. *Crash!*

"What are you doing?" Caryn ducking as pieces of china flew toward her.

He dropped the hammer on a small stack of plates, turning his face away from it as he did. "What's it look like?"

Caryn took another chug of bourbon and set the bottle in the sink. "So this is, like, our house, isn't it? If it belonged to Anna Clare?"

"That's right. She told me her mother died here. No one bought the place. She married Dad because she had no place else to go."

Ekhard took the flashlight from Caryn and shone it inside the cabinets. His free hand swept the pans, cups, and jars of ancient goo to the floor. He ripped off the wall a spice rack with little containers of seasonings. The pile grew.

Caryn looked into another closed cabinet and found a fresh bag of bread. "Eks?"

"What's that?" They gazed in wonderment at the unlikely find.

"It's fresh," she said.

"Does that mean someone lives here?"

Caryn laughed. "This place is a pit. There isn't even electricity."

Ekhard tipped the bottle back again, then set it on the counter. "Let's look around." He led the way to the top of the steep staircase, where he took a sharp turn to the right.

Caryn was already woozy from the bourbon, but she was sure that she smelled smoke. Three doors in the hall were closed, and the smell of smoke grew stronger.

"Smell that?" Ekhard asked.

"I think someone's here," she answered.

Ekhard held the flashlight in one hand and the steel hammer in his other. He nodded to Caryn, telling her to open the first door. A closet. The two bumped into each other in the cramped hallway, and a boozy giggle erupted from her throat.

A floorboard creaked. The noise came from the farthest room.

With his elbow, Ekhard nudged Caryn and pointed the light at that door.

Unafraid, Caryn opened the door like a hurricane wind. She exploded into the room, and Ekhard fell in behind her. On entry, they heard a high-pitched shriek.

Ekhard pointed the flashlight on a small Weber grill. It was staged in the middle of the floor with pieces of wood burning in it. A dirty sleeping bag and a backpack lay to the side of it, as if someone had been sitting there. Candy wrappers and an opened carton of milk lay beside them. He shone the light around the room. The roof was missing from this portion of the house where high wind or a tornado might have taken it some years ago.

Caryn heard shuffling. Ekhard pushed her, and she wobbled, pliant. The flashlight bounced to a point behind them, and she saw a shoe behind the door where they had entered.

It was a dirty blue trainer or jogging shoe, and it was filled with a dirty sock. A leg wearing frayed jeans was attached to the foot. Caryn took the flashlight from her brother. Her breathing was shallow.

Ekhard began wheezing, then he coughed. Someone whined, and Ekhard lifted the hammer into the air above his head. He nudged Caryn toward the open door. With one hand, she slammed the door shut.

Now exposed, a girl about the same age as they were screamed. She was dirty and thin. A runaway, Caryn thought. Her frizzy brown hair looked like it hadn't been washed in weeks.

"What are you doing here?" Caryn asked, trying to sound threatening.

"I don't have no place to go." The girl's voice quavered.

"Get out," she said. "This is my house. You can't stay here."

"I don't have no place else." The girl stepped toward Caryn.

"Stay back," Caryn said, lifting her hand. Behind her, Ekhard held the hammer high. It made her braver.

"You can't stay here," Ekhard repeated.

The runaway looked from Caryn to Ekhard, then lunged at Caryn with her hands at her face. Caryn dropped the flashlight on the floor to fight with her fists. She punched at the girl's heavy coat, then reached for her hair. The girl raised a hand. Something in it glistened. *A knife?* Caryn's heart pounded against her ribs as she stumbled backward and tripped on the sleeping bag. She fell on her back, and right away the girl was on top of her. The knife flashed in the firelight, and she tried to catch the girl's hand. Caryn wrestled to grab the blade, holding her opponent's arm in a tight grip. She struggled to keep her away, but the girl had gravity on her side. She pressed the knife into Caryn's throat, cutting.

"Get off her!" Ekhard screamed. He swung the hammer at the back of the girl's head.

CHAPTER 40

MORGAN

Morgan had waited until she was in her rented Toyota to open the envelope Rebecca wanted her to have. Inside, Rebecca had placed a signed credit card receipt from a steak house in Lafayette, Indiana. The signature was unmistakable. In a tidy cursive, it said *Nathaniel E. Johnson.*

He had paid for a dinner for two and a bottle of wine.

Morgan's heartbeat sped up at the discovery.

It was the weekend before Thanksgiving, and she came in to work early, calling Donnie on the way. His weekends were sacred, she understood. But she had woken up in the middle of the night and compared photos of Nathaniel Johnson from the Baker and Baker website with pictures of Ekhard Klein from his high school yearbook. Ekhard was a blonde, while Nathaniel had darker hair. Otherwise their square jaws were identical. So were the amber-brown eyes and angular noses.

Morgan had filed for a warrant to search Nathaniel Johnson's house. While waiting for it, she sat hunched behind her unusually cluttered desk where file folders and paperwork buried the metal surface. On top, photos of bloody, ravaged bodies were spread in a geisha's fan. At her feet, boxes filled with loose ends were stamped with the year 2004. As she was flipping through a six-inch stack of paperwork in her lap, Lieutenant Holbrooke appeared at her left.

"Morgan!" she exclaimed. "That address you inquired about? A report came in this morning from the city of Lafayette. Last night a woman was attacked with a hammer at that house. Tippecanoe County PD answered the call."

The lieutenant had Morgan's undivided attention. In her pressed navy blue pantsuit, she was an intimidating law officer.

She continued, "The woman escaped but wished to remain anonymous and never gave her name. Go check it out. Now!"

Morgan flew out of her chair. "Tell them I'm en route."

"You'll have the warrant before you get there."

On her way, she called Donnie. "I'm on my way to Nathaniel Johnson's house. Donnie, he *is* Ekhard. Listen, I don't expect you to drop what you're doing with your family today. I'll call when I get done and give you a report."

"Swing by my place. I'll drive," he said.

Over the last few hours, freezing rain had sealed seven counties in a hard, icy crust. But the drive to 6818 Hyacinth Court in Lafayette took twice as long due to incompetent drivers, not weather conditions. Donnie ground his back teeth the whole way.

"Stop that. I can hear you." Morgan was riding in the passenger seat.

"Sorry. Can't help it."

"What's bothering you?"

"Angie is taking a small turkey over to her parents' house this afternoon. We're doing an early Thanksgiving dinner since they're going on vacation next week." Donnie's grip on the steering wheel whitened his knuckles.

"I don't know how you do it all." Morgan gazed out the ice-coated window. Windshield wipers pushed half-frozen slush out of the way.

"Hey, I signed up for this. My girls and Angie are what really matters."

"To me catching this killer is the most important thing. I won't stop till it's done, Donnie."

"I admire that about you. So tell me what we're walking into here."

Morgan told him that she had called Tippecanoe PD. Though no one was home when police arrived, fresh blood on the front doorknob gave officers at the scene enough reason to enter. Based on what they found at the scene, she and Donnie were granted access.

Blinking holiday lights decorated many homes on Hyacinth Court although it was daylight. The holiday decorations gave sparkle to police vans, a dozen black-and-whites, and two television news vans that lined the street. Donnie parked behind a black SUV and shut off the engine. Tree limbs glistened with sparkling ice that reflected a billion red and green lights from someone's holiday display.

Cautiously, they exited the SUV to step onto slippery pavement. Across the street, a half-dozen giant inflatable Christmas decorations filled a neighbor's yard. A cheerful snowman smiled. An oversized Santa waved a floppy arm under the weight of an icy layer. The rest puffed and twinkled—a surreal scene. From the front window of one house a couple smiled and waved at her.

"Excellent. The crime scene has become someone's holiday entertainment." Morgan didn't wave back. Careful of the ice, she took short strides.

Hard ice pellets bounced off Donnie's shoulders and stuck in his hair.

An officer shook a bag of salt on the slanted driveway. "Happy Holidays, right?" his tone was more acidic than cheerful.

"Yeah, whatever," Donnie replied.

The faded-green front door had been taped open and the doorknob removed for evidence. Inside, Morgan brushed the water and ice off her red winter jacket, creating a shower on the already wet floor.

"Checking in?" A female officer sat at a folding table, a makeshift desk in the entryway.

"Detective Jewell from Indy Metro homicide."

The woman in the entrance wrote on a log, then handed the clipboard to her to sign.

"Detective Jewell, I'm Lieutenant Hanne. Call me Henry." Not much taller than Morgan, he shook her two fingers with a limp hand. "Hope the drive wasn't terrible."

"It sucked," Donnie said. "Shall we get on to business? The roads aren't getting any better. And I have to get back by two."

"All right then." With hands on his hips, Henry turned around in the small entryway.

Nathaniel lived simply. Except for one worn-out recliner, there was no other seating in the living room to Morgan's right. Beside the chair there was one small table and, across the room, a large television. There was no clutter. No decorations, garbage, or beer bottles. No newspapers or books. None of the normal stuff of living lay around this room.

"Has the woman who called come forward?" Morgan asked.

"No. We'll get forensics to sweep for DNA." He waved a hand toward the front door. "When we know her identity, the DA may use her as a key witness."

Morgan's fingertips caressed the notebook in her pocket as she remembered the coffee cup she had sent to forensics.

Henry scratched his thinning gray hair. "We're checking with local hospitals. No one has reported injuries like what you've seen with this hammer killer investigation."

Donnie poked through drawers in the kitchen. "Have you arrested the homeowner?"

"Nathaniel Johnson is MIA."

"Nathaniel Johnson is a false identity," Morgan explained. "His name is actually Ekhard Marcus Klein. He's the suspect, the unsub we're looking for. He's been at this for a long time."

Henry added more details. "His car is gone, and he's just changed jobs. Doesn't seem to have any friends. We know of a gym membership, nothing else."

"Send out an APB out on this guy. His picture is going viral," Donnie said. She peered down the hallway at the photos on the wall.

"You'd think he grew up here," Henry said.

"He's only lived here four years," Morgan informed him.

"Where was he before that?"

"We don't know yet. He's changed his identity at least twice in the last twenty years. It's likely that he's moved around the state as his identity changed." The name Larry Milhouse came to Morgan's mind again.

"What did you want to show me, Lieutenant?"

"Come with me." Henry led the way through the kitchen and down a carpeted basement staircase to a lower rec room that had seen better days. Orange carpet dated the room. Dark-red fuzzy wallpaper completed the look. The only furniture, a few dining chairs, sat against one wall. Stacks of boxes had been opened by the police.

"Nice room," Morgan said. "Where's the mirrored disco ball?"

Donnie lifted a photo album out of one box and flipped through it. Morgan peered over his arm at pictures of children on the beach with a woman.

"That's Anna Clare," she said.

"She looks just like Caryn, Ekhard's sister," Donnie said. "Family albums? Is that why we're here?" Donnie tossed the heavy book onto the floor.

"Come this way." Lieutenant Hanne led her through another door to a small utility room with a concrete floor. The furnace and electrical box hid one wall. On the left, white pegboard stretched the length of the room upon which a collection of hammers formed a perfectly straight line.

The breath went out of Morgan.

"I heard about you and that Hallie Marks case. I thought you'd want to see this," Henry said.

Morgan stepped closer to the wall, her hand raised to within inches of a stainless steel, blue-handled utility hammer with something dark smeared on the head.

"Send them to Indy, to Olivia Hawthorne at Metro Homicide. We need DNA testing on the . . ." She couldn't finish. Ten hammers hung in the row. Two new ones with the price tags still attached lay on the bench.

Donnie's mouth hung open.

"There are more than we thought," Morgan said, her eyes wide.

CHAPTER 41

CARYN

Caryn needed to act out. The impulse to hit something or someone overwhelmed her along with that other feeling she hated—loneliness. That was what triggered her anger. Ekhard had betrayed her. He had abandoned her. And Caryn had decided after her mom left that no one would ever do that to her again. Since she kicked Mack out, Caryn hadn't seen him. He'd sounded hurt when he left that morning. What did he expect? He was a married man. In fact, that was the reason Caryn was with him. It kept him at bay. It ensured that his first relationship was with his wife, *not* with Caryn.

Yet, as her anger grew, Mack was the closest thing to a target that she could think of.

In Carmel, a suburb of Indianapolis where the upper crust of the city lived, the Rapture at 86 West was meticulously managed, stroked, and tenderly loved by Gilroy Mackintosh. And to say that this boutique hotel was his baby was an understatement. It was his life. No wonder his marriage was in jeopardy.

Like the pretentious residents of this suburb, Caryn walked in with her head high and her chest inflated. She pretended she was a paying guest. "I'd like a word with the manager," she said to the host at the front desk.

The middle-aged man wore a black suit and a gray vest with a silky dark-blue tie. "Are you a guest at the hotel?" he asked with a bit of a Southern drawl.

"I most certainly am." Torn between making a big show of herself or remaining innocuous and invisible the way Mack liked her, Caryn opted for tactic number one. "Don't you know who I am?" She didn't wish to be swept under the rug.

"I'm sorry, ma'am," he replied, weakly.

"My name's Caryn Klein. I'm staying in the executive suite on the sixteenth floor. I've got a problem, and I need the manager." She doubted he would look up the guest staying in that room. Luckily, she was correct.

"Is there something I can help you with, Ms. Klein?"

"No. Only Mr. Mackintosh can solve this problem. Get him for me, now!" Caryn clicked the heels of her intimidating, pointy black high heels into the tile floor. Her hands remained in the pockets of a long khaki-colored trench coat.

"Yes, ma'am. I'll page him for you."

Joshua Groff, according to his name tag, picked up a phone and dialed three digits. "Mr. Mackintosh, could you come to the front desk please? Ms. Klein from room 1605 is here to see you."

Joshua hung up the phone. "He'll be right out."

Hunched over and glancing furtively around the lobby, Mack appeared with reproach in his eyes. "What are you doing here?" he mumbled under his breath.

Caryn kept up her act. Holding out her hand for a handshake, she introduced herself. Mack left his hand at his side.

She spoke loudly so the reservation desk employee could hear. "Mr. Mackintosh, I have a problem to address with you. The bed in my room is unsuitable."

Mack grabbed her by the arm and, pulling her like a scolded child, ducked into his office. Once the door was firmly closed, he repeated, "What are you doing here?"

Without answering, Caryn unbuttoned her coat. She pulled it to the side and placed her hands on her bare hips. Strategically, she was wearing nothing but a tiny black thong underneath.

Mack let out a moan. "Jesus, Caryn."

"Jesus had nothing to do with this. I came to apologize."

Mack couldn't resist. He rested his cool hands on her warm hips. "Apologies are out of character for you, aren't they?"

"Bad behavior runs in my family."

Mack's frown turned upward as his eyes lit up, but the light quickly dimmed. He looked at his watch and backed away, then fell into the black leather recliner in the corner of his office. "You can't be here. Erin's coming into work at eleven today."

"Tending bar?" she asked.

Mack nodded. "Yes. But she'll come in here first, into my office. She always does."

"So?" Caryn lifted her leg over the arm of the wide, worn chair and joined Mack in the fat recliner, squeezing in behind him. She put her hands on his shoulders and pressed, giving him a light massage.

"So, it's ten forty-five." He leaned back and turned, burying his face in her neck.

Her arms wrapped around Mack as she nuzzled against him. He turned around to face her with one foot on the floor and one knee on the cushion of the chair. His hand moved up her flat belly, stopping at her breasts. Caryn relaxed back into the chair. In doing so, the recliner tilted backward with their weight.

Mack braced himself with one hand on the back of the chair. Then he reached for the tilt lever and, lifting his foot off the ground, laid the chair in its fully reclined position with the footrest out.

Caryn looked up at Mack balanced on his hands and knees over her. "That gives us fifteen minutes." She reached for his belt. While she unfastened it, Mack pressed his lips against hers, then reached behind Caryn with his arm and, in one awkward movement, slid underneath her and switched positions with her. Now she was kneeling over his body as he reclined on his back.

"I'll make it the best fifteen minutes of your life." Caryn peeled back Mack's pants, allowing him freedom from the confines of his jeans and boxers. He sprung loose. The coat came off with a flap of her arms, falling into a pile on the floor beside the recliner.

She hooked her thong with two fingers and straddled Mack. As she settled over his pillar, she rocked with the chair, back and forth.

Mack closed his eyes and moaned.

CHAPTER 42

CARYN

Five, twelve, ten, and ten. Caryn counted the steps to her condo. At her door, she had an unusual sense that something was wrong. It worried her that Ekhard had threatened her. All the way home from Mack's hotel, she had watched in the rear-view mirror for Eks's car following her. She'd looked for it in the condo parking lot, just in case. In his house, he had glared at her as if she were prey. His eyelids narrowed and he focused on . . . *her hands?* His lip curled into a snarl when he threatened her life.

Inside, the condo building was quiet. Not even the sound of her neighbors' TV could be heard. Upon turning the key to her place, she found the deadbolt unlocked. *Have I forgotten to lock it? Not likely. Was Mack inside again?* She turned the handle slowly and pushed the door open.

"Mack? Are you here?" Caryn peered inside, then set her briefcase on the floor before turning on the light. Her kitchen looked exactly as she had left it. She tiptoed to the pantry where she kept a toolbox and silently lifted out a long steel hammer. With it in her hand, she stopped to listen.

No unusual sounds. A used red coffee cup from the morning sat near the sink with a white kitchen towel folded next to it. A dirty pot from boiled pasta on Thursday night remained full of dishwater in the sink. Other odds and ends—a couple of fine-tipped pens, her solar calculator, and a pad of paper, unopened mail, bills, and credit card proposals—were spread out on the island.

The living room looked the same as she had left it too. Still, the door had been unlocked. In her stomach a knot seemed to grow to the size of a golf ball. With the hammer gripped and ready to swing, Caryn checked the voice mail on her landline.

"Hi, Caryn. Are you home?" Annoying Brad. How many times had she regretted giving him her phone number?

"A detective asked about you this morning. What's that about? I hope you're not in any trouble. What did she want? She wouldn't tell me, but I don't like the police asking questions. The other residents might get scared." There was a long pause before he continued. "You know my number, right? I'll try again later . . ." *Beep.*

She hung her trench coat on the coatrack, then slipped out of her high-heeled shoes and kicked them into the corner. News that a detective had stopped by didn't faze her in the least. Confident that she'd given Detective Jewell just the right amount of misdirection, Caryn didn't worry about her.

Beep. "This is Brad again. I told your brother you'd be back soon." Caryn's blood ran cold. *Ekhard was here? Eks found out where I live.*

"He was such a nice guy. I didn't know you had a brother. I invited him over for a brewski. Anyway, when you get in, call me."

Ekhard had been here. The idea of him creeping around her place gave her goosebumps. In the bedroom, her mother's faded white jewelry box had been opened. Dumped out, the contents of the box were scattered across the dresser. Caryn didn't wear the jewelry. What she kept inside were personal items collected from special people in her life. A collection of memories. In order to assess the strewn contents, Caryn set down the hammer with a loud clunk. What would Eks have taken?

She placed the pair of pearl earrings that had belonged to a friend from college back in the bottom corner behind Amy Dufresne's monogrammed pen set. She had stolen the earrings so long ago that she couldn't remember the girl's name. The locket with the initials H.J.M. was here too. She had been fantastic in bed. Caryn counted; seven items collected. One, the most important piece of the collection, was missing. Where was the pink-heart pendant?

Irritation incited ire. Then fury rose, heating Caryn's face and neck. She tore her sweater off and hugged herself, fingernails digging into the backs of her arms. That pendant was part of her collection. Wired and fired up, Caryn paced. He threatened to kill me.

Fucking Ekhard.

* * *

"I'm telling you, Mack, someone broke into my condo." Caryn's tone was frantic, panicked.

Through the cell phone Mack whispered, "I'm in the middle of something right now."

His quiet voice infuriated her. "You're busy?" Caryn shouted. "How can you be busy now? What's more important than me?"

"I can't get away," he said. Then turned away from the receiver he said, "It's nothing, honey. A minor hiccup at work."

I've just been reduced to a hiccup. "Is she there? Are you with her?" Caryn heard shuffling on the other end of the line.

"Call the cops. File a report. I can't help you right now," he said.

"I mean . . ." Caryn inhaled deeply, switching gears. She wanted—no, needed—Mack here. She softened her tone and lowered her voice. "I'm scared, Mack. Can you please come?" She begged with the most helpless, needy voice she could muster. "Please, Mack, I need you."

"Hold on."

Caryn waited. He must have moved out of Erin's earshot.

"Look, you caught me at a bad time. Erin asked the neighbors over for dinner. She just got home from the grocery and I'm cooking dinner. I've got two frying pans going and . . ." He paused. "What was taken?"

"Nothing. I checked the whole apartment. I still have everything." *Except for one very personal part of my collection.*

She didn't tell him she had found her jewelry box opened and its contents strewn across her dresser. In the grand scheme of things, the pendant was insignificant in terms of value. Still, she treasured it. "My class ring from IU is the most valuable thing I own, and it wasn't stolen," she said.

"It doesn't matter. At the least, call the office of your condo association and tell them someone broke in. Maybe others in your building have reported a break-in too. They have security cameras. They might be able to identify the guy."

That didn't matter. She knew Ekhard had done it. The only thing she wanted was for Mack to come over and baby her. For him to prove his devotion.

CHAPTER 43

MORGAN

The Toyota made record time driving to Lafayette. Morgan decided this car could make her very happy.

The Baker and Baker accounting firm was located in a brand-new building on the posh side of town. The glass and chrome furnishings, the quiet conference rooms with long walnut tables and leather chairs, suggested that the firm attracted high-paying customers.

Cheryl Baker had given Morgan access to Nathaniel's notes, computer, and billing software. Sitting at what used to be his desk, Morgan waded through file cabinets full of his clients' information. She was looking for a something—anything—to connect him to Fay.

"He kept very good records." Cheryl leaned on the door jam. Her perfectly sprayed, rounded hairdo looked stiff and unnatural.

"I see that." Morgan leaned back and stretched her arms overhead.

"Have you found anything?"

No one could find Ekhard. And now Nathaniel was missing too. "I haven't found what I'm looking for," she admitted to Cheryl.

"Is there any way I can help?" Cheryl's lace-trimmed blouse made her look much older than Morgan thought she was.

"Have you ever heard of a man named Ekhard Klein?"

When Cheryl shook her head, her hair didn't move.

"How about Hallie Marks?" Morgan asked.

"Oh sure. I hired Hallie to help us redecorate. We recently moved from another location to this one. We needed some updates."

"Mrs. Baker, where did Nathaniel Johnson go?"

"He wanted to branch out. He's started working for himself in Danville. Of course, he wasn't allowed to take any of his clients from here. He claimed to have formed a client base on his own."

"Danville?" Morgan took a breath and held it. Danville was where Hallie lived.

"That's right."

"How long did he work here?"

"About six years."

*   *   *

Morgan took from Ekhard's office what would fit in the rented car. She spent the rest of the afternoon and most of the night looking through his files—looking for any evidence to connect him more than superficially to Hallie or Suzanne. Early in the morning she came across a familiar name. Jennifer Delacourt. It may have been lack of solid sleep, or it may have been a real clue. Donnie would probably think this was way off base, because Morgan's judgment was slipping. She knew he was right.

Six years ago, Jenny Delacourt had owned a flower shop, and Nathaniel—Ekhard—had kept the books for her. That year, she was attacked by blunt force to her face and hands. The case had been big news, and Morgan had heard of it because Stan Williams was the detective at the crime scene. Jenny had lived through the criminal attack but refused to implicate her boyfriend. The case was recorded as a random attack. Now, Morgan didn't think so.

When she returned to work the next day, Morgan told Donnie about it. "When I called this morning, the folks at Beauty Blossoms said he had worked for them. Jenny was the manager at the florist when he did their books. She was attacked and hospitalized the year he worked for them."

Morgan continued, "The assailant crushed her face and hands. Her hands were smashed so badly that one had to be amputated. Poor woman didn't die. Once her insurance money ran out, she wasn't able to afford any of the medical procedures she needed."

Donnie drew his eyebrows together. "Not this again . . ."

"Just give me a second, will you?"

Exasperated, Donnie leaned back and shook his head.

She continued, ignoring his attitude. "In my notes, Delacourt told the Marion County DA that she didn't want to file against the attacker. Claimed she was in love."

Donnie's lips curled in disbelief. "Why don't I remember that case?"

Morgan replied, "Stanley Williams was assigned to it. I read his notes. Her cheekbone was shattered and both her hands."

"Jesus."

Morgan shrugged. "She was faced with fourteen reconstructive surgeries."

Donnie leaned forward. "Did she ever identify the guy?"

"Not even when one of her hands was amputated." Morgan flipped a page in her booklet. "Her boyfriend claimed she was having an affair, which she denied. She told them it was a random attack."

"I don't get the connection. Who was arrested?"

Morgan pushed her black blazer aside and put a hand on her hip. "No one."

Donnie twiddled his pen. "Explain this to me. How did Jenny Delacourt get away?" Morgan's mouth opened wide, letting a yawn escape. She couldn't hide the fact that she wasn't getting any sleep. At this point she didn't care. "Jenny didn't get away. She was left to die."

"I'm not seeing it. I think he would have finished the deed."

Morgan wasn't so sure. "Depends on the circumstances."

"Couldn't you find anything else to implicate Ekhard?"

"No. I want to interview Jenny." She closed her kitten notebook and stuffed it back into her pants pocket.

"Uh-uh." Donnie pursed his lips and shook his head. "Go home and sleep this one off. Stanley won't give you the case."

Morgan knew that Donnie didn't like Stanley because of what he'd put Morgan and every other woman in the precinct through. However, she wanted to at least ask him. Though she didn't know him well, Stan couldn't be as bad as they said.

Donnie's attention shifted to the mess on his desk. As he began shuffling through papers, he reorganized the flat-pile filing system. It was his way of telling Morgan to go ahead and do what she needed to do. "And don't schedule another evening interview, please. The girls have tennis matches every weekend, and Angie wants . . ."

"I know. I know." She took a scolding posture, placing both hands on her hips, though she wasn't much taller than Donnie sitting down. "You have your family. I'll make sure it's during the workday."

He moved piles, avoiding her gaze.

"Thanks, Donnie." Relieved that he'd come around, she lifted the photo of Suzanne Aiken from the top pile. "Jenny was lying. It's here in my notes. It wasn't a random slaying. For certain, she was scared."

CHAPTER 44

MORGAN: 16 Years Ago

The next morning, Morgan showered and dressed as if in a dream. She washed her hair and scrubbed her hands, while wondering where Fay could be. Something about Fay finding a boyfriend had upset Morgan, but now she couldn't remember.

After they'd filled the car with the rest of her boxes and suitcase, Morgan's mother called Mrs. Ramsey. Morgan listened to the muffled conversation from outside the kitchen. When her mother hung up, she came into the dining room and sat facing Morgan. Her furrowed brow and downturned mouth spoke more than she could say.

"She didn't come home, did she?" Morgan asked, dreading the answer.

That day, instead of checking in at the dorms, Morgan and her parents drove to the Ramseys' house. A police officer had swung by at Victoria's request, but it was too early to file a missing person's report. The officer took a few details, gave them business cards, and left.

"This is your fault, Morgan," Victoria accused.

"Now come on, Vic. That's not fair." Morgan's dad defended her.

Morgan shrank. "Mrs. Ramsey, I don't know where she went last night. She didn't call me."

"Mo was home last night," her mother added.

Victoria flew into a tirade, blaming Morgan by default for influencing Fay with alcohol. Morgan shrank from the weight of it. If their parents found out about the pot, they would be in more trouble. The burden and worry sank her even further.

While her parents argued with Mrs. Ramsey, Morgan slinked out of the room. Perhaps she could glean something by looking through Fay's things. She pushed open the door and peered into her sunny, bright-yellow bedroom.

Unlike Morgan's bedroom, Fay's was spotless. Morgan's heart jumped to her throat. The bed was covered with a flowery bedspread without a single wrinkle. Pink and yellow pillows on top supported a handful of stuffed animals: four teddy bears given to her by her dad before he died and one orange monkey that she had won at the amusement park with Morgan. Despite transitioning to college—*that was supposed to be today*—Fay had one box sealed shut on the floor beside her desk. No papers or books covered the surface of her painted pink desk. The only other evidence of moving was Fay's suitcase on the window ledge with clothes folded in tight little squares inside. Socks rolled into perfect balls lined the edges.

Morgan swallowed the dust in her mouth. Fay had a calendar. She did nothing without writing it on her calendar or making a list. Morgan opened the desk drawer, causing a row of blue pens to roll away. On the left, she saw Fay's closed Day-Timer.

"Morgan are you upstairs?" her mother called from the stairway.

Morgan dragged the fat book out and opened it to August as footsteps thundered up the stairs. All three adults were looking for her. She flipped the pages to yesterday's entry, tore the page from the book, and shoved it in her pants pocket.

"What are you doing in here?" Not a slender woman, Vic filled the doorway. "Leave her things alone," she barked. Morgan closed the calendar and placed it back inside the drawer.

"Get out," Vic said.

Behind her, Morgan's parents beckoned her. "Let's go, honey. There's nothing we can do here. Fay will call when she gets home."

"Not if I have anything to say about it. Stay away from her. It's your fault she's gone. I blame you, Morgan Jewell."

CHAPTER 45

CARYN

The sun shone brightly, melting ice on the edges of the pavement and lawn. Caryn could see her breath in the early winter air. A week before Thanksgiving, pumpkins and fall decorations sparkled with the glaze. With her back to the lobby entrance, she stood in the parking lot of the Rapture at 86 West Hotel and heard Mack jogging to meet her.

"Caryn, you okay? Sorry about last night. The neighbors stayed late."

Caryn didn't answer. Her breath puffed lingering clouds as she folded her arms across her heart. No room for access.

"I said I'm sorry." With his hands entrenched deep in his pockets, Mack waited.

She was angry. *Since when does Erin take precedence over my needs?*

"I don't understand why you think your brother did it. I'm sure the break-in wasn't personal. I think it will be okay," Mack said.

She didn't need his feather fluffing. She was no injured bird. She was angry and didn't want him to lift her back up. The urge to take it out on something or someone was a powerful aphrodisiac. Hands balled into rock-hard fists, Caryn stepped away from Mack.

Mack looked down at his feet. In a low whisper, he asked, "Since when do you have a brother?"

Caryn turned with a fist in the air. "Since I was born, asshole."

216

Mack backed away. "I didn't know. How would I know? You never talk about him."

"I don't talk about him because I haven't seen him." Aware she could be caught in her deception, she added, "I don't see him. What do you think? I'm hiding it from you?"

Mack looked her in the eye, doubtful.

"My brother is no longer in my life and there's a reason for that."

"I'm sorry. Look, no one is judging you here. Come back inside, okay? Stop making a scene." Mack surreptitiously looked behind him.

Caryn knew he worried what people thought of him. He'd been careful to conceal their relationship. Arguing with her outside the hotel might ruin his image. And his marriage. She didn't care.

"Erin's not working the bar till five o'clock today. Come in and have a drink. I'm buying."

"No thanks." His lame offer didn't appeal to her.

"I won't let it happen again. I promise," he said. The apology would have had more impact if he had groveled on his knees.

Caryn paced, crunching through the layer of ice near the curb, releasing the water that ran beneath it. "Erin doesn't bother me. It's the fact that you don't care what's going on with me." She let her voice carry.

"Then tell me what's going on." Hotel patrons glanced their way. He lowered his voice to a raspy tone. "Can we go inside?"

"The police asked me questions about him."

His eyebrows drew together. As he peered at the hotel entrance behind them, he asked, "What on earth for?"

She threw a hand in the air. "Nothing. It doesn't matter." She would not tell him the dull saga of Ekhard and Suzanne.

"Then help me. What is going on?"

"I found him! I found my fucking brother! I know where he lives! You don't understand what that means!"

"You're right. I don't. But I'm here for you if you need me." Mack patted Caryn's back through her black wool peacoat.

To Caryn, it felt icky. She slithered away from him. "Don't."

Frustrated, Mack animatedly shook his hands in the air. "Then what do you want from me? I don't know what you want from me. Is it a good thing you found him? Is it a bad thing? I'm drowning, Caryn. Help me out."

Mack could never understand the relationship she had with Ekhard. And Caryn didn't really care about his acceptance. But at the same time she was afraid she was losing Mack too. Because of that fear, rage bubbled just under the surface. To abate it, she wanted—no needed—Mack to come back to her.

Looking him directly in the eye for the first time in a week, she said, "My brother, Ekhard, is a murderer."

CHAPTER 46

CARYN: 22 Years Ago

Their laughter penetrated the bedroom walls. Caryn wouldn't have minded except that Ekhard wasn't getting anything done. With Suzanne around, he hadn't completed any of his college applications.

"And when she stood up, there were smashed potatoes on the back of her skirt." Caryn had listened to the whole story Suzanne told.

Eks laughed as if it was the funniest thing he'd ever heard. They were in Ekhard's room with the door closed. From what Caryn could tell, they weren't getting any homework done. And she wasn't either. Now she was fuming mad.

Caryn slammed her pencil down on her painted white desk. It had become quiet in his room again, but every time Caryn thought she could get back to work, they started in again. Like now.

"Eks, I have to get a good grade or my dad is going to kill me," Suzanne said.

Yeah right, Caryn thought. Our dad used to kill Ekhard on a regular basis. She couldn't count the number of times her brother had nursed a black eye or swollen jaw.

Ekhard told Caryn that he felt sorry for Suzanne. It was his reason for doing her homework for her. Three or four evenings a week they spent together, hanging out, doing her homework, or just talking. When she wasn't visiting, Eks took care of Dad. His health was declining and he needed a slew of medicines. And he could never remember what or when because of the bourbon. Now Ekhard was falling behind. His grades were suffering, and Caryn knew how important it was to him to get into college.

"You need a beginning, a middle, and an end. All the facts are here, but the report needs more organization." Ekhard explained to Suzanne.

"I get that, but I'm no good at writing. It gets jumbled up in my head."

Everything gets jumbled up in Suzanne's little head, Caryn thought.

He said, "I know. That's why I'm helping."

She was a junior and still didn't know how to write a paper. Caryn didn't think Suzanne would get it now. Ekhard was wasting his time.

"Wait, what are you doing?"

Caryn turned her head. She wasn't getting any homework done either. Their voices carrying from the other room were distracting her.

"Let me fix my pants."

"I'll fix them for you."

Pants? This was the last straw. Caryn would not allow her brother to get that stupid girl pregnant. He had more important things to do with his life. Suzanne would ruin it for him if she stuck around. If Mom was here, she'd make sure he got his work done. And if Dad wasn't drunk, he might care about it too. Without parental supervision, it was up to Caryn to draw the line.

Caryn stood up so fast her desk chair tipped over. She rounded the corner and stomped down the hall to her brother's room, where the door was closed. She didn't stop to listen or knock before blasting into the room. The door slammed against the wall, making a round hole where the doorknob hit the wall.

Suzanne shrieked. She was on her knees in between Ekhard's legs. His pants were down around his ankles.

"What the hell are you doing?" Ekhard's eyes were as round as quarters.

"What are *you* doing?" Caryn was livid. "You're not going to fuck up your life for this," she waved an arm toward Suzanne.

Ekhard said, "It's none of your damn business what I do!" While Suzanne wiped her face on her sweater sleeve, Caryn decided she'd deal with the problem herself. She reached for Suzanne's head and grabbed a handful of hair.

Suzanne screamed, "Stop it! Let go!"

But Caryn would not. She pulled her by the hair down the stairs then threw her on the floor. On her hands and knees, Suzanne cried out, "You bitch!" Her hands rubbed the top of her scalp.

Caryn had lost her patience. She opened the door and violently shoved the protesting girl out onto the stoop. Then she slammed and locked the door. Muffled screams came from outside in the yard as Suzanne howled and complained.

"What'd you do that for?" Ekhard asked from the top of the stairs.

Caryn spun around to face him. "She's toying with you, Ekhard. Can't you see that? She is playing you like a guitar. Don't you have enough to do with your own homework and taking care of Dad? Graduate high school. You have to, so you can get a job."

* * *

Two weeks later Suzanne was back at the house. Around her neck hung a silver and pink pendant. A heart. Caryn knew that Ekhard had given it to her. Since Caryn's tantrum, Suzanne had avoided coming over, though Caryn still saw them holding hands in the school hallway between classes. He had told Caryn that Suzanne was coming over and threatened to beat the shit out of her if she did anything this time. He'd done it before, fought Caryn. He'd gripped her index finger and snapped it all the way back like Mom used to do.

In their kitchen, Suzanne helped with dinner. She made spaghetti sauce from scratch and garlic bread to go with it. Ekhard sat at the table trying to get caught up with homework. Next to him, Caryn helped him balance Dad's checkbook while he finished his college essays.

"What's she doing here?" Caryn asked.

With her gaze narrowed, Suzanne looked up from stirring the pasta, "Don't come near me, bitch."

Ekhard put a hand up to stop them both. "She's here to do my calculus homework."

"Beauty queen can do math?" Caryn crossed her arms and glowered at the shiny pink pendant dangling at Suzanne's throat.

"At least he'll have something to turn in," Suzanne said defensively.

"I can do your calculus. And I'll get you a better grade." Caryn pointed past her brother at the sheet Suzanne had left on the table. "That one's wrong. This one, the answer is . . ."

"Stop it, Ceecee. I don't care about the grade." Ekhard put his hands on the table.

To Suzanne, Caryn said, "Why don't you go home to your perfect life and your perfect parents?"

"What's your problem, anyway?" Suzanne asked.

"You're using him," Caryn said.

"Forget it Ceecee," Ekhard stood up and walked over to his girlfriend.

Caryn closed the checkbook and slammed the pen down on the table. "You're using him to get back at your football-player boyfriend. Becky Lewis says so all the time."

"You don't know what you're talking about," Suzanne said.

Caryn couldn't sit still anymore, so got up from the table and confronted them in the kitchen. Jabbing her finger into Suzanne's bare shoulder, she said, "Ekhard does all your homework for you. You won't be able to graduate without him."

"Shut up, bitch." Suzanne cowered behind Ekhard. "You touch me again and I'm calling the cops."

Looking around for something to throw, Caryn lightly grabbed the nearest object, a small plate with a sauce-covered spoon in it. She flung plate and spoon into the corner. As it shattered, Suzanne covered her face with her arms, elbows pulled together to form a shield.

Ekhard grabbed his sister by the arm. "Stop fighting! Stop it, Ceecee! Leave her alone!"

Caryn huffed and stomped out of the kitchen, retreating upstairs to her room.

CHAPTER 47

MORGAN

In the parking lot, Morgan jogged to catch up to Stan Williams. "Stan, wait."

The wiry detective looked back without stopping. His long strides and fast pace indicated he was ignoring her.

"Stan." Morgan ran—four parked cars behind him and closing.

Stan approached his yellow Dodge Charger with a black racing stripe down the center and pulled out the keys.

Morgan jogged up to him. "Hey, Stan, how's it going?"

He turned on her. "What do you want, Morgan?"

Her red blouse was heaving as she caught her breath. "I wanted to talk for a second. I meant to stop by and see you earlier today, but you were out."

Stan's hand rested on the car door handle. "Morgan Jewell wanted to see me? Has the space-time continuum completely shifted? Or was your body abducted by aliens and replaced by a sexier you?"

"It's about work, Stan."

Stan removed his hand from the car door and looked at his watch. "I'll give you one minute."

Morgan jumped right in. "I wanted to ask if you'd give me access to one of your old cases."

"Depends. Which one and how much does it mean to you?"

Morgan faltered. Stan would think this was a crazy idea. So she came right out and said, "The Jenny Delacourt case."

Stan guffawed. "That old case?" He shook his head. "Wait. Why do you want it?"

When Morgan didn't answer, he said, "Oh, I get it. You think it's related to your murder victim in Danville."

"I want to interview Jenny."

Stanley's lips spread into a devilish grin. "Sorry. Like you've said to me so, so many times before, 'not a chance in hell.'"

Morgan looked down at her feet. She had expected this. "You're joking, right? Jenny could have the answers I'm looking for. She lived through it. If I can get her to talk, she might be able to ID my murderer."

"That case was finished and filed six—was it really six years ago? Jenny Delacourt was a wreck then, and she still is. Her boyfriend beat her to within an inch of her life. He scared the shit out of her, but she'll never turn him in. Seriously, if you think her case has something to do with your silly—"

"Is it that you don't see the connection? Or you don't want to give me the case?"

Detective Williams had worked at Metro Homicide for most of his life. He never took promotions. He seemed to enjoy his job well enough but had no compulsion one way or the other to advance. For thirty years he'd been in the same position, and he liked it that way. Morgan wondered why. He must have had some reason for not retiring to the desk.

"Tit for tat, Morgan. You've never given me the time of day. So you're on your own." He turned his back on her and slid into the car.

She stayed next to the car as he started it up and rolled down the window. "Thanks, Stan," she said sarcastically.

"You're very welcome, Detective," he sneered. He put the car in reverse and backed away.

To catch a killer you have to think like one. And she wanted to interview Jenny Delacourt.

* * *

Morgan hopped in the rented Toyota, hoping to catch up to Stan in his yellow Charger. She planned to follow him—to explain her very important reasons for wanting the interview with Jenny. She'd seen him turn left out of the parking lot and, luckily, spotted the bright-colored vehicle about a block ahead. He was stopped at a light, in the left turn lane. *He's headed north,* she thought, *to the interstate.*

Her car, an innocuous gray color, would be less easy to spot—if he was watching out for her. Nevertheless, Morgan remained several car-lengths behind him once they got on the four-lane loop around Indianapolis. On the Interstate, they drove for forty minutes through slow rush-hour traffic before Stan exited on 56th Street on the west side. He continued back toward town, then turned right into an apartment complex.

Morgan kept her foot on the brake, remaining back so he didn't spot her vehicle. Recalling what she knew about Stan, he lived in a two-story house on Indy's north side—a house that was way too big for a single man. Years ago she'd been invited there with the rest of the homicide division when he hosted a holiday party. As he showed off his designer kitchen and complained about the size of the mortgage, she and Donnie had wondered how he could afford it on their salary.

After parking, he got out of his car and locked it. Morgan parked far enough away to watch without being seen. When Stan knocked on the door of one ground level apartment, a thin dark-haired woman answered. Long, pretty hair framed her round cheeks, but she seemed displeased to see him. In the doorway, they argued momentarily. She pushed him away. Stan turned, looking furtively behind him before forcing his way into her apartment.

The door closed.

While waiting, Morgan looked up the address in a database on her cell phone. The apartment was owned by Stan and leased to a woman named Chaybree Wallace. Morgan looked for more information about Chaybree, and it turned out that she had a police record. Chaybree had been arrested four times for prostitution in the last five years. She was only twenty years old.

The last time she was arrested, Morgan remembered, was during a sting operation run by Stan. He and another detective had closed in on the operation by going undercover as the "johns". Morgan thought now that it was probably a job he'd enjoyed. Six women and two men were arrested for prostitution when they broke the case. Chaybree's sentence had been lowered to a class A misdemeanor—her fine of five thousand dollars had been paid off by an un-named party.

An hour passed before Stan came out of Chaybree's apartment walking tall. The sun had gone down but streetlamps dotted the complex with big yellow circles of light. When he pulled out of the complex in his Charger, Morgan didn't follow him. This time, she went to Chaybree's door and knocked softly.

"I don't got time for more of your shit!" A woman hollered from behind the closed door.

"Chaybree, I'm a friend," Morgan said with gentle concern.

About a minute passed before Chaybree opened the door and peeped out with one eye. "What do you want?"

Morgan didn't flash her badge. "I know Stan. I know he's an asshole."

"How do you know him?"

Reluctant to let Chaybree know that Morgan was a cop, she nodded imperceptibly and admitted that she worked with him.

Chaybree let her in, keeping her gaze to the floor and one hand over her left eye. No lights were on in the cramped entryway. She closed the door and left Morgan's side, walking to a living room lit by one lamp. The young woman wore tight white shorts and loose low-cut top. To Morgan, it looked like pajamas. She flopped onto an oversized couch and tucked her legs underneath. Her left hand still covered her eye.

Morgan sat across from her in a wooden chair with a loose back. Her gaze remained full of concern for Chaybree. "Did he hit you?"

"Did you come here to talk about him?"

"If you want to talk."

Chaybree dropped her head to her chest. Silently, she began to cry.

CHAPTER 48

MORGAN

The decor in the iconic diner hadn't changed in about forty years. Jenny Delacourt sat across the table with a yellow paisley scarf pulled over her hair and tied at her chin. She kept her black puffy down coat zipped to her chin. One sleeve end was empty. With her scarred bent hand she caressed the warm cup of coffee in front of her.

Morgan felt bad about how she'd had gotten Jenny Delacourt's case files. She'd reported a fellow officer and gotten Stan suspended. After Chaybree's arrest for prostitution six months ago, Stan put her up in his apartment—appearing to do this from the generosity of his heart. He didn't ask for rent. However, Chaybree told Morgan that he stopped by three or four times a week to collect. And *rent* involved sexual favors.

Jenny Delacourt looked down into the cup, but her waxy features were hard to read. The thin lips of her mouth had been pulled tight, stretched across her face in an expression of mirth, or disdain. Or pain. Though scar tissue was minimal, the skin along her cheekbone was uneven and translucent in places, bumpy and red in others, suggesting an unfinished series of surgeries. "It's been almost six years. Six difficult years."

"I can only imagine." Sitting with one butt cheek on the bench, Morgan Jewell leaned across a Formica table. She and Donnie were sharing the small booth bench, so she couldn't sit all the way on it. He had come along to appease Morgan, though he doubted that Jenny's case had anything to do with Hallie Marks. She thought he was also here to temper her questions.

"I know it was a long time ago, but can you think of anything you didn't tell the police? Anything at all?" Jammed against the wall, Donnie leaned back with his arms crossed over his ribcage because there was no place else to put them. The table pressed against his belly, and even though he had taken his jacket off, he had no room move.

"Look, I told them everything. Everything I wanted to," Jenny said.

Morgan jumped right into her questions. "Nathaniel Johnson was the accountant for Beauty Blossoms. You worked there at the time. What do you remember about him?"

"The accountant?" Jenny shook her head. "He was a quiet guy."

"Anything else?" Donnie asked.

Jenny's mouth turned downward. "I didn't have any involvement with him. My boss met with him a few times. Why?"

"What about Ekhard Klein? Have you ever met a man with that name?"

"No." Jenny answered softly.

More forcefully, Morgan asked, "Then who attacked you?"

Jenny and Donnie simultaneously gave Morgan disapproving looks. Donnie shifted one inch. Maybe two. His untouched coffee splashed the table when he uncrossed his arms then crossed them again.

Donnie said in his mellow voice, "Your boyfriend Robert Montano may have been abusive, but he didn't do that to you, did he? We need to know, Jenny, because there are others. Other women who weren't as lucky as you. Others who died."

Jenny's mouth twitched. "Lucky? You call this lucky? Look at me. I'm a monster. I can't get a job. I don't have enough money to afford a prosthetic." She waved the hollow sleeve in the air, then hid it under the table self-consciously. "I'm not lucky. Do you know how many times I've wished I died?"

"Who attacked you?" Impatient, Morgan asked again. Lack of sleep had made her edgy. Irritable. But lately she knew that what kept her awake at night wasn't Hallie or Suzanne. It was her obsession with finding Fay's killer.

Jenny shook her head no, causing the scarf to shift back and expose another scar along her hairline.

"Robert Montano wasn't the one, was he?" Donnie asked, much more gently than Morgan could.

Jenny's thin lips were slightly parted.

Morgan fidgeted and stomped her foot on the floor. "Either you're withholding evidence because you're frightened, or it's something else. And that would be obstruction of justice, Ms. Delacourt. How about we get a warrant for your arrest. We can take you into the station. We can force you to talk."

Donnie shifted again, nearly pushing his partner onto the floor. "Come on Morgan, let's get out of here. She's not going to tell us."

Morgan hopped to her feet. Standing at the end of the table, she pleaded. "Come on, Jenny. My partner and I are trying to solve more than one murder. We don't want to take you to the station, but if we have to, we will." She knew Jenny was holding back. She could see her holding her breath.

Jenny sat back and looked down at her lap. The scarf hid her face entirely from view. "It wasn't what you think."

Donnie scooted to the edge of the bench.

"Place her under arrest, Donnie. Get this over with," Morgan said, infuriated.

"No, wait." Jenny looked up.

Donnie posed the question, "What are you so afraid of, Jenny?"

"I was cheating on Robert. He'll leave me if he finds out. I still see him, you know. He still loves me, even with . . ." Her hand flew up to cover her face. She wiped tears from the corners of her green eyes with a crooked finger.

Anticipation choked the breath from Morgan. She waited for the confession with her gaze locked on Jenny's destroyed face.

"Robert has been very kind. What I did to him was . . . it was unforgivable. I never wanted to break his heart," Jenny continued.

"He almost went to jail because of you." Donnie slid to the edge of the seat.

Morgan found the notebook in her pocket and encouraged Jenny to go on. "You were seeing someone else, weren't you? Montano is a jealous man, and you're afraid he'll leave you."

"He paid for some of my surgeries."

"Who was it?" Morgan asked. "Who were you seeing?"

"Please. Robert's love is the only thing that keeps me going. If he finds out . . ." Jenny looked from Donnie to Morgan and back again. "His name is Greg Trevesani. He's a close friend of Robert's."

Morgan's jaw went slack. Cold fingers of realization crept down her spine. *I was wrong.*

"You were having an affair with this . . . Trevesani?" Donnie rocked the table as he pushed himself out of the booth. His untouched coffee slopped out of the cup, making a brown puddle and soaking into a napkin.

Morgan lowered her spiral notebook. What had she been thinking?

Jenny pleaded, "Yes, but Robert can never find out, do you hear. He will kill us."

"Seriously? Trevesani did this to you? Why have you protected him all this time?" Donnie snatched his jacket off the nearby hook and put it back on.

"He's Robert's best friend. I couldn't destroy Robert like that. He still loves me." Tears trickled down to her chin.

Disappointed, Morgan slid the notebook back into her pocket. "You should turn him in. He damn near killed you."

"I think about him every time I look in the mirror. God had a reason for letting me live."

Morgan said, "I hope I you're happy with that decision."

Donnie turned to go. "Thanks for your time, Jenny."

*　*　*

Back at Donnie's car, Morgan checked her ponytail in the reflection of the window. The woman gazing back at her had dark circles under her

eyes. She smoothed her hair and reached for the door handle, waiting for Donnie to chew her out. Lieutenant Holbrook had questioned Morgan with the impossibility of a connection between Jenny Delacourt and Hallie Marks, like Donnie and Stan had. *Why didn't I listen?*

"Ekhard Klein had nothing to do with Jenny's attack." he said opening the driver-side door.

Morgan climbed in beside him, embarrassed and worn out. "Sorry about that. I really thought . . ." She looked out the window.

"Mo, it's not your fault. We'll find Ekhard." He put the keys in the ignition. "Focus on him."

"I can't believe she didn't report Trevesani." Morgan shook her head in disgust.

"I'll dig around for dirt on him. There must be something else we can arrest that fucker for."

"It would be the right thing to do." Morgan said.

CHAPTER 49

CARYN

On Friday night, Caryn arrived at Quincey's Pub. Ekhard sat at the bar, working on a near-empty glass of bourbon.

She slid up onto the stool next to him and told the bartender with a braided goatee and tattoos covering his arms that she'd have the same.

Ekhard had grown his beard and hair. He wore a navy-blue baseball cap pulled low on his forehead, shading his features. When he saw Caryn, he wound up tight like a spring. "What are you doing here?"

"Sorry I'm late," she said, removing her coat and scarf.

Football news was on the overhead TV. Sportscasters were comparing teams in the NFL West. With a hand on his glass and his eyes on the screen, he said under his breath, "You shouldn't be here."

Caryn smiled and took a long sip of her bourbon. "Nice to see you too."

Ekhard pulled his cap down, then leaned toward Caryn. In a low whisper, he said, "Someone is bound to connect us."

Caryn leaned back and squawked, "So this is all on me?"

The bartender stared at them with his arms crossed.

Ekhard's gaze stayed riveted on the television. He kept his voice low. "Who else would it be on, Ceecee? You shouldn't be here," he repeated.

She patted Ekhard's back.

He spun in an instant and slapped her hand away, seething.

"Hey!" She cried out.

"I don't want you near me." His arm remained in the air with his hand fisted, poised, and ready for offensive maneuvers. She had only seen rage in her brother once before. The smell of bourbon took her back to the place where it began. Her brows drew together, framing her burning green eyes.

Tight as a piano string, Ekhard's fist remained cocked in the air. "Too much time has passed. Too much stands between us now. There's way too much at stake."

"Is everything okay here?" The hulky bartender picked up Ekhard's empty glass.

Ekhard lowered his fist. "Everything's fine."

The bartender looked from Caryn back to Ekhard.

"I should get going. Could you bring me the tab?" Ekhard pushed his empty glass toward the bartender.

When the bartender stepped to his register, Caryn asked, "How's Hallie?"

Ekhard turned, eyes flashing a warning. "Don't."

Caryn played a note. "Ekhard?"

Ekhard nodded. "You're a cold-hearted bitch. Just like Mom."

Caryn glared at her brother. *He is wrong!* With eye contact, she soaked up his fury and let it feed her own. "And don't put this *all* on me," she said. "I stopped playing your game a long time ago."

Ekhard said, "I can never forgive you for what you've done."

When the bartender came back with Ekhard's bill, she gestured to her glass and asked him, "Did you add this one to it?"

He looked at Ekhard for confirmation.

"Sure." Eks nodded at him. When he'd gone again, Ekhard dropped his gaze to the floor. "Don't contact me again. I can't be connected with you."

"Geez, Eks. You're such a drama queen. Nothing's changed, has it? You're still the same skittish kid." Drawing her hands up and shaking them, Caryn mocked him.

It pissed him off. "And you're still a control freak."

"Admittedly."

Ekhard slapped cash on the bar and shook his finger in Caryn's face. "Stop coming around. Stay away from me, do you hear?"

Caryn didn't confirm or deny. She just smiled and shook her head.

Ekhard slapped cash on the bar and stormed out of the building. It wouldn't be the last time she saw him.

CHAPTER 50

CARYN: 22 Years Ago

Caryn reached for her alarm clock. The blaring awakened painful, pounding throbs in her head. She sniffed. Once the alarm was dead, she rolled onto her back again and swallowed. *I am not going to school.* She had woken up with a cold.

A knock on her door woke her after she had dozed off again. "Hey! You up?" Ekhard entered her room. "What are you doing? Get out of bed. You're making me late."

"I'm sick." Caryn rolled onto her side.

"Yeah, right. Get up. I'm giving you twenty minutes." He slammed the door.

As she pushed her body upright, she realized that she wouldn't make it for five minutes at school. Her skin ached, her head throbbed, and her throat was raw. But she had a test today in fourth period pre-calc.

After climbing into jeans and a yellow hoodie, she made her way downstairs where Ekhard was waiting for her in the kitchen. He had his backpack thrown over his shoulder and keys in his hand. He handed her a cup of coffee. "Where're your shoes?"

"Oh crap." She'd left them upstairs.

"I'll get them." Ekhard slammed his keys down on the counter, then hopped toward the stairway. "I need to be at school early. I told you that."

She shouted back, "No you didn't."

It was just like Eks to yell at her for something he'd forgot to tell her. He blamed her for his inadequacies. And in Caryn's opinion he had more shortcomings than virtues.

She piled books into her purple backpack and thought of her dad. He had bought it for her at the beginning of sixth grade. Now it was torn around the corners and had a quarter-sized hole in the bottom. She wondered if it would last through the school year.

Dad had told her, "Do well in school, Ceecee. Don't be like your mother and waste your life. Make something of yourself. Make me proud." That was when she was in third grade, right after she'd clawed Ellen's face. It was the last time he discussed school.

Ekhard bounded down the stairs with Caryn's shoes in his hand. "Put them on. I'm picking up Suzanne on the way."

"Doesn't she have a ride?" Caryn croaked through the phlegm in her throat.

"You sound like shit."

"I told you I have a cold."

"If you're sick, you won't be able to go with me this afternoon." Ekhard was referring to his interview with an admissions counselor at Butler University.

"Yes I will." Caryn was his coach. She wanted to be there.

"Well . . . I might not go today." Ekhard opened the door for his sister.

"You have to go. They'll accept you to the university if you can raise your GPA by just half a point."

"Suzanne wants me to go to a movie with her tonight."

Caryn climbed into the passenger side of Ekhard's 1979 Datsun. She pushed aside numerous crumpled-up bags from Hardee's piled on the floor to make room for her feet. Dad had bought the car for Eks the instant he got his driver's license so he didn't have to chauffeur them around anymore. It was gray, inside and out, and smelled like old French fries.

"What time is the movie?" she asked.

"Later." Ekhard started the car. He pulled out of the garage and drove down the street without answering any further.

"So?" Caryn cleared her throat. It felt like she'd swallowed broken glass. "The admissions meeting is at four o'clock."

Ekhard gripped the wheel with a hard look on his face. Caryn recognized his way of dealing with anger.

"Ekhard?"

When he didn't respond, she continued. "Your future is more important than that stupid girl. Secure your spot at that college. In four years, you won't be with her, but you *will* have an education."

"I don't care."

"She's no excuse not to go. Meet with that counselor. If you blow it off . . ." This conversation pissed her off. "Goddammit, Eks! That bitch has you tied up so tight you're like her little marionette."

"I am not," he whined.

"When she says jump, you jump." Caryn said with a cough.

Ekhard bit his lip. He stopped at a red light and hung his head.

"Are you sick too?"

As an answer, he wiped his nose on his sleeve and looked out the window to his left.

"Ekhard?"

"What?" The light turned green, and he accelerated. Ekhard white-knuckled the steering wheel as they approached Suzanne's neighborhood. "She said she'd break up with me if I don't go with her."

This was cheerful news to Caryn. "Great. Then break up with her."

"I can't."

"Ekhard, why do you have to stay with her? She isn't worth it. Think about your future."

"I can't help it. I have to do what she says." Tears streamed down his face. He sniffled and wiped his chin with his sleeve.

"Does she really have that much control over you? What is she lording over you?"

Ekhard pulled off the road and parked. He wiped the tears from his cheeks with his bare hands. "Remember those track-team kids two years ago?"

"The guy in the car fire?" Caryn remembered.

"Yeah. Well, he keyed my car. In fact, he humiliated me every day in the locker room. I had to get back at him somehow."

She hadn't known. "You did that?" She waited for the punch line.

Ekhard nodded.

Caryn connected the dots like easy addition.

"Suzanne knows I stuffed socks into his exhaust pipe. She knows it's my fault that his car blew up," he whimpered.

"She's blackmailing you." Caryn couldn't keep the stream of indignation from spilling off her tongue. "You idiot. Why would you tell her that? *I* didn't even know. Me. Your sister. How could you tell *her* and not *me*?"

Ekhard didn't move.

"I knew she was using you, but I couldn't figure out what hold she had on you."

"It's *that*, okay?" Ekhard wiped his nose on his sleeve.

Caryn bored a hole in the side of Ekhard's head with her gaze. "Telling her was the stupidest thing you've ever done."

Ekhard nodded. Beside the car, green grass sprouted from the dormant ground. Tree branch tips swelled with new buds. The sun rose in a blue sky. Along the brick wall surrounding Suzanne's neighborhood, yellow and white daffodils sparkled with dew.

Caryn could ignore her sore throat now. A feeling of new power had replaced the weakness of her illness.

"We're going to your appointment at the university right after school. Then, after that, we'll get Suzanne."

Ekhard nodded.

"Eks?"

He kept his gaze forward. "Yeah?"

"We'll take care of it. We're family. We'll take care of her together."

CHAPTER 51

MORGAN

Metro Homicide buzzed with activity that morning. The noise level in the room was higher than normal. In the days surrounding the holidays the number of violent crimes rose.

When Rob called, Morgan hoped he wanted to go out. Or come over later. She needed the distraction. That notion fell in the gutter when he growled, "Stan? How the fuck could you, Mo?"

She hadn't spoken to Rob since she'd gotten Stan suspended. "What do you mean?"

Rob spoke in short, clipped blurts. "Let's see. Stan's told, um . . . everyone. All the guys at the station are talking about you. Everyone in Mounted . . ."

"That I turned him in for abusing that girl?"

Rob shouted, "Turned him in?"

"He made her pay for his generosity with sex."

"I don't know what you're talking about. Stan has been bragging about his latest conquest. You, Morgan!"

Morgan held her phone with a shaky hand. Known to brag about his sexual experiences, Stan had spread rumors about Morgan. It was his revenge. Blood the color of shame rose to her cheeks. "What did he say?"

"He says that you invited him over. That he stayed all night."

"It never happened. Stan is a liar."

"Why is he telling everyone you're such a good lay?"

When Rob stopped to give her the opportunity to speak, Morgan cringed about the truth. "Because I followed him. I spied on him to get access to a case." She talked fast, as every word counted. It was her word against Stan's, and everything was on the line. "You know how I feel about that slimeball."

"He said you invited him over," Rob argued.

"It's not true."

Morgan sat down in her desk chair. Nearby, Donnie peeked at her over the stacks on his desk. "Rob, I would never . . ." *I didn't mean to hurt you.* "He's a liar, Rob. And he's trying to get back at me."

Rob breathed into the phone, silent.

Morgan didn't feel bad about Stan. She had ordered Chinese food and celebrated the night she took Jenny's files home. The cloying smell hadn't even cleared from the house when Morgan found out the truth. That she'd been wrong about Jenny. And she'd gone about it in a way that made her feel icky. After the meeting in the diner, Morgan had taken three showers. Yet she couldn't wash the disgusting, slime coating her body because she felt like a bad person.

Now, she wondered how a relationship with Rob could last with the level of distrust he had just shown. Perhaps she'd been looking for an excuse. God, he was such a nice guy. It broke her heart to do what she was about to do. She sat in her desk chair and tucked her knees up to her chest. "Rob. . ."

"I'm sorry I doubted you."

"I can't go on like this."

Confusion clouded his tone. "What do you mean?"

"I don't know." *Is this what I want?* Morgan struggled with her feelings.

"Mo. Don't back out on me again. Let's talk this out tonight."

If they did, she would give in. And Morgan needed to remain strong. She was afraid of committing to him. Afraid of loving him. This was as good an opportunity as any.

"I'm on my way. We'll talk in person."

"Please don't. I need space."

"I don't understand. I'm sorry I thought. . ."

Morgan leaned back in the chair, one arm around her knees, the other with the phone pressed against her ear. Things had been going well. There was no denying that. Yet she heard herself saying, "I don't love you."

It wasn't true. The ache in her heart after saying those words confirmed it.

Rob was silent.

She whispered, "I don't want to string you along anymore."

"So be it then," he said.

Both remained silent on the line. Morgan waited.

"Fine. I'll give you the space you need. Call me if you change your mind. But don't expect me to be there for you when you do." His tone was firm.

"I'm sorry."

"Save it. See you around." Rob hung up.

Morgan lost her grip on the phone and let it fall onto her desk.

With her desk facing Donnie's, she had an unobstructed view. Donnie appeared to have been listening in to her conversation with Rob. He stood up and gathered his things together. "Take the weekend, Morgan. Get your head together."

The world closed in on her. The last thing she wanted was for Donnie to come down on her. "Donnie . . ." Morgan couldn't feel any worse. She had been making some bad decisions lately and she knew it.

He put a hand on Morgan's shoulder. "This will be over soon. Go home and get some sleep."

CHAPTER 52

MORGAN: 16 Years Ago

"All right, listen up, people!" A uniformed police officer held a mega-phone up to his mouth. "Here's how this will work."

About fifty people faced the officer, who was standing beside a fire truck. Service professionals and EMTs remained in waiting, just in case they found Fay Ramsey. Near the truck was a poster-sized photograph of her. Next to it Victoria Ramsey huddled under an oversized black umbrella.

Low-hanging clouds leaked a fine mist that seemed to soak the world. It was as if Mother Nature held a giant spray bottle to coat the city in wet, dewy droplets.

Where are you, Fay?

At the back of the crowd, Morgan held her navy-blue jacket tightly wrapped around her body. Because her jacket hood blocked everything on the periphery, tunnel vision was her point of view.

Where are you Fay? Get your ass back here. Can't you see what a scene you've caused? Morgan didn't even hear the officer.

On the way there, she had watched throngs of university students walking over the footbridge toward the IU campus. *I should be one of them,* she thought. *Fay and I should both be attending classes today.*

Fall semester classes had begun, but Morgan didn't move into the dorms. Not yet, not without Fay. Two weeks had passed since Fay went missing.

A blur of thoughts ran through Morgan's mind as she tried to fit together the last days before Fay disappeared. Victoria had pointed fingers, telling police that Morgan knew where Fay had gone. It wasn't true. If Morgan had known for sure that Fay had come here to meet Larry, she would have told them. If she'd known Fay was dating someone else, Morgan would have told them. Wouldn't she?

Morgan had suggested this park because it was one place Fay loved. She was happiest here, walking on the path beside Jackson Creek, sitting on rocks or downed trees with a book in her hand and her headphones on. Morgan felt sick to her stomach when she thought of Jackson Creek Trail, so she mentioned it to the investigators. It was just a guess.

As grief wore her down, anger crept into Morgan's mind. What had Fay kept from her? Jealousy had become part of that emotional cocktail too. *How could Fay want to be with anyone but me?*

Morgan wasn't listening to the instructions from the police officer. His voice boomed, bringing her back to the living. "Are there any questions?"

Four or five hands went up.

Yes, I have a question, Morgan thought. *Why are we doing this? Fay is alive. Fay will come back as soon as she realizes how pointless the drama is.*

"Are you sure you're up for this?" Jeremy nudged her with his elbow.

"We'll find her. She's alive. I think she's run away from her mom, that's all," Morgan spouted her auto-reply.

Jeremy had dodged work to be with her. "Yes, but you don't have to do this if you don't want to. I can take you home." He gripped her arm and ducked into Morgan's limited, restricted view. His scruffy, unshaven face and long, grunge-style haircut were wet with dewy raindrops.

Aware that her hands and jacket were also wet from the continuous spray, Morgan whispered, "I'll find her. I have to find Fay."

The officer continued his instructions. "Form groups of two or three. Stay within visual distance of the groups flanking you. The fog is thick today."

"Stay with me then," Jeremy said.

"In her journal, Fay had written she was meeting Larry. She's probably still with him. God, I wish she would stop this charade." Morgan lowered her head.

Split in two, the groups moved from the swing sets at Sherwood Oaks Park toward the wide Jackson Creek Trail. Parallel to Jackson Creek on the western side was the long walking path and a park named after the creek. The path was ten to twenty feet from the creek's edge due to woods along the water.

Residents of the area used the park for recreation, jogging, bicycling, and relaxing. This time of the year, it was common to see families lying in the grass with books open wide, dogs chasing Frisbees, runners training, and cyclists speeding past. However, the fog and rainy weather had forced most inside. The only people here today were walking with the search group.

A few steps ahead of Morgan, Jeremy had his hands in his pockets and his head tucked low against the drizzle. When they reached the trail, officers leading their group peeled off to the right.

"All right, everyone. Split up here. I want you to stay within six feet of your neighbor because of the fog. Together, we'll cover more ground."

At the front of the group, Victoria Ramsey's black umbrella bumbled forward.

Jeremy turned around. "Are we going over by the water?"

The shroud of dense fog intensified sounds of the creek churning on the other side of dense brush.

"Yes." Morgan knew the creek's edge. Numerous times this past summer she and Fay had walked this trail together. They had sat beside the water and smoked pot in broad daylight under the shelter of the brush. Led by familiarity, Morgan's feet tripped ahead, one in front of the other. Jeremy followed.

"Dimitri, huh?" Morgan hadn't believed Fay was covering for someone at work that day. A broken record of their last conversation played over and over.

"Where are you really going?"

"Work. Like I said."

"I thought your mom didn't let you work the night shift at The Hamburger Stand."

"Today she did."

Victoria strictly enforced curfews. She would never have let Fay go out alone after five o'clock. Victoria blamed Morgan, and Morgan blamed herself.

I should have been more responsible. I should have asked her, "Who is Larry, Fay? Are you dating him?"

The guy Fay wouldn't talk about. Fay had probably run off with this guy named Larry. The guy who no one could find. Morgan's face reheated with anger and regret.

Sporadic drips from the trees above fell on Morgan's hood. Beneath her feet, the grass and rocky ground were soggy from last night's downpour. Closer now, she could see the edge of the creek.

"I'm right beside you," Jeremy said.

Thick fog made it impossible to see ten feet ahead through the trees. *Fay has run away. She is alive,* Morgan thought.

"Keep moving. Everyone keep moving. Make sure you can see your neighbor." The officer shouted from an unseen location in the fog to her left.

In soaking-wet rubber-tipped high-tops, Morgan stepped onward, pushing the dripping brush out of her way. To her right, the foamy water lapped the muddy ground. To her left, wet Jeremy in his dark-gray sweatshirt tangled with bushes and tree limbs.

Heavy brush, a few bent trees, and thick undergrowth loomed on her right. Jeremy closed the distance between them and came up behind her.

Branches tugged at Morgan's clothing as if trying to keep her from something. At one point, when she had to step into the rocky creek bed, cold water filled her shoes and soaked her pant legs.

Jeremy took her arm.

"Hey, neighbors, where are you?" a woman's disembodied voice hollered through the trees.

"On the water's edge," Jeremy shouted back.

"Okay, I see you now." A woman in a purple raincoat waved.

The watery smells were thicker now, more pungent than ever. Among the odors of wet, rotting vegetation and general river scum, Morgan caught a whiff of something else.

"Oh man. What is that?" Jeremy asked.

Morgan made her way to higher ground, stepping on a boulder to get out of the creek. When a branch caught her jacket, it threw her off balance. As she pulled away, the thorny bramble tore it. "Shit," she cursed under her breath. Turning to examine her damaged jacket, a bright, unnatural color on the ground caught her eye.

"God, what is that smell?" Jeremy asked again.

It took Morgan's brain a few seconds to register the familiarity of the yellow object. One of Fay's yellow high-tops lay there covered with mud. Its match lay on its side a foot away.

"Oh God!" Jeremy exclaimed. He grabbed Morgan's arm and shouted something she didn't hear over the sound of rushing blood in her ears.

Attached to those yellow shoes were Fay's unnaturally pale legs. Mud covered her crumpled skirt. She wore a jean jacket over her blouse, but it, too, was drenched and filthy dirty.

"Fay," Morgan whispered. *You must be cold,* she thought. Strength left her legs, and she dropped to her knees beside her friend. "Why are you out in the rain?" The desire to care for her friend, to mother and protect her from harm, filled Morgan's heart. "Let's get you inside." She reached for Fay's hand and found, instead, a shattered and broken appendage.

I'm so sorry . . .

Heavy rain the night before had washed the damaged, bloated flesh clean. Vague awareness registered in Morgan that Fay's face was smashed beyond recognition. Morgan brushed Fay's wet hair out of the dark hole that had been her nose. "What happened to you?"

Jeremy lifted Morgan up and carried her away from the body, but she struggled against him.

"Stop it!" Morgan cried out, kicking her brother, fighting to remain with her friend. "Fay!" She wanted to remain by her side. "I'm sorry, Fay!"

"Come on, let's go. She's dead, Mo." Jeremy held Morgan by the waist and dragged her backward.

"No—she's not! Let me go!" With all her might, she struggled against her strong brother, but Jeremy didn't let her go. Tears streamed down her face. "I want to see Fay. Let me talk to her!" Morgan cried.

Jeremy stood strong, holding her in place until the police and other professionals came running out of the fog to surround Fay's lifeless body.

CHAPTER 53

CARYN

Christmas lights gleamed on the wet pavement. Happy people hurried, ducking away from the wet, slushy mix raining from the sky. Couples, dressed up and decorated like the packages they carried, ran from their cars to the warm, well-lit Rapture at 86 West Hotel.

Mack's holiday party for hotel employees had been scheduled early this year, the weekend after Thanksgiving. With the approaching season, he and Erin planned a long December trip to the Florida Keys. He had told Caryn it was over between them. That was impossible.

Caryn admired the decorated Japanese maples on either side of the entrance. Well-practiced at changing clothes in the car, she slid out of her camouflage pants and athletic shoes, careful of the scabs on both of her palms. At least Ekhard had only pushed her. *He could have done far worse.* She peeled the black Under Armor over her head without mussing up her hair. As she switched to high heels and a skin-tight party dress, she thought about Erin. Mack talked about her a lot lately. *I can't wait to meet her.*

She placed sport trainers sole to sole and put them with her clothes in a medium-sized trash bag. The bag with the shoes fit inside her army-green carryall, which she tucked into the trunk of her car.

Behind a revolving glass door, heavy helpings of glam decorated the Rapture at 86 West. Gold glitz and white lights hung from the Christmas tree in the center of the lobby. A centerpiece in a snowy-white vase held white lilies and pine boughs sprayed with gold glitter.

Since she had not been invited, Caryn had to ask the red-coated attendant at the front desk where the party was. "I'm with the Mackintoshes," she explained.

"Go up in the elevator to the third-floor dining room. You'll hear the party before you see it."

As the elevator slowed, it thumped to the beat of the music. The doors opened to a party in full swing. People filled the dance floor or stood in groups around the bar. Employees of the hotel and guests sat at tables covered in white linen, sipping drinks and finishing their dinners. "Jingle Bell Rock" blared from a stack of speakers.

In the coatroom, Caryn shed her outer layer. Under her jacket she wore a striking, low-cut black number with just the right amount of lacy trim added at the V cut to draw the eye.

She threaded her way through the loud, crowded room, unable to find an empty bar table or unoccupied stool away from the bartender, Erin. So she changed her mind and walked boldly up to her, knowing she wouldn't be recognized.

"I thought I knew all the employees here, but I haven't met you." A tall brunette with soft brown eyes, Erin wore a red sleeveless top showing off muscular biceps. She had a smile as wide and friendly as Christmas morning.

Caryn reached across the bar for a handshake. "I'm Caryn. We haven't met. I'm in accounting." *I'm not lying.*

Erin took Caryn's hand in both of hers. "So nice to meet you. What are you drinking tonight?"

Caryn pulled away. "Bourbon on the rocks."

"Are you having a good time? Did you enjoy the food?"

Some women were like that, mothering others. To Caryn, it felt like being smothered with a cold, wet blanket.

"Yes," she said and placed her hands in her lap.

Erin danced a graceful ballet behind the bar, then handed her the tumbler full of icy bourbon.

"Mack put a lot of effort into this," Caryn said.

"He really did. He was up late every night this week getting the details just right."

He certainly wasn't visiting me, Caryn thought angrily. Before taking a sip, she oozed, "You are so lucky, Erin. Mack is the best. And I've wanted to meet you forever." Only Caryn knew why Mack wasn't a hundred percent devoted to his wife.

Erin asked. "How did you meet him?"

"Mack and I met during an audit twenty-two months ago." This wasn't true.

A confused look passed over Erin's face. "When was that? I don't remember The Rapture getting audited."

Just in time, a bearded man bellowed from the far end of the bar, "Hey, Erin, another cranberry and vodka down here?"

Erin excused herself to tend to the opposite end of the bar.

Mack would go crazy to see Caryn here, and she knew it. She scanned the crowd for her lover, anticipating his discomfort with the excitement of a child at her birthday party. Right on cue, the man of the hour appeared across the room, holding a tray of dessert cups filled with colorful creamy fluff. When he spotted her, his eyes grew wide as dinner plates. He stumbled, tipping the tray, but righted it and turned away.

As she watched, Mack handed out desserts and socialized with his employees. Now and then, he glanced Caryn's way with a panicked and pained expression. *Had he told Erin about their affair?* She suspected that he was ignoring her, so Caryn picked up her drink and slinked toward him.

Once within earshot, she hailed, "I came as soon as I could, darling."

Mack flushed. "What are you doing here?"

A couple nearby smiled awkwardly. As Caryn introduced herself to them, Mack set the tray of desserts on a table.

The woman greeted her with a delicate handshake. "I'm Marian. This is Greg."

"What department are you in?" Greg asked.

"Bedding." Caryn winked at Mack, who blushed bright red.

Mack whispered into Caryn's ear. "Fix your dress. It's too low."

Caryn saw that her dress had slipped, exposing her red bra above the plunging neckline. Greg ogled and Marian elbowed him.

Behind them, Erin approached. Her timing was perfect. Caryn slid her arm around Mack's and used it for support. "Oops!" she said, suppressing a smile. "I might have had too many." She lifted her drink and deliberately sloshed it on the floor.

Mack's eyes widened as his wife stepped into the group. "How's everyone doing? Are you enjoying the party?" she asked.

A true hostess, Caryn thought. "Lovely," she said, lifting her glass in a toast. She snuggled up to Mack and asked in a syrupy sweet tone, "Aren't you going to introduce me, Mack?"

He peeled Caryn's hand off his arm, then pushed her away. His neck went red as he said, "Erin, this is Caryn."

Erin covered for him, "We met at the bar." But her eyelids lowered when she took a step between them. "Who is she, Mack?"

"Erin."

Caryn dipped her shoulder and let the strap fall. "We're lovers, Erin. I really *have* heard so much about you."

Erin stiffened, then looked at her husband.

Mack wiped sweat from his brow with a white linen napkin. In a firm voice, he told Erin, "We'll talk about this later."

The other couple, Greg and Marian, slinked away.

Taking Caryn by the arm, he pulled her out into the hallway. It attracted way too much attention, which was exactly what Caryn wanted.

He snarled, "What are you doing here?"

"I was upset you didn't invite me, baby." Caryn draped a hand over his shoulder.

"Stop that." He brushed her away. "I mean it. What the hell are you doing here?"

"I wanted to share the good news."

"What good news? What are you talking about?" Irritation colored Mack's tone.

"I've taken care of my brother." Caryn pretended she was tipsy, drawing a few onlookers.

Mack shook his head, looking at the bystanders. "How?"

"You'll see," she sang, giving it a flourish. "The police are on to him now."

"Has he been arrested?"

"Not yet. But keep an eye on the news, Gilroy dear." Caryn knew Mack hated being called by his first name.

Erin perched her hands on her hips. Marian and Greg walked past on their way to the coatroom. Mack smiled, pretending nothing was going on, so Caryn threw herself at him. She plastered her arms around his large frame and hung there. While she kissed his chin and neck, he tried to scrape her off. The struggle made a much bigger scene, causing others to stop and watch.

"Goddammit, Caryn." Mack shoved her backward.

In her high heels, she toppled, landing on her butt on the floor. She broke the fall with her hands, already scraped from hitting Ekhard's sidewalk. The scabs on her palms opened up. "You can't treat me this way!" she shrieked, holding up her bleeding hands.

Onlookers had formed a semicircle around them. Mack looked at them, unsure what to do.

Unsteadily, Caryn tried to stand. "You can't humiliate me this way! After all we've been through. Don't make promises you can't keep."

Erin had followed them out to the hallway. She glared at them with her arms crossed. "What did you promise her, Mack?"

"I haven't made any promises." Mack's brow puckered in confusion. Sweat dripped down his temples as he stooped to help her up.

"I'm calling the cops." Erin said.

"You do that. Mack attacked me!" Caryn clamored. And as Mack helped her to her feet, Caryn saw a familiar person standing near the elevator. She spun around to get a good look at him. A tall man with a beard and mirrored glasses, he wore slacks and a suit jacket. Looking right at her, he removed the glasses. His amber eyes bored into her.

Mack was fawning over her. "I didn't mean to. Are you okay?"

"Okay?" Her bleeding palms oozed dark blood where the scabs were torn off. Caryn held them up for others to see just as she craned her neck toward the elevator. It had closed. He was gone.

"Don't call the cops, Erin." Red-faced and tense, Mack said, "It was an accident. Are you okay?"

The man in the elevator had distracted her. A call from home. Every nerve felt exposed. The room grew smaller as Caryn decided she had to leave. She had to get out of here. He had seen her. Ekhard was here.

CHAPTER 54

CARYN

Caryn turned tail and ran past Erin's angry stare. Mack had begun pleading for forgiveness. Telling lies.

When Caryn saw Eks's amber-brown eyes homing in on her, she feared for her life. She had arrived home ignited by anxiety infused with a good dose of adrenaline. Her brother was following her.

Caryn smiled.

Ekhard had left home on the day Caryn graduated from high school. With a new identity, he became chief financial officer of Klemmins' Grocery in the late nineties, and then, a year later, of Goldman's Department store. The two corporations both foreclosed because of procedural inadequacies. Later, after he'd changed his name to Larry Milhouse, he worked for CPA Mike Pritchard. Three more businesses collapsed. In searching the details, she found that those three businesses had assigned Ekhard to be chief financial officer. Before him, the three together had generated over $1.6 million in revenue per year before going bankrupt.

She had followed him ever since he left. *Ekhard.*

Numbers told the story better than any written word. Organized in neat lists and tidy rows, they were precise. Common threads were negative numbers in the thousands and Ekhard Klein—aka Nathaniel Johnson, Larry Milhouse, Derek Smalls, to name a few. Ekhard had caused the ruin of several businesses and innocent people.

He probably had enough money to disappear forever. *Where would he go now?* More importantly, how would Caryn find him again?

Pacing in her kitchen, not knowing what to do, she opened her refrigerator door. Less than desirable frozen choices faced her. But she hadn't eaten all day so didn't care what went in her body. Using a knife, she cut open a cold box, pulled out the meal tray, and stuck it in the microwave, setting the timer for six minutes.

The motions of preparing dinner were automatic. A plate, a fork, a glass of soda . . . She remembered Ekhard cooking for her when Theo got sick.

Absentmindedly, she picked at the wound on her left palm. The bleeding had scabbed over again, but not the bitter anger.

The best thing Eks did was to drive away. But Caryn could never forgive him for abandoning her. She had needed him. And he betrayed her by taking all their belongings with him. He'd left her with nothing. It hadn't been the betrayal that wounded her ego the most. What hurt more than anything was what he had said. Eks told her she was just like Mom. Mom, who abandoned us. Mom who beat us. Mom, who Caryn could never forgive. *He'd said I was just like her.*

The timer on the microwave counted backward: 4:49, 4:48, 4:47. She sipped warm bourbon. 3:57, 3:56, 3:55. And as if expecting it, Caryn turned toward her door. It clicked and began to open.

"Mack?" His warm body next to her would help her sleep.

"No, sister. It's me. You shouldn't leave your door unlocked. Even those pesky police won't keep out the riffraff." Ekhard stepped out from behind the open door. His beard, dyed dark, was longer than the last time and trimmed to perfection. His elegant suit looked expensive. Caryn thought again about the money he'd stolen.

Ekhard set a heavy suitcase on the floor, closed the door, and locked the deadbolt. "I followed your neighbors in through the front door. They're friendly girls, aren't they?"

Caryn held her breath. Now that he stood in front of her, he appeared taller than she remembered. She noticed his shiny leather dress shoes, his good sense of style.

"Did you miss me?" he asked.

Words didn't come. Caryn was, for once, speechless.

"Why don't you pour me a drink? And pour yourself another while you're at it. You'll need it." Eks removed his long coat and hung it on the coat hook beside the door.

The microwave beeped. She slid a clean glass toward her brother. Then, with a towel around her hand, Caryn removed the dish from the microwave. She set it on the counter and pushed it away. She'd lost her appetite. Her heart was thumping so hard it made her nauseous.

"Oh." Eks looked down his nose at her dinner. "After all the years I tended to you . . ."

Was he referring to her cooking? Or the mess?

"I did everything for your survival. I cooked for you, cleaned up after you. Didn't you learn anything?"

"I learned about betrayal," she hissed at him. Whatever Ekhard had up his sleeve, she didn't care for it to go on long.

Ekhard pulled a long object out of his coat pocket. "I brought you something, sister. Sorry, I didn't have time to wrap it. Consider that a throwback to the way old Theo celebrated Christmas. It's a gift in honor of our reunion," he said.

As Eks set a blue-handled rip claw on the counter, Caryn calmly mirrored him and set her glass beside it. It was a thirty-two-ounce framing hammer with a checkered pattern on its face. *Overkill.*

I saw this one in the store and it spoke to me. It made me think of you."

Caryn said, "Honestly, Eks, you shouldn't have."

"Use it well." He took three long strides into the kitchen and opened the bottle of bourbon. "You see? We are both creatures of habit. This is the same brand Theo used to drink."

"What are you doing here, Ekhard?"

"I came to see my baby sister one last time. That's all." He poured three fingers without ice and drank it down. "You're looking good. You're aging gracefully . . . considering."

"And look at you." She shook her head.

He tipped his chin, enjoying the downward view of his own body. "This? The expensive suit is a small pleasure of mine."

"They're looking for you in four or five states. The U.S. Marshals have taken over the investigation. Your picture will be posted all over the country. Think of it, you're famous."

"*You're* famous," he corrected.

"Bonnie Parker?"

"No. Aileen Wuornos. Patricia Hearst. Hell. Dennis Rader."

"Why are you here, Eks?"

One at a time, he placed ice cubes in his glass, then poured more bourbon. "I needed to see you one last time."

"So you can leave me again? Abandon me? Again?" she spit.

His gaze pierced Caryn.

"It took years to get back on my feet." Her hands in fists, Caryn's fingernails dug into sore flesh.

"And look at you now," he said. "It's true, you know? You've grown up to be just like our mother. A cold-hearted, psycho bitch."

Caryn spat, "To think I missed you, brother." Her lips curled.

"There we go. There's my Ceecee. Am I pissing you off, darling? Because I am. Trying. To piss you off." His hand smoothed his dyed black hair.

Caryn looked forward to messing it up.

Ekhard spat through his front teeth. "You set me up. You called the police and sicced them on me."

Fury rose from deep inside her. "You stole from me."

"Suzanne was *my* girlfriend, you bitch," he said, escalating the argument.

"It was *my* trophy." Caryn had turned, placing her right hip against the counter.

"Like that diamond ring on your finger? Is that your trophy too?"

Caryn admired the back of her hand and Hallie's sparkling diamond engagement ring. "I like to collect things."

"Things that belonged to them."

"I didn't realize how much she'd led you on until she told me you'd proposed." As she leaned toward him, Caryn's right hand traveled back toward the hammer that lay on the counter. The hammer that Ekhard had given her.

"I loved Hallie." Ekhard leaned back with the drink in his hand. His lips curled as he hissed, "You psychopath."

"You have no idea what you've put me through." Caryn's fingers curled around the hammer.

"And you're just like Mom."

No I'm not!

CHAPTER 55

CARYN: 22 Years Ago

The moment Miss Popular's heart stopped beating was the moment Caryn first noticed the sound of her own. It beat a dance rhythm against her chest. She was alive.

The woods had grown dark, but she could sense everything. She smelled the earth and the damp leaves on the ground. She smelled the perfumey scent of the girl's clean, blond hair. Mixed into the potpourri was an odor so overpowering Caryn could taste it: the rich metallic iron from the blood glistening on Suzanne's face.

Silence consumed the forest. Suzanne Aiken was warm-dead. Not even the crickets mourned her death. When Eks began crying, the sound was an explosion.

"Oh God. Oh God. Oh God . . ."

The sniveling crybaby, Caryn thought. The hammer slid from her fingers.

"What have we done? What have we done?" He rocked back and forth on his knees. Leaves crunched beneath him.

"Where's the flashlight?" Caryn asked.

"What?"

"The flashlight." Her warm hands were wet and slippery with blood. She wiped her fingers on the blanket spread under Suzanne and cleaned off the handle of the hammer.

"No. No light." His head swung from side to side in dramatic emphasis. "I don't want to see it. Her. I . . ."

Caryn picked up the hammer and turned to face Ekhard. "Give me the flashlight." At that moment, she would have struck him too. She had nothing left to lose.

He stood, wobbly, and backed away. "We need to get out of here." He fumbled, digging an object out of his deep jacket pocket.

The flashlight clicked on. Ekhard sprang backward, dropping it.

It landed near Suzanne's face, illuminating her gruesome expression. Her wide eyes bulged out of their sockets. Red splatters of blood pooled where her nose used to be. Her lip was torn where the hammer had hit her. Caryn wanted to see her shattered teeth. *How many were broken?* She reached for the light.

"Oh God. Oh God," Ekhard sobbed.

Suzanne's chest and North Side High School sweatshirt were soaked. The blanket cradling her held a pool of her blood.

Ekhard's breath came in short gasps. He buried his face in his hands.

"It's a little late to decide that you liked her. Come on, we need to clean up." Caryn handed him the flashlight and pushed leaves aside. She cleared the ground so they could dig a hole, then rolled the body in the blanket.

Caryn decided she was in charge. Her older brother had lost it. "Get the shovel, Eks. Start digging."

Suzanne was way out of Ekhard's league, everyone knew that. And when she blackmailed him to do her homework, Ekhard became her little slave. In Caryn's mind, that had to end. Suzanne wasn't university bound. Her agenda had more to do with making babies. But Eks would never have gotten that far with her. Suzanne would have used him and spit him out when she was done. She would have dragged this on until she graduated, then left Eks heartbroken and miserable. *That will never happen now.*

Ekhard had been there to take care of Caryn when their mother left. Dad, too, had been unavailable. Unhelpful. Useless. This was a way for Caryn to help Ekhard launch. The only way she knew how.

Ekhard wiped his nose on his sleeve.

"What's your problem?" Caryn put her hands on her hips the way she remembered their mom doing.

"Shut up, Ceecee. Just shut up." He plunged the shovel into the soft earth.

They could only find one shovel in the garage or Caryn would have helped. She flopped onto the ground in the leaves beside Suzanne's body and picked up a plastic pink jelly shoe. Caryn played with it and poked her finger through one hole. "We have to talk about our alibis. Everyone knows you were dating her. Tell me where you were tonight."

His voice thick and gravelly, Eks said, "I was with you."

"Good. Where did we go?"

"We went to Butler University. To the admissions office. We were there till six, then we took a tour of the campus. Then we drove home. I helped you with your science project." Ekhard puffed while he worked hard, digging fast. The hole was nearly long enough.

Scrawny yet strong, Ekhard worked out, lifting weights at the school gym every day. That's where he had met Suzanne. While practicing a routine with the other cheerleaders, she had noticed him. Said she thought he was cute. Caryn knew the relationship had begun as a super-ficial attraction.

"What about Suzanne? Did she call the house?"

Ekhard threw the shovel to the side and then stooped to push the blanketed body into the hole. "Yeah. She rode her bike. She was going to meet Becky at the movie theater."

Caryn tossed the shoe on the blanket. She stood to get out of the way while Ekhard put the finishing touches on the mound, kicking leaves over it. He leaned on the shovel, and Caryn chucked the hammer into the woods.

The siblings made their way back to the car, but not before stripping off their blood-spattered clothing and putting it in a large garbage bag. They wiped themselves with a solution of watered-down bleach, some-thing Caryn had seen on an episode of *Law and Order,* then dropped the towel and bottle into the bag too. They placed the bag in a dumpster behind the drugstore on the way home. The next morning, they took Suzanne's bicycle apart and dropped it into a different dumpster.

Caryn saw that Eks was never the same afterward. He became quiet, opting out of entertainments like school football games. He avoided hanging out with his friends and mostly stayed in his room until the end of the school year. Only Caryn knew that guilt saddled him. It rode him like a deadly virus.

CHAPTER 56

MORGAN

Over a week had passed since Jenny's interview. Morgan had gone to Bloomington for Thanksgiving and spent a few extra days there. Being away from work, she had actually slept. It had been good to see her family again. Morgan had helped out in the kitchen when her mom came down with a respiratory virus. And it was nice cooking for family and feeling useful. There, she wasn't alone. When she returned to the station, Morgan texted Donnie. While staring at her phone, she walked right into Rob.

"Hey. No texting and walking," he joked.

Embarrassed, Morgan hid her phone.

He greeted her with a friendly smile. "I wanted to call. Figured the only way to talk to you is to see you in person."

Rob looked good—a tall, refreshing drink, complete with all the nutrients she needed. Out of uniform, Rob's tight red T-shirt rippled as he tucked his hands into his pockets. She couldn't keep from gazing at his muscular shoulders and chest. She'd missed him.

Offering an open invitation, he asked, "Are you free later?"

Rob moved fast, but Morgan had grown used to that.

"Let me take you out to dinner," he said. "I don't like the way we left things last time."

So many things spun through her head. *I'm not ready. I'm not good at relationships.*

"Gretta wants to see you," he urged.

"Really? Gretta?" The smile on her face grew. Rob knew how to coax her. For that, she liked him against her will.

"Well, if Gretta is coming to dinner, then I'm in."

Her sarcasm didn't get past Rob. "She has a new bone to show you."

"I'd love to see it."

"How's my little minx?"

Hot embarrassment crept up Morgan's spine at the sound of the voice. Behind her, Stan Williams had put a hand on her elbow.

"Look, Stan . . ."

"What are you doing tonight? You owe me. Let's finish where we left off."

And to think she was going to apologize for getting him put on administrative leave. She guessed he was returning to work now. But the thought of Stan near her made Morgan want to shower.

"Sorry, Stan. I can't." *Won't. Not ever.*

"Too bad. I'll check in with you again soon, you hear?" He nodded at Rob.

It became clear that Stan felt he had gained the right to make Morgan's life a living hell. What he was dishing out, Morgan had had enough of. "No, Stan. You won't. You won't call, you won't check in with me. I don't want you near me. If you so much as look at me sideways, I'll report you for sexual harassment. Do you understand? Leave me alone!" Tension lifted from her shoulders.

Stan stepped backward. "Okay," was his quiet response. His cheeks reddened. Then he strode past Rob, saying, "Good luck with that," as he brushed elbows with him.

Rob merely nodded at him and watched him go. To Morgan, he whispered, "I'd beat him up, but you have it handled."

Morgan felt satisfaction fill her chest. She stood a little taller.

"Do you want to talk?" Rob asked as his hand took hers.

She nodded. "I do." She looked down the hall.

Olivia Hawthorn jogged toward them. She pushed past IMPD officers and civilians. Some of her hair had escaped the confines of a tight bun. "Morgan, there you are. I've been trying to reach you and Donnie. I have something really important to show you regarding DNA evidence."

Torn, Morgan looked up at Rob.

Olivia pleaded. "Come back to the lab with me. You've got to see this. Now. It has to do with Suzanne Aiken."

"Talking will have to wait," Morgan said to Rob.

Kindly, he smiled. "It's okay. I understand."

More than anything, she wanted to spend the rest of the day with him. As she looked up at his dark, forgiving eyes, she knew everything would be okay. "I'll be in touch. I swear I will. I just have to . . ."

"Tonight?"

"Morgan?" Olivia called.

Morgan reluctantly pulled her hand from Rob's. "I will. I promise."

"If you don't call, I know where you live." He smiled.

She returned the grin, regretting, for a change, that work took so much of her time. "You do," she said as an invitation.

"Okay, you two." Olivia's overbearing impatience pulled Morgan away. "Put the love affair on pause. This evidence can't wait."

Morgan followed Olivia, feeling Rob's magnetic pull the entire way to the lab.

"Early this morning results came back, and I've been dying to tell you. Where's your partner?"

Morgan checked her phone to see if Donnie had returned her text. He hadn't. "I've texted him, he's probably on his way here."

When they arrived at the lab, Olivia closed the door. "Results from your DNA test came in today. Normally, we can't get much DNA from a hair sample. Luckily—for us, not for the blonde—the hair was ripped out with follicles intact. The DNA from that coffee cup you gave me matches the hair in Suzanne's hand." Olivia stared at Morgan as if waiting to deliver a punch line.

Morgan's heart skipped a beat. "It is Caryn Klein's hair."

"Yes." Olivia said.

This was what she had waited her whole life for. Morgan wanted to jump for joy. The killer was Caryn! Elation washed over her, followed by dread. It hadn't been Ekhard all along. Then he couldn't have killed Fay. "You're positive?" Enthusiasm drained from her.

"It's Caryn Klein's hair. Do you want to see the test results?" Olivia asked.

"No. I believe you."

The urgency of the situation fell on Morgan. She thanked Olivia and ducked out of the lab, heading straight for her desk. There, she gathered her things and beelined to her rented car. Donnie still hadn't replied to her text, so Morgan dialed his number. The call went straight to voice mail. *Where is Donnie?*

On the way to Caryn's condo, Morgan called for backup.

CHAPTER 57

MORGAN

Two Indianapolis Metro Police cars followed Morgan to arrest Caryn for the murder of Suzanne Aiken. What else had Caryn done? Had she murdered Hallie Marks? Did Caryn know where Ekhard was? He was still implicated in Hallie's murder.

U.S. Marshals were hunting Ekhard down. It was only a matter of time before they caught up with him. Morgan wanted to be the one to grill Ekhard in the interrogation room because her dream of becoming a U.S. Marshall was growing brighter all the time. After this case closed and Donnie moved up to Lieutenant Holbrooke's position, she would send in her application.

The impending sense of closure allowed Morgan to exhale.

A wet frozen mixture had been falling again today. She looked at the empty seat next to her and sank down a little lower. Donnie would have driven his SUV with four-wheel drive. *Where the hell was he?* She regretted doing this alone—Donnie would want to be by her side when she made the arrest—but she had to bring Caryn in now.

Morgan and the other cars arrived with their sirens off, not wanting their suspect to flee the scene. With the engine still running, she got cautiously out of the car and skated to the door across slippery pavement. Four police officers fell into step behind her.

When she found the outer door locked, Morgan backed away and ordered another officer to open it. A hulky officer with a shaved head ran back to his vehicle and returned with a crowbar. In the silence that followed, Morgan's heart pounded against her chest. He jammed the metal crowbar between the door and its frame. With a satisfying crack and crackle, the glass of the outer door broke. An alarm shrieked throughout the building as the security wires signaled entry.

Morgan darted into the building past people in the lower level who had opened their doors. She dashed up the stairs, taking them two at a time; the officers followed.

At Caryn's door, Morgan stopped to catch her breath. With one hand on her weapon and the other knocking, she shouted, "Caryn Klein, this is Detective Jewell." She knocked again, this time harder. "Ms. Klein, this is Detective Jewell. Open up!"

The deafening sound of Morgan's breath split the silence. She nodded at the bald officer and quietly asked his name.

"Officer O'Brian, ma'am," he answered.

"Open the door, O'Brian," Morgan commanded.

He leaned forward and pressed his ear against Caryn's door. With one hand holding a pistol against his chest, he turned the knob and threw his weight into it. He stormed in ahead of Morgan with his pistol out in front of him. Morgan followed, her weapon at the ready.

Lights were on, and the odor of food filled the air. The condo was quiet. With her weapon raised, Morgan surveyed the living room ahead of her and turned to her right, toward the kitchen.

On the floor between the sink and island, a man lay crumpled face-down. Blood pooled under his head.

Morgan holstered her weapon and dropped to her knees beside Ekhard Klein's dead body.

CHAPTER 58

MORGAN

The call came from Donnie's wife, Angie. She said the accident was bad. The driver of a Chevy pickup had slid through a red light going forty mph and hit the passenger side of Donnie's car. Etta had been driving.

Morgan drove as fast as possible on slick roads—only forty-five on the highway—to Community Hospital on the north side of Indy. When she arrived at the surgery center, Angie and the girls were sitting huddled together in the stark gray waiting room. As she approached them, Annabel rushed to give her a warm, loving hug.

"His shoulder was shattered," Angie said. "He's been in surgery for an hour." She looked like she was about to cry, then held it back.

Etta wore a brand-new supportive collar around her neck. She slumped in a chair, resting at a stiff angle on Angie's shoulder.

Morgan shook her head in disbelief. "God, Angie, I wish you'd called me earlier."

"I know. I wanted to, but we were in the ER with Etta." She pulled her daughter closer.

"Is it whiplash?" Morgan sank into the chair next to Etta and touched her arm.

Weakly Etta replied, "I don't know."

"They said it's muscle strain. The doctors are just being cautious." Angie looked at her injured daughter and brushed Etta's long brown hair out of her face. "She's exhausted. Painkillers are probably kicking in. They did X-rays. Nothing's out of place."

Morgan gave Etta a squeeze, then shrugged off her coat.

Angie peeled herself out from under Etta, who looked at her fearfully. "I'm not going far, baby. I need to talk to Morgan."

Annabel took her mother's seat on the bench and cuddled her sister.

Morgan followed Angie to the window at the far end of the waiting room. "How is he?"

"Etta feels so bad. They used the jaws of life to get him out of the car. It wasn't her fault at all. I keep trying to explain that to her." Angie looked down at her hands where she toyed with her wedding ring.

"His right shoulder?"

"Shattered. His upper arm, the shoulder blade and this one," she pointed to her clavicle, "are destroyed. This surgery is only to reset the bones temporarily. The plan is to eventually replace the entire joint once the surrounding tissue is healed."

Morgan shook her head. The implications about Donnie's career and future job security hit her in the gut. She felt nauseated.

Angie stared out the window. "I always expected to be in the hospital waiting room someday. I just figured it would be work-related."

Morgan nodded. "He's been very lucky."

* * *

It was eight o'clock before the surgeon emerged from Donnie's three-hour operation. Morgan offered to take Etta and Annabel so Angie could stay with Donnie, but Angie remained a pillar of strength for her girls. Since there was no chance Donnie would wake up, she chose to take the girls home for the night, as Etta needed rest.

Shaken up by the event, Morgan stayed. By 2:00 AM, Donnie still hadn't woken, and no progress had been made in the hunt for Caryn Klein. At 5:00 AM, Morgan sat near Donnie's hospital bed. Unable to sleep, she needed to talk to her partner and get his feedback.

"Caryn is our killer, Donnie. Think of that. Suzanne's case is solved," she said.

It took another minute for Morgan to muster the strength to continue. "Ekhard is dead too. Caryn killed him." It meant that Morgan's search for Fay's killer was over too.

"I've been meaning to tell you this. We knew that Ekhard had been changing his name every few years. Anna Clare remembered that he'd once used the name Larry." Or Linus, she'd said. Morgan took it as the clue she'd been looking for. "Donnie, even if Ekhard wasn't the one who killed Fay, I'd be happy to settle it. I think I can finally stop searching for her killer."

She exhaled and dropped her gaze to the silver ring that her brother had given her. "I know I've put you through a lot over the years. I've been too . . . obsessed. You were right. It's time to put that part of my life behind me. Time to let it go."

The peaceful rise and fall of Donnie's slumbering chest comforted Morgan. His right arm was fitted with a sling below the heavily bandaged shoulder. The only noises in the room were Donnie's sleep-breathing and the occasional beep of an automatic IV drip timer. "Now all that's left is to find Caryn Klein."

For Donnie, Morgan thought, *this is the pits.*

But it is different for me.

CHAPTER 59

MORGAN: 15 Years Ago

Dr. Taylor sat in a pale-yellow antique chair facing Morgan from across the room. Between them *Psychology Today* magazines covered the glass coffee-table, leaving only a corner available for the pitcher of water and a stack of plastic cups.

Morgan slumped in the couch with her arms crossed and her hoodie pulled so far over her head it almost covered her eyes.

"PITS, or Perpetration-Induced Traumatic Stress, is a very real condition, Morgan," Dr. Taylor continued, her voice smooth and caressing. Like silk. "You are experiencing one of the symptoms right now."

Morgan shook her head so slightly it felt like a jiggle. Inside, her inner voice was screaming *No!*

"That symptom is loss of memory. Morgan, the very fact that you don't remember leads me to believe that you saw something so terrible, so horrific, that your mind has shut that event down."

"I didn't see anything," Morgan grumbled.

"From everything you've told me, I believe that you went looking for your friend."

"I would remember." Morgan sat up. Ready to leave, she put her hands on her knees.

Dr. Taylor held up her hand. Thin fingers raised toward the ceiling in a universal sign for *stop*. Morgan did.

"Perpetration-Induced Trauma isn't the end of the world." The doctor said this so gently—as if giving Morgan a gift. "Before you go, I want to explain to you what other symptoms you may eventually experience with this disorder."

Morgan's face puckered with anger and resentment. How could this be happening? She decided not to believe a word Dr. Taylor said, yet she remained frozen by her held-up hand.

"Your brain has responded to seeing something that it doesn't want to believe. You may feel like you need to avoid Fay's house and her mother. You may even want to avoid your friends because they remind you of her. I believe that if you seek those friends out, it may trigger the memory."

"Not happening."

"Since this has been going on for more than six months, I don't know when you will regain your memory of the event. It has reached the chronic stage."

Morgan shifted weight to her feet, preparing to stand up. The doctor reinforced the hand signal and Morgan fell to her seat again.

"When it does surface, you may be unable to sleep. You may experience a renewed flood of memories associated with your friend Fay. You may become uninterested in your normal activities, and you may decide to put some distance between yourself and your friends."

"Why are you telling me all this irrelevant bullshit?"

"I want you to know there's no telling when your PITS will manifest. But someday you will remember what happened to Fay."

Morgan stood up to go. "There is nothing *wrong* with me. I am not sick." She crossed the small office in four strides. Her black Doc Martin boots thumped on the floor.

"Try not to think of it that way, Morgan."

As Morgan put her hand on the doorknob, Dr. Taylor asked, "When do classes start?"

"They already have."

"Criminal psychology?" Dr. Taylor asked.

"Yes."

"Are you sure that's a good idea?"

"Yes. I have to find out what happened to Fay."

"You know what happened to her."

Right when Morgan pulled the door open, a thought entered her mind and she pushed a strand of dark-brown hair away from her chin. She turned to the doctor seated in the yellow chair that surrounded her like a big glowing halo.

"What is it?" the doctor asked.

Morgan let the door close without shutting it completely. "You can't tell anyone, can you?"

"Of course not. Do you want me to?"

"No," she said, too emphatically.

"Morgan," Doctor Taylor clasped her clipboard to her chest, and she stood up slowly. "I can't share any of our discussion unless I think you are a danger to yourself or to others. From what I've seen, you are neither. I don't believe you have harmed anyone. But you need to take this seriously. When the symptoms manifest—and they will—things will get hard for you."

"So you can't tell anyone? Ever?"

The doctor closed her eyes and bent her head in a nod. "Not a peep."

Morgan opened the door and strode through it without looking back.

Since then, the doctor's words had haunted Morgan. Someday something would trigger those memories to open. A jack-in-the-box. *Surprise!*

CHAPTER 60

MORGAN

Donnie's surgery was successful. The shattered pieces of bone had been removed and the bones pinned together. If the surrounding tissue healed as expected, joint replacement surgery would take place before next spring. He was home now, under the watchful care of his wife and girls, but would return before the new year to begin his transition to lieutenant. Morgan had mixed feelings. She was sad to lose the best partner she could have asked for, but happy for him. Monday morning the department would choose a new temporary partner for her.

And Caryn Klein hadn't been found. It had been two weeks.

Morgan parked the rented Toyota in the Raffertys' dark garage, then sat for a moment. Her life seemed on the edge of a precipice. She could accept that Ekhard might have killed Fay and now he was dead. But had Caryn killed Hallie? There was no evidence in her favor.

I have been so wrong. About Fay, about everything. But Morgan pushed these thoughts aside. She had to if she was going to move on.

The morning after Ekhard Klein's murder, a neighbor had found the condo manager Brad Olafson naked and tied to his bed with leather bondage gear. He refused to implicate Caryn but did tell Morgan that she had visited him the night of Ekhard's murder. He claimed it was a night to remember. Caryn had likely escaped in Brad's vehicle. That day, he reported his truck stolen too.

Morgan called an old friend, Keith Broderick, a U.S. Marshal, and shared details. If anyone could find Caryn, Keith could. A full-scale manhunt with Caryn's viral photo was in place. Would US Marshals catch her? She had evaded police thus far.

In the meantime, Morgan had taken the seven-hour test for admission to U.S. Marshals. Now she would wait. The process could take months, or years, depending on what they needed when they needed it. Morgan was hopeful, given her record and the good references put in by Holbrooke and Donnie. She had begun training much harder at the gym, knowing that if she was accepted, she would still have to pass the eighteen-week training program in Georgia. Physical fitness was imperative. The USM standards were much higher than law enforcement.

She took the keys in her hand and got out of the Toyota. The automatic overhead light on the garage-door opener had burned out this fall, so it was dark once she turned off her headlights. She felt her way around the car.

Focused on Ekhard, *and Fay,* for too long, Morgan had ignored mundane chores like replacing light bulbs. The bathroom sink was dripping, and a knob had fallen off the bedroom closet door. Repairs needed to be made.

After closing the garage door, she went inside and found the laundry room light on. *No wonder light bulbs are burning out*, she thought. Morgan dropped her keys on top of the dryer, and then hung up her coat. One by one, she pulled off her ankle-high boots and kicked them under a bench that Bill had installed last summer.

Now that Morgan had a few minutes to relax, she remembered she had promised to call Rob. She dug her cell phone out of her pants pocket and checked the time. Rob might be home from work. She wanted him to know the truth about Stan. When she'd bumped into him at the station the other day, he seemed to have forgiven her. Hope filled her heart.

Phone in hand, she took two steps into the kitchen. A movement to her right caught her eye when she pressed the call button. *Crack.* Something struck her in the head. As her knees buckled, the phone fell out of her hand.

From the floor, she couldn't see the intruder. She tried to reach for her gun with a hand that was pinned to the floor by a woman's shoe. Her last thought was that a hammer had hit her.

CHAPTER 61

MORGAN

Head hurting like it was in a pressure cooker, Morgan emerged from blackness. The strong odor of menthol burned her sinuses.

"That's it. Wakey, wakey."

Morgan didn't recognize the voice. She tried to lift a hand to touch her head. *Fuck, it hurts.*

That's when she remembered getting hit.

Consciousness blew away the fog. Morgan peeled open her eyes. Her vision, cloudy at first, grew clear, and she made out a person standing in front of her. The light in the room seemed exceptionally bright. *Is every light bulb pointing at me?* She blinked.

The woman standing in front of her had her arms folded over her chest. She looked down at Morgan. "There you are. Welcome back, Detective."

Morgan closed her eyes and flinched. A wave of nausea rose from her belly. She held it back by struggling to get up and realized she was seated in a chair.

"Oh, don't bother. You're not going anywhere." The woman moved out of Morgan's field of vision to set something heavy on the edge of the bar-height kitchen counter.

The turn of her head caused a shot of pain in her eye socket. Morgan closed her eyes. The woman remained out of sight behind her. Rope bound Morgan's wrists to the arms of the dining-room chair she was sitting in. And though she couldn't see, her bare feet felt heavy. Perhaps they were also tied to the chair. She wiggled her toes.

Dizzy, she opened her eyes to get her bearings and the floor swam up to greet her. The breakfast table floated on her left, the kitchen on her right. In front of her, the stairs moved like something out of a Harry Potter film. The nausea rose and fell in waves. Morgan kept her breathing steady. Out of the corner of her eye, she saw her aggressor and flinched.

"It's okay, darling. I won't hurt you . . . yet." She squatted beside Morgan, then with a long, slender finger turned Morgan's head. "I want you to look at me."

Morgan opened her eyes again. She wore thick makeup—foundation, eye shadow, and bright-red lipstick. False eyelashes fluttered against her soft features. Her jet black hair made her pale complexion look sallow. Sickly.

"Do you know who I am?" The woman teased. "I ought to make you guess. Let's see if the neurons are still firing in your damaged, pretty head." She poked at Morgan's temple.

The realization made Morgan's stomach lurch. "Caryn Klein," she said.

"Not anymore. I'm following my brother's lead and changing my name. No looking back." Caryn stood up. She pulled another chair in front of Morgan and sat down.

"The surveillance unit." Morgan's tongue felt thick. "They would have followed you. They're right outside."

She laughed. "I don't think so."

In an effort to stay awake, Morgan kept talking with her. "You killed Suzanne Aiken. Did you also kill Hallie Marks?" she asked.

Caryn's head snapped around, her gaze locked onto Morgan. "Oh no you don't." She leaped forward and placed her hands on the ropes binding Morgan's wrists. "I get to ask the questions." Her breath smelled sickly sweet, like she'd been eating fruit or pie, and underlying that was a distinct smell of alcohol.

Morgan recoiled. With the movement, another lightning bolt of pain shot into Morgan's face.

"I miss her, you know." Caryn backed away.

"Who?" The sound of her own voice vibrated in Morgan's skull. An internal explosion.

"Hallie Marks. Don't be an idiot. I loved her, too. Everyone did." She kicked the chair back under the table and paced back and forth. "Even though she fucked everyone . . ."

Nausea surged again. Morgan struggled to keep down the contents of her stomach.

"Hallie made us all feel special. She loved romance. How she strung Rebecca along. And Ekhard. I'll never figure it out. They had no idea what she was up to." She backed into the steps across from Morgan and sat down. "But I got the last laugh, didn't I. And I broke everyone's hearts."

"How did you meet?"

"Don't you know? Hit the Mark Design was hired to redecorate my office downtown. Hallie flirted with everyone, even Harry the Dick. I think she even fucked him. But I liked her attitude. She was no victim, if you know what I mean. In so many ways, she was like me. Obsessed."

Morgan said something just to keep awake. "So you became friends?"

"We did. Until . . ."

Caryn clapped her hands together right in front of Morgan's face. "Stay awake, Detective. I'm telling you the story!"

What Morgan would give for a couple ibuprofen, or something stronger. "What happened with Hallie?"

"Hallie and I used to go to the Blue Room together. As friends. We would dance. I never had any friends like Hallie before. She loved to party. Do you know how I found out she was going to marry Eks?"

"No. Tell me." Morgan's eyes closed for a moment. She forced them open again. Caryn slid off a pair of metallic-blue, high-heeled shoes, trading them for a pair of trainers.

All of Morgan's hostage negotiation training told her to keep Caryn talking, no matter what. She wanted her confession. "How did you find out she and Ekhard were engaged?"

"That was a stroke of luck. Hallie and I were out at a club. Drinking and dancing. She went off to the bathroom or somewhere. It seemed like she was gone a long time, so I went looking for her. I found her at the bar doing shots with—none other than—my brother."

Morgan could hear the anger in Caryn's voice.

"I left. I was so angry that he'd shown up there."

"So you killed her?"

"At one point Hallie told me she was dumping Rebecca to be with him. In so many ways, she reminded me of my mother. In the end, she would have left me, too. I could never let that happen."

"Who else did you kill?"

"Others. Many others. They all reminded me of Anna Clare."

Morgan wanted to ask, but the names of victims she and Donnie had investigated eluded her right now.

"How many?"

"Twelve. You would think that would make sixty blows. Three strikes to each face, one to each hand. But in total there have been eighty-seven hammer strikes. I counted. Sometimes I didn't quite *hit the mark.*" Caryn laughed. "It didn't matter. They looked like my mother. They all looked like her. And so I smashed their faces." She walked over to the bar-height counter and toyed with something heavy.

Unable to turn her head to see, Morgan assumed the hammer was there. "Have you ever been to Bloomington?"

With fire in her eyes, Caryn looked down at her.

"Fay Ramsey was my friend and I think you killed her," Morgan guessed.

She put her hands on her thin hips. "Is that what this is about? Some old girlfriend?" Caryn laughed a crazed, loud cackle.

Ire rose in Morgan, swelling her painful head. "What's so funny?"

"Oh, darling! Did your heart get broken too?" Caryn leaned over Morgan, placing both hands on top of her tied wrists and asked, "Detective. Do you think you've found your friend's killer?

"We've all lost someone, isn't that true? I lost my parents. Then. . . Ekhard left me. He said he would never ever do it. After all that we fought against, he fucking abandoned me. And I could never forgive him for it. After all we went through. . . "

Caryn's last words faded to a whisper. It seemed like she had gone somewhere in her mind. Morgan wondered about Fay again. "What about the others, Caryn? Who else did you kill?" Morgan wanted the whole confession, but her eyes were closing, and her head throbbed with pain.

Caryn's head jolted up again and she slapped Morgan in the face. "I'm done answering your questions!"

A wave of nausea rose, and Morgan wanted to throw up. She had to keep Caryn talking at all costs and so rephrased the question as a statement. "Ekhard dated Fay Ramsey."

"Ekhard thought he could get away from me, but he couldn't. He thought that by changing his identity, he could have a life that was all his own. But he underestimated little Ceecee."

"How so? How did he underestimate you?"

"I am *not* like my mother. My mom was a cold-hearted bitch. She would take us by the hand and squeeze. She broke Eks's fingers once. She would take the back of a spoon and smack the bones till you were black-and-blue."

Morgan turned her head and vomited on the floor. The violent retching sent knifelike stabs through her skull. When she was through, she said weakly, "Anna Clare left when you were young."

"I am *not* like that. I am not like *her!*"

Every nerve in Morgan's body had woken up with the tone of Caryn's voice. Her skin prickled. The hammer was in Caryn's hand. Morgan knew the damage that tool could do. The threat was very real now. *I have to talk her out of this.* "I'm on your side, Caryn. I understand how you feel. Your brother betrayed you. He hurt you."

"He said I'm just like her. *He* said *I'm* a psychopath. He abandoned me. He's more like our mother than I am. I've been proving him wrong ever since. Just because he left didn't mean he could get away from me."

Caryn continued to smack the handle on her palm as she moved behind Morgan with the weapon. "So I proved him wrong! I proved that I'm not like our mother!"

Morgan sat up straighter, pulling hard against the ropes binding her. "Tell me more about him. Tell me about Ekhard." She disguised her fear by using her best interrogative voice. The sound rattled her aching head.

A loud explosion of shattered glass sounded behind Morgan. As far as she was able, she shrank away from it. Caryn had hit the china hutch, breaking glass and the Raffertys' fine dishware. Out of sight, the threat of the hammer remained behind her. She tucked her chin to her chest and cringed.

"Ekhard can't hurt you anymore! You don't have to do this!" Morgan noticed the panicky tone of her own voice. And she heard something else. Knocking? *Is someone at the door?*

Caryn must have heard it too. On Morgan's left, Caryn appeared with hammer raised, her gaze directed at the front door.

"You don't have to do this!" Morgan yelled. If someone was at the door, she wanted them to hear her.

"You are mistaken, Detective." Caryn swung around to face Morgan.

"I can help you. Let me help you," Morgan pleaded with as loud a voice as she could tolerate. "We can get through this together." What fear she had felt before grew exponentially in seeing the weapon—the long, gleaming, steel hammer—raised over her head.

Caryn had cracked. Her eyes were wild, darting from Morgan to the door and back to the hammer in her hand. Morgan kept her gaze locked on Caryn. The pounding at the door became louder. Muffled voices called through the door.

With all her might Morgan tried to back away, but she was unable to pull out of the bonds on her wrists or the ropes holding her legs in place. She couldn't escape. Sweat broke out on her neck and chest. *Keep her talking.* "Caryn, I can help you."

The hammer swung in a big arc over Caryn's head.

An explosive sound filled the room when the tool came down on Morgan's left hand, crushing the bones. Her broken left hand splayed in an ugly sprawl with fingers going the wrong directions.

A high-pitched scream threatened Morgan's consciousness. At first, she thought the scream had erupted from her own throat. Pain radiated up her arm to her shoulder.

Now a fuzzy image, Caryn turned toward the garage entrance with her lipstick-red mouth opened wide as she let out an ear-splitting howl. As she backed away with the hammer held high in the air, police officers—three, four—stormed into the dining room, pointing guns at her.

There was shouting. Then gunfire.

And Rob asking Morgan if she was okay.

CHAPTER 62

MORGAN

Morgan lay in her bed, grateful that the cold, dark night swallowed daylight early on this winter day. Light sensitivity gave her occasional migraines since the encounter with Caryn, as did reading on the computer for longer than fifteen minutes and watching fast-paced movies. Though the road to recovery would be long and bumpy, Morgan was grateful to be alive.

On the bedside table, her cell phone vibrated. She pushed up on one elbow to see who the caller was. Jeremy. They had been talking more often.

"Hey there, how are you?" he asked. Jeremy's voice soothed her, like a cool bubbling brook washing over Morgan's exhausted mind.

"Never better," she lied.

"Hope you've been resting, taking it easy. Are Adrienne and Bill taking care of you?" As soon as they had learned of the attack on Morgan, Adrienne and Bill had returned from Florida.

"As much as I'll let them. When are you coming to visit?"

"Aw, you know I can't come to Indy right now. We're getting the baby room ready. I'm painting and Dierdre picked out a crib."

Morgan forgave him. Deirdre was seven and a half months pregnant. "How is Deirdre?" Without turning on a light, she set the cell phone on her bedside table and pressed the speaker icon.

"Deirdre's good. She's still going to yoga every morning. She'll bounce back from this quickly. Yesterday she said she can't wait to get her old body back."

Surprised by this, Morgan said, "I thought she loved being pregnant."

"I think she's ready for it to be over." He laughed. "But she's got two months to go."

Morgan realized how little she knew about pregnancy. "Yoga? Is that okay for the baby? Isn't she supposed to be resting?"

Jeremy laughed. "Have you met my wife? *Rest* isn't a word in her vocabulary."

His laughter had made Morgan smile. "I miss you."

"I miss you too, Mo."

"Mom said you're not moving back to Bloomington. Why not? You can't be working, not with . . ."

His reminder drew Morgan's gaze to her bandaged left hand. "I'm not working *yet*. *Yet* is the key word here," she said with lifted eyebrows.

"How is your hand?" Jeremy asked with the sensitive, probing tone only a sibling can muster.

"Better." A recent surgery had reset four bones in her hand and wrist. But until the tissue healed, doctors didn't know how her mobility would be affected. At least it was her left hand, not her shooting hand. Naturally, the thought drew her mind to images of other crushed hands: Hallie Marks's, Jenny Delacourt's, and Fay's.

"I'm proud of you, Mo. You've mastered your trade. Remember when this started?"

"How can I forget?" *I'll never forget Fay. I'll never forget how we betrayed each other, how much I loved her, or how jealous I was of Larry.*

"And you've come a long way." Jeremy hesitated. Morgan sensed he wanted to say something she didn't want to hear. "I think you should quit. Get a desk job. Open a deli. Do something that doesn't involve police work, guns, and crazy people."

"A deli? I can't cook. That's *your* dream job. And besides, crazy people are everywhere." *He doesn't realize . . .*

"Oh, right," he admitted.

"It's cute how protective you are, big brother."

"I'm serious," Jeremy said. "Mom and Dad agree, you are very lucky. You could have been killed."

"I'm not quitting, Jeremy. I've applied for a position with the US Marshals." *And I have a debt to Fay that I can never repay.* Morgan cradled her left hand. The surrounding bandage was a soft, football-sized pillow.

"Doing what?"

"Finding missing people, escaped convicts, wanted criminals."

"Sounds dangerous," Jeremy said.

"Probably will be." Morgan knew too well what it took to hide from a broken past.

Jeremy chuckled. "Okay, Mo. I've got to get some sleep. Deirdre and I will come visit this spring with little Dylan Brianne."

"She's a girl?"

"She is."

"I'm going to love her!"

"I love you, kid," Jeremy said.

"Call me again soon."

As Morgan hung up, she couldn't imagine ever estranging Jeremy. Life without him would be lonely and difficult, she thought. She wondered if it had been that way for Caryn.

CHAPTER 63

MORGAN

"Thank you," Morgan said as Bill Rafferty passed her with a smile on his face and his arms loaded up with two heavy boxes. He placed them in the bed of a Ford F150, Morgan's new pickup truck. Rob had taken great care of the roadworthy vehicle. And because she liked driving it, he sold it to her and bought a newer model.

"There isn't much left," Bill said. The bed of the truck was half full. A bookshelf lay on its side supported by three boxes of books, a small antique desk, and two black garbage bags full of clothes. "Are you hanging in there?"

Bill jogged back toward the house with the energy of a much younger man. After he and Adrienne returned, and while cleaning up shattered china and glass, they decided to sell the house.

"I wish I could help," Morgan said. With her left splinted hand cradled in a sling, she looked up at the trees bursting with green leaves. Three bushes in front of the Raffertys' brick house hung heavy with lilacs. The light-purple blooms filled the fresh spring air with their fragrance.

"Do you want this too?" Adrienne asked, following Bill with a tall floor lamp. Ready for a workday, she wore her silver hair bundled in a knot at the back of her head.

"That would be great." From her heart, Morgan said, "Thank you for setting me up with so much furniture." She had said thank you often and frequently, but it hadn't been enough. Gratitude for her Indianapolis family filled her heart to the brim.

Adrienne stopped to catch her breath. "Oh, when this place sells, we won't need any of it. I'm glad you can use it." A spry, birdlike woman, she spoke fast. "The apartment we're moving to in Florida is fully furnished. We don't need all this stuff! And as they say, 'You can't take it with you.'"

Morgan gave her friend and stand-in mother a hug. "Thanks for everything."

"We will miss you, Mo. You must come visit us in Florida. I'm not sure I'll be able to talk Bill into driving that far north."

"But Wisconsin is beautiful in the summertime."

"Hold that thought. We can't say goodbye just yet." Adrienne raised her eyebrows with a knowing smile, then walked back to the house.

Morgan was excited about the move to Wisconsin. Though it was far from her family, she had always loved visiting her brother on the isthmus in Madison. She was finally ready to put more distance between her and Bloomington too. She had paid her dues and come to terms with her past. And as part of her new life, she wanted to spend time around water. Fay had loved the water.

"How's this?" Rob stepped out into the yard with a cushioned chair from the living room. He set it down in the grass beside where Morgan stood next to the "For Sale" sign. "Take a load off."

"I'd rather take a load to my truck," she admitted.

"You can't do that. We won't let you."

"I know." Morgan's hand itched under the splint. Until it healed, she had limited use of it. To date, two surgeries before had set broken bones with pins. The third, to remove the pins, the doctor had promised, would be the last. Morgan wouldn't play guitar with Bill again, but that was no big loss. Bill had said so too.

Fay wouldn't play the piano again either. When she raised her hand to protect her face from that rock, it took the blow. Morgan thought three fingers were broken with that hit. But that wasn't the blow that had killed her.

"We've got this covered for you." Rob took Morgan by the shoulders and pressed her back into the chair.

"Timing could have been better." She waved her left hand.

"Could have been worse." He looked over Morgan's shoulder. "Gretta! Gretta, come here, girl!"

In the next-door neighbor's yard, Gretta had made friends with a small, fluffy teddy-bear mix.

"She'll miss you."

"I don't think so," Morgan said. "In fact, I'll bet Allie has all the right kinds of treats."

A sweetheart, Allie had moved in with Rob. They were perfect for each other. Allie loved children and animals, and she wanted the same things Rob did. The same future.

"Where is Allie, anyway? I thought she'd be joining us."

Rob looked down the street. "She had to work today, but she'll stop by before you go."

"I hope so," Morgan admitted. "Plus, I want to tell her to take care of you. She's got something special, Rob. I mean that from the depths of my heart." The words sprinkled regret onto the growing pile of emotions . She owed Rob everything. If it hadn't been for him, Morgan would be dead.

In the days following the attack, Morgan found out that, as she entered the house, she had dialed Rob's number right before Caryn attacked her. He had tried returning the call, but because Caryn had smashed her phone after knocking her unconscious, Rob got nothing but dead air. He grew worried and asked friends in patrol to meet him at her house. The officers arrived just in time to hear the glass hutch shatter. Phone lines had been cut, and no one responded to their pounding on the front door. They entered with guns raised. When Caryn shrieked and threw the hammer, Rob shot her.

Helpful throughout her hospitalization and subsequent surgeries, Rob made himself available. But Morgan kept her distance. This chapter of her life had ended. Though a great friend, Rob wasn't the person she wanted to settle down with. She wanted adventure, and he wanted to get married and start a family.

Morgan loathed leading him on. So right before Christmas, and just in time for the IMPD Christmas party, she told Rob it was over. He'd seen it coming, and he gave her space. By mid-January, he and Allie were dating again.

"What have you got in here? Bricks?" Bill joked. He and Adrienne hustled past with more boxes.

"Thanks, Bill," Morgan said.

Birds in the grass flew upward when a brand-new green SUV parked behind the Ford truck. Donnie, no longer wearing his arm sling, stepped out of the passenger side, his daughter Etta from the driver's side. The surgery to replace his shoulder joint had been successful.

Tall and as thin as a runway model, Etta bounced across the lawn. "Hi, Morgan." She waved, then bent to pet Gretta who, with a smile and wagging tail, greeted everyone.

Morgan pushed herself out of her chair. Excited and nervous, she didn't want to sit. "How was the track meet, Etta?"

Etta shrugged and tossed her long braids to the side. "I don't know."

"She did great!" Donnie, the proud papa, answered. "Beat her own record in the hurdles by two and a half seconds."

"Congratulations!" Morgan said.

"How can I help?" Etta asked.

"I have a few more marked boxes upstairs," Morgan told her.

As Etta danced into the house, Donnie gave Morgan a kiss on the cheek. "I'll miss you, Mo."

"Hey, no goodbyes. Not yet," she said. The surge of emotion tickled her nose and curled her lips as a tear caught in her eye. The weight of her decision might bury her alive if she let it. But a sense of purpose floated over her misgivings, just as it had after Fay's death.

Thinner, Donnie shifted to the other foot. Hours of rehab had inspired him to go to the gym more often, and it had paid off. Morgan knew the slower pace at work was exactly what he wanted so he could be with his girls.

Rob, standing nearby, asked, "How are you? Enjoying the new job, Lieutenant?"

Donnie patted Rob on the back. "Being lieutenant is not boring if that's what you mean. Though at my age, boredom is welcome," he admitted.

"I know what you mean," Rob said, looking up at the sky. "Someday . . ."

Morgan hoped things would work out for him with Allie.

"Adrienne and Bill are doing all the work. I'd better go help them." Rob returned to the house.

"Thanks, Rob," Morgan called after him.

"So. Are you ready for this?" Donnie asked, with a nod toward her bandaged hand.

"Wisconsin?" Morgan asked.

"Yes. Going undercover is never easy. You'll be cut off from your family and friends."

"I don't mind." The psychiatrist had been right about PITS. Morgan needed more than ever to get away from people. She still wasn't sleeping. Medication didn't help, it just made her feel groggy in the morning. "I need a vacation anyway," she told Donnie.

"This'll be no vacation! Lieutenant Detective Callen Roth from the Madison violent crimes unit has told me how dangerous he thinks Honey Drake is. You'll be living under her roof."

"I know. I was briefed." Morgan wanted to stop him from worrying but didn't know how to achieve that. They'd been friends for too long. "Are you going to be my contact back here?" She asked.

"Only when necessary. You'll be working for the Madison PD from now on." Donnie shook his head. "If I could have sent someone else, I would have."

"It's ok, *Lieutenant*. They requested me."

Donnie gazed across the lawn, searching for something. "You're perfect for the job."

Morgan thought his eyes teared up. So she took the compliment silently.

"Heard back from the Marshals?"

"I've heard the process is long," she explained. "My friend Keith Broderick put a recommendation in for me, but all I can do is wait.

It could be another twelve to eighteen months before I hear anything. In the meantime, this undercover work will look good on my resume."

"The training . . ." Donnie said, lifting his eyebrows.

Morgan shook her head. "I know about U.S. Marshals training." Too loudly, she defended herself. "Eighteen weeks of sheer physical hell. I'll have to be in my best shape. And I'll have to be healed." She waved her splinted hand.

"Okay. As long as you'll be ready." Donnie stuffed his hands into his pockets and looked up at the lilacs.

"I'll be ready."

Trustworthy, dark-brown eyes gazed into Morgan's. "If anyone can do it, you can, Mo. I have faith in you," Donnie said.

She knew he was saying he cared.

"Thank you, Donnie. That means a lot." She hugged him. Of all her friends, she'd miss Donnie the most.

The threat of tears having passed for now, Morgan beckoned Donnie inside to check that nothing important got left behind.

With a strong odor of new carpet, the Raffertys' charming home had been reduced to a shell, as most of the furniture had been sold or given away. The rest was scattered or piled in the living room for their upcoming garage sale.

"Careful with that," Donnie said to Etta as she brushed past them with a boxed coffeepot.

Today's unopened mail sat on the kitchen counter. Morgan picked through it. In between a cell-phone bill and a Netflix DVD, she found a thick envelope from Victoria Ramsey.

"Look at this." Eager to see what was inside, Morgan tried, unsuccessfully, to rip it open with her teeth.

"Give me that." Donnie took it from her and dug a knife out of a nearby drawer. When he slit the envelope open, a get-well card and a stack of pictures fell out. Donnie helped sort them. "Who's it from?" He handed the card to Morgan.

"It's from Fay's mother." She opened the card. Inside, Vic had written:

Dear Morgan,

It has taken me years to come to terms with Fay's death. Now I know that I held her much too close. When my husband died, I tried—too hard—to keep Fay from leaving me. I should have known she'd fly from the nest eventually. I just didn't know she'd grow those wings so early. Her fate was sealed. Now, I can't blame you for her death. It's in the past, and it's time to move on. Please take these photos as a small remembrance of her. She'd want you to have them. Thank you for being such a good friend to my daughter.

Victoria

With one hand, Morgan spread the photos across the countertop. The first picture, from Senior Prom, was of Fay and Morgan standing on the grass outside her parents' house. In a slinky blue prom dress, Morgan's arm was around her taller friend. Fay's white dress reminded Morgan of how innocent Fay had been. It also reminded her that she had wanted to marry Fay.

"Is that . . .?" Donnie asked.

"Fay." Morgan nodded.

The next was a shot taken in front of the IU Student Union. Another with their orientation backpacks. Many photos from the Kodak 110 camera were blurry, but not in Morgan's memory. In the back of her mind, she heard Fay's giggle as if she were standing in the Raffertys' kitchen.

From the bottom of the stack, Donnie pulled out a picture of Fay and a brunette girl, a younger Morgan Jewell. Their happiness then was reflected in their smiles. The background to the last photo on the reel of film was dark. It had been late at night when the photo was taken beside Jackson Creek. Their faces were close to the camera and off-center.

And Morgan remembered holding a jagged, heavy rock in her hand.

DISCUSSION GUIDE QUESTIONS

1. Many people develop crushes on their best friends. For Morgan, Fay was the closest and best friend. What would you do in that situation? Would you reveal your feelings or keep quiet for fear of making things awkward?

2. One triggering event in Morgan's life changed her entire life path. What has or what would alter the course of your life? Not necessarily connected, if someone close to you passed away, would you move on or hang your life on figuring it out?

3. Caryn and Ekhard didn't have a stable home environment. Is it nature or nurture that made them the way they are?

4. They say you can't choose your family. Morgan's adult relationship with her brother is vastly different than Caryn's relationship with Ekhard. How has your relationship with a sibling help form who you are today?

5. Several characters play a role in Fay's death. Who do you think is most to blame?

ACKNOWLEDGMENTS

This book would not be in your hands were it not for the insights and dreams of my editor, Jenny Chen, who found me at #pitdark, a Twitter pitch event. Her helpfulness and extraordinary attention to detail are what made *Best Kept Secrets* rise to excellence. Warmest heartfelt gratitude to you, Jenny, for making my dreams come true.

My husband Michael put up with my emotional roller-coaster through tears of failure and the elation of success. You have been my rock. Thank you for your strange devotion to researching dark matter and legal matter. And thank you for not killing me with a hammer.

Dear children, Dylan and Erika, thanks for your insights. And for sitting through discussions too dark to fathom. And for all the time you put into my online presence and your many read-throughs, ideas, and unfailing belief in me. You both connect me to the younger set. I so admire and appreciate your talents and enthusiasm. Thank you both for standing by me.

Many thanks go to my critique partners, Gisele Lewis, Anne Feldman, and Kirsche Romo, for making BKS glimmer and shine. Your insights were key to my publication. Marianne Flynn, your last-minute advice was crucial. Amber Boudreau, you put up with my dark writing, even though it's not your thing. And to my dear friend Diane Boles, without you, I never would have dreamt this possible.

Acknowledgments

To my first readers, I'm sorry. You never should have had to suffer through that, Diana Schramer, Joan Donovan, Ginny Hansen, and Dave Klingan. I thank you for your many encouraging words.

And Katherine Ramsland, even though you don't know me, your teachings and books have been instrumental in the creation of Caryn. I thoroughly enjoyed your classes in the WPA, Appleton.

Much like raising a child, writing and publishing a book takes a village. I am only one woman in the village. The biggest thank you goes to you readers. You make up the rest of my village.